STARLETS AND SAVAGES

ROSE GRAVESTONE

DKS PUBLISHING LLC

To all the anxious girlies who want to be dominated in bed and taken care of outside of it, Mason Sieger is ready to make you his good girl.

Author's Note

Author's Note:

Hello, lovely reader! Thank you for picking up Starlets and Savages, book three of the dark and sensual Greywood Elites Series. Chloe and Mason are a wonderful, unique pairing, and I hope you enjoy reading their story as much as I enjoyed writing it.

Please be advised that this book contains dark and potentially triggering content. If any of the following themes are unsettling to you, it might not be the right book for you.

- Mentions of S/A.
- Mentions of child abuse (NOT perpetrated by main characters).
- Unapologetic alpha-hole hero.
- Depictions of intense anxiety and panic attacks.
- Light dub-con.

Contents

CHAPTER ONE

Chloe Richardson

My entire body trembles as I rush out of the entrance to my dorm building, the rhythmic slaps of my Vans echoing on the pavement. My heart pounds like I'm running from a killer—*which I think I actually might be.*

Being accepted to Greywood last year was a dream come true. I was ecstatic to be invited into the school's elite dance program while also taking biochemistry classes. I knew it'd be tough to balance the rigorous schedule, but I managed during my freshman year. Of course, the peace couldn't have lasted; nothing good ever lasts in my life. Discovering the state of my dorm room after returning from a rigorous physics class mere minutes ago was just a stark reminder of that.

Somebody wants me the hell off campus, and they made quite the statement in my room to prove it.

I half-speed walk, half-jog down one of Greywood's paved walking paths that lead from the program dorms and over to the campus café.

Elia and April, two of my good friends on campus and fellow students in the dance program, invited me to join them for a coffee tonight. I told them I couldn't make it because I have an obscene amount of homework to do, but now I'm desperate to get to them. The thought of going back to my dorm room makes me want to throw up.

The small student café is only a ten-minute walk from program dorms; at a speedwalk, it's cut down to seven minutes, and at a full-paced sprint like the one I break into, it's about four. I made all the calculations during the first semester of my freshman year, when I had to either figure out how to juggle a ridiculously busy schedule or fail out of all of my classes. Since the latter wasn't—still isn't—an option, I decided on the former.

I burst into the one-story café, probably looking as panicked as I feel, and sweep my eyes around the shop, trying to muster my nerves. Timber beams hold up the A-frame roof; tables covered with green and red checkered cloths stand on the polished oakwood floorboards; a Christmas tree is propped up by the barista's counter, and bells have been hung on the display case showcasing baked treats. Everyone's getting into a festive spirit for the holidays—at least, those who aren't terrified for their lives.

I spot April Stein and Eliana Pierce sitting at a table in the corner of the room, right by a large window that overlooks Greywood's scenic campus. I cut a path through the crowd toward them, needing to talk to them and ask for their help. They're my only real friends on campus, and both of them happen to be coupled—or in Elia's case, throupled—up with men who have dangerous reputations.

April notices me as I approach; her amber eyes light up, then dim as she takes me in. Elia smiles as she spots me, though the smile is quick to recede as I speedwalk over to them.

I collapse on the seat beside Elia and manage to blurt a single sentence that sums up my situation: "I think I'm marked for death."

April's totally unmoved. "You mean, like, death by orgasms? Half of the boys on campus do look at you like they're dying for a piece of that hotness, so—"

"April," Elia says with a censuring look, before offering me a kind, small smile. "I got you a gingerbread latte in case you were going to join us tonight. Sit, drink, tell us what happened."

Elia was in the center of a campus serial killer debacle last year, and April has skin made of stainless-steel armor, so they don't appear to be as fazed by my statement as most others would be. I inhale several consecutive deep breaths and accept the red takeout cup Elia slides over to me, taking a gulp of the scalding liquid, barely tasting it.

I set down the cup, then slap the note I found on my pillow in front of Elia; she takes one look at it and pales. "Oh, shit—*what the hell?* Chloe, what happened? Where did you find this?"

April snatches up the note while I try to calm my racing heart, only to find I'm unable to. I'm too anxious and keyed up, with old memories creeping into my thoughts, threatening to send me into a panic attack. *Not again*—I thought I'd gotten over those already. I should've gotten over those, but apparently, one incident is all it takes to bring them back. Having a diagnosed anxiety disorder is not a walk in the park, though I'm usually good at managing it.

"Damn, sis, this is *fuuuucked*," April says, eyebrows raised. "*A small taste of what's to come if you don't get off campus. Get lost, or get dead,*" she reads aloud. "Who did you piss off, girl?"

"No one!" I shriek, then feel my cheeks heat as several people from nearby tables turn to stare at me. I lower my voice, and say, "No one that I know of. I—I don't know who would've left this... I came back from my physics class, and..." I trail off, shaking my head. Eliana puts her hand on my shoulder, giving me an encouraging nod, her brows creased with worry. The physical contact helps, which is surprising; I'm not someone who generally enjoys being touched. "After my physics class, I went back to my dorm room, and there was a knife sticking out of my mattress. My books were scattered, the table of elements poster that hangs above my bed was shredded, and this note was laid on my destroyed pillow. I don't know what to do—I can't afford to find somewhere else to stay, and I can't leave campus because I need to graduate, but... but..."

"But someone wants you dead," April finishes for me, nodding her head with understanding as if this is a commonplace occurrence. She's so coolheaded, I think she could give an iceberg a run for its money. "I guess that'd be a tad off putting. Have you reported it?"

I nod. "I called the admin office while getting out of the program dorm building. They told me they'd *look into* it. I don't think they're going to take this seriously; they'll just assume a prank's being played or something. They never take stuff like this seriously." In my high school, they wouldn't even take sexual assault seriously.

"You could go to the police," Eliana suggests gently. "They might be able to—"

"*No police,*" I cut her off, feeling bile crawl up my throat yet again. Three years ago, I went to the police after a horrible party gone wrong; they said things I'll never forget, attributing my dress and smeared makeup to the fact that I must've been *asking for it.*

"No police," Elia agrees with a nod, rubbing my arm. There's a nurturing energy emanating from her that I'm in desperate need of. Despite being the star of our dance program, she's probably the nicest girl I've ever met, so kindhearted and *good* it's hard to believe.

"You two are both dating men with certain reputations," I hedge carefully. "Seth Balor and Ian Vargas are both kind of known for..."

"Maiming and killing?" April supplies, unblinking. "Yeah, they do have those reputations. They also both know how to get shit done when it comes to protection. I'd offer up Ian's services to you, but honestly, he won't get out of bed for anyone who isn't me. If I asked him to help you, he'd probably try to break up our friendship so he'd have more time with me—he's possessive like that."

Elia nods sagely. "Yeah, Ian tried to push me away from April last year. Seth stepped in because he doesn't like anything to upset me. My man threatened to fuck Ian's shit sideways."

"Then, Ian fucked me until I couldn't breathe in response," April says with a little laugh, like it's amusing. "He thought that would be good revenge for me having the audacity to make friends; joke's on him, I *love* it when he gets feral. I never come harder."

Sensing my discomfort at the direction of the topic, Elia gently steers the conversation away. "If Seth were in town, I'd have him look into it—he likes you as much as he's capable of liking anyone, since you've defended me being in a ménage relationship more than once."

"I only did what was right," I mumble, taking another sip of my latte. Too many people gave Elia shit last year when it became clear that she had *two* boyfriends: Seth Balor, one of Greywood's resident menaces, and Carson Ajax, son of an oil tycoon. "But Seth's out of town," I say dully, realizing that's exactly why Elia's here tonight. Otherwise, Seth would've whisked her off campus after her classes.

Eliana nods. "He is, and Carson and Ian are working late together at the Ajax company building in the city."

Something they're probably doing as part of their course credits in Greywood's acclaimed business program. All students accepted into any of the elite programs at Greywood—from fine arts, to business, to political science—are required to work in their chosen field to complete their course credits, so they can get real-life experience alongside their studies. As a member of the dance program, I'm part of one of the Greywood Dance Company's productions, Pandora's Box. The show, written and directed by an instructor in the dance program, premiered last year to a slew of incredible reviews. It went on tour over the summer, something I was honored to be a part of, and has continued running this year.

"I can't go back to my dorm," I say, fighting tears. "Jesus, I haven't been this terrified in years." Even on *that* night in my junior year of high school, when I lost all my faith in the male population and any naïve romantic sentiments, I wasn't this scared. My life wasn't on the line, only my innocence.

"Seth's back on Monday, four days from now, I'll tell him to look into it then," Elia says resolutely. "For now, I can talk Carson into letting you use the couch in our apartment—"

"No," I interject, shaking my head. "Thank you, you're the sweetest for offering, but I can't impose like that. I'll just..." hell, what am I supposed to do? I have *just* enough in my bank account to put myself up in a local hotel, but that won't work indefinitely. It would also drain funds that I need for other things, like school and dance supplies.

"You can take my old dorm room, if you want," April offers, twisting around a gorgeous engagement ring settled on her ring finger. "I'm totally moved out so it's empty, and Ian installed a whole bunch of techy precautions when I was refusing to move in with him at the beginning of the year because he's ridiculous like that. Nobody can get in there unless they have a key—the lock's not pickable, the door and window are both reinforced. You'd be safe there."

The thought of sleeping in the program dorms tonight absolutely terrifies me, but I understand that I might not have another option. At least I'd be safe in April's room, though I doubt I'll actually get any sleep if I stay in that cursed building, and I need sleep to get through my super-packed days. *God, I can't deal with insomnia again...*

"Seth and Ian aren't the *only* two on campus with a certain skillset," Elia says, sounding somewhat hesitant. "There's also... oh, Jesus, I can't believe I'm stooping to this, but have you heard of Mason Sieger?"

My blood runs cold. Everyone's heard of Mason Sieger; he's the son of the billionaire businessman Grant Sieger, who's rumored to have ties to organized crime, the mafia. Mason's a senior in the business program, and it's said that last year he nearly beat a fellow student to death, landing the poor kid in the ER because he had the gall to look at Mason the wrong way.

"Everyone's heard of him," I reply. "He's bad news."

"He totally is," April agrees. "Ian's had dealings with Mason; that alone is a bad sign, my man doesn't deal with *nice* people. From what I know, Mason will do favors in return for favors—he likes to make deals, and he sticks to his word religiously. If you go to him with a solid offer, Chloe, I think he'd help you out. It wouldn't be from the kindness of his heart, but it would be a fair exchange."

I've heard about the deals Mason makes, and his effectiveness in both holding up his end of the deal and making sure the other person holds up their end. What could I have that I could offer to someone like Mason? *Doctor.* I have being a future doctor under my belt, and I already acquired some ER experience the summer before I started Greywood, shadowing doctors who worked in trauma care. I'm proficient with most forms of first aid, I can tend to all sorts of nasty wounds... that could be useful to someone like Mason, considering the darker edges of the world he lives in. I can only pray he'll take an IOU from a future doctor who'll have discretion and not ask questions.

Being in the debt of someone like Mason sounds profoundly dangerous, but he's a future danger I might have to deal with, which is better than the danger I'm currently facing. Logically, he's my best option, if he agrees to help me—which is a big if. *It can't hurt to ask.* I have nowhere else to go and nothing else to do.

"He lives a floor below me in that posh as fuck apartment building in the city," April says. "I can give you a ride, point you in the right direction. Worst comes to worse, if Mason refuses, you'll still have a safe place to stay in my old dorm room while you wait for Elia to convince Seth to help."

As ever, a list of pros and cons takes shape in my head as I weigh my options. Pros of asking Mason for help: if he agrees, my problem could be taken care of very quickly. He's known for getting shit done. Cons: being in his debt. Having to face someone as scary as Mason Sieger. Still... the current pros outweigh the cons.

"Okay," I say. "Thank you—both of you." I turn to April. "I'll gladly take your old dorm room. If I could catch a ride with you to your apartment building, I'll see if Mason's willing to make a deal to take care of whoever broke into my room. If not, then I'll just stay in your room until Seth's back in town and hope he'll help."

"He will," Elia assures me, sounding confident. "I'll tell him it'd make me sleep easier, which is the truth, and he'll get right on it." A fond smile spreads on her lips, and her eyes shimmer with a dreamy glint. "Seth will do whatever to make sure I'm comfortable—he always has. He gets adorably pissy when I'm out of sorts, takes whatever steps he can to fix the problem. Usually with violence—he considers anything that worsens my mood to be a personal offense."

I blink at her a few times, wondering what it must be like to be loved so fiercely, with such protectiveness that your lover would kill for you, live for you, do anything for you. It must be intoxicating. I almost envy her for the briefest moment, before remembering that I have zero interest in lovers or any semblance of romantic love.

What I have interest in is both of my career paths, dancer and doctor. In two years, I'll graduate with a biochemistry degree and a classical/ contemporary dance degree. If a dance company takes me on as a principal dancer, then I'll dance and go to med school when I'm older. If not, then I'm off to med school immediately. To achieve that, I have to stay alive, and to stay alive, it looks like I'll be making a deal with the devil.

Chapter Two

I'm not terribly religious, but as I stand in front of Mason Sieger's door, I have to wonder if this is what the door to hell looks like. It's painted dark grey with a golden handle jutting out from the smooth surface, and no less than three locks on it. There's something sinister about it, and something even more sinister emanating from within the apartment beyond the door.

"Best of luck," April calls out from the elevator at the end of the hall. "Text me when you need a ride back to dorms—as long as Ian's not in a bondage mood tonight, I should be able to respond."

I blink at her several times as the elevator doors close, unable to summon a response. Bondage mood? Last year, April had a big reputation on campus for going through men and women like they were water, and she was damn good at the game before Ian came along.

I think I'll be taking an Uber home when I'm done here. I don't want to impose on April or Elia when they're already doing a great deal to help me.

I inhale a deep breath, steel myself, and heft my bag higher on my shoulder. Then, I raise my finger and ring the ornate doorbell above the handle of the door, praying to whatever god might exist that I escape this encounter unscathed. All I have to do is make a simple deal: offer my future services in return for Mason's agreement to look into and help solve my problem. I think, I *hope,* that he's sensible enough to see the value I could offer him going forward. If not, I'll just be keeping vigil in April's old room, praying that whoever broke into my room can't get to me until Seth returns and Elia convinces him to help.

Several grueling moments of silence pass before I hear locks clicking, and the door swings open. When I see the giant of a man in front of me, it takes considerable effort to stop my jaw from dropping.

Mason Sieger is... *stunning.* Dark auburn hair curls over his head in an unruly nest; piercing golden eyes with flecks of green fixate on me, and his perfectly sharp, angled jawline clenches as he regards me with a glimmer of mild curiosity and interest in his eyes. A black t-shirt is stretched over his abdomen, perfectly outlining his six-pack and rock-hard chest. *His biceps are the size of my calves...*

Low-slung sweatpants hang on his hips. Dressed casually, as if he just returned from the gym, he appears sort of like an avenging angel. *So this is what the devil looks like up close.* Deceptively beautiful.

"I asked for a blonde," he says curtly, jaw clenching as he looks me over. "And I wasn't expecting my blonde for another two hours. The agency's gone downhill, it would seem. You are... *unexpectedly* stunning, though, so you'll do."

Realization hits me; I think he might've been waiting for a stripper, or even worse, a prostitute. *I need to backtrack fast.*

"I wasn't sent by an agency or anything like that," I rush out, trying to mask the sheer horror in my voice. "I'm not... yeah, I don't know who you were waiting for, but I'm not her. I'm Chloe—I go to Greywood. Sophomore."

Mason's eyebrows raise by the slightest margin as he regards me with deepening interest, the sort that makes my skin tingle and sends a shiver up my spine. I don't think it's a good idea to be an object of interest for a man like this. He's too... much. Just too much in every way; too big, too strong, too masculine, too *powerful*.

"Well, then," he says calmly, "if you're not looking for a ride tonight, *Chloe*, what the fuck are you doing at my door?"

I think I made a mistake coming here—no, I'm *positive* I did. This is a male who clearly sees women as a means to an end—in addition to being a notorious campus player, he evidently utilizes the services of an *agency* to have women sent to him. Any interest I might've felt in his physique evaporates; when I look at him again, it's from under lowered eyebrows and through a jaded lens.

"I have a problem," I say lowly. "I've heard from friends that you're someone who makes... *deals*. Of sorts. Favors for favors, I mean—not sexual favors, I'm not in that market, but—"

"Cut to the chase," Mason says, folding his arms over his chest and leaning against the doorway as he regards me, eyes running up and down my body, gaze lingering on my breasts and hips. The golden color of his irises brightens as he takes in my form. I need to redirect immediately, before he gets the wrong impression.

Clumsily, I take the note from whoever broke into my room out of my pocket and extend it to him. "This was left on my pillow, in my dorm room. Someone who doesn't want me around broke in. I am very afraid for my well-being, and I don't know who to turn to for help. The rumors about you indicate that you might be into certain dealings... dealings that would potentially make someone with medical experience valuable to you. I'm proficient with injuries; cleaning, stitching, and fixing them up. If you could help me out with my bind, I'll trade for a favor in the future. Call on me whenever, to tend to whatever wound you or one of your associates might sustain, and I'll be there. No questions asked, no reports made, a clean favor with no strings attached."

Mason takes the note from my hand, his fingers deliberately lingering on my skin, and I have to stop my breath from catching at the contact. Even his hand is overly masculine—big and veiny and burning with heat, his skin almost feverish. Every self-preservation instinct I have screams at me to get away from him, but I hold firm. I'll do whatever it takes to find out who wants me off campus enough to threaten my life, even if it means coming to the most unsafe man on campus.

"I see," Mason murmurs as he reads over the note. "And where did you hear about me?"

Since April gave me the go ahead to use her as a reference, I say, "April Stein. She's engaged to Ian Vargas. I'm friends with her, and when I told her what happened, she referred me to you."

"Ah, April," Mason says with a nod. He pockets the note, then turns his burning stare back to me. I feel like a butterfly pinned in place by the weight of his gaze, trapped, dying to flutter away but unable to. "I recognize you—aren't you in Pandora's Box? I've seen you on stage, though you were wearing a much different getup..."

I feel my cheeks burn. "Yes, I'm in Greywood's dance program," I tell him, trying to ignore the fact that if he's come to the show, he's seen me mostly undressed. In Pandora's Box, my costume is a skimpy leotard that leaves little to the imagination. I play the trickster god Hermes in the production, and I have two solos, both of which are quite seductive in nature.

"Huh." He pauses for a beat, giving me another once-over. "Tell me, how does a dancer come to acquire medical experience?"

Good question. "I'm a double major," I explain. "Dance and biochemistry. If dancing doesn't work out, I intend to go to medical school. I took a bunch of AP courses applicable to a pre-med track during high school, starting my junior year. Summer after my senior year, I interned at an ER, where I got some hands-on experience with tending to nasty wounds. I was also raised by a doctor who trained me extensively in first aid throughout my youth."

Mason's head slowly tilts to the side as he regards me with a deepening interest, the kind that makes me *very* nervous. "That so?" he questions, sounding amused. "Smart *and* beautiful. You don't see that mix often."

"My looks aren't our topic of discussion," I say tersely. "I'm here to see if you'll make a deal. If not... I guess I'll go to the police and hope they do something about it." Even as I say the words, the thought makes my skin crawl—I'd rather wait for Elia to ask Seth to look into my problem.

"They won't," Mason assures me. "They're notoriously unreliable and rarely take cases like this seriously. They'll assume the note is a prank, just like Greywood admin will. You came to the right place. Now, in terms of the favor I'll ask for... as much as your knowledge of medicine could prove useful, that's not my interest right now. I appreciate your proposal, but I'm going to counter it with the deal I'm willing to make."

As he speaks, I start to grow genuinely anxious, my nerves heightened by the heat of his gaze and the way he stares at me—like I'm a meal waiting to be devoured. If he's not interested in my medical abilities, I have an inkling as to what he'll ask. Probably something along the lines of whatever he's expecting from the girl that the agency's meant to send, the one that'll be here in two hours.

He reaches forward to pick up a lock of my hair; I can't entirely hide my flinch, which makes his eyes narrow before his expression smooths and he continues talking. "It's a deal as old as time, really. I find whoever broke into your room, and make sure they don't do it again. While I work on that, you make yourself available to me."

I step back, and the hair he's holding falls from between his fingers. His brows furrow while I swallow hard. "Available to you how?"

"Available for me to use," he says, rather flatly. "I mean sex, Chloe. I want to find out what you look like beneath those clothes, and I want to find out what you feel like impaled on my cock. You give me what I want, I'll give you what you—"

"No!" The word bursts out of me, cutting him off; a scowl darkens his features at my interruption. "No, I'm not going to do... *that*. I won't whore myself out. I—I think I made a mistake here. No, I definitely made a mistake here—"

"The other option is for you to drop to your knees and wrap those pretty, plump lips around my cock a couple of times," he interjects in a voice that's butter smooth. "I'll accept that as payment, too."

While half of me wants to run for the elevator and forget about Mason's existence, take my chances with Seth, the other part of me considers his proposal. This won't be the first time I've gone down on a guy, and while I absolutely *despised* it last time because I had no choice in the matter, doing it again here might not be the worst thing in the world. It'll certainly nip whatever strange attraction I feel to Mason right in the bud. I'll definitely see this deal as nothing more than a necessary evil, a temporary arrangement I'm taking part in for the sake of my safety.

Besides, this won't go on forever; a few blowjobs in return for my physical well-being... I think I can handle that. If Mason hasn't taken care of the threat by the time Elia's man is back in town, I trust that she'll put Seth on the problem; while I don't personally trust Seth, I do trust his commitment to Elia and his dedication to making her happy in any way he can.

Seth will be back in four days, which leaves a gap. I'd rather not spend the next days terrified and looking over my shoulder. I inhale deeply, trying to switch from thinking desperately to thinking logically. Mason strikes me as an expert deal maker and a tricky guy; I need to set ironclad terms that he won't be able to find a loophole in, along with an escape clause in case things go to shit.

"I need solid terms," I say, trying to make my voice firm. "How often do you want..."

"A blowjob?" Mason supplies, lips curling with amusement. "I'll take one for each day that I'm looking into your problem. It shouldn't take too long, so we can start out with just one and take it from there. I'm gonna demand payment up front, right now. You get on your knees, I'll get right into your situation." Slowly, he extends a hand for me to shake.

I think over his wording carefully. *One a day for each day he's looking into it*, which would be a maximum of four days, until Seth gets back and takes over. If it's terrible, I'll leave it at one time and tell him to fuck off. Unlike *that* night, right now I have a choice in the matter. At most, I'll only have to do this a few times. I'll get safety from whoever broke into my room and a guarantee that I'll never feel any warped attraction to Mason Sieger again. He gets to have his dick sucked before going back to his usual supply of girls on campus and, apparently, women sent by some agency. The fact that I'm considering agreeing to this speaks to just how frightened I am.

"Are you clean?" I ask him. "Any STI's?"

He shakes his head. "Nope, I'm clean. I always fuck with a condom, and I get tested regularly. My last test was yesterday, if you want to see the bill of health. All negative." He tilts his head to the side, considering me. "Are *you* clean?"

A laugh bubbles out of my lips. Since I've had no sexual contact since that awful party, after which I frantically got tested, there's no way I wouldn't be. "Oh, yes, I'm definitely clean. To clarify, the deal's contingent. It starts out with one time, today, then negotiations going forward. The maximum you can ask for is one... *you know*, per day, as long as we're both satisfied with each other, until such a time where the deal is terminated or naturally comes to an end."

Again, his lips curl, this time into a genuine smile. "I think I like you, Chloe... what's your last name?"

"Richardson," I say absently.

He nods. "Chloe Richardson. I agree to the set terms. Now, do we have a deal? We'll need to shake on it to make the verbal contract official. And, Chloe, you should know that I don't go back on deals. If someone else tries to renege, it won't end well for them."

I can't renege, I think grimly. After all, if that note is to be believed, my life is at stake. Thanks to the serial killer that stalked campus last year, I've already learned that Greywood is a dangerous place.

I take Mason's hand reluctantly, biting back a gasp at the firm way he grips my hand and gives it a single shake.

"Excellent," he says.

Then, he uses his grip to yank me into his apartment, sending me crashing into his chest.

CHAPTER THREE

Mason Sieger

Chloe tumbles into my chest; her teal eyes widen as she braces her palms on my pecs for balance. The door shuts behind her, and she quickly tries to step back. Her second-hand bag tumbles off her shoulder and to the floor. I don't allow her to back away—I wrap an arm around her waist, lift another into her silky-soft hair, and lower my head to slant my lips over hers.

I'm not usually a kisser. I'm also not someone who usually demands sex as a favor; I don't need to. When I'm bored of the girls on campus, I have sources that send a ready supply of women my way. There are, in fact, a great number of irregularities about this moment, all of which began the moment I laid eyes on a pixie-looking thing ringing my doorbell to ask for a deal.

Chloe is unusually gorgeous, with an appearance reminiscent of a fairy from folklore. She's petite, with strawberry-blonde wavy hair, and entrancing teal eyes that are like a sucker punch to the gut. She has small, perky breasts beneath her loose shirt, ample hips, and a tiny waist that I'd like to wrap my hands around. There's something particularly delectable about her, and a strange attraction sparked in the air the moment I saw her.

I've needed to feel her lips on mine since she licked them nervously out in the hall; now that I can, I groan at their softness, how they feel like two clouds. She's stiff in my arms, surprised since I never mentioned kissing as part of our deal, but I can't help myself. I probe at her lips with my tongue, oddly desperate to find out what she tastes like. She keeps them firmly sealed together, which only makes a chuckle rumble out of me. I give her hair a sharp tug, and she gasps; that's all the opening I need to push into her mouth. Her taste explodes on my tongue—sweet and minty and edged with a strange innocence—which turns me *ravenous* for her.

A haze of desire descends over my mind, so consuming it nearly robs me of my sanity. My kiss turns from hungry to *savage*. I suck her tongue, keeping one hand in her hair to hold her still while the other wanders down to her ass. *Fuck. Me.* Full, firm, and luscious, her ass fills my palm and makes my cock stiffen against Chloe's flat belly. Her hands on my chest slowly turn from stiff to pliant, and she reluctantly begins to sink into our kiss, which invigorates me. I need to feel those lips wrapped around my cock; I *have* to find out what she looks like when she's choking on me, what it feels like to fuck her face. I'd much prefer her pussy, but that wasn't part of our deal. *Oversight on my part.*

With great reluctance, I pull my mouth away from hers, nipping her lower lip. I watch her as she blinks several times, and my gaze wanders over her delicate features. My lips curve when I notice a light smattering of freckles over the bridge of her nose. *Adorable.*

I release her ass and hair in favor of taking hold of her shoulders and pushing her down to her knees. I'm too far gone right now to wait or be gentle; I need to feel her mouth around me *immediately*. I need to get whatever I can out of our deal, which she so cleverly negotiated. I have to see if reality can live up to the fantasies scorching a path through my thoughts.

"Pull down my pants," I tell her, my voice gravelly. "I'm eager to get started."

A flighty look overcomes her features as her eyes come into focus and widen. Her body tenses in a strange way, as if she doesn't like this particular act or isn't familiar with it. If I had more presence of mind, I might try to understand the meaning behind the strange expression she wears; right now, though, I've been robbed of all intellect. All I want is to feel her sucking me.

"Now, Chloe," I tell her when she pauses.

She follows my orders with furrowed eyebrows and thinned lips. Her fingers slide along the waistband of my sweats, and she slowly pulls them down. She looks startled when she realizes I'm not wearing any boxers; even more startled when the length of my cock bobs in front of her face, the tip pointing at her lips. I'm as hard as I can ever remember being, which in itself is markedly rare. It usually takes some heavy fantasizing for me to get hard and ready for a fuck; with her, all it takes is a goddamn *kiss* of all things. *I think there's something about this girl...* something I want to explore.

With her brows furrowed and lips swollen, she reaches up a hesitant hand to grab the base of my cock, making me hiss as tingles explode along my length. *If her hand feels that good, her mouth is going to feel incredible.* I'm willing to bet her pussy would feel even better. It really is a shame I didn't push harder to have full access to her.

"How do you... want me to do it?" she asks uncertainly, as if she's never given a blowjob before, which I just don't believe. She's too beautiful, too seductive, like the walking personification of a siren.

"Take the tip in your mouth and suck," I tell her, my words little more than a growl. "Don't use any teeth or we're gonna have problems."

She nods, leans forward, opens her puffy lips, and wraps them around the tip of my cock just like I told her to. Her mouth is hot, wet, absolute fucking *heaven*. We've barely gotten started, and this is already the best blowjob I've ever received. I'm having trouble remembering the last time I felt such pleasure, which should, frankly, be illegal. I wind a hand into her hair, desperate to feel more of her, *have* more of her—as much as I can get. She's tentative at first, moving her head back and forward, tongue laving over my tip, then seems to get down to business. Her cheeks hollow as she takes more of my length into her mouth and sucks me so firmly, I think she might just suck the soul out of my body. I need more, *now*.

A red fog of pure need clouds my vision. My hand tightens in her hair, and I start controlling her movements, forcing her to swallow more of me. Her hands fly up to grip my bare thighs, fingernails digging in, but I barely notice the pinch of pain—I'm too caught up in the pleasure, which is overwhelming. This is almost *too* good.

She slaps my legs, and her teeth scrape against the underside of my length. I pull out with a hiss. "What did I say about teeth?" I demand, then pause as I *actually* look at her.

One glance is all it takes to tell me that something's very wrong here. There are tears streaming down her cheeks, ones that don't come from deep throating but something else entirely, something I do *not* like. Her head lowers as her shoulders shake with sobs, and I take a step back, startled. *She's crying over a blowjob?*

This would usually be the point where I usher the hysterical girl out of my apartment, shut the door on her, and let her figure out her problems on her own. I am not a knight in shining armor; I don't lower myself to deal with the emotions of others. But there's something different about this situation, something fundamentally wrong.

I frown at the little pixie who's crying on my hardwood floor, trying to figure out what the hell is going on. We made a deal, and now she's doing... this. Tears from a woman *can* be a turn on, but only when they're born of pain or pleasure that works for both of us. I'm pretty sure I'm witnessing a genuine breakdown right now, and there's nothing sexy about that. I pull up my sweats to cover my softening cock, blinking repeatedly, unsure of how I'm supposed to proceed.

Her tears combined with her tiny, trembling frame affect me in a way I'm entirely unaccustomed to; I have an urge to fix whatever's wrong, if only so I have the chance to see her again. I *will* be seeing her again, outside the bounds of our deal, because there's no goddamn way I'm not going to explore whatever's between us. It's too intense, too genuine, too *real* for me to let go of. A single kiss was more than enough to tell me that.

For the first time in my life, I check on a woman's welfare rather than giving her the boot. I bend down and reach out a hand to brush Chloe's hair away from her face before cupping her cheek.

She shoves me away with a fierceness and strength I didn't expect, screeching, "Don't touch me!"

What. The. Fuck?

Her eyes are wild but unseeing, glazed over as if she's in a different place and time. She scrambles backward until her back hits the wall, leaving me frozen with confusion and surprise. As I peer at her, noting her twitchy movements and gasping breaths, it finally hits me. I'm able to put together a tenuous picture of her, one that makes a lot of sense.

I think that this little pixie has had some bad experiences in the past, experiences that probably had to do with being forced to perform sexual acts when she didn't want to. My intensity might've brought back those experiences, hence her current state of panic.

Her tears and the obvious pain evident on her features bother me on some fundamental level I'm unused to, which pisses me off. I shouldn't care about her meltdown, but I do, and my chest tightens with an unfamiliar urge to fix whatever's wrong.

"Hey," I say, keeping my voice even as I squat down to her level. "Calm down, you're good." I slowly reach out to take her hand—she tries to jerk it away, which irritates the hell out of me. I tighten my grip to prevent her from pulling away. I like the feel of her small hand in mine too much to let go. Some instinct inside me wants to calm her, tame her, and *keep* her, even though I've never wanted to keep a girl before. *Looks like this is a night of firsts.*

Her eyes drop down to our intertwined hands, and her tears slow as her sobs turn into occasional hiccups. I stroke my thumb over her knuckles, marveling at the softness of her skin, at how very delicate she looks—so small and fragile, yet she possesses a quiet strength. After all, it was courage born of strength that made her negotiate with me out in the hallway, and bravery that brought her to my doorstep in the first place. I'm almost tempted to berate her for agreeing to a deal that reduced her to this state, but I hold my tongue.

I watch as Chloe blinks several times, still staring at our hands. She yanks her hand again with such strength that I release it, and then she scrambles to her feet. There's a flighty look in her eyes, but the desperate edge to her demeanor is gone, which relieves me more than I'm willing to admit.

"Chloe," I start slowly, "what was that?"

"A mistake," she says, wiping her cheeks with the backs of her hands, clearing the tear tracks. "This was... very much a mistake. *My* mistake," she hastens to add, as if not wanting to offend me. "I'm terminating the deal. You don't have to look into anything, and we don't have to see each other again." She nods resolutely. "Yes, that's the best course of action."

The fuck it is. To not see her again? She's stirred up strange yet addictive feelings within me, and she just wants to go? I'm not ready to let her go. There's a monster inside of me that's rearing his head and roaring with the need to possess her, perhaps even *keep* her. While I'm not a slave to my desires, I'm also not one to ignore them unless I have a good reason to. With her, I have zero reason to ignore them.

"That's not going to happen," I tell her, trying to keep my voice even. "I will be seeing you again. What just happened? Why did you lose it like that?" I'm reasonably sure I already know, but I want to hear it from her.

"I didn't lose it!" she snaps, cheeks burning. "I am terminating our deal. Hope you enjoyed the freebie; it won't *ever* happen again." She shakes her head. "Never *that* again."

She scoops her bag off the floor, turns to the door, and pulls on the handle, opening it and slipping out without a backward look. I'm tempted to reach for her, seize her, and keep her here with me regardless of her sentiments on the matter, but I restrain myself. Just barely, and mainly because I need to learn more about her, but I don't think she's in a chatty mood right now. What I need right now is to regroup and make a game plan.

I know with absolute certainty that I am not ready to let her go, but I hated the sight of her misery and don't want to incite it again. If someone hurt her, which seems increasingly likely, I am going to find and destroy them.

I also know that I will come for Chloe. I'll chase her down if I must, because I'm not done with her. Not by a longshot. First, though, I need to make sure she's safe from whatever fuck dared to threaten her.

Chapter Four

Chloe

I order an Uber that I can hardly afford back to dorms and spend the ride trying to calm myself down. It's not easy; I'm trembling and nauseous, mortified by the way I lost it in front of *Mason freaking Sieger*. I shouldn't have agreed to go down on him; I should've known that the act would bring up visceral flashbacks to the horrific party, but I wasn't thinking, so I made a fool of myself. I am *not* equipped to handle Mason—I don't think I'm equipped to handle anyone when it comes to sexual things, but certainly not him. There's something untamed and savage about him, and his sexuality is obviously off the charts, while I'm a virgin with no intimate experience aside from one time that cleared me of any desires or fantasies.

My driver notices my discontent and repeatedly glances at me in the rearview mirror. He even offers me a bottle of water that I politely decline. As soon as we arrive at the program dorms, I rush into the building and hurry up the stairwell to April's old room. My hands tremble as I rummage through my bag to find the key card she gave me, then lift it up to the scanner by her door. The rest of us have plain old locks, but Ian installed an entire security system for April. He is the very embodiment of overprotectiveness.

As soon as I'm in, I switch on the lights and shut the door behind me. The room's been stripped bare, all of April's belongings moved out. On the bed there's a neatly folded pile of sheets still in their packaging, obviously new and unused, sitting on top of a small pillow. A chest of drawers is set up along the wall. Tomorrow, I'll need to start moving my things out of my old dorm room and into this one.

After making the bed, I toss and turn for hours, my mind set on tormenting me. When I'm not hyperventilating my way through flashbacks to one of the worst times of my life and its terrible after-math, I'm thinking about who exactly broke into my room—who wants me off campus so badly they're threatening to kill me for it. I know that the threat might not be feasible; it could be a nasty prank, but my gut tells me it's more. The one time I disregarded my intuition, I got assaulted, so I'm not keen to ignore it again, especially with a threat on my life looming.

Somewhere in the early hours of the morning, I finally manage to fall asleep. My phone alarm goes off only a short time later.

Exhausted and dazed, I head to my dorm room to prepare for dance. The room's in the same state as when I left: a knife sticking out of my destroyed bed, my treasured periodic table of elements—the one my father gifted me when I was very young—hanging in tatters from the wall, and my textbooks scattered across the floor. At least they aren't ripped; I can't afford to re-buy all of my textbooks this semester.

Although I barely have time to spare, I load my backpack and take my most essential items to April's room, which I guess is now my room. Then, I run off to the dance headquarters building, which is luckily just a short jog from program dorms.

Heading to the studio where we do warmups before classes, I spot Carson Ajax sitting in a corner, scrolling through his phone. Every few seconds, his gaze flicks over to Eliana, who stands at the barre with April, as if he can't keep his eyes off his girl. He's been shadowing her dance classes since the beginning of freshman year; Elia hated it at first, but now she finds it kind of endearing.

I drop my backpack and dance duffel bag by the door, then join April and Elia at the barre.

"Morning," Elia greets brightly, giving me a smile that's too damn cheery for 6:30 a.m., especially when I'm running on a few hours of sleep.

"You look like a bucket o' fuck," April observes bluntly. "Did you not sleep at all?"

"I think I got two or three hours in," I mumble, propping my leg on the barre and beginning my usual stretches.

"So, tell me, how did your little chat with Mason go? I'm *dying* to know," Elia says.

I feel my cheeks heat as unwanted memories assail my mind. I'm close with Elia and April, but I wouldn't call us *best* friends, so I go for a surface-level explanation. "Deal didn't end up going through."

Elia's eyebrows furrow. "Really? Huh. That's weird. I ran into Mason in the elevator this morning, and he mentioned your name, asked me about you."

I feel myself stiffen. "Did he, now? What'd you say?"

"The basics," Elia responds with a shrug. "You're Hermes in Pandora's Box, and you're also majoring in biochemistry." A smile spreads on her lips. "Most people think I'm crazy for doing an art history degree on top of dance, but you take it to a whole new level. Do you have time for anything but classes and studying?"

"There's lots of homework to do, but I'm pretty good at staying on top of it," I tell Elia.

I inherited my father's excellent memory, which helps me with tests, but big projects are still pretty time-consuming. Last year was a steep learning curve, since I'd taken enough AP and college courses throughout high school to start my freshman year at Greywood with sophomore biochemistry classes. Now, as a sophomore, I'm taking junior year biochem classes.

April shakes her head, looking baffled. "I don't know how you two do it. I have a pretty good head on my shoulders, so I take some extra courses. But having an entire major *on top of* Greywood's insane dance program? That sounds like too much."

Elia chuckles. "It can be, but it's also super rewarding."

"Definitely," I agree. While I'd love to think that I'll make it in a dancing career, there's no guarantee, especially since I won't accept anything less than being a principal dancer, which is a stretch. I'm very good at ballet, but I'm not one of the greats of my time, so the competition would be tough. Elia and April aren't just good; they're otherworldly. Companies will probably compete to have them as principal dancers once they've graduated.

We chat a little more before our instructor walks in. I try not to let my mind wander to darker topics, allowing my body and muscle memory to take over as I spend the next hours dancing.

***

After dance, I go right to my biochem classes, exercising my mind after spending six hours working out my body. At the end of a lab class that I quite enjoy, I try not to drag my feet as I head out of the classroom. One of my lab group members, Mira, walks beside me as I mentally prepare for my next class, an anthropology elective.

"I just don't understand why dissection is always so smelly," Mira says, wrinkling her nose as she unwinds her platinum-blonde hair from its bun. "That pig we worked on today was *foul*. Formaldehyde is not a pleasant scent."

"You're an animal science major, on track for vet school," I remind her. "I imagine unpleasant scents are going to be a big part of veterinary medicine. You'd better get used to it."

Mira chuckles. "Yeah, you're right." She checks the time on her phone. "Shoot, I need to get going—I'm visiting my wolf pack tonight."

I smile faintly. "Has anyone ever told you you're insane for visiting a wild wolf pack?" I ask her.

She pauses to consider this, then nods. "Yes. Multiple times. My dorm roommates never shut up about it," she sighs. "You're lucky to be a program student—you all get an entire room to *yourselves* in that shiny program dorm building. My roommates won't leave me the hell alone. Hey, have you ever wondered if poison gets more or less poisonous when it expires?"

My smile widens. Even though I only share a few classes with her, I adore Mira. She's quirky and random and absolutely lovely. "I think that'd depend on the poison." I open the squeaky front door of the science building for her, then follow her into the late afternoon sunlight. "Let's meet up for a coffee soon, yeah? I feel like we never see each other outside of class."

Mira nods. "Yeah, I should be free soon. I'll text you to set something up." She gives my arm a squeeze, then flits off down the paved walkway. As I veer onto the path leading to the history building, another one of my lab groupmates strolls up beside me.

"Hey," Daniel greets quietly, running a hand through his short chestnut hair.

I glance at him, a little startled that he's walking with me; Daniel's never approached me outside of class before. We chit-chat before class starts often enough, and he's nice to look at—he has that sleepy, bedhead sort of sexiness going for him. He occasionally teases me for being clumsy with beakers, but he's never really shown any interest in being my friend outside of school.

"Hey," I return.

"I'm going to see Pandora's Box tonight," he tells me. "I'm really looking forward to it. It sounds like a great show."

I'm confused as to why he's bothering to tell me this, but I still say, "It is pretty great, though I might be a touch biased."

"Right." He pauses for a beat, following alongside me as I turn toward the entrance of the history building. "You want to grab dinner after the show's done?"

Woah—that feels like it comes straight out of left-field. At the beginning of the year, I thought that Daniel might've been interested in me, but he's never been anything more than distantly friendly, so I decided that I was just fooling myself. Maybe I wasn't, though.

I pause, slowing my stride as I consider him. I haven't gone out with anyone since starting Greywood last year. Partly because I'm still hung up on old fears and partly because I'm afraid I wouldn't be able to stay on top of my classes if I dated. I'm doing pretty well with my classes, though, and after my encounter with Mason last night, I want more than ever to get past my shit. Eventually I want a family; I'd love to have kids someday. Though that goal is a while away, to get there I need to get over my aversion to physical intimacy. Daniel's a bit of a troublemaker, but he's also ridiculously smart and we share a major—possibly even a career track. I've never gotten a bad vibe from him—there's no real reason for me to turn him down.

"I'll take your prolonged silence as a no thanks," he says with a somewhat sardonic smirk.

"No, not that, it's just... there's a lot on my plate right now. Last night someone broke into my dorm room, stabbed my mattress, and left a death threat on my pillow, so I'm using a friend's room. It's been a long day."

"Shit," Daniel says, eyebrows raising. If there was any question in my mind about whether he was somehow the one responsible for the break in, his expression of genuine surprise dulls it. "Are you okay? Did you tell campus security?"

"I got an email that they'd be checking into it today, and I should be hearing back from them soon," I say, thinking back to the email I got from admissions after dance. From what I was told, they intend to clean up my room and look into who broke in, though it didn't sound like they considered this to be a pressing matter.

"I hope they take care of it quickly," Daniel says, frowning. "I'm sorry that happened to you—that's fucking terrible. If you find out who broke in, I can beat the shit out of him for you."

I feel a faint smile spread on my lips. "Very noble of you. What makes you think it's a guy?"

I come to a stop below the stone steps leading up to the history building. With its stained glass windows and arched wooden doors that are carved with ancient engravings, the history building on campus certainly represents it's studies.

"In my experience, girls tend to be pettier while guys tend to be deadlier," Daniel says. "So, fuckwad who'll hopefully soon get found out and expelled aside, dinner?"

I bite my lip, once again thinking back to last night. I don't know if Daniel would be interested in someone with my kind of baggage. Then again, I don't expect we'll do more than share a meal if I agree to go out with him. Maybe there'll be a kiss at the end of the night. I usually hate kissing as much as anything, but I didn't hate it last night with Mason. It's what came after that I couldn't stand. *God, I need to stop thinking about him.*

"I can't do dinner tonight—I usually try to get a good night's rest after a performance," I say. "I could do something tomorrow, in the first half of the day. Since word has it you're lagging on our group project, maybe we could meet at the library? Work on your share?"

"Nah," he says, shaking his head. "I'll get it done in time—I always do. What about a picnic? We could go to the campus park for brunch."

"That works," I agree with a nod. Daniel's attractive enough; square jaw, pretty blue eyes, a strong build that tells me he takes care of himself, probably hits the gym regularly. *Not like Mason, though, who looks like he benches cars in his free time...*

Once again, I have to remind myself that I am *not* attracted to Mason. The harsh way he gripped my head, twisting my hair around his fist while he basically fucked my mouth was not attractive, it was triggering. He's just too intense for my tastes. Daniel might have some rough edges and like to stir up trouble, but he's a decent guy—he certainly doesn't have ties to any mafia.

Out of the corner of my eye, I think I spot a swath of auburn hair, which makes me whip my head to the side to check. Seeing nothing—certainly no six and a half foot hulking man with golden-green eyes—I subtly exhale a breath of relief.

"What's your number?" Daniel asks, pulling my attention back to him as he draws his phone out of his pocket. I reel it off and he plugs it into his contacts before giving me a grin. "I'll text you in the morning. I'll also probably text you a thorough critique of my thoughts on Pandora's Box tonight, too."

"I look forward to it," I say with a small laugh. "I need to get to class, but I really do hope you enjoy the performance tonight. See you tomorrow."

"See you," he agrees.

Chapter Five

After my final class of the day, I walk out of the history building, my eyes focused on the textbook in my hands. It's still light outside, with plenty of students and faculty members milling about, so I'm not particularly worried that whoever broke into my room last night will accost me. Even in the evening, Greywood's campus remains crowded with ongoing classes until around 8 p.m.—a side effect of having so many overachievers at the university—so there'd still be plenty of people to provide a sense of protection. It's late at night, after 10, when the campus is deserted, that I'd feel concerned about walking alone.

I'm so engrossed in the passage I'm reading that I don't notice someone stepping into my path and don't have enough time to stop myself from crashing face-first into them. My textbook clatters to the ground, falling down the steps leading from the building, but I forget all about that when vaguely familiar hands grip my shoulders to steady me. I inhale a deep breath, taking in a familiar scent of subtle spicy cologne over fresh earth and something sheerly masculine, knowing who I have the misfortune of running into even before I look up into a pair of golden-green eyes.

I shove out of Mason's hold with a yelp and stumble back. A few passing students glance at us; several stop to stare at Mason outright. I can't blame them—he is as physically attractive as a man can get, but if they knew who he truly was beneath the looks, I hope they'd have the sense to run in the opposite direction.

"Gotta say, that's not a reaction I usually get," Mason comments calmly, his gaze burning with the heat of a million suns. The way he looks at me is so blatantly possessive that it raises goosebumps on my arms.

A faint, "Oh shit," escapes my lips. *How did he find me?* We go to the same school, sure, but Greywood has a huge campus. Mason's in the business program, and business buildings are across campus, so I think he might be here... *for me*. The way he looks at me only backs up my sinking suspicion.

"Chloe, lovely to see you again," Mason says, as if we're old friends reuniting.

Huh? "Um... our deal's off," I say, brushing past him to trot down the stairs and grab my textbook before it gets trampled by passing students.

Mason gets to it before I do, picks it up, and makes a show of dusting it off. He doesn't hand it back to me, though; instead, he keeps it in his grip.

"Wrong," he says, raking his gaze over my body. "Our deal's just getting started."

"No, it's not," I say emphatically, keeping my voice low to avoid any more attention. "It's really, *really* not. I terminated it—"

"You *tried* to terminate it. Termination would have to be agreed upon by both of us." He pauses for a beat while anxiety curls in my stomach, and a profound need to run away from him sweeps over me. That would just look odd, and I get the sense that it won't work. Everyone who's heard of Mason knows he is a very powerful man with even more powerful connections.

"I'm not doing… *that* again," I hiss. "Get yourself off somewhere else. It was my mistake for agreeing to it in the first place—"

"I'm not asking for you to blow me again, Chloe," he cuts me off. "While you do look particularly erotic on your knees, I get the sense that you don't like *that* activity. We can adjust terms."

"No," I say emphatically, shaking my head. "Absolutely not." The unyielding look in his eyes tells me that trying to take a firm approach with him won't get me anywhere; I need to be careful. Softening my expression and posture, I say in a more mellow voice, "Look, I'll figure my situation out some other way. You're off the hook—there's no reason for us to see each other again, which is for the best."

"We disagree on that point," he says smoothly, stroking his thumb over the glossy cover of my textbook. "I think there's every reason for us to see each other again."

I blink several times, barely able to comprehend his words. "What are you *talking* about?"

"You and me, Chloe. That's what I'm talking about." He steps closer, leaving less than a foot of space between us. Before I can step back, he slings an arm around my waist like a boyfriend would—a gesture that might look affectionate from the outside. Held against his chest, I feel only menace and impending danger. I could try to push him off, but that would just draw the wrong kind of attention.

"Please remove your arm from me," I murmur lowly, trying to keep my voice steady.

Mason makes a humming noise, as if he's actually considering it. "I don't think so," he finally says. "I like touching you very much."

"*I* do not like touching *you*. It is making me deeply uncomfortable; *you* are making me deeply uncomfortable. Please, for the love of god, *let me go.*"

Panic rises within me, making my breaths turn into pants and inciting a sudden sensation of cold, as if I'm stranded in Antarctica without so much as a sweater. I start to shiver in his hold—Mason notices this and his brows furrow almost thoughtfully. I look away, trying to think of how I can escape him, but he props my textbook under his arm and then uses his free hand to redirect my gaze to him.

"I'm not him." His words slip through my stupor and add shock to the turmoil swirling around in my chest—*how does Mason know there's another* him? A guy who made me like this?

Still so damn calmly, Mason tells me, "Breathe."

The word is smooth and assertive, hitting me like a siren's call, impossible to ignore or resist. My breaths even out, but my shivering doesn't lessen; I still feel chilled to the bone. Mason shifts his hand to stroke his thumb over my cheek, then pushes it into my hair, tenderly cupping the base of my skull and rubbing the back of my neck with his fingers. This isn't like last night, when he ruthlessly held me in place—it's a lot more caring.

Inadvertently and completely against my will, my body starts to relax. Warmth replaces the cold, and I feel my heartbeat slow to a semi-normal pace. The fact that it's *him* calming me down when he's the one who worked me up in the first place is a mindfuck of cosmic proportion, but I really don't want to have a panic attack in public, so I take what I can get.

"That's it," he breathes out.

I don't say anything, too ashamed, embarrassed, and confused to respond. I'd like to find a hole to hide in and stay there for the next thousand or so years, away from people and stress, but I have a performance in just a few hours that I need to start preparing for.

"I got carried away last night," he tells me lowly. "If I had known you had some problems in that department, I would've been more careful." It's not an apology, but I get the feeling his words are as close to an apology as Mason can offer.

"You're not a nice or careful person," I mumble.

"You're right," he surprises me by admitting easily. Tension gathers within me at the admission, but it's quickly dissipated by the way he continues holding me, rubbing the back of my neck soothingly, lulling me under his spell. "I'm very rough when it comes to certain things, but I'm not an animal. I can control my desires. Oftentimes, I just don't see a reason to or even want to, but that doesn't mean I'm incapable of it."

"That has no bearing here," I say quietly. "I would very much like for you to let me out of the deal we made." Seeing his displeasure at that, I add, "Unless you'd like to revert to my original offer: I give emergency first aid at some point in the future, no questions asked." I'd really prefer not to have any entanglement with him whatsoever, but I get the feeling he isn't keen on letting me out entirely—it might be a blow to his ego or something.

"You're a very clever little negotiator, aren't you?" he questions, sounding amused. "No, Chloe, I don't want your medical services in the future. I'm going to give you two options, and you can choose between them. First option, we revert to *my* initial offer of you making yourself available for my use." My jaw drops in horror at his audacity. He's just saved me from a public panic attack, only to do a complete one-eighty and put *that* on the table. There's something very wrong with this man, and I realize I need to get away from him permanently.

"Are you fucking kidding me?" the words escape my lips in a barely audible whisper.

"Not in the least. I'm more serious than either of us can fathom. The second option is we go to dinner. We can negotiate terms more to your liking then."

"No," I say, aghast.

He nods, expression placid. "So, option one it is. Open your dorm room door when I knock—trying to keep me out will only piss me off."

Louder, I snap, "*No!*"

His eyebrows raise, and faint amusement flits across his expression. "Then we'll be having dinner tonight. Do you have any preferences for where you'd like to eat?"

I can't wrap my mind around how twisted this whole interaction is; it's overwhelming. *He's* overwhelming, and it strikes me again that I am not equipped to handle him. "What if I say fuck your deal making bullshit and tell you to stay away from me?"

"Then we revert to option number one. Don't test me, Chloe. I'm neither gentle nor forgiving by nature. You made a bargain with me, and I'm being quite nice by offering to alter the terms to something that works for both of us because I like you, but I don't have to be nice. I can be mean instead, though I doubt you'd like that." He pauses for an infinitely long beat, gazing down at me. "Would you like me to be mean?"

His tone carries a silky menace, making it clear I have no choice but to choose option two. I'm not giving myself up for his use, so instead I have to resign myself to spending more time with him. I'll go to dinner with him and hope that he doesn't take advantage of me.

"You're being deeply unfair," I say bluntly, lowering my gaze to his chest, not wanting to look at his deceptively beautiful face any longer.

Mason tightens his grip in my hair—not as harshly as last night, as if he's mindful of not setting me off again—but enough to tilt my head up and force me to look at him.

"This world is an unfair place. That's why your room was broken into, your mattress destroyed, your textbooks scattered, and a death threat left on your pillow. If the world were fair, that wouldn't have happened. If the world were fair, campus administration would do something about that break in and take the threat seriously, but they won't devote any significant resources to you because you haven't been hurt, and you are a nobody to them." I wince at the harshness of his words, and his gaze softens. His grip in my hair loosens, and he strokes his fingers along my skull. "You are a somebody to me, and I will protect you. I'll find who's fucking with you and take care of them. All I ask in return is that you give me some of your time, let me take you to dinner. Is that really such a steep price?"

"When the alternative is rape, yes," I mutter.

Instead of getting angry or indignant, Mason chuckles. "Oh, Pixie, I wouldn't have to rape you. That holds no appeal for me. You'd be begging for my touch, *dripping* for it. I'd make sure of that."

"I am sincerely glad that your theory will never be tested," I reply snippily.

"It's not a theory, you'll find that out eventually. Whether that happens sooner should you take option one—I'll tell you now, I'd come for you tonight if that's the case—or on a looser timetable with option two is entirely up to you. The ball's in your court, Chloe. Are we going to dinner, or are you spreading your delectable legs for me tonight?"

"Dinner," I say, deeply disturbed. Between going out to eat with him—where I might get a chance to divert his attention, try to convince him to take *my* initial offer, or perhaps even find a way to make him lose interest in me—and having to lose my virginity to this monster tonight, I choose dinner.

"Very good," he purrs. He still doesn't release me, as if he's not ready to or he simply doesn't want to. His eyes drop to my lips, his gaze igniting with hunger, causing anxiety to roil within me again. It's not panic, though—for some reason, the way he's holding me is keeping true panic at bay, even though his touch is completely at odds with his words and clear intentions. *What the hell is wrong with me?*

"How did you know about my mattress and books?" I blurt out, trying to deflect his attention from my mouth. "I didn't tell you that."

His eyes once again meet mine, but the hunger and darkness in them doesn't lessen. "I have my ways, and they are very extensive. Keep that in mind if you're thinking about wiggling out of our deal or trying to get away from me—it won't work. I have eyes, ears, and connections everywhere. Be a good girl and I'll continue being nice; be bad, and I'll get mean."

Left with no other option and shaken to my core, I whisper, "Okay."

"Good." He releases me slowly, first letting go of my hair, then leisurely unwinding his arm from around me. I nod toward my textbook as he takes it in his hands.

"Can I have that back?"

"After dinner, yes. I'll meet you in the theatre lobby—I'll be at the show tonight." He steps away, giving me one last lingering stare before turning and melting into the crowd.

Fuck.

CHAPTER SIX

Mason

I attend Chloe's performance that evening. Reclining in my box seat at the historic local theatre, I watch with rapt attention as Chloe pours her heart into her every movement on stage. I've seen Pandora's Box once before, after donating a substantial sum of money to Greywood's Dance Co. to earn a favor from Ian Vargas and Carson Ajax. I noticed Chloe then, but now I direct all my attention to her. Objectively, she's one of the most talented performers on stage—that's why she has not one but *two* solos. Subjectively, however, I believe she outshines every other dancer by miles.

She looks unreasonably gorgeous in a skimpy leotard that reveals her bare belly, with silver highlighter that makes her high cheekbones glimmer, and dramatic blue eye makeup. Her lips curve into a seductive and mischievous smile throughout both her solos—the dances themselves exude mischief and seduction, leaving me *enamored* as I watch.

As the dancers take bows after the show has concluded, I notice that Chloe gets an extra round of applause from the audience as she takes an individual bow for her solos. Her cheeks blush prettily at the praise, visible even beneath layers of makeup. I can't help but wonder how I might bring that blush back to her face.

Once the applause and shouts of adulation have died down, the dancers make their way backstage, and the audience members begin sifting toward the lobby. On the stairway, I run into both Ian and Carson—they're also coming from their own box seats.

"Mason," Carson greets with a nod, looking me over. "Strange seeing you here."

"Is it?" I query flatly.

Carson shrugs. "Maybe not, since you asked my girl about Chloe this morning. You angling to make a play for her?"

"Yes," I say honestly.

The sooner people know Chloe's off-limits for the foreseeable future, until I've had a thorough taste of her and discovered the root of my unfurling obsession, the better. I have a history of permanently eliminating competition in business matters—while that's never applied to a woman before, this just might be the exception.

"Richardson doesn't seem like your usual type," Ian comments. "Too smart."

It's true that I often go for girls with specific physical attributes, and few of them have the intellect to match. Maybe that's what has me so wrapped up in my Pixie; her intelligence shines through in her eyes, and everything I've learned about her so far tells me she is indeed very bright *and* absolutely stunning. She's not the usual buxom beauty with exaggerated curves; she's more sensual and sultry than the overtly sexual girls who often catch my notice for a quick ride. Then again, I take them for just that: a quick ride and decent release. Chloe's company is far more stimulating, both physically and intellectually.

"April's loud compared to your usual type, yet you did shit that raised even my eyebrows to lock her down," I tell Ian calmly.

When I noticed his unfurling obsession for the pretty raven-haired dancer, I was surprised at the lengths he was willing to go for her, not to mention the favors that he called in with me. I thought he might've been losing his mind at the time—I still thought so, until recently. Now, I think I'm starting to understand exactly what makes men like us lose all sense and reason, and turns us single-minded in pursuit of a woman. I've known Chloe for all of one day, and yet I feel disturbingly certain that she's someone I *must* have.

Just the idea of being in her presence again is invigorating. I've only had a few hits of the drug that she's proving to be, and I'm already in withdrawal. I need more.

Ian shrugs. "April's it for me; always has been. It took me some time to see that, but once I did, I was unstoppable. She was always going to be mine."

"Fair play," I concede with a nod, while internally wondering what it might be like to lock Chloe down permanently the way Ian did with April. The way both Seth and Carson did with Eliana. *Not a bad thought*. The idea of something permanent is ludicrous after knowing Chloe for such a short time, but the prospect of losing her feels equally untenable.

As we reach the entrance to the lobby, I tell Carson, "When Seth gets back next week, Eliana might ask him to look into something for Chloe. Have him come to me instead."

I've already gathered that I wasn't Chloe's first person of choice to turn to with her problem, and I intend to ensure that I'm her only option. I haven't had as much time as I'd like to study Chloe, but I've been able to glean a few things.

"Any reason why I should help you?" Carson questions, arching an eyebrow at me.

"Of course. You do me a favor, and I'll owe you a favor. I am a very useful asset."

"Are you going to hurt her?" Carson asks.

That would be my last method of choice. I like Chloe's discomfort, *love* the reluctant interest I've seen in her gaze, but I do not like her pain or panic. I think I might enjoy it in certain sexual situations, but not at any other time. Seeing her misery last night ignited a burning need to protect her.

"Not intentionally," I decide. If I were just speaking with Ian, he wouldn't ask any questions that don't pertain to him, but Carson is more noble than both of us combined.

"Fine," Carson agrees with a nod as we step into the crowded lobby. "I can't promise anything, but I'll tell Seth to go to you. Whether he'll listen is a whole different matter."

I nod at Carson, then let my gaze wander over the marble floors and walls, admiring the room's blend of old and refurbished styles. Stone pillars support a high domed ceiling adorned with stained glass detailing. A warm glow emanates from old lamps, casting a calm light on the many audience members chatting with each other.

Several minutes pass before the dancers start trickling out of the dressing rooms, having changed out of their costumes and wiped off the over-the-top makeup. I spot a head of blonde hair rushing toward Carson, just before Eliana wraps her arms around his waist and beams at her boyfriend. Carson smiles down at her, tucking her hair behind her ear.

"Hey, Princess. You were the best out there, as ever. Ready to get some food and go home?"

I turn and stroll deeper into the crowd. Watching their exchange tugs at something in my chest—a desire to find what they have for myself. Though their unity inspires envy within me, the vibe between Eliana and Carson is a bit too sweet and wholesome for my tastes. Just as I have the thought, I watch Ian step out of the crowd and snag April's waist from behind, startling his fiancée. She lets out a yelp, then turns in his arms and slaps his chest, snapping something about him being an asshole—he cuts her off with a kiss that bends her backward at the waist, drawing more than a few looks from passerby's. Their dynamic seems appropriate for their relationship; they both have rather loud personalities.

Knowing that it's only a matter of time before Chloe emerges into the lobby, I keep my eyes fixed on the hallway leading backstage. I don't have to wait long before she appears, her strawberry-blonde locks spilling over her shoulders in waves, her face free of makeup, and her eyes shining with exhilaration. She's wearing skin-tight black jeans that highlight her small waist and toned legs, along with a dark blue sweater that makes her skin look ethereally bright, almost glowing. *Absolutely stunning.* It's more than just her physical appearance that I find entrancing; it's also the cleverness and intelligence in her teal eyes, which currently look more green than blue.

She parts ways with the girl she's walking with, then turns around as someone calls her name. I watch as she walks over to a familiar boy, the kid I saw her talking to before her last class of the day. They looked far too cozy and familiar for my liking. From what I've gathered, Chloe isn't dating anyone, but if she were in a dating mood, I think this fuck might fit the bill. I'll need to look into him further to determine if he's a threat to my pursuit.

I watch as Chloe walks up to the boy and starts talking to him. Jealousy burns in my chest, unfamiliar and overpowering, pushing me to go over there and break up their conversation, make it clear that Chloe's mine, even if she doesn't yet agree with my claim.

Patience, I remind myself. There's a reason I'm known in my circles as the strategist; I'm very good at watching and analyzing people so I can understand them on a fundamental level. It's a helpful skill in business, and even more helpful in the few dealings my family has with mafias. Though my father doesn't officially work with any one organization, he's associated with several and is known as a mastermind. I've been trained from birth to take over his role, and my training has been very thorough.

I call on that training to keep me from storming forward like a fool and instead force myself to hang back and watch. *Assess the threat; don't intervene until the time is right.* I want to see what Chloe does—she knows I'm here somewhere, waiting for her. She should know to tread carefully.

Thankfully, after another minute or so she says her goodbyes to that fuck, who gives her a longing look as he walks to the exit of the theatre. Meanwhile, Chloe's wide-eyed gaze sweeps the crowd, undoubtedly looking for me. Once the boy's gone, I start to slowly slink toward her. She notices me when I'm closing in, and her entire posture goes rigid. She gets that flighty look she often wears around me, but she doesn't run. *Good girl.*

"Hello, Chloe," I greet once I'm in front of her, gazing down at her lovely features. "You danced beautifully tonight."

Her brows furrow, perhaps in disbelief at my words or confusion at my niceness. She'll learn soon enough that I'll only get mean when she makes certain choices—the *wrong* choices. Otherwise, I can control myself, even though what I'd really like to do is take her back to my apartment and spend the night getting thoroughly acquainted with her body. The air of innocence surrounding her makes me quite sure that she's a virgin, and while that would usually put me off, the idea of being her first and only is very appealing to me. *All mine.*

"Thank you," she says lowly, watching me like one might watch a predator in their vicinity—with an abundance of caution. She has no idea the things I plan on doing to her; spreading her out, tasting her everywhere, fucking her until she screams and pleads.

"You like Indian?" I ask her, though I already know the answer from thoroughly stalking her social media. Indian food is her favorite, thanks to a family trip she once took to India. Last year, she posted a photo of a much younger version of herself riding an elephant, wrapped in her father's arms and smiling widely.

"Y-yes," she says, clearing her throat with a frown.

I offer her my arm. "I've made reservations, let's be off. We can talk more once we're there."

She glances at my arm but doesn't take it, instead she wraps her arms around her waist in a protective cocoon. I wonder how long it'll take her to figure out that the only way to be protected from me is to cleave to me. The nicer and sweeter she is, the nicer I'll be. If this beautiful Pixie acts closed off, it'll only prompt me to go after her harder to break through her defenses.

"I can meet you at the restaurant if you tell me the name," she says with admirable firmness.

A smile tugs at my lips. "That won't work for me, Chloe. You'll be riding with me. I'd like to get to know you more." I step closer to her, and her gaze darts around. I get the sense that the only reason she doesn't step back is because we're surrounded by people who might find it odd to see her backing away from me. *Interesting that she cares.*

Depending on how much she values the opinions of others, I can use that to control her.

I take one of her arms, gently unwinding it from her waist and threading it through mine. She doesn't protest physically or verbally, but a helpless look appears in her eyes, as if she's realizing just how powerless she is to stop me from doing what I want, taking what I wish. *You're only powerless for so long as you resist,* I think. If she drops the resistance and gets clever, focuses on negotiating rather than blocking, she'll get a lot farther with me.

CHAPTER SEVEN

Mason

I lead Chloe out of the theatre and into the parking lot, heading toward my BMW. The closer we get to the car, the more reluctant she becomes, her stride slowing. Several times she opens her mouth, presumably to protest, only to stop when she thinks better of it. Once we're in front of my sleek, matte-black car, I open the passenger-side door for her. She exhales a long breath before climbing in and folding her hands on her lap, posture stiff. I close the door for her like the gentleman I can be when I feel like it, then round the car to the driver's side and climb in.

Since she hasn't put on her seat belt, I reach across to do it for her; she panics and grips my arm, crying, "*Wait!*"

"Easy," I tell her. "I'm just putting on your seatbelt, Pixie." Still, I rest my hand on her hip for a beat, silently letting her know that if I want to touch her, I'll touch her—there's nothing she can do to stop or sway me. She's tense under my touch, chest rising and falling with heavy breaths. I give her hip a squeeze before clicking her seatbelt into place, then shifting the car gear into drive and pulling out of my parking spot.

"So, you're a biochemistry major," I say, sliding her a glance. She clutches her seatbelt as if it can save her from me, which brings a faint smile to my lips. The only thing that would save her from me *is* me. "What career path are you thinking of pursuing if you don't end up in a dance company?"

"Medicine," she murmurs quietly. "I'd like to be a doctor—cardiologist, I think, with an emphasis on surgery."

I nod. "Solid choice. Tough schooling and residency. You'll have a lot of work to do."

She shrugs delicately. "I don't mind hard work."

I can see that, and it's a respectable quality. Between her dance courses and biochemistry classes, Chloe must have very little free time—she's wholly dedicated to her studies and classwork. Very admirable.

"You a genius or something, Chloe?" I ask her, my tone faintly teasing but also genuinely curious about her self-perception. From what I've seen so far, she is *very* intelligent, with a bright future ahead of her. She's extremely driven and focused, as well as talented and gorgeous to boot. A very desirable package, indeed.

She frowns. "No, not even close. I just... like what I do, I guess. Getting good grades is like a rewards system; praise follows hard work."

Interesting. I wonder if she might have a praise kink, both in the bedroom and outside of it.

"You like getting praised?" I ask.

"Who doesn't?" she replies. "It's a way to know you're doing well and achieving your goals."

So she's goal-oriented, just like I am. I intend to find as many commonalities with her as possible, so we can build the foundation for a relationship. I'm realizing more and more that my interest in her isn't just sexual; I'm intrigued by her as a person. *Very* intrigued—more so than I have been with anyone else in a long time.

"You gonna ask me any questions of your own?" I wonder aloud.

She shakes her head. "No, I think what I've learned about you is enough. I'm not eager to learn more."

I get the sense it runs deeper than that; she doesn't *want* to like me, even though she could. I know she's attracted to me, even if she doesn't want to be—maybe she's trying to suppress that attraction. That could be why she consented to give me a blowjob last night, even though that should've been the last thing she agreed to, considering she obviously has trauma in that area.

"Contrary to what you might believe, I'm not just an asshole," I inform her. "If you get to know me more, you might find you like me."

She shrugs. "If I wanted to get to know you, I would, but I don't. All I want is to get away from you; getting to know you won't help with that."

Her candor makes me chuckle. "You won't get away from me, Pixie—there's nothing you could do to make that happen. My interest will either burn out on its own, or it won't." I'm starting to think that it won't—it'll only grow. She's too fascinating to grow bored of, and everything about her pulls me deeper into her allure. "So there's no use in trying to put me off. It won't work. I'm too persistent, too focused."

She gazes down at her lap, that miserable look returning to her eyes, reminding me how much I dislike seeing her that way. I remain quiet, giving her the rest of the ride to process and collect herself in silence.

A few minutes later, we arrive at the restaurant; as soon as I've parked the car, I get out and round the hood to her side, opening the door for her. She takes off the seatbelt but doesn't move, looking like she'd rather be anywhere but here. *Too fucking bad.* I take her hand in mine and use it to pull her out of the car, then keep hold of it as I lead her up to the restaurant and through the wooden door marking the entrance. The interior is decorated minimally but tastefully, with vibrant scrolls of artwork on the walls, lamps hanging from beams beneath the ceiling, and a dim, intimate ambiance.

A hostess lingering behind a stand at the front of the restaurant looks up from her computer, does a double take when she sees me, and licks her lips. She's pretty enough; at another time I might flirt with her, even consider pulling her into a back room for a quickie. I don't now—I'm too intrigued and attracted to the Pixie at my side to pay attention to another woman.

The hostess clears her throat, giving me a look filled with blatant lust. "Do you have a reservation?"

I nod. "Under Mason Sieger, table for two."

The hostess clicks around on her computer, sliding me several inviting glances that I pointedly ignore. After a moment, she nods. "Got it. Right this way, Mr. Sieger."

As she leads Chloe and me through the rows of tables and to a booth in the back of the restaurant, I watch my Pixie, curious to see if my getting attention from someone else bothers her. It doesn't; in fact, she appears hopeful that I might instead switch my focus to the hostess or another woman, giving her a reprieve. *Adorable,* and so very misguided.

I'm tempted to seat myself beside Chloe so I can be close to her and touch her, but I also want a clear view of her face to gauge her reactions as we talk. I opt for the seat across from her. As soon as the hostess is gone, Chloe focuses on the napkin in front of her, placing it on her lap, then folding and unfolding it repeatedly.

"So," I say after a few minutes of silence, "back to our deal. I'll admit I'm glad that you took option two; option one would've been hard on you."

"As if you care," she mutters, shaking her head and avoiding my gaze.

"I care very much, Chloe, far more than I'm used to caring. Otherwise, I wouldn't have given you an option two, and right now I'd have you bent over somewhere, plunging my cock in and out of you, listening to your moans of abandon."

Her cheeks flame at the scene I depict, gaze darting up to lock with mine, once again filling with that reluctant interest. *Yes, that's what I want.*

"I'll be blunt," I start frankly, "I'm going to take you eventually. Whether that happens sooner or later is entirely up to you. I'm willing to give you time and take less than I'd like to if you cooperate."

"I really, *really* don't want to be taken," she says lowly.

"That'll change," I tell her, because it will. I'll ensure it. Even if it doesn't, I don't know that it'd stop me; I'm too committed to having her. "Here's my offer. I'm looking into your problem; it'll take me a bit longer than usual to figure it out, since whoever broke into your dorm room left me little to go on." Oddly, the security cameras were disabled during the break in. "While I'm working on that, we're going to spend some time together."

She shifts uncomfortably in her seat, folding her arms across her torso, drawing my eyes down as the gesture perks up her breasts. When she catches my line of vision, she quickly drops her arms, folding her hands in her lap.

"What will we be doing if we're going to be spending time together?" she questions cautiously.

I allow a smile to pull at my lips. I'm going to be doing my level best to seduce her while enjoying the resistance she presents. Usually, I wouldn't put in the effort of chasing after someone, but it seems that with Chloe, all my usual rules are being rendered inapplicable. There's something profoundly unique about her and it's causing me to stray far outside the lines of my normal behavior. So, I'll relish chasing my gorgeous Pixie around until I've caught her. She is lovely prey to hunt, after all...

I shrug at her question, as if it doesn't matter what activities we partake in, which is true to an extent. I don't really care exactly what we do, so long as I'm doing it with her.

"We can choose that on a case-by-case basis, but I'd like time with you regularly," I tell her. "I'll also be taking one kiss a day to satisfy the terms of our deal."

"One kiss a day," she repeats, sounding deeply unnerved at the prospect, yet somewhat resigned. She knows by now that refusing my kinder offer would mean reverting to the option that I would prefer. Having her spread out beneath me, taking my cock while I listen to her erotic moans as I ride her to within an inch of her life.

"Yes. As for our dates—"

"Dates?" she repeats, a shrill edge to her voice. "You didn't say anything about dates, only spending time together."

My eyes narrow at her words, but I quickly smooth my expression. I don't like the idea that she's repulsed by going on a date with me. Still, my aim tonight is to *not* spook her, to perhaps entice her, which is precisely why I'm affording her so much leeway.

"What do you call it when a man and woman spend time together?" I ask her.

"Hanging out," she says, frowning. "We're not compatible for... *dating.*"

"I happen to disagree, but we can touch on that later," I respond, fighting to keep my tone calm. "So, let's say we'll *hang out* a few times a week. I'll also be coming to you daily to collect on my kiss."

"I don't have time for a kiss every day," she tells me. "I'm ridiculously busy; when I'm not in classes, I'm studying. When I'm not studying, I'm working ahead in my biochem courses. Finals week is about to start, I'll barely have time to sleep, let alone kiss."

"I think I'll manage to find time for myself in your schedule," I say drily. "Don't worry about the details, I'll figure them out. Still, every day, I'm going to find you and demand my kiss. You will give it to me, regardless of the place or time."

"And if I don't, you'll revert back to your first idea for our arrangement," she says flatly.

I smile. "You're starting to catch on."

"Why are you doing this to me?" she asks. "I'm not the prettiest girl on campus, and I am certainly not the easiest or most willing. You could point to any other girl and she'd come running, yet you're putting time and effort into cornering me and bending me to your will. Why? Where did I go wrong?"

"You didn't go wrong anywhere, you are perfectly *right*," I tell her plainly. "That's why."

An adorable frown creases her brows. She tilts her head, staring at me as though I'm a puzzle she wants to solve. I think Chloe's one of the few people I've come across who could actually understand me, if she put her mind to it. I'll have to step carefully around her and do a great deal of preparation. I need her to be firmly ensnared by the time she does figure me out and finds out more about my life than just the rumors floating around campus, which barely scratch the surface.

I come from a shadowy world filled with immensely dark people. The wealthiest 1% of the business world is the very definition of cut-throat—I have more sociopaths and psychopaths in my social circles than I care to admit. By the time Chloe learns enough about my life to be *truly* afraid, I need her to be firmly ensnared.

I realize belatedly that my line of thinking means I intend to keep her around long enough to cross paths with the more dangerous individuals in my world, which is startling, because it indicates that I want her on a permanent basis. As soon as I have the thought, it's followed by several compelling ideas: Chloe, going to sleep wrapped in my arms. Me, waking up to the sight of her. Having her with me at all times, letting her into my world and keeping her there... all incredibly appetizing and enticing prospects.

The server comes around to take our drink orders, interrupting my train of thought. After he's left, Chloe abruptly stands from the table, and then mutters that she needs to go to the restroom.

While she's gone, I try to formulate how to best approach spending time with her in a way that doesn't scare her off too quickly. I'd already decided on the kissing part of our deal before bringing her here, and she seems so damn averse to the dating aspect that it makes me want to push it all the more. As I think, it strikes me that Chloe is an ideal candidate for a girlfriend. Smart, beautiful, already on her way to great accomplishments... she could be just what the doctor ordered. My family, specifically my father, is already pushing me to marry a girl in our circles, to make a match that would be advantageous for business.

He himself married my mother when he was twenty and she was nineteen, a strategic union, but also a dismal one. Mom and Dad hate each other and cheat flagrantly. They only had me out of a sense of duty and the need for an heir. Both of them are pushing me toward a similar path already, but what they don't understand is that I'd rather douse myself with gasoline and strike the match that burns me to a crisp than end up in a similar arrangement. I'm not sure that I would want love in a marriage; I don't know that I entirely believe in it, but I certainly want solid companionship, someone I'm attracted to and enjoy speaking to. Chloe fits the bill perfectly.

She's averse to dating me, while I'm growing increasingly more desperate to spend time with her; I think I might've found a solution to that little conundrum.

When Chloe returns to the table, I appraise her in a new light, considering her less as someone I want to fuck and get to know in the process, and instead as someone I'd like to play the long game with. Sex is short term; I don't just want that with her, I'd like a great deal more, and I think I might've figured out a way to make that happen.

"There'll be one more thing as part of our deal," I say.

Chloe groans. "Oh god."

"I prefer Mason, especially once I'm so deep inside you, you'll scream."

Her cheeks flame at that, but the edge of panic is gone from her expression—I think she might've splashed water on her face or given herself a pep talk in the bathroom, because she seems calmer and more collected. Although I like seeing her flustered, love *making* her blush, I also want to find out what it's like when the full power of her brain and wit are at the table.

"There are several functions I have to attend for the sake of my family. Oftentimes, I'm pushed toward girls during such gatherings, which is becoming fucking irritating. The last part of our deal is that you'll attend these events with me, as my date. We will act as if we're dating." We *will* be dating, but I think saying that to her might make her flighty again, so I refrain.

Chloe tilts her head to the side as she considers that. "I'm going to need more details." She seems more interested than opposed, which bodes well.

I shrug. "My family is a prestigious one. My father and grandfather both married young so that they could produce heirs and ensure the succession of our empire. I'm getting strongly encouraged to do the same. I'm not interested in marrying a bimbo who doesn't have two braincells to rub together, which is where you come in. With you on my arm, my parents will be quiet, if only temporarily. You're smart, accomplished in dance, on your way to being accomplished in medicine... a very appealing package they won't be able to outright dismiss. Come with me as my date to certain events, act the part of my girlfriend."

Chloe thinks for several moments before asking, "What exactly will you want me to do while acting the part of your girlfriend?"

I shrug. "The usual; holding hands, taking my arm, kissing, having conversations that don't make me wish to throw myself off the nearest cliff. Greet my family and associates—make it clear I'm unavailable." All while I'll be making it clear she's off-limits for anyone who isn't me, and paving the path to making her mine outside of this 'fake' arrangement. The more I think about it, the more I believe this is the right course of action.

Chloe hums. "Where exactly would we be going? Is your family in Vermont?"

I shake my head. "No, they're spread around New York and D.C. areas. My family has a private plane I usually use to get to the gatherings they participate in, which happen once every few weeks." And will be happening more and more soon, which makes the timing of my plan perfect. "The next events will be the Christmas party and then New Year's party; we'll go together to kick off the fake dating portion of our arrangement. Outside of that, we'll spend some time together when our schedules allow so we can get to know each other."

"For the sake of the fake dating?" Chloe asks hopefully. "You know, so we don't slip up?"

I barely contain a snort. "Sure. Those two items and a kiss will satisfy my deal."

"It sounds like this will go beyond the duration of however long it takes you to find the person who broke into my dorm room," Chloe comments, frowning.

It most certainly will.

"I doubt I'll be able to find whoever did that before they make another move, which I expect will be soon," I explain. "In any case, our arrangement will go a bit longer, but that's the deal I'm offering."

"What do you mean, make another move?" she asks, sounding worried.

"I expect they'll do something else to try to rattle you, which will give me an opening to catch them," I tell her. "I don't believe I'll find them from their vandalism of your bedroom or the note they left—it's not enough to go on, and the security cameras didn't pick up anything. This person wants you gone badly; they'll try to do something else to scare you off soon. That's when I'll have an opportunity to pin them down and take care of them."

Chloe's knee jiggles beneath the table with anxiety, but she doesn't fall into panic; instead, she appears thoughtful and focused, which I like far more than her fear. I don't mind being the one to soothe her fear, and in certain circumstances, I don't mind being the one to cause it, but not generally. It affects me negatively in a way I'm not used to.

"So, while waiting for whoever's after me to strike, what should I do?"

"Trust me to protect you," I say simply. "I won't let any harm come to you so long as you're under my protection."

She frowns, not seeming like she entirely believes me. "I guess I shouldn't walk around campus after dark, leaving myself vulnerable…"

"I don't think they'll directly attack you," I say truthfully. "For now, they want to scare you. Before that escalates into something more, I'll take care of them. In return, you spend time with me weekly, attend functions as my girlfriend when the need calls, and give me my daily kiss."

"For how long?" she questions.

"Let's say until the end of spring semester," I tell her. That way, I'll have plenty of time to lock her down, an idea I'm steadily growing more fond of.

"That's a long time," she mutters, frowning. "Hundreds of kisses, lots of time spent together, several fake-dates…"

"That's my offer," I say immovably. "Alternatively, we revert to option one. Take it or leave it."

At the mention of option one, she quickly says, "I'll take it."

She doesn't realize that we'll still get to the point where I fuck her as often as I like. With this deal, I'll be giving her the time she needs to get accustomed to me and come to want me, while also getting the bonus of her time and daily access to her lips. *Very appealing, indeed.* The path to making her mine is already as good as paved; now I only need to lead her down it without scaring her away.

CHAPTER EIGHT

Chloe

Mason looks unaccountably pleased by the deal we've made. I'm just relieved that I won't end up being used as a sex doll for him to get off in. At least with this deal, there are boundaries. Yes, I have to spend time with him, which is unnerving. However, as I've already learned, things could be much worse with him.

The problem is, the parameters he set out almost seem a little too favorable. The daily kissing is a concern on its own. When he pressed his lips to mine in his apartment, I was initially frozen with shock—then his tongue probed at my lips, his dominant touch crumbled my defenses, and I melted beneath him, helpless to resist. I could almost be grateful that things went sour after that, because his kiss was drugging.

Now I'll have to experience a kiss like that every day while trying to stay away from him. I have a niggling sense that it won't be as easy as I might've hoped; he's a phenomenal kisser.

Before the incident that robbed me of any will to engage in intimate or sexual activities with men, I'd kissed a few guys. Those kisses were nothing to write home about; they were all sloppy and tactless. Mason's kiss was consuming, ravaging, passionate, and *very* skilled. I don't know how I'll hold up against having to deal with more of those—not just a few, but a kiss *every day.*

The waiter comes to drop off our drinks—wine for Mason, water for me—and take our orders. As soon as he's gone, Mason resumes staring at me. The weight of his gaze is a physical force; it feels like fingers ghosting over my skin, raising goosebumps on my arms.

"What made you want to go into medicine?" Mason asks me, seemingly out of the blue.

I blink at the line of inquiry. It's a question I receive often enough, especially from people who think I'm crazy doing a double major of dance and biochemistry.

"My father," I answer. "He was a doctor—cardiologist and surgeon, very well respected in his field. He's the reason I fell in love with the idea of being a doctor, with helping save lives and improve someone's quality of life."

"Was," Mason repeats. "He passed away?"

As ever, a pang of pain travels through my chest at the memory, but I nod nonetheless. "Yes, when I was fourteen."

"I'm sorry to hear that," Mason murmurs, sounding surprisingly genuine. "I take it you two were close?"

The pain dissipates, replaced by a longing, nostalgic ache. "Very," I say quietly, memories of my favorite times spent with Dad flitting through my mind. "He was an incredible person, and an even better father."

"Tell me more about that," Mason requests.

I'm not sure I want to divulge a great deal about myself, but I'm learning that Mason's go-to when I resist is to make threats, which I'd rather avoid. I don't want to test the bounds of his tolerance.

"He had a really demanding job that sucked up most of his time, but he always made room for me," I say, smiling a little at the memories. "He was head of the department at the hospital he worked in, so he instated a biweekly, optional bring-your-kids-to-work day. Every other week, my nanny would take me to his office after school. He had a little room next to his personal office set up for me. I'd get my schoolwork done, and in between patients, he'd help me with homework.

"Afterward, he'd sometimes take me to patient appointments with him—his long-time patients knew me by my first name. I'd observe those meetings and learn more about his practice each time. Once he was done with patients, we'd sit side by side as he did his charts for the day, and then he'd take me to dinner. We spent every weekend together with my mom doing fun activities. Despite being very busy, Dad still put a lot of work into making me one of the centerpieces of his life. Watching him, I learned that I wanted to be like him when I grew up, wanted to be a doctor. Someone who genuinely cared for their patients, but also made time for their family. He was... the best dad ever."

"He sounds like quite the man," Mason says, though there's an edge to his tone that might be jealousy. "My dad's also very accomplished and busy, but he never carved much time out of his work life for me. When he wasn't working, he was fully present for me, but the rest of the time I was sort of on my own. We're close enough, but nowhere near as close as it sounds like you were with your dad."

The tidbit of information is interesting, and I'm startled to realize that I don't mind talking with Mason when he isn't threatening me.

I'm curious to know more about him, which I know I shouldn't be. I already know enough; he has no qualms with making terrifying threats, comes from a family with organized crime affiliations, and is a seriously scary person when he wants to be. Nothing else should be relevant, and yet, I want to hear more about him. Maybe it's so I can humanize him to better get through our deal.

"What about your mom?" I ask him.

His expression shutters. "We're not close. She's a bit vain for my taste. A stay-at-home mom who doesn't work, yet never made room for me in her life."

That must be difficult. I don't have the best relationship with my mom, either, but it isn't the worst. We simply grew apart after my father passed away.

"Are you close with your mom?" Mason asks.

I shrug. "We were close when I was younger. After my dad died, she fought to move on quickly, started dating other men within the year... I couldn't really understand that. So we sort of drifted. I love her, but I lost a lot of my respect for her."

Mason nods, as if he understands perfectly.

Conversation flows easily enough after that, and we mostly talk about surface-level things. He asks me about dance and biochem, and I ask him about the business program. When the food arrives, we continue talking between bites, and I dislike just how easy it is to converse with him.

When the bill comes, I offer to cover my half even though my bank account can ill afford it, but Mason firmly insists that when we go out together, he'll foot the bill. I don't waste energy arguing, because I don't feel like finding out how he'll retaliate.

After he drives me back to campus, he insists on accompanying me inside the program dorms to make sure that there aren't any threats lurking about, and also asks me to show him my old room firsthand. Somewhat reluctantly, I do. The knife's been removed from the mattress by campus security, who investigated and sent me an email stating they'd continue looking into the matter. My bed's still destroyed, as is the pillow, though I cleaned up the books earlier. Mason paces around the room, spending a long time studying the bed, nodding to himself. Once he's done, he walks with me to my new dorm, watching as I unlock it. Then, we stand outside of it, awkwardly staring at each other.

"I'm going to cash in on our first kiss now," Mason says, taking a step forward. "Let's go into your room."

"We can do it out here," I respond nervously. I really don't want to kiss him, but I understand my options are to either acquiesce to the kiss, or face something much worse.

Mason shakes his head, a smile pulling at his lips, then swings open my dorm room door and steps in, taking my arm and pulling me in behind him. I flash back to the previous night, when he forced me on my knees, and my breathing quickens with anxiety. I *certainly* don't want to go down that road again.

"Wait—"

"Shh," Mason cuts me off. "We have a deal, Chloe, don't renege on it." He wraps his arms around my waist, tugging me close so that we're chest to chest, and stares down at me. "You're so damn gorgeous it's almost painful."

Although he says the words kindly, they only make me more nervous. I don't want to attract his attention or notice, but it seems I've got it, and that's a reality I'll need to grapple with.

After a beat, Mason asks, "Aren't you going to say thank you?"

I shake my head. "No, I don't like the compliment coming from you. I'd prefer it if you thought I was ugly and decided to leave me alone."

His lips tug up with amusement. "Cute." Then, he lowers his head down to mine; I freeze, holding my breath.

Unlike last night, he doesn't crash his lips on mine; instead, he's confusingly gentle. He slides one hand into my hair, massaging my scalp like he did earlier, then gently brushes a kiss over one corner of my mouth, followed by the other, making my eyes flutter shut. Once he feels me relax, he slowly slants his lips over mine in a much softer kiss than I was anticipating.

His tongue runs along the seam of my lips, and his hand on my waist slips lower, until it's cupping my ass. The gesture isn't forceful; *he* isn't forceful right now—he's being persuasive and sultry, which works to put me at ease. My lips part, allowing his tongue entry, and he sweeps it into my mouth. His minty, masculine taste assaults my taste buds as he deepens the kiss, sliding his tongue along mine before sucking on it, making my toes curl in my shoes as my hands rise to clutch at his shoulders.

The kiss goes on for what feels like an eternity as he leisurely sips from my mouth. I grow more and more pliant the longer it goes on, eventually sagging against him. Only when my head's spinning and I feel thoroughly disoriented does Mason pull his lips away from mine.

"I'll see you tomorrow, Chloe," he says, giving me a look so filled with heat it makes me think I might just burst into flames.

With that, he turns and leaves. I rush to lock the door behind him, then sag against it, trying to catch my breath.

***

I think someone might be watching me. Sitting in the campus park on a picnic blanket, I half-listen to Daniel droning on about our upcoming projects and tests. The bulk of my attention is taken up by glancing around, as I have the distinct impression that somebody's staring at me.

The suspicion is unsubstantiated. Each time I look around, I only see fellow students enjoying a mildly chilly Saturday afternoon together.

I was hesitant to go on a date with Daniel today, especially given my new arrangement with Mason, but that's ultimately what drove me to join Daniel. I don't like my attraction to Mason, the fact that I don't mind spending time with him when he's not being an asshole. I agreed to join Daniel today to get my mind off Mason and keep my options open. After all, Mason and I are only fake dating, and only on certain occasions. Yes, there's the kissing deal, but it's just that; a deal. Nothing more.

Daniel's company is intellectually stimulating, and we get along well, but I can't help but notice that there isn't really a spark between us. I think we could be good friends, but I'm not attracted to him. I like his brain and his sense of humor, but there's no chemistry between us—just an ease one might have with an old friend.

"You looking for someone?" Daniel asks, pulling me from my thoughts.

I turn my gaze back to him and offer an apologetic smile. "I'm just feeling a bit paranoid, you'll have to forgive me."

He grimaces. "Yeah, if my room was broken into by some asshole, I might be paranoid, too. Have you heard anything on that front?"

I shake my head. "Unfortunately not. Campus security has not been particularly helpful—they took away the knife and told me they'd look into the break in, and that's about it."

Daniel sighs. "Hopefully whoever wanted to fuck with you will leave you alone."

I'm not so sure, but I agree, "Hopefully." Glancing at my watch, I realize it's getting late—nearly 3 p.m. I have to be in the theatre by 6 for tonight's performance, and I'd like to have some downtime before then.

Looking at the wrappers from the sandwiches we picked up at a café on the far corner of campus, I start collecting them. "This has been nice," I tell Daniel, "but I should get going. I have a performance tonight."

He nods easily. "Sure. I'll help you clean up." Together, we gather the soda cans and other trash, and toss them into a nearby trashcan. Then, Daniel rolls up the blanket he brought and picks up his backpack. "I'll walk you back to dorms."

We stroll in companionable silence. Again, I can't shake the feeling that someone is watching me, so I scan my surroundings for the umpteenth time, finding nothing out of the ordinary.

At the entrance to dorms, Daniel takes my hand in his, stopping me from walking into the building. Before I can ask what he's doing, he lowers his head to mine, going in for a kiss. For a moment, I'm frozen in horrified shock because I did not see this coming. Then, the thought unfurls in my head that maybe I should just see where this is going, see if I have a similar reaction to him as I did to Mason last night. As soon as Daniel's lips touch mine, any hope that I might be attracted to him deflates—I feel nothing but mild discomfort. No spark, no need, no desire... just nothing. I quickly pull away, fighting the urge to wipe my mouth on my sleeve.

Daniel frowns, but his expression quickly smooths out. "Sorry if that was too fast, but I've been wanting to do that since I first saw you at the beginning of the year."

Oh. "It's okay," I say with a shrill laugh. "I'm just… not big on kissing." I give my head a shake as a little voice in my mind whispers that I liked kissing just fine last night. "Today was really nice, thank you for the sandwiches, but I don't think we should try a date again." There was just no spark. "We can be friends for sure," I add.

If Daniel's offended, he doesn't show it. Instead, he gives a casual shrug. "I'd like to go out with you again, but I won't push it. If you do want to go on a date some other time, let me know. I like you a lot, Chloe."

I don't want to be an asshole while shooting him down, so I say, "I'm pretty busy between dance and biochem… and in any case, I'm just not really in a dating place right now."

"Fair enough," Daniel says. "If you change your mind, I'll be here." He gives me a two-finger salute before turning and strolling away.

I rush into the dorms, mortified by the kiss and that awkward interaction, feeling only mildly appeased that Daniel didn't take anything to heart. I'm frustrated at the fact that I'm not attracted to him while I *am* attracted to Mason. I don't want to be, but I am. Daniel's far more my type, yet when he kissed me, nothing. When Mason kissed me, *fireworks*.

Grumbling to myself, I push into my new dorm room, promptly grab a book from the top of the wardrobe and take it to my bed, hoping to get lost in the words and escape reality. This is just college; a single stop in the road of my life. It'll be over soon enough, and then, I'll move onto what's next—most likely med school, since I doubt I'll get picked up as a principal dancer for any dance company. After a few minutes, the distraction works, and my body relaxes as I focus on the text in front of me.

Several loud knocks on my door draw me away from my reading. A wave of nervousness washes over me at those knocks; it could be

Daniel, though I don't know how he'd have gotten into the building. I can't imagine it'd be whoever broke into my old dorm room, since it's broad daylight.

Shaking off the sensation of paranoia, I stand from the bed and cross the room, unlocking the door before swinging it open. Then, my blood runs cold. It's not Daniel that greets me on the other side, it's a much less pleasant figure. *Mason*, who looks livid as he glares down at me. *I guess someone was watching me, after all.*

CHAPTER NINE

"How did you get in here?" I gasp, taking an instinctive step back at the expression of sheer menace carved into Mason's features.

Mason doesn't respond; instead, he pushes me into the room with a firm hand on my shoulder and kicks the door shut behind him. His chest heaves with each breath he takes, eyes blazing with an intensity that suggests he's either just returned from a killing spree or is on the verge of starting one. A cold wave of apprehension grips my chest, tightening like a vice.

I open my mouth to ask what his problem is; he snaps a hand around my neck, cutting off my words.

"You don't get to ask questions here, Chloe," he growls. "Right now, *I'm* the one asking questions, and you will answer honestly if you want to escape this encounter somewhat intact."

Everything about him exudes fury. It dawns on me that Mason might've been the person I sensed watching me earlier—*stalking* me—and he must have seen Daniel kiss me. I can't quite grasp why that would trigger such a reaction; our deal never specified exclusivity.

His hand gripping my throat, he forces me backward until we're hovering by my bed. With a cruel shove, he throws me down on it with such force that the breath whooshes out of my lungs. I gasp, startled, and immediately try to rise, but he climbs onto the bed, straddling my hips. His hand wraps around my neck again, pinning me down. Though he doesn't squeeze hard enough to cut off my air, the message is unmistakable: he holds all the power here, and if he wants, he can cut off my oxygen supply.

"Tell me, Chloe," he starts slowly, his voice deceptively calm. "Exactly what in the *fuck* were you doing with Daniel Graves today?"

"Hanging out," I say weakly, staring up at him with wide eyes. Panic whirls within me like a storm, and a fine sheen of sweat breaks out over the back of my neck as my breaths shorten. Mason's expression remains unchanged—he's either oblivious to my distress or indifferent to it.

"Hanging out," he repeats, not sounding like he believes me. "Do you always let people's lips touch yours when you fucking *hang out*? Is that a common occurrence I'll need to look out for?"

"No!" I say quickly. "I didn't know he was going to kiss me. The moment I realized what was happening, I pulled back—"

"*Don't fucking lie to me*," Mason snaps. "You let another man touch what's mine. A man who's clearly interested in you, even though you know you're off limits."

"What are you talking about?" I breathe. "We're *fake* dating on certain occasions and we have a *deal*. How does that make me yours?"

"I thought you were smart enough to understand that our arrangement means you aren't available to anyone who isn't me, but obviously not," Mason seethes. "You went on a *picnic date* with that imbecile. This displeases me greatly, Chloe, and it shows that you either don't understand the nature of our deal or don't grasp the consequences of your actions. Let me make something abundantly clear." His hand on my throat tightens—not enough to rob me of breath, but enough to drive home his point. "As long as our deal stands, you are mine. If you let another man touch you, I will kill him, and nobody will ever find the body."

The longer he speaks, the more my fear grows, and I begin to shiver. He doesn't seem to care; in fact, he looks like he's savoring my fear, as if it fuels him.

Mason releases his grip on my throat, lowering his hands to my shirt. He seizes the fabric with both fists and yanks it apart—I gasp as a harsh tearing sound reverberates through the room.

"Wait!" I cry, reaching up to clutch his wrists—he doesn't even flinch as he yanks my bra down, freeing my breasts. His gaze sharpens, stark hunger igniting in his eyes, making the green flecks in his golden orbs blaze more vividly than ever. I tug at his hands, pleading, "Mason, please, I didn't mean to anger you. I didn't know about the expectation of exclusivity. I'd already had plans with Daniel, I didn't want to cut them off."

That turns out to be the wrong thing to say; Mason snarls and pins my arms above my head. "Our deal last night should have canceled any plans you had with other men for the foreseeable goddamn future, Chloe. You are mine and mine alone, and I do not appreciate you leading anyone else to believe you're available."

My chest heaves, breathing labored, but strangely, I don't fall into a panic attack despite my terror. Something about *Mason* being the one to do this to me is holding the truly debilitating fear at bay. Perhaps it's because he calmed me yesterday, even if he's in no mood to do that today; or maybe my survival instincts around him have shifted from freaking out to staying present, if only so I'm able to defend myself.

Mason transfers my wrists to one hand and uses the other to palm my breast, pinching my nipple harshly and making a squeak of pain escape me. "Apologize," he demands. "Do it *very* nicely, and I might be more lenient than I intended to be when I saw that *fuck* put his lips on yours." He twists my nipple so hard that tears of pain spark into my eyes.

I know I shouldn't *have* to apologize; he's being unreasonable, punishing me for something I didn't even know was wrong, but I don't think he'll be receptive to me pointing that out right now. "I'm sorry," I blurt. "I didn't mean to offend you or give the wrong impression. I'm committed to our deal. I'm sorry, Mason."

His touch softens at my words. His fingers switch from torturing my nipple to running over it gently. A wave of shock courses through me as I feel an unexpected tug of arousal in my core, as if this is somehow... *turning me on*. It can't be—some wires in my brain must be crossed. I am being pinned to my bed by a man who viciously fucked my mouth the other day, which sent me hurtling into a panic attack. Getting aroused by him in any way would be sheer madness.

"Do you really mean your apology, Chloe?" he asks, his voice a silky purr. "Maybe you're just saying it to calm me down, to get me off your back. If that's the case, let me make something clear; I am not going away. I have decided that, for the time being, you are mine. You can either fall in line and get to enjoy the perks of my decision, or you can fight against me and do stupid shit that'll only get you punished and other people dead."

A chill runs through me at his suggestion that he'd *kill* someone for touching me, filling me with worry for Daniel. We just went on a pleasant picnic date; there was nothing nefarious or sexual about it. When I turned him down, he accepted it easily, without any anger or protest, *unlike Mason*. He doesn't deserve to *die* for being interested in me.

"I mean my apology, I *am* sorry," I say, struggling to keep my voice steady. "It won't happen again."

Mason nods slowly, though a hint of dissatisfaction lingers in his eyes. "Good." He abruptly releases my hands and climbs off the bed, standing beside it and staring down at me. For a moment, I think he might be leaving, but my hopes are dashed when he says, "Undress. I want to see what's mine."

See what's mine. The possessive, proprietary tone of his voice has a dual effect on me; it terrifies me, making me question his sanity, yet it also sends another tug of arousal through my core, as if his possessive words and demeanor are somehow turning me on.

I swallow hard and sit up, adjusting my bra to cover my breasts, which earns a displeased frown from Mason. "Are you just going to... look?" I ask. "Or are you, um..."

"Going to fuck you?" Mason supplies, arching an eyebrow. "I want to, Chloe. I really, *really* want to. I want to shove my cock deep inside you and hear you scream my name. I want to show you exactly what *I* can make you feel, claim you so thoroughly you won't be able to think of another." He pauses for a beat to let that sink in, seeming amused by my shiver. "But I'm not going to fuck you. I'm just gonna play a little."

"What do you mean?" I ask, trying to temper the subtle tremor coursing through my limbs. My heart gallops like a racehorse, so quickly that I wouldn't be surprised if Mason notices my chest shaking.

"Take off your fucking clothes, Chloe. My patience has limits."

Mortified to my very bones but not wanting to provoke him further, I follow his instructions. I've never let another man see me fully undressed; the closest I ever came to full nudity in front of a boy was the night of the party. Even then, I was only down to my bra when I managed to divert my assaulter's attention from full-blown rape to something I thought I could live with.

As my thoughts flick back to that terrible moment in my life, I start noticing the differences. *He* was all groping, grubby hands, sweaty grunts, and sloppy touches. Mason, even in anger, is in cool control, steering this interaction with his usual confidence. This moment is nothing like *then*, and the horrifying fact that I'm somewhat turned on right now only reaffirms it.

Slowly, I reach down to unbutton and unzip my jeans and shimmy out of them, leaving me only in my bra and panties. Mason's eyes follow every inch of skin I reveal, his gaze focused, drinking in the sight with rapt attention.

"Stand up," he tells me.

I swallow hard, moving to comply with his wishes. He doesn't step back to give me room as I stand; he seems to relish crowding me, especially now, as though it appeases some part of him. The part that has no qualms with pinning me to my bed and tearing off my shirt like an animal.

He steps forward, closing the small distance between us, and reaches his arms around me to unhook my bra. Instinctively, I lift my arms to hold the cups over my breasts, not used to being seen like this. Mason gives a single shake of his head, and his mildly admonishing look forces me to comply with his unspoken command. I drop my arms, hanging my head as the bra falls to the ground.

I have a mixed relationship with my body. I appreciate it because I've spent years honing it to be as strong and flexible as possible, bending, contorting, and exercising to mold myself into a powerful ballerina. At the same time, I *hate* it because it draws attention to me for all the wrong reasons. I don't like that people look at my physical appearance and decide my only value is my prettiness, or that because I'm pretty, they have the right to come onto me or treat me like a doll.

Mason ushers me forward a few steps, then circles around behind me. He hooks his fingers in the waistband of my panties and tugs them down, telling me to step out of them. Breath hitching, I comply. My initial hint of arousal simmers down, replaced by sheer embarrassment and shame as Mason examines me like I'm livestock being sold at an auction. I feel extremely devalued, like my only worth is tied into my physique.

I jump when he smooths his palm down my back before clutching a handful of my ass, releasing a low grunt of pleasure. He steps in front of me and takes my chin with his thumb and forefinger, tilting my head up. I let my eyes flutter shut, not wanting to see the expression on his face.

"Open your eyes," he commands softly. Since he tends to get forceful when I don't comply, I reluctantly lift my lids, meeting his intense gaze. "You're stunning, Chloe. So breathtakingly beautiful it leaves me speechless, but that's not what I like most about you. What I like most is your eyes; not just the unique color, but the intelligence in them. They captivate me more than anything else about you."

That... wasn't what I expected him to say. My lips part as I stare at him, questioning the sincerity of his words. He's a very blunt person, unafraid to speak his mind, making me inclined to believe he's being honest. From what I've observed, he's too indifferent to lie for the sake of anyone's comfort.

"A moment ago I was so angry I wanted to spank your ass until it turned bright red. Now, all I want to do is worship you."

If it's between being spanked and being worshipped, I choose the latter. But I don't think he cares for my desires right now; he's driven by his own needs. I can either roll with it and appease him or resist and risk upsetting him again.

After a moment of silence, he commands, "Get on the bed." I can't hide a wince at that, but I obey.

I take a seat on the bed, fighting the urge to cross my arms over my chest, knowing he'll just tell me to lower them. And, while I'm loath to admit it, what he said about my intelligence struck me harder than I expected, softened my sentiments toward whatever's happening here.

"Lie down and spread your legs for me." Letting out a shuttering breath, I do, embarrassment whipping through me along with something else; a low pulse between my legs that I can't ignore. As much as part of me is frightened right now, another part is undeniably turned on, which shames me. Mason has outright admitted he's a killer and threatened to kill other men for touching me, and here I am getting hot and bothered by him. *What does that say about me?*

"You've been a very good girl for me, apologizing and following my instructions," Mason murmurs, walking to the foot of the bed. "You've been such a good girl that my earlier ire has dissipated, and I want to reward you."

"I don't need a reward," I say quietly. "If you want to reward me, give me a free pass."

He shakes his head, lips tilting up. "The thing is, I also want to taste you, Chloe. Very badly, in fact, which is unusual for me. Don't worry, you'll enjoy it." The mattress dips beneath his weight as he places one knee on the bed, then the other.

He slowly shuffles forward. He gently cuffs my ankles, spreading my legs wider, and places my feet flat on the bed, bending them at the knees and holding me open for his hungry eyes. I've heard enough girl-talk from April to guess what he intends to do, but I've never been on the receiving end of oral. A thread of curiosity travels through me, keeping me from making any protests.

"Such a pretty pussy," he says, his voice gravelly. My cheeks flame, and I turn my head away. "Ah-ah. Look at me, Chloe. I want you to watch what I'm doing to you. You're going to realize that while I might scare you, I can also make you feel *really* good." He pauses to cup my pussy in his hand, and a hiss escapes me as the heat of his palm sparks warmth in my core. "Tell me, has anyone else ever touched you here?"

I shake my head.

Dark satisfaction glimmers in his gaze. "Very good. The thought of being the first excites me, probably more than it should. There's a whole world of pleasure out there that you've been missing out on, and I'm eager to be the one to guide you through it."

I lick my lips. "I've never done this before. I... this feels uncomfortable."

"I know," he says. "That's okay. Your discomfort will soon be replaced by pleasure." He releases my pussy only to spread it open with his forefinger and thumb. Then, he brushes the thumb of his free hand over my clit; I gasp, core clenching as his finger smooths over the most sensitive part of my body. Mason smirks. "Have you ever touched yourself here?"

I shake my head again.

His eyebrows raise. "Ever made yourself come?"

"N-no," I say, holding in a moan as his thumb rubs a lazy circle over my clit, making my back arch.

He gazes at me for a long, thoughtful moment, continuing to rub my clit. I bite my lip and try to keep my hips from bucking.

"Let me get this right, you've never orgasmed before?"

My cheeks burn even brighter as I hesitantly shake my head. I know most girls and guys masturbate; I've just never really had the urge. Never wondered what I was missing out on.

"Then this is going to be all the more satisfying for me," Mason murmurs, lifting his thumb from my clit. My eyes widen as his head lowers to my pussy. I open my lips to utter a protest; it gets caught in my throat as his tongue runs a long, slow path over my slit. It's hot, wet, and feels so insanely good that I can't hold back a moan.

My noise of pleasure intermixes with his low groan of satisfaction. His tongue probes at my entrance, the tip slipping inside me, making my toes curl as a higher pitched moan escapes me. "You taste so fucking good," he mutters, pulling back an inch. "Better than I fantasized. As sweet as you look."

He gives me another slow lick before swirling his tongue over my clit; my hands grasp at the bedsheets and my back bows. One of his fingers nudges at my entrance, making me tense, but the feeling of liquid heat insistently twirling along my sensitive bundle of nerves slickens my channel, allowing him to slide his finger in. He twists it around inside me, and I bite my lip. A knot of tension winds inside my belly, and a fine sheen of sweat coats my body from the stimulation. Confusion thoroughly intermixes with arousal, and I think I suddenly understand just why people lose their minds over sex and orgasms—it feels *amazing*.

"You're already about to come, aren't you?" Mason asks against my flesh, a smile in his voice. "My beautiful little virgin." A second finger wedges inside me, stretching my channel and making me gasp in a breath before exhaling it in a long, low moan.

The tension in my belly coils tighter and tighter as he plays with me, lavishing his tongue over my clit while slowly starting to thrust his fingers in and out.

"Wait—I don't—" I cut off with another moan at the clever swirl of his tongue, and the muscles in my stomach tighten. "What is *happening?*"

"You're getting ready to come," Mason murmurs. "Let it happen, beautiful girl; I want to feel it. *Taste* it."

He fixes his lips around my clit and suckles, drawing a cry from me as sensations so intense they're almost *too* intense envelope my body. "Oh—*fuck*," I whimper as his fingers inside me curl upwards, hitting a spot along my walls that makes everything within me tense.

A moment later, unbearable heat sweeps over my body as his suction over my clit turns firmer. A low cry spills from my lips as the coil of tension in my belly explodes, sending rounds of convulsions coursing through me. My inner walls tighten and release around Mason's fingers, my clit pulses, my legs shake, and I can't seem to stop the noises spilling out of me as unimaginable pleasure explodes in my body. Mason doesn't stop or back off; he continues torturing me through my orgasm, prolonging it, until it's too much and I reach down with my hands to push his head away.

I pant in the aftermath of my first-ever orgasm, dazed and drunk on pleasure, staring at the ceiling and feeling like I just had a revelation of some sort. Mason licks and kisses a path up my body, braces his hands on either side of my head, and smiles down at me, seeming deeply pleased and slightly amused.

"That was an orgasm, Pixie," he tells me, licking his glistening lips. "The first of many."

Trembling from aftershocks, I stare up at him, at once confused and titillated. The curl of his lips is genuine, his eyes are sparkling with desire and mirth, and he seems to have relaxed despite having stormed into my room with all the anger of a tempest. He brushes the back of his hand over my cheek, lifting a lock of my hair and rubbing it between his fingers. "So silky."

"This wasn't..." I trail off, shaking my head. "This wasn't part of our deal."

Mason's eyes shutter as he drops my hair. Mentioning the deal causes something to shift within him; he switches from lazily satisfied to darkly intense in an instant.

"Our deal is flexible," he tells me. "Malleable. It's loosely worded. We agreed we'd spend time together—no clarifications on how we'd spend our time. We agreed you'd give me a kiss every day—no specifications on *where* I'd kiss you. And we agreed that you'd act the part of my girlfriend, which means *no other men.*"

"I don't understand you," I tell him quietly. "I don't understand any of this."

He rubs his thumb over my bottom lip. "The only thing you need to understand is that you're mine. Act like it."

"For the duration of the deal?" I whisper.

A smirk tilts the corners of his lips. "Sure, Pixie. For the duration of our deal, until the end of spring semester. Then we can renegotiate."

"Renegotiate?" I repeat, shaking my head. "No, everything will end then—"

He leans down to kiss me, silencing me. I taste myself on his tongue as he thrusts it into my mouth, which is odd but also erotic. "We'll renegotiate at the end of spring semester," he confirms, pulling back.

"What game are you playing?" I ask him. "What's your goal?"

He shrugs. "I'll reveal my endgame when I'm ready. Until then, be good and you can enjoy the ride. Be bad..." he trails off, wrapping his hand around my neck, exerting the lightest pressure, which still makes my breath catch. "And next time you won't get a gentle reminder, you'll get a punishment."

He leans down to brush his lips over mine once more, then stands and breezes out of the room, leaving me a puddle of confusion on the bed.

Chapter Ten

Finals week drifts by in a slow haze of tests, projects, and performances. The pressure is so immense that Mason becomes a small blip on my radar rather than someone taking over my life.

Every day, he finds me somewhere on campus and demands his kiss; the longer it goes on, the more accustomed I become to his lips on mine. I even begin to crave the contact.

He doesn't rage at me again or demand more than a simple kiss, and my fear of him starts to melt away. As my anxiety fades, rational thoughts return, and I shift my focus to what I *can* do rather than what I can't. I can't get away from Mason before he grows tired of me, but I can try to change our arrangement to something more reasonable.

So far, Mason's only seen me at my worst—panicking, afraid, or so damn confused by him I can't think. That's not how I always am; usually, I'm quite crafty. I understand that our strange arrangement will last until the end of the school year. Unless I stop letting him steamroll me and show that I have a backbone, I get the sense that the school year will consist of me being jerked around like a puppet on strings.

On the Friday after my last test of the semester, Mason finds me as I'm heading back to my dorm room. He's wearing a polo shirt, khakis, and a smirk I'm becoming terribly familiar with. It's the same smirk I see every day, in different locations, when he tracks me down for our kiss. Yesterday, it was as I was running from one building to another between tests; I was so worked up over class that I was willing to do whatever he asked to get to my next test on time. The day before, it was in the cafeteria while I was trying to choke down a stale plate of chicken. Since our deal began, he's always caught me off guard, giving him an advantage that I'm growing tired of.

Today, I'm not wound up or worrying over my next project or test; all my work is done. I feel good about the tests I took and the finals projects I officially submitted to professors. Now, my only problem is having been severely sleep deprived this week, but I'm still in a much better frame of mind to deal with Mason. I'm sick of bending to his every wish just to avoid stress—if he wants our arrangement to continue, he needs to start treating me like a human rather than a pair of lips.

"Chloe," Mason drawls, coming to a stop in front of me. "Funny seeing you here."

"Is it?" I ask dryly. "Look, Sieger, we need to talk. This whole cornering me at any time of the day or night isn't going to work anymore. A lot of what's been going on isn't going to work anymore."

Mason appears intrigued rather than put off by my words. He tilts his head to the side as he considers me, as if he's seeing me in a new light. Finally, his lips curl up, and a glint of pleasure brightens his expression. "*There* you are."

I frown, trying to ignore the headache that starts prickling at my temples. *I really need to sleep.* "Pardon?"

"I think I'm finally getting acquainted with the Chloe beneath the fear," Mason clarifies. "I've seen glimpses of her in your eyes, but she never breaks through. You're always too afraid, too confused, or in too much of a rush. I'm surprised it only took a week for the real you to come out."

Not sure what bullshit he's going on about, but also not wanting to waste the rest of my afternoon trying to understand his brand of crazy, I purse my lips. "You set the ground rules when I was at a disadvantage; now I'm going to add some rules of my own to our arrangement."

Mason arches an eyebrow. "Is that so?" He takes a step toward me, and sizzling tension fills the space between us. After a week of being kissed senseless by him every day, my body's begun to light up each time he's close enough. When we're *this* close, and I can see the finely honed muscle beneath his white polo, feel the heat emanating from him... I can't stop my own body from responding. Not now that I know exactly what his wicked mouth can do. "What's to say I won't automatically revert to option one if I don't like your demands?" he asks softly. "I'm still waiting for whoever vandalized your dorm room to make another move so I can catch them. Until I have them, I could demand you make yourself available for my use."

A week ago, that threat would've terrified me. But late last night, as I was thinking about my upcoming tests and problems with Mason, I realized a few things. A few reasons why he won't make good on his threat.

"First of all, if you go back on our agreement, you won't have someone on your arm at those family functions you mentioned. From what you told me, the first one is next week, and you've made clear you want me there to stop your parents from throwing other girls at you. I absolutely will not go with you if you try to change the terms of our deal. Second, if you change the deal now that we've agreed to the terms, you'll undermine your own reputation with future deal-making—people won't know if they can rely on you to keep your word. Third, and I think this one's the real kicker..." I pause to examine Mason's expression. He looks partly irritated, partly impressed. "You know that I'll run like hell if you try to cross certain boundaries, and for some reason, you don't want me to run. I'm not sure what twisted logic or endgame is driving you, but you could've taken me any day in the last week, and you didn't. That means something."

After a long moment of staring at me, Mason inclines his head. "Alright, Ms. Richardson," he says in a mockingly professional tone. "Let's hear these demands of yours, and we'll see what we can agree on."

I nod. "I have a few things, and they're all common courtesy." I lift a hand and start ticking off a finger for each item. "I want to arrange times and places for these kisses you're so desperate for—no more surprising me with them. You will tell me about your family before we go to the party so I know what to expect and how to approach them. You will stop treating me like my body is my only important quality, or I will make you look like shit at the Christmas and New Year's party out of spite." I pause, shaking my head. "There's a reason I've made it this long without sex, and it isn't just because I learned how unreliable and untrustworthy men are; it's because I get objectified enough that I have no appetite for physical intimacy."

Mason nods mildly. "Here's the thing, Chloe. Nobody knows about our deal, so I can change the terms whenever I want to, and my reputation won't suffer." He tucks a lock of my hair behind my ear. "You can try to run as much as you like, but it won't work. I'll chase you, I'll find you, and then I'll take pure delight in punishing you."

Goosebumps of alarm rise on my flesh, and the headache that's been threatening to consume me for the last two days finally takes hold, pounding away at my skull, causing the sun to suddenly seem *too* bright. I don't know if it's because of Mason's bullshit or the fact that I've been running on two hours a sleep a night since Sunday, but my vision wobbles, and I realize I need to go to my room and lie down. I have ibuprofen there; I'll pop a few pills, take a nap, and pray to god I'm ready for the Pandora's Box performance tonight.

"Fine. Do whatever you want; I'm done wasting time agonizing over it. I've dealt with worse than you, Sieger, and considering my track record, I'll probably deal with worse in the future. You want an air-headed doll on your arm, like the ones you're being pushed toward? I can be that. You want a smart, educated, and cultured woman by your side to make you look like you have some worth beyond prettiness? *Treat me like one.*"

I'm sick of my value stemming solely from my appearance. Ever since I was fifteen and my body started changing, I've attracted the wrong kind of attention. Hair too pretty, eyes too vivid, ass too sculpted, body too well-proportioned. Instead of being interested in my brain, people were captivated by my looks. It irritated me like no other because I've always longed for someone to look beyond the surface, to understand the depths of my thoughts and dreams.

Even before that cursed party, I avoided anything sexual because I didn't want to feed into the narrative that pretty girls should focus on their looks rather than their intellect. I immersed myself in my studies, pursuing ballet alongside science and medicine. I rarely joined my peers when they snuck into bars or clubs to waste time getting drunk—I've been focusing on my future since before my father passed away.

"I wish I'd seen this side of you sooner," Mason says, surprising me. "You're gorgeous when you're dazed and a little afraid, but like this, you're a vision." He wraps an arm around my waist, pulling me close.

"No," I growl, shoving at his chest. "Not now. Not while we're discussing something and I'm getting increasingly pissed off with your responses. You're missing the point."

"I get the point," Mason replies in a velvety voice. "You're the beauty and the brains. I see it, Chlo. I've seen it ever since I opened my door and saw you standing there. The looks are great, but I can get plenty of girls with good looks. It's what's in here," he taps my temple, "that really enthralls me."

He lowers his head to mine, bringing our lips together. All of my anger flees instantaneously, leaving behind tingles that erupt on my skin and penetrate deep, accompanied by scorching heat that surges through me like a tidal wave. Stuck between irritation and flaring arousal, I fist my hands in his shirt, trying to take over our kiss and make the statement that I'm not someone he can constantly steamroll.

Mason chuckles as I battle him for dominance, fisting a hand in my hair and yanking my head back, holding me still as he plunders me, forcing his will on me. Fed up with that shit, I bite his lip hard enough to make him jerk back. When my eyes drift open, I see that a thin trail of blood is running from his lip down onto his stubbled jaw—he brushes it away with a thumb, appearing shocked as he stares at the red smear on his digit. A mixture of anger and arousal takes over his features, and he shoves his blood-stained finger between my lips.

"Lick it off," he tells me coolly.

Startled and left with no other option, I do, surprised that the metallic taste is almost erotic. *I* did that to Mason; *I* made him bleed. There's power in that. Mason's eyes brighten with heat as he watches me suck his blood off his thumb. Slowly, he withdraws his hand and says, "Good girl."

I hiss. "Don't call me that."

His lips tip up at the edges. "You don't want to be my good girl?"

"I want to be what I'm working to be: brilliant and successful. Being your *good girl* doesn't tie into that, and it never will. I don't care about being *good;* I care about being *smart.*"

"Which you already are," Mason says easily. "So now all that's left is for you to find the path to success. I could help you with that, you know. Our arrangement could have more benefits for both of us. I have friends in high places, a wide net of social connections that extend into every industry in this country. I could make sure you get into your med school of choice, hook you up with a great internship—"

I shove him away, hard enough that he's forced to release me, and glare at him. "*Fuck you*, Sieger. I neither want nor need your connections. I'm doing fine on my own. The only benefit from our arrangement I want is for you to find whoever broke into my room. Do not insinuate that I can't get places on my own, because I *can*, and I will prove to everyone who doubts me just how wrong they are."

My headache, forgotten with the heat of our kiss, returns with a vengeance. I barely keep from swaying on my feet, and I'm struck anew by the need to get to my dorm room. I spin on my heel and storm away from Mason, blinking against the brightness of the sun. Fury courses through my veins, fueling me, causing my heart to race.

Over the past few years, my mother has often told me that I should pursue modeling or look for a good husband to pay the bills while I indulge in dance. When I told her I wanted to be a doctor if I wasn't chosen as a principal in a respected company, she *laughed.* Mom's insult years ago is now underscored by her engagement to a startlingly wealthy businessman who's constantly showing her off as his new trophy fiancée. I've only met Bradley a few times, and I don't think he's ever truly noticed me.

Mason catches up with me in a few strides, and I let out a low growl. "Go away. Our arrangement is satisfied for the day; I'll see you tomorrow. Text me the details of the parties—where they are, when they are, how we'll be getting to them, and who'll be there. I was planning to stay at Greywood for winter break, so lucky for you, I'm available for whichever bullshit gatherings you need me to go to." It's a struggle to keep my voice clear; I'm so exhausted it's a wonder I'm still upright.

"I didn't mean to offend you or imply that you can't make it on your own," Mason says. "I only meant that everyone can use help when working toward their dreams. Networking is as important as hard work and good grades. More, in many cases."

"*Shut. Up.*"

"Your anger is something of an aphrodisiac to me, so you might want to tone it down," Mason comments. I turn onto the path leading to the program dorms, determined to ignore him, but Mason doesn't let up. He says, "Come to dinner with me, I'll give you the party details in person. We both seem to have some free time now."

"I have a performance in a few hours that I need to prepare for. You have innocent lives to go terrorize; you should get to that and leave me alone," I snap.

"Our deal also includes spending time together," Mason interjects. "I'm cashing in on that now. I'll get you to the theatre with plenty of time to prepare."

"You really don't get the concept of letting up, do you?" I ask him as I trudge up the stairs leading to my dorm building and root around my backpack, looking for my student ID badge that doubles as a key card. "Read the writing on the walls; I am not in the fucking mood right now. I just got done with a ridiculously stressful week of finals. My headache is making everything fuzzy and amplifying my anger. I've slept a total of two hours each night. I need to take a handful of ibuprofen and hope that I'm in dancing shape in three hours. Seriously, Mason, right now is not a good time."

Mason places a surprisingly gentle hand on my arm as I find my keycard. "Look at me, Chloe."

Knowing that he won't back off until I do, I turn to glare at him with a huff. He studies my face, his eyebrows drawing together. "You're flushed and pale at the same time. White lips, unsteady on your feet," he mutters, clasping my shoulders. "You're probably dehydrated and exhausted. Let's get you inside."

CHAPTER ELEVEN

I blink several times, trying to clear the fog clouding my vision so I can focus on Mason. The genuine concern etched in his expression is the last thing I expect considering the fight we just had. I don't want to be around him right now; I thought I was in the right frame of mind to go toe-to-toe with him, but my full-body exhaustion says otherwise. I want to curl up in my dark room and sleep off the worst of my headache.

"I'm fine, I just need water and rest," I mumble

"When was the last time you ate?" he asks.

I frown as I try to remember. "Yesterday morning? No, Wednesday afternoon, I think. Maybe. I don't know, finals are hectic."

"Obviously," Mason drawls, pressing the back of his hand to my forehead. "Well, I can't have my pretend-girlfriend passing out on me. We'll raincheck on going out, but for now, you really should get some food and water."

"I'll get right on that, doctor," I say snarkily, unable to tone myself back. Mason's worry for me is surprising, but I'm still irritated with him. Not just for today but for this week and last weekend, for making me so flustered I can't think straight. I feel like the worst version of myself when he's around, and I hate it.

"Go to your room. I'm gonna grab some food and bring it to you."

What's his game here? I haven't known Mason to do anything out of the kindness of his heart—everything with him is a deal, a trade-off of services or favors. I'm not inclined to find myself in his debt. "That's really not necessary, and not part of our deal. I can take care of myself." As I speak, I try and fail to tap my student ID against the keycard reader by the door, missing the scanner entirely. Mason plucks the ID from me and seamlessly taps it against the reader, then opens the door for me.

"Clearly," he says, giving me a pointed look. "Don't worry about our deal. Right now, I need to make sure you don't die on me. In you go, I'll be back in a few minutes."

He hands me my card back and nods toward the elevator. Frowning, I ask him, "How are you going to get back in here? How did you even get in here on Saturday?"

He smirks, eyes glinting with mischief. "I can get into wherever I want, Pixie. Connections come in handy." With that, he turns and strides away.

Fifteen minutes later, I'm in my room with all the lights turned off, lying on my bed and waiting for the ibuprofen to kick in. It *has* to work—I need to dance my best tonight. It's our last show before winter break, and Sanders said there'll be a huge turnout of patrons and donors, so I *must* give a perfect performance.

The last time I was this exhausted was in my senior year of high school, when my chock-full AP schedule and the additional college courses I was taking overwhelmed me so much that I passed out in the parking lot of my school. An acquaintance rushed me to the nurse's office, and my mom was called to pick me up and advised to take me to urgent care. When Mom showed up, she took me home instead of to see a doctor, grumbling that I'd pulled her away from her day date with Bradley. I don't think she actually asked me how I was feeling; she just gave me a brief lecture on the importance of beauty sleep.

It's shocking to realize that Mason, the asshole who's spent most of our time together threatening me in a bid to gain my compliance, is being more caring than my own mother. Mom didn't even stop for food that day when I asked her to, she was too wrapped up in herself.

When Mason's knocks echo through my door, I stumble across the room to open it, then trip right back into bed. Mason doesn't say anything, but he does turn on the lights, prompting me to shriek, "No lights!" as the pounding in my head sharpens and intensifies.

"No lights," he repeats, turning them off. He sets a plastic bag that emits the delightful aromas of cheeses and meats on my desk, then walks over to the windows and closes the blinds. "Light sensitivity along with your headache?"

"Yes," I grumble, curling up on my side and burying my head in the pillow. "Thanks for the food. You can go. I need to sleep."

Instead of leaving, he pulls something out of the bag he brought, then drags my desk chair over to my bed and plops down on it. "Sit up."

"Fuck off."

He releases a low chuckle. "I really wish I'd seen the real Chloe come out to play sooner; you're a delight when you're sassy." He sobers with his next words. "Your blood sugar is low and you're dehydrated. If you don't hydrate yourself and get some nutrients before you sleep, you'll feel even worse when you wake up. I got a BLT with Swiss cheese from the campus café—a little birdy told me that's your favorite. Sit up, Chlo."

I don't bother asking him where he got his information, because as he likes to remind me, he has connections everywhere. It's no wonder he always knows where to find me—he probably has my class schedule by now. I force myself to sit up, propping my single, flimsy pillow against the headboard and leaning back on it.

"Why are you being nice to me?" I ask as he hands me the sandwich. "You need a fake girlfriend, and you want daily make-out sessions with me, which is baffling, considering you can get them from anyone on campus. Why put so much effort into me? I promise you that I'm not worth it."

Instead of answering my question, Mason asks casually, "Who's made you feel so unworthy in your life?" Seeing my startled look, he explains, "You're tetchy when it comes to talking about looks or anything that you perceive to subvert your intelligence. Why?"

His observation strikes too close to home. I unwrap the foil around the sandwich, my mouth watering at the sight of crispy bacon and toasted baguette. "Answer my questions, and I might answer yours."

"I'll answer yours when you're ready," Mason says. "You can answer mine then, as well. I don't mind waiting; we have months for me to figure you out."

I don't have the energy to decipher the subtext of his words or question why he thinks I'm not ready for the answers. At the end of the day, it doesn't matter. Still, I say, "You're an asshole."

"An asshole you seem to enjoy kissing," Mason observes. "An asshole who's face you rode, an asshole who gave you your first orgasm. I've gotta say, that had to be one of the hottest moments of my life."

Ignoring that, I take a big bite of the sandwich, groaning as the flavors of bacon, tomato, fresh lettuce, mayonnaise, and melted cheese burst on my tongue. After chewing and swallowing, I murmur, "I'm surprised that a brief interlude with an inexperienced college student overshadowed your many other exploits."

Mason shrugs. "Those were quick, fun rides. One-time occurrences. I think I'm going to want a lot more from you, Chloe."

"You'll get what the deal says you'll get, and nothing more," I say firmly.

Mason grins. "I'm going to seduce you sooner or later. I'm irresistible like that, as you'll soon come to see. I give it a few weeks, tops, before you cave under the force of my charm. I have a feeling you'll be worth the wait."

"You're insufferable." I take another bite of the sandwich, glaring at him. He stands, retrieves a Gatorade from the bag on my desk, then sits back down and hands it to me. "Drink. Get your electrolytes balanced again."

I begrudgingly accept it, trying to ignore the fact that it's my favorite flavor—cool blue—as I take several sips. "How do you know all of this health stuff?" I ask him.

"I played football in high school," Mason tells me. "Every year, the team went to football camp in the month leading up to the start of school. It was intense—lots of drills, not enough food or sleep. Many guys would get dehydrated while running fifteen miles in scorching heat, and some even ended up passing out. I myself dropped like a sack of potatoes once or twice. I learned to prioritize hydration and proper nutrition."

Something about his explanation humanizes Mason. Since I've met him, he's been a shadow haunting my thoughts and days—elusive and almost like a legend rather than a man, especially considering the rumors about him that flit around campus. Hearing that he did something as mortal as passing out after overexerting himself makes him more real. He's a flawed man who breathes and hurts and experiences all the downsides of humanity.

"Were you any good?" I ask.

"Decent enough that I got some scholarship offers," Mason says. "Didn't take them, though, since I always wanted to come to Greywood."

"Why's that?"

"The environment. It's quieter here than it is in most cities, and the mountains are a short drive away. I like going on hikes, enjoying the fresh air and beauty of this world."

"Which is home for you, New York or D.C.?" I ask him, curious.

"New York City, though my family has a penthouse in D.C. and several residencies in other states and overseas. NYC is where I grew up, though. I enjoy the bustling energy of the city, but I also love the tranquility of the outdoors. Once I finish college, I'd like to have a house in the country along with an apartment in the city. I'd work from both places, but in the country, I'd be able to relax. In the city, I always need to be Mason Sieger, son of *Grant* Sieger—the legendary businessman and strategist whom I've been raised to emulate."

My brows furrow as I listen to Mason. There's a hint of resentment in his voice when he talks about his father, which reminds me of our dinner last Friday. He spoke of his father with grudging respect, and I remember sensing his jealousy when I talked about my relationship with *my* father.

"Where's home for you?" Mason asks.

I smile faintly. "Ithaca, upstate New York." My smile dims. "I haven't been back home since coming to Greywood. My mom's moved out of our house and in with her fiancé. We still own my childhood house, but it's no longer used." Blinking, I try to brighten the mood. "I'm a big lover of nature, as well. I used to go camping with my dad regularly."

Mason studies me closely, seeming thoughtful, though he doesn't say anything else.

I eat in silence for several minutes while Mason watches me, playing nurse and handing me the Gatorade every few bites. By the time I'm done, I feel better—my headache has started to recede, courtesy of both the medicine I took and the sustenance Mason brought.

"Thanks for this," I tell him, a touch awkwardly because this is the most civil, genuine interaction we've had so far. I can't help but feel like that means something; *changes* something. There's more to Mason than he lets on. "While you're here, want to tell me about the party details?"

"Not particularly, but I will," Mason says with a sigh. "The venue is a hotel in downtown New York City, the party will take place there the night before Christmas Eve. My father, Grant, and my mother, Jade, will be there. I'm not sure how they'll react to you—they'll certainly be civil given the public setting, but they might try to grill you about our relationship and your accomplishments. There will also be many of my father's business associates in attendance, and I'll be expected to mingle with them. You'll attract attention and scrutiny since I've never brought a girl to an event before, but I have a feeling you'll handle everyone just fine. We'll stay two or three hours, then head back to our hotel in midtown."

"Doesn't your family have a home in the city?" I question.

"Yes, but I prefer to stay in a hotel." Mason shrugs. "My parents' apartment is massive and soulless, and they're rarely home. A hotel has more character and life."

"We'll have separate rooms, right?" I ask.

He shakes his head. "Same room, separate beds." When I open my mouth to protest, Mason cuts me off. "I'm a well-known person in the city and at the hotel where we'll stay—I always use the same one. If I'm taking you as my girlfriend, people will wonder why we're not staying together. It could ruin the pretense."

I sigh. "Fine. When do we leave and when do we return?"

"We'll leave Sunday morning and fly to NYC on my family's private jet. The first party is on Sunday night, so we'll have most of the day to explore the city and find you a dress for the gatherings we'll be attending. There's also a family-only party on Christmas Eve at my parents' place that we'll need to go to, followed by the New Year's party. We can fly back here on January 1st, or stay in New York a bit longer if you'd like."

"I don't want you to spend money on me, I can bring my own dress," I say.

Mason chuckles. "You don't have to worry about my bank account, Pixie, I can afford to get you a damn dress. I've had several streams of income aside from my trust fund for years now." He sighs, glancing down. "What the wealthy never talk about is the fact that having a certain amount of money tends to create one shitstorm after another. Everyone wants to use you for it—family, friends, and strangers alike." He meets my eyes, his gaze uncharacteristically open. "Spending it on someone I like might actually make it seem like a bit less of a burden."

I can imagine that money often comes with a pair of golden handcuffs. Great wealth buys incredible privileges, but those privileges have nasty side effects. Bradley is richer than god, and he has to employ a team of security personnel to keep him safe.

I clear my throat. "You're not supposed to like me, we're only using each other."

Mason shrugs. "Fair enough, but at least we're upfront about it. You'll make my parents stop throwing women at me, I'll find whoever vandalized your room and ensure they can't pull such a stunt again. Even after I've taken care of your problem, you'll continue being my pretend girlfriend in front of my family and associates until the end of the school year."

"Right," I agree.

"Get some sleep, Chloe, you have a few hours before you need to be at the theatre. I'll drive you when it's time to go."

"There's no need," I say as a yawn cracks my jaw. "I'll take the bus, like always."

"Nope, I'm driving you. Then I'm driving you home afterwards. Don't argue, Pixie; it won't get you anywhere with me."

Yawning again, I wipe my hands with antibacterial wipes I keep on my bedside table and drop the sandwich wrapper beside them. "Why do you call me that? Pixie?" I ask as I scoot down the bed and lay my head on my pillow, rolling onto my side so I can look at Mason.

"You remind me of a fairy from folklore," he replies. "A Pixie. That was my first impression of you; strawberry-blonde hair and bright teal eyes that shine with cleverness."

I open my mouth to ask another question, but it doesn't come—the call of sleep pulls me under.

***

A warm hand rubbing along my arm stirs me from the darkness of slumber. Blinking blearily, I nuzzle closer to the comforting warmth, resting my head on it. A noise breaks through the fog of my sleep; with a start, I recall exactly what happened before I fell into a dead sleep and bolt upright in bed. Mason's still sitting in the chair beside me, chuckling and staring at me with mirthful eyes.

"Any time you want to cuddle, just let me know," he says, laughter in his voice. "I'm proficient in many physical activities besides fucking."

"Shut up," I groan. "What would you know about cuddling? Rumor has it you never spend a night with a girl. Besides, I wasn't cuddling you."

"Of course not, you were just clinging to my arm like it's a lifeline and rubbing your cheek against it," Mason replies. "And I might not have cuddled much in the past, but I'm very good at it. Sorry to wake you, but we should get going soon—it's 5 p.m. How are you feeling?"

"Much better, thank you," I reply honestly. My headache is gone, and the worst of my tiredness has lifted.

I throw my thick comforter off me. I don't remember pulling it up, which means Mason must have done it after I fell asleep.

It's heartening to see this side of him. So far, I've known Mason as the domineering asshole—yet today, he took care of me even though it had no personal benefit to him. He fed me, spoke to me in a soothing voice, watched over me as I slept. I'm not sure what to make of these two conflicting sides of him; on one hand, he's a jerk who seems larger than life and is too rich for his own good, exerting an almost godlike influence. On the other hand, he's remarkably human.

He waits patiently as I gather my things for dance, and then drives me to the theatre. Before we part, he tells me to be ready to leave Sunday morning.

During the performance, despite an auditorium full of people, I swear I can feel his eyes on me. For once, that feeling is less unnerving and more... thrilling.

CHAPTER TWELVE

S unday morning comes around, bringing with it a whirlwind of anticipation and anxiety. I pack a duffel bag with all my basic necessities and throw my nicest dress in with the mix, though I doubt it'll be good enough for Mason's ultra-rich family. My mind swirls with a maelstrom of thoughts and concerns, but I barely have time to dwell on the potential pitfalls of the trip before Mason picks me up from the program dorms.

Mason is unusually subdued during the ride. Quiet as he drives, silent as he parks the car, and still wordless as we bypass TSA and all the usual flight requirements. Instead, we head to a private section of the airport. The wing is devoid of crowds and waiting; as soon as we arrive at a small, empty gate, a flight attendant promptly ushers us onto the airplane.

The plane's interior is primarily adorned in crème tones, with warm paneled walls and elegant lamps embedded in the curved ceiling. The seats are upholstered in smooth, plush leather, appearing buttery and luxurious, inviting passengers to sink in and relax. Mason settles into a seat beside a window, and I take the one across from him, tucking my shoulder bag beneath the small, dark wooden table that separates us. On it is a vase filled with delicate daisies interspersed with valerian blooms.

Mason's focus goes to his phone, and his eyebrows draw together as he rapidly types away on it. An attendant comes to announce takeoff and asks what we'd like to drink; Mason orders a scotch for himself, while I request a bottle of water. As the plane starts to taxi, my heartbeat quickens. I've never been a fan of heights and have always hated air travel, but I've done it enough times to learn to keep my composure. Still, as departure begins, my breathing shallows and sweat forms on my brow. Mason notices, the way he seems to notice everything. He sets down his phone and tilts his head to the side.

"Not a fan of airplanes?" he asks.

I shake my head. "I don't like heights."

Mason nods. "Ah. Then you probably won't enjoy the penthouses my family frequents."

I shrug. "I'm fine with tall buildings, but being in a metal box in the sky is disconcerting. The chances of crashing, especially in a small jet, vastly supersede the likelihood of a structurally sound tall building tumbling."

"Fair enough," Mason allows, then switches topics. "At the party tonight, your main job will be to stay close to me, smile, and engage in bullshit small talk. Are you good with people?"

"Good enough," I respond. "I don't like pointless interactions or small talk, but I'm familiar with both. How much deference should I show? How much of a kiss-ass do I need to be?"

"No deference, no ass kissing, especially with my father. He'll respect you more if you aren't a suck-up. Be courteous, but you don't have to go out of your way to please anyone." He pauses. "Other than me, of course, if you're in the mood to."

"I'm really not," I tell him. "Stop coming onto me, Mason, it won't get you anywhere."

"I disagree," he responds easily. "It's already gotten me somewhere. I can still remember your taste on my tongue—*delicious*. I had a dream about you last night."

Feeling my cheeks heat, I murmur, "Good to know. Can we switch topics?"

Mason chuckles. "You're not going to ask about the nature of my dream?"

I shake my head. "No. I'm not interested."

"I think you're lying," he replies softly. "You are interested, you just don't want to be. That's fine; we have plenty of time to work on your reluctant interest."

I hate the fact that he's right. Hearing that he's fantasized about me is thrilling—I know from his reputation alone that Mason has slept with plenty of women, all of them likely far more experienced than I am. Despite myself, I am curious to find out what he dreamed of—if he might've imagined us together, *how* he might've imagined us together. He hasn't yet appeared in *my* dreams, but that could be because I haven't been sleeping well lately.

"Since you won't ask, I'll tell you," Mason says.

"That's not necessary," I say sharply. "I don't want to know."

"I dreamed that you were naked and spread out in front of me, like a virgin sacrifice waiting to be sullied," Mason tells me. "I dreamed of eating your pussy until you were nice and slick, limp from coming. Then I took you—languidly at first, because I have no interest in hurting you. Your soft moans filled my ears, your sweet pussy clenched around me until I thought my cock would break off, and you asked me to fuck you harder." He pauses, emitting a low, rumbly chuckle that makes heat gather between my thighs. "I was more than happy to comply. We came at the same time, and you cried out with pleasure. I woke up and jerked myself to the strongest orgasm of my life, just from a dream."

My mouth runs dry, my thighs clench, and my cheeks and neck burn. I find his words way sexier than I should; I find *him* far more attractive than I should.

"That sounds a bit too explicit for me," I manage to murmur, trying to quench the sudden thirst that's overtaken me. "I didn't need such details."

"Yes, you did," Mason says softly. "You wanted them, too."

"I did not," I lie, turning my gaze back toward the window.

Mason's low chuckle taunts me. "Whatever you say, Pixie."

The attendant returns, saving me from the immense discomfort of this conversation, and inquires what we'd like for brunch, reciting an extensive menu. I ask for fresh fruit while Mason orders an omelet. We eat in silence, broken up only by the sound of our chewing and the rumbling engine of the jet. After the attendant clears our dishes, I recline my seat and settle in, trying to fall asleep. It doesn't take long before I do, and I'm pulled into a dream that's startlingly similar to the one Mason described having.

***

I wake up to a gentle hand stroking my cheek; blinking my eyes open, I'm surprised to find Mason standing above me, leaned over my seat, staring at me with heated eyes. When I shift, returning my seat to its upright position, I'm even more startled to find that my panties have somehow, inexplicably, grown damp.

"What were you dreaming of?" Mason asks as I stand and grab my bag. "Something erotic, I hope. You were making these lovely muffled moans and gasps. I do hope I was the star of whatever dream had you reacting so...*vividly*."

"I can't remember," I lie, even as flashes of the dream cross my mind. *Dirty words whispered in my ear, calloused palms gripping my hips to guide my movements, velvety tongue running over every inch of my* body. I shove the images away before they can take a hold of me.

"Hmm," Mason says, not entirely sounding like he believes me. "Limo's here to pick us up and take us to the hotel; let's get going."

I follow him off the plane and into a sleek black limo parked on the tarmac. The dark, smooth leather seats and unnecessarily spacious interior exude luxury. A bucket of champagne with accompanying crystal glasses sits by the window, waiting for us.

Mason barely spares it a glance before taking a seat by me, with just a few feet of distance separating us—nowhere near enough for my comfort. I'm tempted to switch seats to the other side, but that would be the same as admitting my discomfort, and he'll probably try to grill me more on my dream. I'd rather tar-and-feather myself than admit the erotic scenes that played in my mind while I was sleeping.

Mason checks his phone, then turns to face me. "When you meet my father, look him in the eye. He might ask you about your academic background, aspirations, and accomplishments; don't brag, but don't be modest either. Mention Pandora's Box. Explain that you're a year ahead in your biochemistry studies thanks to your work ethic in high school. My father will respect your ambition and motivation. It's critical that he sees us as a good match so he'll back off and stop my mother from playing matchmaker."

"He won't care that I don't come from money like you?" I question.

Mason's lips thin. "Not as much as my mom will. He values hard work and intellect as much as family fortune." He exhales. "I want Dad to respect you, even if you aren't his choice for me."

"Why do you want your father to approve of me so much?" I ask, frowning. "We'll be broken up by summer, what does it matter?"

"It matters a great deal," Mason tells me. "He needs to believe in us for me to get a break."

"I'm not versed in talking myself up," I admit. "I don't really like speaking highly of myself, even in a modest sense."

"Why is that?" Mason asks me.

I shrug. "Because there's not much to boast of. I'm not *great* at anything. I'm a proficient dancer, but not a star. I'm a diligent student, but that's because I inherited my father's intelligence and learned to work hard from him. I don't have many accomplishments that aren't explained by me being an overachiever with a high IQ."

"You're very bright and very talented," Mason says, sounding incredulous. "You have every right to talk yourself up."

I look away, recalling the many times my mom made me feel subpar simply because I didn't follow in her footsteps and become exactly what she wanted me to be. Many times, she'd tell me some variation of, "*You're wasting yourself on frivolous endeavors, darling. You should really focus on your appearance; you could be so beautiful if you tried. A model gracing the covers of the most famous magazines in the world.*"

"I'll do my best," I murmur. "I'll treat your father like a potential employer I need to impress."

A puff of laughter escapes Mason. "Whatever works."

After sitting in traffic for two hours, we enter the heart of Manhattan. I take in the countless skyscrapers, magnificent bridges, eclectic architecture, and hustle of people on the streets with wide eyes. Everyone seems to be in a rush to get somewhere; the environment is so taut with excitement and tension, I can feel it even in the car.

My lips curve as I watch a man on a streetcorner wolf down a hotdog in two bites. Beside him, a young couple argues animatedly, hands waving and feet stomping. The streets are crowded with people in all stages of dress and undress, some of them nearly naked.

"This place is... wow," I murmur quietly, sneaking a peek at Mason, who's watching me with a smile of amusement. "You grew up here?"

He nods. "It gave me a certain set of valuable skills. Mainly, situational awareness and crowd navigation to help get through busy streets—important abilities in this city if you don't want to get run over."

"It must be easy to get lost here," I say, turning my attention to the many different avenues and streets as we pass them.

Mason shrugs. "Not really, at least not in Manhattan. It's set up in a grid: avenues and streets. Once you know the order of avenues on the east and west side, everything else is straightforward." He checks his phone again. "We made pretty good time, so we'll have a few hours to explore today. I want to show you some spots I think you'll like. Luckily, our hotel is in walking distance from all of them. We'll also stop by some stores to get you appropriate clothes."

I glance down at my blouse and jeans, growing defensive. "My clothes are fine."

"They are," Mason agrees easily. "They'll also make you stand out like a sore thumb with my family. You can dress however you want with me, Chloe, *I* won't judge you. *They* will. I'm not trying to demean you, I'm trying to spare you."

I open my mouth, then shut it, unable to come up with a rebuke because he's being fair. I don't want to stand out any more than I already inevitably will with his obscenely wealthy family.

The limo pulls to a stop in front of a magnificent hotel that resembles a revamped old manor. Standing on the edge of a large park bursting with greenery and filled with pedestrians, the hotel is stately and tall, though not a skyscraper. Its architectural style is reminiscent of French Renaissance—made of light stone, built with perfect symmetry, and topped with a mansard roof.

Even though I know I'm only here to participate in an act to uphold my end of the deal with Mason, I start to grow excited, which is a welcome reprieve from the nerves that have been wracking me all day.

"It's one of the best hotels in the city, if I do say so myself," Mason says. "Many famous families have stayed here, and they pay a hefty price to experience the heights of luxury and excellent service. C'mon, Pixie, let's go check in."

The driver opens the limousine door for us, and a bellhop dressed in a green uniform rushes out of the hotel to greet us. "Mr. Sieger," the young man says as we step out, gathering our luggage. "Your room has been prepared in advance, and your check in has been completed. If you'll kindly stop by the front desk, the concierge will give you the keycard."

My eyebrows rise at the realization that hotel staff members know Mason by name—I already knew he comes from a prominent and affluent family, but I'm beginning to wonder just *how* influential and wealthy they are.

I follow behind Mason as he takes us through a gorgeous vestibule with a towering Christmas tree standing proudly in the center, weeping pine needles onto a plush red circular rug surrounding it. A chandelier drips crystals from above, and the ceiling is meticulously painted with gold detailing. Mason breezes right through the vestibule and into a lobby with marble floors, walls, and even pillars at the corners of the room.

Glancing at the other hotel guests bustling around, I suddenly understand Mason's insistence on adjusting my wardrobe. Even in the lobby of this hotel, I feel obscenely underdressed—everyone here is wearing designer clothing.

Walking up to the reception desk, Mason offers the woman seated behind it a charming smile that she returns with a dreamy one of her own. "Mr. Sieger," she greets. "We have your usual suite prepared. One bedroom with an en-suite bathroom, living room, kitchenette, balcony, and one king-sized bed—"

"*One* bed?" I repeat in a shrill tone.

Chapter Thirteen

Mason glances at me from the corner of his eye. "Roll with it, Chloe," he murmurs softly.

The concierge stares at me like I've sprouted a second head, as if protesting sharing a bed with Mason is the epitome of irrationality. To most of the female population, my reluctance might seem ridiculous, but most women haven't seen the parts of Mason that I have. While he's acted like less of an asshole recently, I won't soon forget the rocky start of our relationship. Staying in a single suite with him would've already pushed the limits of my comfort, only having one bed is a step too far. Knowing that the lobby isn't the right place to discuss this, I seal my lips and swallow hard, pasting a brittle smile on my face.

Mason collects the keycards for the room, then leads me through the hotel lobby and to a bank of elevators in a brightly lit hallway. A short ride to the top floor later, he unlocks our hotel room and ushers me inside.

I step into a dark toned wooden entryway with intricately carved boiserie paneling on the walls, and a brass chandelier adorned with alabaster cups hanging from the ceiling. Our luggage sits on the floor beneath an upholstered wooden bench, above which hangs a painting of an impressionistic New York City skyline at sunset.

Mason shrugs off his jacket and hangs it up in the coat closet by the door, while I try to keep my astonishment under wraps as I walk through the elegant vestibule and into a large sitting room.

The ceiling is high, featuring a contemporary chandelier with suspended asymmetrical glass crystals. Decorated in teal and silver tones, the room has a light carpet embellished with hand-sewn silver and blue detailing, a teal velvet sofa flanked by two armchairs facing a flat-screen TV, and a dining table long enough to seat eight people by the right wall. Three of the walls display expertly crafted paintings of New York City in eras past, and the fourth is made almost entirely of glass panels, with a doorway leading to a balcony that overlooks an expansive park.

Shaking my head in bafflement, I make my way into the bedroom. There, the teal theme of the living room transitions to hues of gentle crèmes and off-whites. A four-poster bed frame carved from pale wood features a mattress with a crème bedspread and an array of meticulously arranged pillows, accompanied by a chaise lounge at the foot of it and two antique bedstands on either side of the headboard. I wander into the bathroom, which boasts of gleaming white marble floors, a spacious bathtub that could comfortably fit four people, a glass shower enclosure, and a two-sink counter with *gilded* faucets.

I walk back into the bedroom, finding Mason seated on the chaise lounge. "Impressed?" he questions.

"Overwhelmed," I reply honestly. "This is... a lot. I'm not used to this sort of splendor."

"Get used to it, Pixie," he responds. "You'll be seeing a lot more of it. Are you tired? Do you want to take a nap?"

I shake my head. "I'm brimming with energy. I'd like to shower, but then I'm keen to explore."

He nods. "Go ahead. Once you're ready, we'll head to Madison Avenue for some shopping, and then to Central Park if we have time. I think you'll like it. Did you bring a warm coat?" At my nod, he says, "Good."

An hour later, I've showered, applied a touch of makeup, and pulled on the best outfit I packed—dark jeans and a beige sweater. My clothes are nowhere near as elegant as the blue cashmere sweater and black slacks that Mason wears; he looks at once sophisticated and comfortable.

As promised, he takes me to Madison Avenue, which is lined with luxury boutiques, some with names I've never even heard of. Each store has window displays with mannequins dressed in gorgeous outfits, surrounded by cute Christmas decorations. I like the bells and little trees far more than the luxurious fabrics covering the mannequins, but I don't protest as Mason pulls me into several stores.

As soon as the staff glimpse Mason's American Express black card with his family name, they're all too eager to help us. I try on more outfits and dresses than I ever have before, and even though I discard most of the options because I just don't need so many clothes, Mason purchases far too much for me. While I feel second-hand guilt at his splurge, I also understand that the cost of this shopping trip is likely peanuts for him.

"Why so much?" I ask him, cheeks burning as he swipes his card at yet another store. "We're here for a few days."

"I'm prepping for the next months," Mason tells me. "You can't wear the same outfit or dress twice in front of my family; it would raise questions as to why I'm not looking after my girlfriend properly."

"Your family sounds like it's made up of pretentious snobs," I say, earning a gasp from a cashier.

Mason merely chuckles. "Yeah, Pixie, that about describes them. Don't worry, I'll protect you from the vultures." After arranging for the clothes to be delivered to our hotel, he checks his watch. "We have a few more hours before we need to get ready for the party. You hungry?"

I shake my head. "Too excited for hunger."

His brows draw together, but he doesn't comment. "Up for a walk around Central Park?"

"Definitely," I agree.

As we walk the few city blocks to Central Park, I'm struck by the realization that, when he isn't being a jerk, I *like* Mason. We talk about everything and nothing, from the quirky pedestrians on the streets to our opinions regarding holiday decorations, to the intense snowstorm that's forecasted to hit the city at the end of the week. Mason has a relaxed demeanor that almost makes me forget he's as sharp as a hawk and meticulously calculated, traits I assume are useful in the upper echelons of New York.

We enter the park on a paved pathway bordered by low metal railings. Old streetlamps stand at intervals—I imagine they'd look magical in the evenings, once the sun is down, with snow drifting around them. On either side of the walking path, hills are blanketed in a few inches of snow, with kids of all different ages playing on them. I smile as I watch a group of children gather at the top of a steeper hill, armed with sleds. One by one, they hop on their sleds and slide down the hill, shrieking with laughter and giggles.

"Those two are really cute," I comment, tipping my chin at a brother-sister duo sharing a sled as they speed down the hill.

"You like kids?" Mason asks me.

"I adore them," I respond. "I started taking on babysitting jobs from the time I was eleven years old and only stopped when I left for college. The money was good, but I would have done it for free. Children are full of energy and a bit challenging to keep up with, but they're also so uncomplicated and delightful to be around. They see the world in an innocent way, everything's wonderous and fascinating to them."

"Hmm," Mason says. "I guess that makes sense. How old were your charges?"

"Any age up to twelve. I once had to look after a six-week-old; that was terrifying because I had no idea what to do at first. I caught on quickly enough with a bit of help from Google and the baby's twelve-year-old brother, who was kind enough to guide me."

Mason smiles. "You're good at picking up on things."

The compliment sends a rush of warmth through me. "Thank you, I do try."

We walk in companionable silence for a while as I take in the people, trees, snow, and ambiance of the environment, breathing it all in. After a while, we come upon a skating rink that's teeming with people of all different ages.

"Want to skate?" Mason offers.

I shake my head. "I broke an ankle during a lesson when I was young, didn't bother trying again."

Mason nods. "Fair enough, I'm not much of a fan of skating either. I prefer skiing. Do you ski?"

A pang of nostalgia washes over me as some of my fondest memories with my father flit across my mind. He was an avid skier who traveled to various mountains in the States every winter and spring for a week of skiing, and always took me with him. He'd put me in ski school during the day, then when school ended, he'd pick me up and we'd hit the slopes for a few runs. Since Mom wasn't athletic, she'd stay in the lodge or hotel room, leaving the two of us to enjoy our skiing time together.

"Yeah," I say, my voice faintly choked. "My dad and I went skiing every year. He was very skilled and taught me most of what I know." A faint smile tugs at my lips. "I remember one time when I was twelve, we got lost in a blizzard so severe we couldn't even see the signs. We ended up going down a triple black without realizing it. I was so scared I thought I'd pass out, but Dad told me to trust the mountain and trust myself, that everything would be fine if I stayed in tune with nature. He was right. When we got to the bottom, the sun broke through the snowstorm long enough for us to see the slope—it was littered with fallen trees and cliffs, any one of which could've killed us." My father was big on nature and the outdoors, and he believed there was a harmony between people and the earth that could be tapped into—he instilled that belief in me, and it's saved my life more than once.

"Wow," Mason says. "Triple black diamond, huh? So you're good, then."

"At anything that doesn't involve moguls," I confirm. "Never did figure those shitty bumps out, always fell on them. I dislocated my knee once and decided to avoid them after that."

"Have you ever raced?" Mason asks.

"Took first place six years in a row in annual ski school races," I tell him.

"We have a champion on our hands," Mason murmurs. "It sounds like your dad was an incredible person."

"He was," I say with a touch of sadness. I still miss my dad terribly whenever I think of him—sometimes so much so that I can barely breathe. The pain has eased over the years, but it hasn't gone away, and

I don't think it ever will. He had too much of a profound impact on me; in many ways, the person I am today is owed to him.

"We should go skiing some time, race each other," Mason suggests, a smile tugging at his lips.

I feel a frown crease my forehead. "Unless your family is throwing a skiing party that I need to attend, that isn't part of our deal."

"Always going back to the deal," Mason mutters, lips thinning. He doesn't say anything else, but I can sense the shift in his mood from lighthearted and somewhat hopeful to somber and serious.

"That's what we decided," I remind him gently. "I don't dislike you as much as I did, say, a week ago, but this is business. Right?"

Mason gives me a long, lingering look, then says flatly, "Sure, Chloe. Just business."

From the corner of my eye, I see a young child—maybe five years old—weaving through the crowd and giggling, a split second before the little girl runs headfirst into my legs, then falls on her butt. My heart aches as tears well up in her big blue eyes, and I crouch down to her level.

"Aw, it's okay sweet girl, just a little tumble," I coo at her. "No harm done, right?" Gently, I extend my hands toward her, and when she doesn't recoil or cry—merely stares up at me with wide eyes—I smile and lift her into my arms, coming to a stand. "Where are your mommy and daddy?"

She extends her hand and points ahead of me, just as two frazzled parents push through the crowd, eyes wide, looking panicked. The mother, brown-haired and blue-eyed, lets out a sigh of relief upon seeing her daughter and quickly rushes forward.

"I'm so sorry about Alicia," she tells me, reaching for the girl. "She likes to run off when she gets too excited."

"Absolutely no problem," I say sincerely, gently handing Alicia over to her mom, smiling at the little girl. "She's adorable—I don't mind at all."

The mother gives me a weary smile. "This is our first time in New York; we thought Alicia might enjoy a walk through the park, but didn't anticipate just how much she'd enjoy it."

The father nods at me. "Thank you for helping her."

I smile at the parents and Alicia, who's begun playing with her mother's hair, tugging at it hard enough to make her mom wince. "It's no bother. Enjoy the city, and happy holidays."

I walk past the trio with a soft smile. I miss my days of babysitting and resent that I'm far too busy for it now.

"You're going to be a hit with my little cousins," Mason comments.

I glance at him. "You have youngsters in the family that'll be at the party?"

"Not tonight's party, but they'll be at the family gathering to-morrow," Mason tells me. "They're little demons; far too energetic, constantly getting into trouble."

I laugh. "That's the nature of children. I don't mind, I'll happily amuse the kids while you attend to whatever family business there might be."

"Trying to leave my side already?" Mason asks. "It won't be so easy, Chloe."

I can't help but sense a double meaning to his words; one that extends far beyond the events we'll be attending.

Chapter Fourteen

Mason

A few hours later, my agitation at the upcoming party has risen to dangerous levels. As I sit in the living room of the hotel suite, adjusting my cufflinks and waiting for Chloe to finish getting ready, my thoughts are mainly on the politics that'll be at play tonight.

My father hosts and attends these types of parties not for enjoyment, but to gather many important people in one room at the same time. He conducts business with the relevant men and women while the other attendants mingle, drink, and engage in menial gossip. The only thing to look forward to tonight is that once my parents meet Chloe, they will temporarily cease throwing women at me in hopes that I'll marry. They might not like Chloe due to her modest background—Mom will *certainly* put up a fuss—but Dad should respect Chloe's intelligence and work ethic.

Soft footfalls sound on the floor, drawing my attention toward the bedroom. My heart stops when Chloe steps out wearing a stunning green dress made of silk. The neckline is modest, revealing the barest hint of cleavage, and the straps drape off her shoulders in a cascade of sheer silk that gently caresses her fair skin. The upper half of the dress is so tight it almost resembles the corsets I've seen at costume parties, but beneath the sash-marked waist, the skirt flows to the ground in a curtain of silk and lace.

Chloe's added soft curls to her long hair and pulled the top layer back, giving a clear view of her face, which has been gently accentuated with makeup. Subtle pigments enhance her eyes, making them look larger; a faint shimmer shines on her cheekbones, showcasing their elegance, and her lips are painted a dark pink, accentuating their poutiness. All in all, she is *stunning*.

The interest she always stirs in my gut magnifies tenfold, and I rub a hand over my jaw, inhaling sharply as my cock starts to harden in my pants. I shift my position to alleviate some of the pressure, praying to whatever god might exist that Chloe doesn't notice the hard-on she's inspired.

"Is this..." she trails off, cheeks flushing a lovely pink. "Appropriate? Acceptable?"

"More than," I say, swallowing roughly. "You're breathtaking. You'll be the envy of every unmarried man at the gathering." I'll have to keep a close eye on her tonight. Many people in my circles are weary of airheaded socialites; Chloe's conversational skills and intellect will draw them like a beacon. I'm almost tempted to say fuck the party and spend the night here with her.

"Thank you," she murmurs, adorably bashful. "Should we go?"

"Yes." I take a moment to think about party politics and family bullshit until my hard-on dies down, then stand. I extend my hand to Chloe, pleased when she crosses to me and takes it without protest. I like to think that's a marked improvement from the times when she flinched away from me. I don't think Chloe's entirely comfortable around me just yet, it'll take some work to get there, but my efforts to put her at ease and get to know her this afternoon appear to have chipped away at some of the ice between us.

After sitting through forty minutes of city holiday traffic, we arrive in front of the hotel where the party is being held. A doorman escorts us across a monstrous marble lobby entirely devoid of character and through several hallways, up to a grand double-door entrance leading into a ballroom. One of the guards standing by the doors recognizes me, and waves us in without asking to see our tickets.

I keep a tight hold of Chloe's hand as I lead her through the doors and into the proverbial fire. I cast a cursory glance around the ballroom, barely suppressing a grimace at the overdone opulence of the space that lacks any depth or interest. Three crystal chandeliers hang from a domed ceiling, an orchestra plays classical compositions on a small, raised platform in the corner, and stone columns are placed around the room for no apparent reason. Well-dressed people from the most prestigious families and backgrounds mingle together, politicians and mafia men alike enjoying the hors d'oeuvres being offered by waiters weaving through the crowd.

I spot my mother and father standing in the corner of the ballroom just as Dad notices me. He's looking as sharp as ever in a pristine black tuxedo, his auburn hair parted to the side, his posture regal, and his stare slicing through me like a blade. A glance at Chloe causes his eyebrows to inch up ever so slightly, though his expression quickly melts back into the cool mask he always wears. He waves a hand to beckon me over, his ruby cufflink glittering with the gesture.

"Grant and Jade Sieger," I murmur to Chloe, who gazes at my parents. "My mother and father."

Chloe nods, straightening her back and lifting her chin. "Showtime."

Her observant eyes scan the room as we make our way toward my parents, and I notice that they flash with surprise and recognition several times, likely at the sight of famous politicians mingling in the space.

"Mason," Father greets as we stop before them. He stares at me intently for several moments, then shifts his gaze to Chloe. "I see you've brought a friend."

"A date," I correct, keeping my tone steady. "My girlfriend, actually. Chloe Richardson."

"Hmm. I've never heard of her." Father watches Chloe with a faint expression of distaste, and I quickly understand that he's attempting to gauge if she's a weak girl who'll wither under the weight of his harsh stare and jab.

"Mr. Sieger, it's a pleasure to meet you," she says gracefully. "Mason's told me a great deal about you."

"I can't say the same," Father responds tersely, making me tense.

Chloe, however, doesn't tense; she gives a light, echoing laugh. "Mason and I were friends up until recently, I don't like diving head-first into relationships." Her smile takes on a decidedly impish slant. "I made him wait quite a while before agreeing to a date."

Father blinks slowly at Chloe, looking like he's not quite sure what to make of her.

"You made my son wait?" Mother demands, glaring at Chloe with sheer disdain. "Why would that be?"

"An abundance of caution," Chloe replies smoothly. "It's also a pleasure to meet you, Mrs. Sieger. You are as beautiful as Mason described. Your dress is absolutely *stunning*. Such a perfect blend of elegance and boldness."

I can tell that Mom doesn't *want* to like Chloe, but she can't resist compliments on her appearance; she's the vainest person I've ever met. "Thank you," she says primly. "It's a limited edition by Oscar de la Renta."

I'm more than a little impressed by how Chloe's handling herself, especially since my family has the art of demeaning people down to a fucking science. Chloe's not deterred or put off by the coldness; she's flattering my parents without being sycophantic and refusing to buckle under their scrutiny.

Father slowly extends a hand to Chloe, which is as close to a mark of approval as I'll get from him. Chloe accepts it with a smile, and her eyebrows lift as he lifts her hand to his lips and brushes a kiss over her knuckles.

"I hope the two of you enjoy the evening," Father says, gaze flicking back to me. "We'll speak tomorrow."

Chloe respectfully inclines her head. Before we can turn to walk away, a new, shrill voice says, "*Chloe?*"

Chloe stiffens beside me, becoming still as a statue, before turning to glance over her shoulder. Her gaze shutters and her entire demeanor changes to cold and closed off.

"Mom," she greets, her voice strained as she turns away from my parents. I turn with her, my eyes fixing on an elegant woman with red-blonde hair cutting through the crowd, clinging to the arm of a man I recognize as one of Dad's most prestigious business associates, *Bradley Rodgers*.

I glance back at my father, watching as recognition flashes in his eyes. We both piece together the puzzle of what's going on here at the same time—Bradley's fiancée, whom we hadn't yet had the pleasure of meeting, is Chloe's mother. Everyone heard that the billionaire mogul, head of a luxury conglomerate, got engaged a few months ago. But

Bradley hadn't yet brought his fiancée to any of our gatherings, so this comes as quite the shock.

Dad's recognition is quickly followed by a look of deepening interest as he reaches the same conclusion as I do; when Bradley and his fiancée marry, Chloe will become part of our circles by default. In other words, she just transitioned from an acceptable temporary date to a potential match. A match promising a sturdy business alliance that's guaranteed to be advantageous for my family.

"I didn't know you would be in New York this week!" Chloe's mom says as she comes to a stop by her daughter, a wide smile splitting her red-painted lips. I notice that she has the same teal eyes as her daughter, lined with dark eyeliner. Chloe releases my hand to exchange stiff-looking cheek kisses with her mother. "And you know to call me Grace in public, dear," her mom adds with a laugh.

Out of the corner of my eye, I see Dad's eyebrows twitch again

"Of course, my mistake," Chloe says, somewhat stiffly. "Good to see you, *Grace*. Mr. Rodgers—"

"Bradley, please," Bradley corrects, glancing between me and Chloe with a speculative, not altogether pleased look.

I thought my relationship with my parents was strained; it looks like Chloe doesn't even communicate with her mom about holiday plans. *Jesus.*

"Right," Chloe says, giving Bradley a smile that appears perfectly polite to an outsider, though I can see the strain on her delicate features. "This is a pleasant surprise."

Grace's attention quickly turns to me as I take her daughter's hand and tuck it into the crook of my arm. "I wasn't aware that you're with Mason Sieger, this is wonderful! We *must* meet up for a girls' lunch to catch up while we're both in the city," Grace says excitedly.

Without waiting for Chloe to respond, Grace turns to my parents, while Bradley exchanges an amicable greeting and handshake with my father and kisses my mother's hand. A conversation of pleasantries quickly ensues—when I glance at Chloe, I notice a placid smile plastered on her lips, though I get the sense she would rather be anywhere but here. She hasn't told me anywhere near as much about her mother as she has about her father, and I think I'm starting to understand why. For Grace to ask her daughter to refer to her by first name in public means she probably rivals my mom in the vanity department.

My heart speeds at the understanding that, after tonight, word will spread of Bradley's soon-to-be stepdaughter. A young woman who's beautiful, clever, and about to enter into one of the most prestigious families not just in this country, but in the entire world. A young woman who's about to become one of the most eligible single women in my circles, which means the vultures will begin their descent in no time. *Fuck*.

CHAPTER FIFTEEN

Mason

While Bradley engages my mother in a light conversation, paying his respects to the hostess of the party, Grace pulls Chloe a few feet to the side, speaking to her daughter with an absent smile.

My father takes the opportunity to step forward and place a hand on my shoulder. "Rodgers is one of the most influential men here tonight," he tells me, speaking quietly so as not to be overheard. "His future stepdaughter is beautiful and clearly intelligent. He has no other children. His family will be a good match for ours." He pauses, giving me a meaningful look. "I am not the only one who will think that. Many will want a connection to Bradley Rodgers."

"I understand," I tell Father.

Chloe's already beginning to attract curious glances from onlookers. Before her mom arrived with Rodgers, Chloe was a pretty date on my arm. Now, she's transformed from a beautiful date to a desirable match.

"Good," Dad says stiffly. "Do what you must."

Bradley finishes exchanging customary pleasantries with my mother and joins his fiancée and her daughter. He casts an inscrutable glance at Chloe, then gives her a subtle nod. Chloe offers a stiff formal incline of her head in return, appearing a bit pale. A moment later, Bradley and Grace flit away, followed by my mother and father, who begin making their rounds to greet all the notable guests.

I walk to Chloe, taking her hand again. I don't have a chance to speak to her before we're approached by a well-dressed man and his wife, associates of my father. Accompanying the couple are their son and daughter. While I make light conversation with their parents, the daughter stares at me like I'm a juicy steak fresh off the grill, and the son stares at Chloe with undisguised lust in his gaze. Irritation curls in my gut, and I slip an arm around Chloe's waist to make a statement: she's mine.

I was already angling to alter my arrangement with Chloe into an actual relationship—she's the first woman to catch and hold my interest. Prior to the unexpected events of tonight, I thought I'd have until the end of the school year to woo her, but now my time will be extremely limited. While there are those in attendance who will look down on her middle-class origins despite her connection to Bradley Rodgers, most eligible young men won't care and will swiftly begin pursuing her. I need to lock her down to ensure that no one else is successful in winning her hand.

My goal comes with its own set of complications; most notably, Chloe's not comfortable with me. The greatest compliment she's paid me to date is telling me that she doesn't hate me as much as she did a week ago. Fortunately, I can sense her desire for me—even though she tries to conceal it—and I intend to leverage that desire to draw her closer to me.

For the next hour, Chloe and I are approached by a continuous stream of my father's partners and associates. All those who have children bring their kids along; I keep a possessive arm wrapped around Chloe's waist, a silent message to the unattached sons who practically drool over her.

Finally, a man I enjoy speaking with walks up to Chloe and me, accompanied by a raven-haired woman wearing an elegant blue dress. "Sergei Novikov," I greet with my first genuine smile of the evening, clasping the offered hand of the Bratva boss who owns the majority of Eurasia. "It's been too long."

Most people cower at the mere mention of this Bratva Pakhan's name and shit themselves at the sight of him, but I first met him when I was all of thirteen years old. Sergei conducts a great deal of business in the states, and many of his legitimate dealings are done either with or through my father. Dad had me sit in on one of their meetings when I was younger, and I found Sergei *fascinating* instead of terrifying—I still do. He may be a cold-blooded killer whose staggering fortune comes from drug and gun trafficking, but he is also one of the most honorable men I've ever met.

"Mason," Sergei replies, squeezing my hand. "It's been too long." He gestures to the woman at his side. "This is my wife, Kira."

I kiss Kira's hand, resisting the urge to shiver under the calculating weight of her green gaze. "Congratulations on your nuptials," I say. "I'm sorry I couldn't make it to your wedding. I hope my father was a pleasant guest."

"He was as entertaining as always," Sergei says drily. "In other words, I've found more amusement in watching paint dry. Regardless, he makes me a stunning amount of money, so I won't complain."

"You must be Chloe," Kira says, turning her appraising gaze on my girl. "The whispers about you have been relentless in the last hour. Are you looking forward to your mother's marriage to Bradley Rodgers?"

Chloe's smile is lukewarm. "So long as Mom and Bradley are happy together, what occurs between them is hardly my concern. I will be glad of my mother's joy, but I'll be too engrossed in my studies to take much notice of either my mom or future stepfather."

Kira blinks slowly. "I see. You go to Greywood with Mason, if I'm not mistaken."

"According to the chatter in the room," Sergei adds.

"That's correct," I reply in Chloe's stead. I tighten my arm around her, this time in a show of protection rather than possessiveness. While I might appreciate Sergei, I'm under no illusions that he's a very dangerous man, and both he and his wife are currently gazing at Chloe with calculated coolness, which unnerves me.

"What's your major?" Kira questions.

"I'm a double major in biochemistry and dance," Chloe replies.

Sergei tilts his head to the side. "That's an unusual mix."

Chloe shrugs delicately. "I enjoy dancing, but I'm a realist. I'd like to have a secure plan for my future, not an idealistic one. Dance might be one of my passions, but it's not an especially practical career path." She turns to me. "Please excuse me, I have to use the restroom." I reluctantly release her waist, watching as she glides off to the bathroom, attracting many stares as she passes through the crowd.

"Looks like you've got yourself a good one," Sergei comments, casting a glance in Chloe's direction.

"An uncommonly intelligent one, too. I can see it in her eyes. You'll want to hold onto her, Sieger," Kira advises.

"She'll certainly be a valuable asset," Sergei adds.

"I intend to hold onto her *very* tightly," I say with complete honesty.

Sergei nods. "Good for you." He claps my shoulder. "It's good to see you. I do hope we'll collaborate together in the future, you've grown into quite the man." He strides away with an arm around Kira, holding her closely against him.

Before I can be pulled into yet another meaningless conversation, I cut through the crowd and make my way to the bathrooms, returning the many polite smiles I receive from guests, and casting subtle warning glares at the men who've spent the last hour staring at Chloe.

I enter the bathroom hallway just as one of the doors to the private restrooms open and Chloe steps out; before she even notices me, I act on sheer impulse, swiftly pushing her back into the bathroom and locking the door behind us.

"Mason, what the fu—" I cut Chloe off with a kiss, spinning her around and pinning her against the door, claiming her lips with mine. I gorge myself on her sweet scent, sweeter taste, and give her a punishing kiss that's a fierce reminder of the fact that she's here with *me*.

I've never dealt with jealousy over a woman until this evening, so I don't know how to handle the urge to destroy every single man who now wants to take her from me. If they try, the simple truth is that I will kill them, regardless of their last name or station in society. The need to rain fire on anyone who even thinks of touching her burns bright within me.

Chloe pulls her mouth away from mine with a gasp, turning her head to the side. "Mason—"

I cut her off with another, deeper kiss, sucking on her tongue and fisting a hand in her hair to hold her still for my exploration. When that isn't enough, I palm her breast through her dress, enjoying the breathy little moan that escapes her as she inadvertently arches her back, pressing her chest into my hand. My cock hardens into a steel pipe that nudges against Chloe's stomach, demanding attention, but I ignore it. This isn't about me, it's about her, and I intend to ensure she is *very* satisfied by the end of it.

Now more than ever, I need Chloe to want me as much as I want her. She's susceptible sexually—if I need to exploit her innocence to make sure she's addicted to me, make sure she *needs* me just as I'm starting to need her, that's precisely what I'll do.

I release her breast in favor of gripping the skirt of her dress, bunching up the silk until I can get my hand beneath the hem. I run my palm up the soft skin of her thigh before cupping her pussy. She releases another moan that goes straight to my cock as I rub my fingers over her panties, gratified by the bucking of her hips. I continue kissing her as I stroke her through the silky fabric, loving the little whimper she releases. Everything about Chloe appeals to me, and I *need* to get under her skin the same way she's gotten under mine.

She rips her mouth away from mine; I allow it, taking the opportunity to run my lips along her jaw and kiss a path down her neck, loving the sweet taste of her skin and the way she clutches my shoulders, sagging against me.

"Mason, this is wrong—" she cuts off with a yelp when I slip my fingers beneath the fabric of her panties. I hiss against her neck when I find her hot and slick, primed for my touch. I'd love nothing more than to get on my knees and eat her little pussy until she's shaking and screaming, but I can tell Chloe's in a flighty mood, and she might come to her senses and try to push me away in the short time it would take to get my lips and tongue between her thighs. I can't have that.

"Does this feel wrong, Pixie?" I ask her, rubbing leisurely circles over her clit with the pad of my thumb. "It feels perfectly right to me."

"*Oooh god,*" she moans lowly when I slip a finger inside her, then two. Her head tosses from side to side as her back bows and her eyes flutter shut. Unable to resist, I scoop one of her breasts from the dress and fasten my lips around her nipple as I slide my fingers in and out of her and play with her clit. This is more than a scandalous interlude in the restroom; this is my way of staking a claim on her, even if nobody else is around to witness it. I want to imprint myself on her body as much as her mind, and I have the perfect way to do it—make her come so hard she sees stars.

"You're so fucking tight," I murmur, releasing her nipple. "Your pussy is going to feel incredible when I plant it on my cock."

Chloe's pliant and limp in my hold, panting harshly, too over-whelmed by pleasure to rebut my words. Her brows draw together as she pulls her bottom lip between her teeth, trying to suppress a moan.

"Come for me, pretty girl," I say when I feel her tight walls start to flutter around my fingers with an impending orgasm. "Let me feel you."

"*Fuck,*" she whimpers. A moment later, a full-body shudder wracks through her as her pussy clamps down on my fingers, the tight heat of her channel clenching convulsively around my invading digits. I claim her lips again, swallowing her moan as she starts to tremble and shake. Determined to draw every drop of pleasure I can from her, I don't cease my ministrations until she falls limp against the wall with only a subtle tremor coursing through her limbs. Only then do I withdraw my fingers and suck them into my mouth, groaning at her taste, willing to burn this entire fucking venue down if it means I can have my way with her like I want to, here and now. "Good girl," I tell her. "Very good girl."

As Chloe attempts to catch her breath, I leisurely run my hands over her body, my hold going from firm and restraining to tender and supporting. I stroke my fingers through her curled hair, trail soft kisses along her jaw, and help her right her dress as she comes back to herself. Her eyes are glazed with pleasure, her lips swollen from my greedy kisses. To see her so undone is nearly as erotic as making her come—knowing that I'm the one who gets to introduce her to the sensual world of pleasure is a heady sensation.

"Where did that come from?" she asks after a few moments pass. She's not trying to wriggle away from me, which I take as a sign of progress. She's also not scolding me or mentioning the fact that I didn't exactly give her a chance to stop me from touching her, which is certainly interesting. Not too long ago she would've panicked and lost her cool at a situation like this, but right now her expression is hazy and satisfied.

"I've wanted to do that since the moment I saw you wearing that dress," I tell her honestly. After a beat, I ask, "Why didn't you tell me that your mom is engaged to Bradley Rodgers?"

That sobers Chloe too quickly for my liking. She stiffens in my arms, then places her hands on my chest, and tries to push me away. After a moment, I reluctantly release her and step back to give her space.

"I didn't know it was relevant; didn't know Bradley was prestigious enough to be here tonight. He's rich, sure, but that's about the extent of what I know of him. I've only met him a handful of times, and..." she trails off, shaking her head and pressing her lips together in a thin line.

"And?" I prompt. There are dozens of questions resting on the tip of my tongue, but I bite them back. Mostly, I want to know if she understands the implications of being Bradley's soon-to-be stepdaughter. If she understands that, after tonight, she will be a sought-after member of my circles that many men will try to woo and marry.

"Nothing." Chloe slips past me and heads toward the mirror, combing her fingers through her hair to tame it and correcting the edges of her smudged lipstick with a paper hand towel. "I'll be having lunch with my mom tomorrow, so I'll be out in the afternoon." Her tone suggests she's not looking forward to lunch with her mom, but I decide that now isn't the best time to push or comment.

I can't resist saying, "You know you can talk to me, right?"

Chloe meets my eyes in the mirror, her gaze sharpening. "Can I, Mason?" she questions. "We're pretending to be together as part of our deal. You're the one who keeps crossing lines with kisses and... *more*. I never wanted this; I'm here to uphold my end of the bargain. We aren't friends, we aren't lovers, we aren't anything except two people in a mutually beneficial business arrangement. Though I'm starting to question if it really is advantageous to both of us; I'm coming through for you, but you've yet to come through for me."

Her words serve as a cold slap to my face, reminding me that I have a short window of time to either change Chloe's mind or find a way to cement my place in her life and affections. Otherwise, someone else will, and then I'll have to kill them.

"This is more than just a deal, Chloe," I tell her. "You know it, I know it. Soon enough you'll need to admit it; if not to me, then to yourself."

With that, I turn and walk out of the bathroom, slamming the door behind me.

CHAPTER SIXTEEN

Chloe

After I fix my appearance in the bathroom mirror, I locate Mason in the bustling ballroom. We spend another hour at the party, engaging in small talk with unfamiliar people who I have little interest in. Once the party begins to dwindle, we bid farewell to both our parents and finally make our way back to the hotel.

I take a quick shower to scrub all the makeup from my face and wash away the lingering stickiness between my thighs, trying to suppress the blush that rises at the memory of Mason kissing the breath from my lungs while treating my body like his personal playground.

When I emerge, I find Mason lounging on the bed. He's changed out of his form-fitting tux and into a low-hanging pair of sweatpants, no shirt in sight. I can't stop my eyes from traveling over every ridge and valley in his six-pack, admiring his finely-honed muscles and the immense effort that must have gone into sculpting such a magnificent physique. Mason is a modern-day Adonis, perfectly proportioned and so unbearably sexy I can hardly keep from biting my lip.

Mason glances up from his phone, and a smirk curls his lips when he catches me ogling him. "Enjoying the view?" he teases.

I clear my throat. "Hardly. I'm, um… I'm going to sleep on the couch."

Mason tosses his phone to the side, sitting up. "The fuck you are. This bed is huge, there's plenty of room for both of us."

The problem isn't the spaciousness of the bed, it's my inexplicable urge to climb Mason like a tree.

"I'm not sleeping in the same bed as you," I say firmly.

Mason releases a long sigh, lips thinning. Instead of arguing like I expect him to, he rolls out of bed with a grumble. "You don't make things easy, Richardson." His jaw tightens. "I'll take the goddamn couch; you can have the bed.

I frown. "No, that's—"

He holds up a hand to cut me off. "Do me a favor and don't argue. It's late, we're both exhausted, and despite all the horrible things you might think of me, I am a gentleman." When I raise my eyebrows in disbelief, he chuckles. "I'll call the front desk for more bedsheets and take the couch."

I blink slowly, watching in a daze as he picks up his phone and laptop before walking out of the room, closing the door behind him.

After a long moment of staring at the door, I climb into the bed and flick off the nightstand lights. I toss and turn for a long time, trying to reconcile the two sides of Mason I've seen so far: the asshole and the gentleman. It takes me over an hour to fall asleep, because all I can think about is that despite our rocky beginning, I'm *definitely* starting to like Mason.

***

I'm up at 5 a.m. the next morning. Even though it's winter break, I have to get in at least three hours of exercise and dance every day, or I'll fall behind in the dance program when Greywood resumes. I pull on my leotard, throw sweatpants and a long-sleeved shirt over it, and quietly step into the sitting room. Mason is sound asleep on the couch, his breaths deep and even, so I try to stay quiet as I exit the room, taking care to open and close the front door as gently as possible.

I spend the next three hours in the hotel's 24-hour-gym. The first hour, I warm up on the treadmill and stretch; then, I make use of the small, empty dance studio meant for ballroom dancing classes to go through my Pandora's Box solos and variations. By the end, I'm sweaty and tired, but also gratified.

When I return to the room, it's 8 a.m., but Mason's still asleep. After I've showered and prepared for the day, I emerge into the sitting room to find that the dining table has been set with a variety of breakfast foods. Mason sits at the head of the table, still wearing only sweatpants, reading something on his phone. Before him is a plate loaded with sausages, bacon, and *two* large waffles topped with berries and whipped cream.

"Good morning," he greets, taking a sip of coffee. "I ordered room service."

"Morning," I return as I approach the table, taking a seat at Mason's right. "Thank you. Everything looks delicious."

I pour myself a cup of coffee, load up a plate, then go through my email on my phone as I eat.

"Check local gossip websites," Mason tells me.

I glance at him. "Why?"

"We're in them," Mason replies, a slight smile on his lips. "I've never shown up to an event with a date before, and the fact that my date is Bradley Rodgers's future stepdaughter has caught some attention."

A quick google search produces at least half a dozen articles that speculate about my relationship with Mason. There are no pictures, but both of our names are mentioned, and I grimace as I read over the poorly written pieces. I'm not someone who enjoys attention—I only thrive in the spotlight when I'm dancing on stage. Otherwise, even being congratulated on a good performance makes me uncomfortable. Seeing my name splashed across trashy tabloids is a thousand times worse.

"Lovely," I mutter, scanning an article that details Bradley's engagement to my mother, which only briefly mentions me. "Will these sorts of reports die down quickly?"

Mason arches an eyebrow at me. "Quickly enough, sure, but they'll be replaced by new ones each time we go to a notable party together. You have to admit, we do make a striking couple, and the cameras and reporters love to chronicle young love—especially when it's between two particularly attractive people."

"Is there any way to avoid the cameras and reporters?" I ask him. "It's not like I actually intend to be part of your world."

Mason shakes his head. "Sorry, Chlo. Since nobody's bothered to tell you yet, I will; your mother's engagement to Bradley Rodgers is a big deal. It shines a spotlight on both you and her. Frankly, I'm surprised you haven't been mentioned in the tabloids sooner. The best way to keep your private life private is to give the cameras an occasional show to appease them, then turn around to do what you will behind closed doors. They shouldn't bother you in your day to day life, only when you go out to high society events."

I let out a long sigh, trying to suppress my mounting frustration at Mom's choice in fiancé. I quickly gulp down my cup of coffee, then stand and head toward the vestibule.

"Where are you going?" Mason asks.

I toss him a frown over my shoulder. "Out. I want to explore and decompress before lunch with my mom."

"You're not going anywhere without me," Mason says sternly, rising from his seat. "Give me twenty minutes to shower and dress, then we can go."

"Mason, we spent all of yesterday together; we can take time for ourselves today," I say slowly, speaking to him the way I would to a child that needs a clear explanation. "I'm sure you have things to do in the city; you do your thing, I'll do mine. There are already too many blurred lines between us, there's no need to add to them."

Mason crosses the room, stopping in front of me and reaching out to tuck a few strands of hair behind my ear. "You'll want me with you, Chloe. Otherwise, the vultures will descend. I'm a good line of defense for you; use our arrangement to your benefit. I can shield you from a whole lot of crap—few people are suicidal enough to cross my family."

"I don't need shielding," I tell him plainly.

"The fact that you think you don't just proves how much you do," he replies, a half-smile flitting across his lips. "Last night was your societal debut. You're a hot topic right now, and people will want to know more about you. There are those who might try to approach you if they see you out and about on your own."

What he's saying makes a certain amount of sense, but I can't shake the feeling that there's more to it. Mason's been relentless in his pursuit of me, and while our deal might have temporarily calmed him, it hasn't done so permanently. He's constantly making innuendos and trying to get closer to me—he always seems to be wanting more than I'm comfortable giving.

"Why else?" I ask Mason. "Why are you going through all of this effort? You're going above and beyond the terms of our deal, which hints to you having a greater plan. I know you're trying to get in my pants, but is that it? Do you just want sex tossed into our arrangement?"

Mason tilts his head to the side. "I'll reveal what I really want from you when you're ready. For now, of course I want to seduce you—you're beautiful and intelligent—and I want to use our arrangement to our mutual advantage. Now that you're out, you're not the only one who will be shielding the other from unwanted proposals. Trust me, many people will want a connection to Bradley, and you're the easiest, most readily available way of getting that." He drops a kiss on my forehead, a gesture that feels oddly natural. "Give me twenty, Pixie. I have some spots in mind that I think you'll like. Oh, and wear comfortable shoes; we'll be walking."

Seeing no better option, I sit at the dining table and pick at my food while Mason gets ready.

After we leave the hotel, the morning flies by as Mason whisks me around the city. Once again, I find it surprisingly easy to spend time with him. First, he takes me to a chocolate shop offering fine chocolates imported from all over the world. We sit in a cozy café at the back of the store, and Mason orders the taster menu. We share half a dozen pieces of chocolate, two brownies, and a slice of fudge. Once we're done, he leads me down several historic streets, pointing out old townhouses and telling me about the famous people that have lived there. Then, we visit a museum, and I thoroughly enjoy walking through beautiful galleries displaying stunning paintings and sculptures crafted by master artists.

My mood is significantly brighter when the time comes to start walking in the direction of the restaurant where I'll be meeting my mom. Even the text she sends, telling me that Bradley will be joining us, isn't enough to bring me down. There's just something wonderous about the city; the eclectic mix of people, the many energies buzzing in the air, the countless scents... I don't know that I'd ever want to live here, but visiting is wonderful. I'm almost sad I'll only be here a few days; there's so much to explore, see, and do.

"What's the story with you and your mom?" Mason asks as we cross a crowded street.

"There's no big story," I respond, raising my voice to be heard over the chatter of pedestrians and the many honking car horns. "We've just decided to take different paths in this world."

"You went pale as a sheet when you realized she was at the party last night," Mason points out, using a hand on my waist to pull me out of the way of a man who nearly plows right over me. I try to step out of Mason's hold once we've reached the sidewalk, but he doesn't release me. Since I don't mind his touch as much as I probably should, I let his arm remain curled around me.

"Because I didn't know she would be there. She didn't tell me her plans for the holidays; of course I was surprised at her sudden appearance," I say.

The years have strained my relationship with my mother in ways that I'm not sure can be undone. She has never supported my choice of going to college instead of pursuing modeling, and her relationship with Bradley has furthered the distance between us. Not because I have anything against Bradley, but because neither of them make a conscious effort to invite me into the new life they're building.

The truly low point in my relationship with Mom was the night of the horrible party when I was assaulted. After I returned home from the police station, Mom's greatest concern was subduing any potential gossip by burying the incident. I desperately wanted her to hold and comfort me; instead, I received a lecture on keeping private matters private. I learned then that I'd have to act as my own primary caretaker. While that mindset has served me well, it's also created a natural distance between me and my mother.

"When did your mom get engaged to Bradley?" Mason questions.

"He proposed when they were vacationing in Thailand at the beginning of August. She texted me a picture of the engagement ring a week later."

"That's cold," Mason murmurs. "She didn't give her only daughter a call?"

I shrug. "It is what it is. Very little surprises me when it comes to her. Bradley and I mostly ignore each other, which suits both of us."

Mason nods, sliding me a glance from the corner of his eye. "I've never been really close with my mom, either. I was the heir that was expected of her, not a son that she wanted—the only value I have in her eyes is the prestige I can bring our family, or the scandals I might create."

My heart pangs for him, and I give his arm a squeeze as we slow to a stop on the sidewalk in front of the restaurant where I'm supposed to meet my mom and Bradley. For several long moments, Mason and I stare at each other, a silent understanding passing between us. There may not be many similarities between us, but we do share strained relationships with self-absorbed mothers. The difference is that my mom and I were close when I was younger, back when I'd get excited over her dressing me up like a doll because it was our form of bonding. I don't know that Mason ever shared a closeness with his mom.

"Chloe, darling!" my mother's voice draws my attention away from Mason, and I turn to watch as she steps out of a sleek black SUV double-parked by the curb bordering the sidewalk. She's wearing a modest knee-length skirt, high heels, and a silk blouse, woefully underdressed for the winter chill.

Bradley follows her out onto the sidewalk, looking impeccable in a navy suit, blond hair parted to the side. His hazel eyes give me the briefest glance before narrowing on Mason. He takes my mother's hand in his as they make their way toward me. I inhale a deep breath, praying that lunch with them won't be too strenuous.

Chapter Seventeen

"Hello, Grace," I say, accepting a cheek-kiss from Mom before shaking Bradley's outstretched hand. Mason shakes it, as well, also exchanging greetings with Bradley and my mother.

"Mason Sieger," Bradley says, a practiced-looking smile stretching his lips. The thin smile doesn't reach his eyes; they remain cold and calculated. "I wasn't aware you'd be joining us."

"Mason was just kind enough to walk me here," I explain. "He's heading back to the hotel now."

"Oh no, you must stay!" Mom exclaims. "Our reservations are for three people, but I'm sure the waitstaff can squeeze you in as well, Mason." She looks to Bradley, as if for permission; when he inclines his head in agreement, a wide smile spreads on her lips.

My stomach churns as the four of us walk into the upscale restaurant, which is lavishly adorned with extensive Christmas décor. A Christmas tree stands to the right of the entrance, decorated with glowing lights and countless multicolored ornaments. Mistletoe curls down from wooden beams propping up the ceiling, twining over little silver bells laid along the rafters. Colorful streamers weave around the frames of the scenic paintings and photos that decorate the polished hardwood walls.

A hostess greets us from her stand at the front of the restaurant, graciously agreeing to add another chair to our table. She promptly ushers us to the back, where she seats us at a square table covered in a white tablecloth and set with fine dishware and glasses. Mason and I take seats across from Mom and Bradley; I concentrate on trying not to fidget under the weight of Bradley's scrutinizing stare.

It doesn't take long for Mom to start chattering on about everything and nothing; the weather, the fashion season, the upcoming trips she has planned with Bradley—none of which I've been invited to join. She only pauses in her animated, one-sided conversation when the waiter comes to take our orders, then continues prattling on. Not once does she ask any questions about how Greywood's going, the show I'm currently in, or my grades. She doesn't even seem to remember the fact that I'm in college, bending over backwards to secure a steady future for myself.

After a while, Bradley shifts in his seat, placing his hand on Mom's arm; she cuts off midsentence, sealing her lips and offering him a small smile. I don't miss the fact that she seems to be completely under his control. Outside the restaurant, she waited for his agreement before officially inviting Mason to join us. Now, a simple touch from him is enough to silence her after nearly half an hour of empty rambling.

"How long have the two of you been dating?" Bradley asks, flicking a glance between me and Mason. It's telling that he doesn't inquire about my general well-being or how my time at Greywood is going; instead he's more interested in my supposed relationship with one of New York high society's most eligible bachelors.

"A few weeks," Mason says, slinging an arm on the back of my chair, casually stroking my shoulder with his fingertips. Despite his relaxed demeanor, I can sense the tension radiating from him. I've learned that Mason is extremely observant, so I doubt he'll miss the fact that neither my mom nor her fiancé seem to give a single fuck about me as a person.

"I see," Bradley says with a nod. "Have you been enjoying each other's company?"

A lazy smile tips up Mason's lips. "Very much. Chloe's intelligent, beautiful, and an excellent companion. I'm surprised she finds room for me in her schedule, having a double major leaves her with little free time, but we manage to sneak in dates whenever we're both free." Mason turns to look me in the eye, warmth filling his gaze. "She's sharp, talented enough to be a soloist in Greywood's most successful dance production of the decade, and smart enough to intimidate lesser men. What's not to love?"

I have to blink several times to clear the mistiness in my eyes. Unlike my mom or Bradley, Mason looks beyond the surface of my appearance and appreciates what lies beneath. I give Mason a grateful smile, half tempted to lean in and give him a thank-you kiss. Instead, I turn to face my mother and Bradley again.

Bradley's eyebrows lift as he gives me a look of faint surprise, as if this is the first he's hearing of my accomplishments and aspirations in college. Mom probably hasn't mentioned anything to him about my studies. She didn't even ask what major I planned to pursue when I disregarded her modeling advice and requested access to the college trust fund my dad set up for me when I was barely five years old. I knew she wasn't going to pay for my education, but thankfully, my father spent my childhood planning for my college career.

"I didn't know that," Bradley murmurs, casting Mom a disapproving glance that visibly makes her wilt. "Greywood does have a rather prestigious dance program, from what I've heard. I assume you're a part of that program, Chloe?"

This feels more like an interview than a conversation, but I clear my throat and nod. "Yes, I am. I'm fortunate enough to be one of their soloists."

Bradley inclines his head. "And what else are you majoring in?"

"Biochemistry. If I don't receive any principal offers from dance companies after I graduate Greywood, I'd like to pursue a career in medicine."

Bradley gives me a slow once-over, as if he's seeing me for the first time. I think that, previously, he saw me as an irrelevant entity loosely attached to my mother. Now, I might be an actual person, one who deserves consideration and perhaps even respect.

"Very sensible," Bradley says.

"Chloe's already in the third year of her biochemistry studies," Mason adds on, making something warm unfurl in my chest.

"How's that?" Bradley questions. "You're a sophomore, aren't you?"

"I took AP and college courses during my junior and senior years in high school," I explain. "I started Greywood in my second year of bio-chemistry classes, with several of my core courses already complete."

"That's very impressive, Chloe," Mom says, her eyebrows drawing together as she also looks me over as if she's seeing me for the first time in years. There was a time when realizing her complete lack of interest in my life would've hurt; now, there's only a faint echo of pain in my chest. More the remembrance of pain than the actual sensation.

"My girl's talented," Mason says, making the warmth in my chest spread until I'm practically tingling with it. He sounds genuinely proud as he speaks, and he seems content to brag about me instead of himself. *I can't remember the last time someone focused on praising me rather than putting the spotlight on themselves.* It makes me want to cuddle up to Mason and curl myself around him.

Fuck, no. I can't let that happen. We might be good together in public, good at putting on an act, but that doesn't mean that Mason and I are *actually* good. We're not enemies, but we're not friends either, and he's *certainly* not someone I should want to be around outside the bounds of our deal. We're just playing roles right now, I can't get attached simply because he's good at acting.

"Apparently so," Bradley says with a nod, casting another disapproving glance at Mom. She turns her gaze down to her empty plate, remaining silent. "How did your finals for the fall semester go?" he asks, turning back to me.

"Fairly well. From the grades I've received so far, I should finish with all A's," I respond. Then, I add, "Mason's doing really well in Greywood's business program, too." We spoke about our classes and courseloads while we were walking around earlier; he told me he's also maintaining perfect scores and a 4.0 GPA.

Bradley fixes his gaze on Mason. "Word has it you're planning on joining your father's business once you've completed your degree."

"For once, the gossip is right," Mason confirms. "I might pursue business school if I feel like I need more preparation, but the plan is to join Dad and eventually take over his many business dealings."

"Your father's a very skilled businessman," Bradley says. "You'll have a great deal to live up to, if you can manage it."

Protectiveness surges through me like a tidal wave, unexpected and intense. I don't mind Bradley scrutinizing *me*, but his implication that Mason won't be able to live up to his father's work does not sit well with me. I've known that Mason is intelligent, perhaps *too* intelligent, since our first encounter. While I don't know the ins and outs of his father's dealings, I have complete faith in Mason's ability to carry the torch after his father.

"Mason's one of the smartest people I know," I tell Bradley. "Considering my biochem major, that's saying something. I'm sure he'll do *very* well when it's time for him to take his father's place."

Mason casts me a startled glance that quickly morphs into a warm smile. He gives my shoulder a squeeze of gratitude before turning back to Bradley.

"Like I've said, if I feel underprepared after I've graduated Greywood's business program, I'll go on to business school," Mason says, turning back to Bradley.

"Naturally," Bradley responds. Then, he asks, "Are you serious about Chloe?"

For a moment, I wonder why he cares so much about my relationship with Mason, but then it dawns on me. Now that I have Bradley's attention, I might become a potential bargaining chip for him. Mason has made it clear that the function of marriage in high society is often business-minded; if I've proven myself worthy, even inadvertently, Bradley could see me as a conduit to strengthening certain business ties.

"I care about her and like spending time with her very much," Mason replies.

"And you, Chloe?" Bradley asks. "How serious are you about Mason?"

"Bradley, they're just kids," Mom intervenes. "They're too young to know—"

"They're old enough to make their own decisions and know their minds, Grace," Bradley interrupts, not taking his eyes from me.

"I'm just seeing where things go," I blurt out. I can't say I'm serious about Mason because I'm *not*, and I don't want to set future expectations that I won't be able to meet.

Mason tenses beside me, and his fingers stop doodling nonsensical patterns on my shoulder. I don't think he's pleased with my response, or the way that Bradley's looking at me with increasing interest, as if pondering what uses I might have as a pawn on his chessboard.

Bradley's lips curl into a faint approximation of a genuine smile. "Very sensible, indeed."

"Please excuse me," Mason says, "I need to use the men's room."

A strange coldness replaces the warmth in my chest as I watch him stand and walk away without a backward glance. I think I might have offended or even *hurt* him. Mason has alluded to wanting more from our arrangement on several occasions and always seems displeased when I remind him that all we have is a deal. I don't like the idea that I might've caused him pain, but I also don't want to lead him on.

Distracting me from my thoughts, Bradley says, "Now that you've debuted in society, it's wise to keep your options open. Mason might be one of the big fish, but he isn't the biggest or most advantageous."

I blink slowly, swallowing past the knot of discomfort in my throat. "I have little interest in the dealings of high society," I tell Bradley plainly. "I'm with Mason because I enjoy his company. Right now, I'm focusing on school and my future."

Bradley tilts his head to the side. "Given that I'm to become your stepfather, you should be interested in high society dealings, Chloe. Once I marry your mother, until we have children, you'll be my next of kin. Even after we start our family, you'll still be one of my heirs. An advantageous match is critical."

Shock suffuses me, causing my eyes to widen as I look at Mom, whose gaze remains glued to her plate. I never considered the idea of her wanting more children; she's still of child-bearing age, but the possibility of her birthing more kids never crossed my mind. It *shouldn't* be surprising that Bradley wants heirs from her, but the thought of having half-brothers or half-sisters stuns me, hitting me with the impact of a freight train. A blessed numbness quickly overtakes my shock, and I sink into it, allowing it to wash over me and replace my pain.

"I'm sure your children will give you the advantageous matches you seek," I tell Bradley, my voice surprisingly calm. "The fact remains that I was not raised in your world, and I have no intention of entering it. When and if I marry, it will be for love and for the sake of family, not for business."

"You're obviously smart, which is why you shouldn't be so damn naïve," Bradley says, lips thinning. "Almost everything in this world has to do with business. There are advantages to my last name, Chloe, you'd be foolish not to use them."

"If those advantages come with requirements such as marrying to better *your* business dealings, then I don't want them," I respond bluntly, my numbness dissipating in favor of irritation. "I like my last name. I like my life; I've worked very hard to get where I am. I'm happy so long as you make my mom happy, but please don't expect me to change my entire lifestyle for her marriage. I can't." *And it's not like she'd ever do the same for me.*

Bradley draws in a deep breath. "You're young. You'll learn as you go along. I'm going to set up some dates for you with a few boys around your age, ones who you might enjoy spending time with."

His words show his complete disregard for my sentiments and desires; before I can tell him off like I'm itching to, Mason returns, and I fall silent. While Bradley and Mason strike up a conversation about the stock market, I try to catch Mom's eye to see if I can get *any* support from her. She pointedly avoids my gaze, unwilling to get involved, even to defend my choices. It's not surprising, but it still hurts.

By the time our food arrives, I've lost my appetite entirely. I pick at my pasta with the tines of my fork, only eating a few bites. I'm grateful for the conversation Bradley and Mason hold, because it gives me a chance to silently grieve the sense of family I once had with mom. Now, I can see that it's gone for good.

CHAPTER EIGHTEEN

After the hellish lunch, Mason and I walk back to the hotel in silence. I can't stop replaying the way Mom stayed quiet while Bradley spoke of setting me up with other boys, completely ignoring my protests.

I'm not even halfway to the hotel when a text from Mom pops up on my screen; my heart sinks when I see she's sent me information for a date she and Bradley have *already* arranged. Apparently, I'm to go out to dinner with a young man from the party last night later in the week. It seems the matchmaking efforts have already begun.

"What the fuck?" Mason asks me, reading the text over my shoulder.

I pocket my phone, sliding him a glance that's part irritated, part exhausted. The lunch took a lot out of me, and I'm not in the mood to spar with Mason.

"Bradley wants to send me on dates with men he thinks will be appropriate for me—in other words, appropriate for his last name." I don't want to talk or even think about that right now, but the unfortunate timing of Mom's text combined with Mason's utter lack of respect for my privacy means that Mason would keep hounding me until he gets an answer. I figure I might as well save myself time by telling him up front.

Mason's features contort into a scowl. "Rodgers didn't get the hint when you showed up *with me*?"

"Evidently not," I respond. "He suggested I go on other dates while you were in the bathroom and ignored my clear disinterest in dating for his advantage."

"Are you going to date other men while we're together, Chloe?" Mason asks, his voice laced with a silky threat that raises goosebumps on my skin.

I frown as I think it over. "I'll probably end up going on a few dates to appease Bradley since I'm not interested in finding out what happens when that man is displeased," I decide. "But I don't foresee the dates leading to anything. They'll just be a waste of time."

"Don't," Mason clips. "Do both of us a favor, and don't go out with anyone else."

I give him a tired look. "Why do you care, Mason?"

We stop a street away from our hotel as the pedestrian light turns red. I startle when Mason sneaks an arm around my waist and uses it to pull me directly into his hard, sculpted torso, which radiates tension and hums with unspoken threats. My breath hitches and my nerves tingle as I gaze into his eyes, which are darkened with irritation and intent.

"Because I—*don't*—*share*," he says, enunciating every word. "Our arrangement is exclusive, Chloe. I thought you learned that lesson after you went on a fucking picnic date with that dickwad from your biochemistry classes."

My eyes widen as Mason leans down, slowly and deliberately, until his lips hover above mine. I half expect him to kiss me, and some part of me wants him to. Tension lights the space between our mouths, making my lips tingle with desire.

Before Mason can close that final inch between our lips, we're jostled by pedestrians as the light turns green. Mason releases me as abruptly as he grabbed me, then stalks across the street, his posture rigid. The rest of our trek to our shared room is silent. I try to ignore the way Mason glares at me during the elevator ride, quietly wondering how I'm going to make it through yet another gathering with his family while such palpable, intense tension hums between us.

***

The Christmas Eve party is held on the top floor of a high-rise building, in a beautiful penthouse that's a study of lavishness and opulence, but also has a sense of coldness. Mason's relatives gather in three large rooms: two sitting areas adorned with designer furniture and extravagant Christmas decorations, and a ballroom. *What is it with his family and ballrooms?*

I wear a red dress and matching lipstick that gives me the boost of confidence I'm in desperate need of. Mason puts on a bespoke Brioni suit that makes him even more devastatingly handsome than usual, and completes his appearance with a scowl.

His parents greet him with lukewarm smiles, while I receive cheek kisses and gushing compliments from his mother—a side effect of my impending relation to Bradley Rodgers, no doubt. Grant kisses my hand again and offers me a deceptively warm-sounding welcome, telling me to enjoy the evening and try the eggnog.

For the first half hour of the gathering, Mason and I greet several of his relatives, none of whom seem like remarkable people. Frankly, it strikes me that his family is made up of silver-spoon-fed divas.

Then, Mason's cousins run up to us. There are two little girls—a seven-year-old named Raegan, and the most adorable three-year-old named Amara—along with an eight-year-old pair of twin boys, Brandon and Thomas.

Raegan tells me she likes my lip color. Smiling, I stroke a hand over her honey-blonde hair and tell her I like her pink dress. Five minutes later, the kids pull me away from Mason and onto a large, uncomfortable divan beside a Christmas tree decorated with silver and gold.

I've always enjoyed the company of children more than that of adults, and years of babysitting have taught me the tried-and-true methods of entertaining little ones. Although we live in a digital era where most children are more captivated by screens than human interaction, animated stories rarely fail to get and hold their attention.

Four pairs of young eyes stare up at me as I recite Dr. Seuss's *Oh, the Places You'll Go!* Midway through the tale, Amara climbs onto my lap, while Raegan begins playing with my hair. When I'm done with that story, the boys and Raegan quickly demand another, so I dive right into *The Lorax*. After I'm done with that recitation, I start improvising stories, weaving tales of these kids embarking on mythical journeys to slay dragons. Amara falls asleep after a few more stories, clinging to my neck with her head resting on my shoulder.

An hour later, the twins are lecturing me on how they'd *really* slay dragons or krakens or whatever monsters I conjure in my stories, and Raegan has woven at least a dozen sloppy braids into my hair. Adults breeze by us, ignoring the children, making my heart ache for the little ones. To be raised in a family where their parents don't spare them a second glance is horrible for their development.

After a while, the twins run off to stir up mischief somewhere, and Raegan does me the courtesy of beginning to unwind the many lopsided braids in my hair while chattering away in my ear.

The divan dips as Mason takes a seat on my free side, reaching around me to ruffle Raegan's hair. "Hey, Sanity-Eater. Guess what?"

"What?" Raegan asks, eyes widening with excitement and awe as she stares at Mason.

"I glimpsed some chocolate chip cookies and milk in the kitchen. You might wanna grab your share before Santa eats them all up."

Raegan disappears from the couch so fast she's nearly a blur, and I watch with an amused smile as she weaves through the crowd of adults, racing to seize the treats before a fictional bearded man can steal them away.

"Are there really cookies?" I ask Mason doubtfully. "Or are you just trying to get me all to yourself?"

Mason glances at Amara. "Considering the state of the baby of our family, I don't think I'll be getting you alone tonight. Yes, there are cookies—ones I may or may not have ordered for the benefit of the kiddos." He gently strokes a lock of Amara's light-blonde wavy hair. "How did you get her to fall asleep? She's always fussy at parties like this, gets nervous in large crowds."

I lift the shoulder that Amara isn't slumbering on. "I don't know. Maybe she gets fussy when she feels alone in these crowds? Nobody's paying attention to the kids, and little ones don't do very well without attention. She fell asleep quickly enough after climbing onto my lap." I smile gently at the adorable girl clinging to me.

She stirs a little, then starts shifting restlessly, her breathing speeding up and hitting my neck in harsher bursts. With a sudden jerk, her eyes snap open and start filling with tears. *Poor child had a nightmare.*

"Hey," I say gently. "Just a bad dream, sweetheart."

She inhales a shuttering breath, her eyes widening as they scan the room. I can *feel* the distress emanating from her, but strangely, she doesn't make a single noise—she's entirely silent as the tears welling in her eyes start rolling down her cheeks. I feel my heart ache for this angelic child who's obviously uncomfortable in a crowded room.

I brush Amara's tears away with my thumbs, then ask Mason, "Is there somewhere quiet we can go?" I think a change of scenery might help her settle.

Amara's father, who I was introduced to earlier, walks right by the couch with a tumbler of amber liquid cradled in his hand. Amara's eyes turn to her dad beseechingly; a heartbreaking hiccup escapes her when he just keeps walking, not even noticing his own child. Mason's lips thin as he watches his uncle walk by with no regard for his daughter.

Mason says, "Follow me."

I stand, cradling Amara in my arms, and trail behind Mason as he makes his way through the crowd of his well-dressed family members, few of whom even spare me a glance. None of them ask after Amara or check on her welfare. *Are these people made of fucking stone?*

At the end of a long hallway boasting of famous art, Mason opens the door into a small library. Decorated with dark brown tones and filled with plenty of comfortable armchairs and walls made up of bookshelves, the library is cozy and quiet. I take a seat on a plush chair and settle Amara back on my lap, feeling close to crying myself at the way she clings to *me,* a virtual stranger, because her dad didn't notice her.

I murmur to her in soft tones and wipe her tears while Mason flicks on the electric fireplace in front of us. After a few minutes, Amara's tears slow, and she eventually falls back asleep. I keep my arms around her, one hand softly cupping the back of her head, wondering if I can steal her away from these lizard-people who shouldn't even have children if they can't give them attention. *Is this what Mom's going to be like when she gives Bradley the heirs he wants?* God, I hope not. Otherwise, I'll have to kidnap my half-siblings so I can make sure they're getting the attention they need.

"You're good at that," Mason murmurs quietly. "Soothing kids, making them feel at home."

"Better than everyone else here," I agree, shaking my head with distaste at the thought of his cold-as-ice family. "Look at this little angel—she needs warmth and love, not people who don't even look at her."

Mason smiles sadly. "Unfortunately, growing up in this family often means the absence of all affection."

CHAPTER NINETEEN

Mason and I spend Christmas exploring the west side of Manhattan. We visit Times Square, stand on an observation deck in a dizzyingly high building that offers a breathtaking view of New York, and go to see a Broadway musical. I enjoy the day so much that I almost invite Mason to share the bed with me that night. Almost.

I'm just stepping out of the shower on Thursday morning when my phone rings with a call from my mother. My eyebrows raise as I lift my phone from the marble counter and pick up the call. It's been years since Mom called me, so I assume she has a good reason to go through the effort of dialing my number.

"Grace," I greet, trying to keep the wariness from my tone.

"Chloe, darling, you can call me Mom when it's just us," Mom says with a light, ringing laugh.

Her words serve as a stark reminder that with her, everything revolves around the perception of others. In public, she insists I call her by her first name so people within earshot don't think she's old, but in private, it doesn't matter.

"Of course," I say tersely, putting my phone on speaker and setting it down on the counter. "How can I help you, *Mom*?"

"I'm calling to talk about how *I* can help *you*," she says, her words brimming with excitement. "I have the most wonderful news for you. Bradley and I spoke last night, and he offered to pay your tuition for Greywood! We've gathered that you have a partial scholarship, but Brad would be happy to help you with anything that isn't covered by Greywood. Isn't that so *kind* of him?"

I bite my bottom lip, a spark of hope lighting up my chest. It'd be a relief to stop using the college fund Dad set up for me, since there isn't enough money in it for both undergrad *and* medical school. My Greywood scholarship covers the dance program and part of my biochemistry major, but I've still had to dip into my college fund to pay for the remaining tuition and all school supplies.

"Any help would be wonderful," I say slowly, suspicion beginning to temper my hope. What I've learned of Bradley so far makes me assume he doesn't give out favors for free. I'm not sure what he'll want from me in return for him paying my tuition, but I am certain that he'll want something.

"Bradley's *so* generous," Mom gushes. "There's just one thing..." *Here it comes.* "I know you aren't crazy about the idea of Brad setting you up on dates, but we both want what's best for you. In return for his help with your college tuition, he'd like you to go out with a few boys of his choosing. We understand that you're with Mason *right now*, but there's no guarantee your relationship will last, and we believe it'd be good for you to have other options in case things don't work out with your *current* boyfriend."

And there it is. Now the timing of her phone call makes sense. I didn't respond the text she sent me about the date she wanted me to go on tonight—I'd hoped that my silence would reinforce my complete disinterest in dating around high society. Now, Bradley's found a way to bribe my compliance. He's making me an offer that I can't refuse, since I don't want my education to leave me with a mountain of debt.

"Just dates?" I question. "You won't ask me to get married or anything?" I can handle a few dates in return for tuition payments, but anything else is out of the question. I'd rather spend a decade paying off student loans than permanently tie myself to someone in the cold, impersonal world of the rich and elite.

"Of course not!" Mom exclaims, sounding offended. "You're a bit young to marry. I mean, we do hope that you'll accept our advice when you're ready to get married, but that's several years away. For now, dates."

If it's several years away, then by the time Bradley deems me old enough to marry, I'll have graduated Greywood. If he pays for the rest of my Greywood tuition, I might be able to scrape through medical school with just my college fund.

"Right," I say, briefly weighing the pros and cons of accepting Bradley's offer. It only takes me a moment to realize the pros far outweigh the cons. "Um... yeah, I accept the offer. A few dates in return for tuition."

"We're so glad to hear that," Mom says. I find my eye twitching at her easy use of '*we*' when referring to herself and Bradley. I don't think there really is a '*we*' between them; it seems to me that Bradley calls the shots and Mom goes along with whatever he says.

"Right," I repeat dumbly.

"I think you'll really like these boys, Chloe," Mom continues, oblivious to my discomfort. "I texted you about the first one, George Anderson, on Monday—you'll be meeting him for dinner at a French restaurant tonight. I assume you missed my text since you never responded." I barely stop myself from laughing at that. "Check my message for the address of the restaurant and the reservation time."

"Okay," I agree, resigned.

"I took the liberty of sending him your phone number, so you two can coordinate where he'll pick you up—"

"No need for that," I say quickly. "I can meet him at the restaurant."

Mom pauses. "If that's what you'd like," she says after a long moment. "I want you to know that I am *so* glad you're settling into our new family. This will be good for us, Chloe. Brad's a great guy. So is George, from what I hear—his father owns Anderson Jewels, a company that controls most of the diamond trade in North America."

My eyes flutter shut. She really doesn't know me at all if she thinks I'm *settling*, when in reality, I'm merely *tolerating*. If Bradley hadn't offered to pay my tuition, we wouldn't be having this conversation, which is precisely *why* he made such an offer. Paying for something important to me is a way to get me under his control.

"Yeah," I say noncommittally. "Sure. Great talking to you, Mom. Thank Bradley for his generosity." I force out the last sentence through gritted teeth.

"Of course. Have fun tonight, Chloe. Bradley really thinks you'll hit it off with George."

I hang up before I accidentally blurt out the cutting comments buzzing around in my mind. The efforts that Mom and Bradley are making just to get me out on dates with random guys are offensive, devaluing, and ridiculous, but I can't say that. I need the help Bradley's offering, so I'll do what I have to. I try to take my mind off my upcoming date as I brush my hair and teeth, then get dressed for the day.

Just as I come out of the bathroom, I hear the front door of the hotel room unlock. Mason strolls into the sitting room, dressed in grey sweatpants and a white shirt damp with sweat, the material clinging to the outlines of his muscles. I walk to the doorway of the bedroom and lean against it, waving at him and silently wondering how I'm going to break the news of my date tonight. Mason's already made it clear he doesn't want me seeing other men, but I don't have much of a choice—I need help with tuition.

"Hey," I greet. "How was your workout?"

He smiles at me. "It was good. Probably not as intense as your 5 a.m. ones, though."

I shrug. "I went a bit later this morning, at 6 a.m."

Mason snorts. "That's still several hours before I wake up."

"I have to stay in dancing shape." I pause, worrying my lower lip. I know I need to tell Mason about my date tonight, but I don't want to upset him. We had such a good day together yesterday, and despite my better judgment, I'm starting to enjoy our deal. I *shouldn't* be liking Mason more and more, but I can't help myself. Maybe my date tonight can serve as an opportunity to put some much-needed distance between us.

"What's wrong?" Mason asks, sensing my distress.

I let out a long breath. "My mom called. Bradley's becoming very persuasive about me going on that date tonight."

Mason goes entirely still, as if he's suddenly turned into a marble statue. He doesn't blink, doesn't even appear to breathe for several infinite moments.

"I see," he finally says, chest expanding as he sucks in a deep breath. "Naturally, you declined."

Something about his tone makes me clam up. It strikes me that if I tell Mason why I'm going on the date, he might try to leverage my tuition over me as well.

"I didn't decline; I agreed. I want to keep the peace with Bradley, and this is the easiest way to do it." *Partially true.* "I'm going out with a guy named George Anderson. If you have any info about him you care to share, I'd appreciate it," I say.

Mason lets out an empty laugh. "Info," he repeats. "Sure, Chloe, I have some info. If you go out with him, I will make it my personal mission to ruin his life. Fuck keeping the peace—stay here with me, where you belong. *I'll* take you out to dinner."

Irritation churns in my belly. Mason and I might be enjoying each other's company, but we're not *actually* dating, so he has no right to be possessive. Under different circumstances, his territorialism might secretly excite a small part of me, but it doesn't right now. I'm already stressed about tonight; I don't need him adding to my anxiety.

"Stop," I say, holding up a hand. "You don't get to interfere in my life. I let go of the way you reacted to Daniel; I won't let go of this." Especially not when my tuition's on the line.

"If you think I overreacted to Daniel, someone so far beneath my notice it's almost comedic, you'll hate to see how I react to good old Georgie," Mason says. "Anderson's someone I could see as actual competition, Chloe. Believe me, I am not known for being kind to the competition."

"There *is* no competition, because you and I aren't together," I snap.

"Yes, we are," he grits out. "According to the arrangement you so love to cling to, we are. Fake dating or not, the arrangement makes you mine, Chloe. You need to start acting like it."

I shake my head, my temper rising. "No, *you* need to stop acting like a goddamn psychopath. I'm getting sick of your shit, Mason. If you want our deal to continue, you need to give me space to live my life. That's not a request, it's a demand. I am going out to dinner tonight to appease my mother and soon-to-be stepfather."

"Since when do you care about appeasing your mother?" Mason fires back, taking a few steps forward. "You don't like her."

"I love her," I respond adamantly, which is true. Despite our differences, I do love my mother—a leftover from the good relationship we had when I was young.

"I didn't say you don't *love* her, I said you don't *like* her," Mason replies.

I fall silent, because we both know he's right. I don't like my mom as a person, and I haven't for many years. What I *really* dislike is the way Mason sees me so clearly. I've been too open with him—I need to start building more walls between us. If he gets too close, he'll have too much power over me.

"My relationship with my mother is none of your business," I growl. "Whether you like it or not, I am going out."

Mason works his jaw, turning to glare at the sofa where he sleeps. "If you go out with Anderson, Chloe, I guarantee that you'll regret it."

"He can't be that bad," I say, exasperated.

Mason's eyes meet mine again. "I didn't say *he'd* make you regret it, though I'm sure you'll hate that soft fuck. *I* will make you regret it. You're tempting my jealousy, which is a bad move on your part. I've never been possessive over a person before, Chloe, but I am possessive over you. That means I can easily become the monster you were so afraid of at first."

His threat makes me hesitate, and I swallow hard as I recall how unpleasant the beginning of our situationship was. Still... "You have no right to be possessive. I don't belong to you, Mason. I'm not stopping you from going out with other girls; don't stop me from going out with other guys."

"Fine," Mason says, his soft tone in sharp contrast to the harsh lines of his face. "Go. Tempt my monstrous side."

"Show that side, and our arrangement is done," I hiss. I step back into the bedroom and slam the door, locking it for good measure. If Mason wants to be an asshole who throws tantrums, he'll have to deal with the fallout.

Chapter Twenty

It takes about fifteen minutes for me to realize that dinner with George was a bad idea. He shows up to the restaurant drunk, his eyes glazed and breath reeking of whiskey. After we're seated, he spends the entire fifteen minutes we wait for our drinks ogling my cleavage, despite my breasts being well-covered by the modest neckline of my dress. He asks me nothing about myself, instead he prattles on about his family's business and the position he'll take in Anderson Jewels once he's done with undergrad.

Mason isn't set on joining his father's business after undergrad—not unless he really feels he's ready. As soon as I have the thought about Mason, I shove it out of my mind; I'm still pissed at him. He left the hotel room shortly after our argument and hadn't returned by the time I emerged from the bedroom to go on my date with George. Hopefully, he spent the day calming himself down.

"You should come by our jewelry store soon," George says, *still* staring at my breasts.

I give him a faintly distasteful once-over, noting the roundness of his midsection and the lack of muscles underneath his white collared shirt. He's not *ugly*—he has a nice enough face with dark hair and light brown eyes—but he's not particularly handsome, either.

A waitress walks up to our table, delivering a whiskey for George and a tonic for me. As she sets our drinks in front of us, George's eyes shift from my body to hers. She doesn't even seem to notice the direction of his gaze; I imagine she's probably used to this behavior from diners.

"Are we ready to place orders?" she asks with a lukewarm smile

I open my mouth to respond; George cuts me off and orders salmon for both of our main courses—*I hate salmon*—and *snails* of all things for our appetizers. My stomach sinks as I realize that I won't be eating dinner tonight. *Lovely.*

"So, as I was saying, the jewelry store," George says, looking back at me as the waitress walks away. "There are some limited-edition pieces that all the girls like. Bracelets, necklaces, cocktail rings. I can let you try some on, if you want."

All the girls like. He's just given away his routine of trying to woo girls with diamonds. He doesn't even *buy* diamonds for his dates; he only lets them try the pieces on. Does this shit work with the others?

"Maybe," I respond noncommittally.

George's bushy eyebrows inch up at my words, and a salacious, sloppy grin overtakes his lips. "Maybe, huh? Playing hard to get? I like that."

I'm not playing hard to get; I *am* hard to get, especially for someone like George. He might be wealthy, but he does not have a desirable personality, and I much prefer a good conversationalist to someone obsessed with jewels, money, and sex. I much prefer someone like Mason—*no, I'm not thinking about him.*

The appetizer arrives shortly, and George digs into his food. He doesn't even notice that I don't eat, only push around the snails with my fork and half-heartedly mime eating. Then, the waitress brings out our salmon, and I wrinkle my nose at the pungent scent of fish, not even bothering to pretend to eat this course. Again, George doesn't notice. It feels like an eternity passes as he eats and talks and drinks, growing increasingly inebriated until his words become noticeably slurred.

Finally, the terrible dinner comes to an end.

"Why don't you come back with me to my place?" George asks as we say our goodbyes in front of the restaurant.

Hell no. "Actually, I'm quite tired, so I think I'll be returning to my hotel," I say, trying to keep my tone polite. I told Mom I'd go out for the sake of getting my tuition paid; I did not promise to go home with anyone, especially someone as gross as George.

George's eyes darken with irritation. "Why t'fuck not?" he demands, too drunk to properly enunciate. "We had a good time at dinner."

No, *he* had a good time at dinner, while I was one part bored out of my mind, two parts disgusted by him.

"Yeah, I'm just tired. It's been a long week," I say. Then, not wanting to invite his anger or cause a scene, I add, "Why don't you text me about the store? I'd love to accompany you sometime."

That appears to pacify him, though only slightly. "I'll see if I have time in my schedule," he slurs, a smirk playing on his lips. "I've already got three tours of the shop set up in the next few days."

In other words, there are three girls he's going to try to seduce with diamonds. *Ew.* "I hope you'll be able to fit me in," I quip.

"As long as you'll let me fit in you," he says, and it takes me a moment to realize his blatant sexual come-on. *Jesus.* At least Mason is somewhat suave in his teasing—George is straight-up disgusting.

Thankfully, I manage to hail a cab moments later. George tries to lean in for a goodbye kiss as the taxi pulls up to the curb; I manage to dodge and give him a pat on the shoulder paired with an awkward smile that I'm sure looks more like a grimace. I dive into the cab, slam the door shut, and engage the lock before telling the driver the hotel's address.

As the car pulls away from the restaurant, I sag low in my seat, ruminating on just how much I wish I'd stayed with Mason today. My determination to keep him from my thoughts has crumbled—while I'm still irritated with his earlier reaction, I kind of... *miss* him.

When the cab pulls up to my hotel, I'm quick to pay the fare and stumble out. Minutes later, I'm striding down the hallway to my hotel room, ready to talk things over with Mason and then sleep away my shitty date.

I pause just outside the door when I realize that music is playing from inside the room, *loud* music. *I guess Mason's back, and in the mood to make a racket.* Sighing, I tap my keycard against the scanner, open the door, and step into the room.

The first thing I notice is that there are three pairs of high heels lying by the coat closet—heels that don't belong to me. A long breath escapes me as I stare at them, a ball of dread forming in my chest. Slowly, as if in a daze, I walk toward the sitting room, then stop cold at the sight that greets me.

Mason is seated on the couch, surrounded by *three* girls. Two scantily-dressed blondes sit on either side of him, and a brunette lounges on the arm of the couch. All three women gaze at Mason with fuck-me eyes as they talk amongst themselves, their words drowned out by a speaker blaring music in the corner of the room. Several beer and liquor bottles litter the coffee table, most of them tipped over and dribbling liquid onto the wooden surface.

This must be Mason's way of getting back at me. I went out with a guy, so he invited three girls over to *our* hotel room. A sharp pain pierces the ball of dread in my chest as I stare at the four of them, lost for words. That pain is quickly replaced by cold determination. I will *not* let Mason see that I'm hurt by this.

I wanted to talk to him and tell him that I regretted going out on a date not fifteen minutes into it, maybe even confide in him as to *why* I went out, but now I can see that it would be a pointless endeavor. He's just a petty, childish asshole, and there's no use trying to reason with a man who'll pull a stunt like this.

Mason glances over his shoulder, then does a double take when he sees me. After a beat of staring at me, he offers a lazy smile. "Hey, Chloe. Since you had plans tonight, I decided to make some, as well. Hope you don't mind." A challenge gleams in his eyes—he *wants* a reaction from me.

All three women turn to look in my direction, each of them appearing irritated with my interruption, as if *I'm* the intruder here.

I swallow past the knot in my throat and straighten my posture. "Of course, I don't mind." The lie scrapes along my throat like sandpaper. "Just try not to get too many STDs on that couch. After all, you're the one who'll be sleeping there." With my head held high, I march into the bedroom, closing and locking the door behind me.

I fall face-first onto the bed, roll over to my back, and force myself to blink away the tears prickling at my eyes. I know I *shouldn't* be hurt by Mason's juvenile bullshit, but I am, and I only have myself to blame. Getting comfortable with him was a mistake.

I desperately want to get the hell out of this hotel room, away from the pounding music and knowledge that Mason's probably about to have a goddamn *orgy* in the sitting room. The cold truth is that I have nowhere to go.

I should've never come to New York. I should've found a way out of my deal with Mason.

When the sun comes up, I'm going to inform him that I'm terminating our deal. I'll point out that since he hasn't delivered on his promise, I have no obligation to continue delivering on mine. I'll find a way back to Greywood, then hope to god I never have to see Mason again.

CHAPTER TWENTY-ONE

The music coming from the sitting room turns off about an hour after I lock myself in the bedroom. The sound of the front door opening and closing follows shortly after, most likely signaling the exit of the women Mason invited over. I half-assume he leaves with them, until loud knocks start rattling the bedroom door. Those pounding knocks sound every ten or so minutes until the early hours of the morning. Eventually, I drown them out by putting on my headphones and allow my classical music playlist to lull me into a restless sleep.

I wake up well before dawn and go about my usual routine of preparing to go to the gym. With any luck, Mason will be asleep, allowing me to sneak out without having to talk to him. Hopefully, my workout will help me get my emotions in check, so when I face Mason again, I can put on a believable act of nonchalance.

As soon as I open the door to the bedroom, I realize that things won't be quite so simple. Mason is wide awake, sitting at the dining table and typing away on his laptop. I cast a glance around the room, mildly surprised to realize he cleaned up the mess from last night. The coffee table in front of the sofa is clear of all bottles, the speaker that was blasting music has disappeared, presumably taken by whichever girl brought it, and there's no evidence that the women were ever here, which relieves me more than it should.

I contemplate making a run for the door, but the thought dies a quick death when Mason stops typing and slowly turns to look at me. Dark circles shadow his eyes, and he looks to be a mixture of exhausted and *furious*. I fold my arms over my chest, returning his stare with a cold one of my own.

Moving slowly, Mason shuts the laptop and stands from his seat. He begins to walk toward me with measured steps, not saying a single word. I resist the urge to cower or slam the bedroom door to prevent him from coming near; I'm done shying away from him. My lingering anger from last night gives me the confidence I need to face him. *Now is as good a time as any to terminate our deal.*

Mason stops just a few steps away from me. "You ignored me last night."

I lift a shoulder, trying to act casual. "You seemed well-occupied with your company; I didn't want to interrupt your fun."

He crosses his arms over his chest. "I don't like being ignored, *especially* by you. It makes me very angry."

Is he kidding? "And *I* don't like being humiliated. I didn't want to talk to you after the petty tantrum you threw, so I ignored your knocks and crude demands for me to let you in. I even put in headphones and blasted Chopin to drown you out. Your anger isn't my problem; *you're* not my problem. You probably got plenty of attention and enjoyment from the girls you invited over, so I'm not sure why you went through the effort of knocking on my door."

"Is that jealousy I detect in your tone, Chloe?" Mason questions.

I gape at him. "I'm not *jealous*, I just feel pretty goddamn *disrespected*. I don't care what you do behind closed doors, but you could do me the courtesy of keeping it discreet."

"My party was discreet," Mason rumbles.

I throw my hands in the air. "It was in *our* hotel room, which *you* insisted we share!" I growl, shaking my head. "I don't understand what you want from me, Mason. I've been trying to keep to our deal and do my part, but there are times when you make it *so fucking difficult*."

"You went out on a date with a slimy fuck, so why does it matter that I decided to have some fun in your absence?" Mason challenges.

"Why do *you* care that I went out on a date?" I burst out. "We have a *deal*, Mason. An *arrangement*. I help you, you help me. Clearly, it's not working out." I inhale a deep breath, steeling myself. "We need to call it off," I say firmly. "You can pretend to have a broken heart—or bruised pride, to make it more believable—so people in your circles leave you alone for a while. That should give you enough time to find someone more suitable to play the role of your girlfriend. I need to get away from this madness and back to Greywood; your world isn't for me."

I hope Bradley will agree to pay my tuition since I played ball and went on that terrible date last night. If one date isn't enough for him to help, then my scholarships combined with my college fund will be enough to get me through undergrad and a semester of medical school. I'll try to secure grants and use loans to cover the rest. I'll be a slave to paying off my debt for quite some time, but at least my life will be my own.

"I'll be out of here tonight," I go on, calculating how much my bank account will suffer from buying plane tickets. I have a few thousand saved up from babysitting in high school, working as a counselor for summer camps, and teaching occasional dance classes for young girls. I try to use my money very sparingly, but I think getting away from Mason is worth the cost of tickets. "Thank you for this trip, it has had its moments, but I think it's best if we part—"

My words are cut off when Mason closes the gap between us and places a hand over my mouth, using the other to push me against the doorframe. He leans over me, eyes blazing with intensity and barely leashed fury. His grip on my mouth is harsh and unyielding, and I'm frozen in place like a deer caught in headlights.

"Stop. Talking," he growls, nostrils flaring.

Fear creeps into my system, but it's accompanied by another, more dangerous emotion: arousal. The look in Mason's eyes is feral; he stares at me like a predator who's finally caught his prey and is savoring the win before going in for the meal. I swallow on a dry throat, then tentatively lift my hands to move his palm away from my mouth, but he doesn't allow it. He catches my wrists and pins them above my head, trapping me. His hand lowers from my mouth, sliding down my jaw and neck, coming to a stop at the base of my throat.

My eyes widen as I stare up at him. My instinct is to struggle and try to break free, but something tells me that a fight will only spur him on. So instead, I say quietly, "Mason, please let me go."

His hand tightens around my throat ever so slightly as he shakes his head. "No, Chloe, I don't think I will. I am fucking *sick* of you attributing everything to our deal. I'm done with that deal. So, we're going to make a new one." He dips his head to run his lips along my jaw until they hover right by my ear. "You are no longer my *fake* girlfriend, you are my real one. No more dates with other guys. No more bullshit. No more trying to get away from me at every turn; no more running unless you want me to chase you, pin you down, and fuck the fight out of you. Enough. I'm not going to pretend like you don't belong to me, and you are going to stop acting like you aren't really mine, because *you absolutely are.*"

The fear coursing through me intensifies at his declaration, but it's accompanied by a surge of exhilaration, as if some part of me *does* want to be with him.

A whirlwind of thoughts muddles my mind. I can't deny I've had some good experiences with Mason the past few days—our walk through Central Park, the way he made me come so hard I saw stars at the party, his warmth toward Amara on Christmas Eve. Those memories are quickly followed by flashes of our fight yesterday and his absurd reaction. It hurt to walk in on him surrounded by three bimbos, and I might've even experienced a flash of jealousy. If I give into his ludicrous demand for me to be his *real* girlfriend, I'll be giving him *real* power to hurt me, which would be an idiotic move.

"No," I say. "Thanks for the offer, but no. Next time you want a relationship with a girl, don't offer it after a stunt like the one you pulled last night." I turn my head away from him and tug at my hands, trying to free them; his grip hardens to steel and he presses his body against mine, holding me in place.

"I wasn't offering you anything," Mason says darkly. "I was informing you about what's going to happen next, Chloe. Don't fight me on this. You want me, even if you don't like that fact; I very much want you. Stop resisting."

"No," I growl, tugging at my wrists and even trying to kick out at him, but my fight proves futile. He has me firmly trapped, and I'm not as disgusted with that fact as I should be. Mason shifts his head to the side and dips it down to my lips; I turn my head away to avoid his kiss.

"Don't touch me with those lips!" I snap. They were probably all over another woman mere hours ago, so I don't want them anywhere near me.

"Why?" Mason asks. "Because you think they spent the evening on another's body? You *are* jealous."

"I'm not!" I insist—*lie*. "I'm serious, *let me go!*" my voice rises in pitch and volume as I start to struggle in earnest, but Mason easily keeps me in place.

"I only invited them over because I was pissed and wanted to make you jealous," he tells me calmly. "I can admit, that was the wrong move. I shouldn't have reacted that way; you have my word that it won't happen again. I didn't touch those girls *at all*, certainly not with my lips. I kicked them out not long after you locked yourself in here."

"I don't care," I hiss. "You think I want a relationship with someone who barely grasps the concept of consent and throws tantrums like a petulant child? Newsflash: I don't want a relationship, period, and I *certainly* don't want it with someone like you."

What I don't say out loud is that Mason's right; I don't want to want him. I *am* drawn to him, but I know he's dangerous and capable of wreaking untold havoc in my life and on my emotions.

I make a split-second decision to say the one thing that can stop this madness before it goes any further. "I'm not going to stop appeasing my mom and Bradley with dates. Even if I wanted to, I won't."

"Wrong thing to say, Chloe," Mason says, releasing my neck in favor of gripping my chin so he can angle my head. I don't have the chance to move away or protest before he slants his lips over mine.

Squeezing my eyes shut, I seal my lips and try not to sink into the kiss—try to ignore Mason's blatant desire, his passion, his will to fight for me. He bites down on my bottom lip, causing me to gasp, then uses the opportunity to push his tongue into my mouth, sensually rubbing it over mine, eating away at my resistance with each languorous lick and rub. My eyes drift shut under the sensual assault and my body softens against his; my struggles cease as I get caught up in him. In his taste, his scent, in his intensity and hunger and the way he seems so desperate for me. The kiss feels at once like a punishment and a revelation, and it doesn't take long for my head to start spinning.

"You're mine, Chloe," he breathes, pulling back to kiss a path down my neck. "You can't change that. I couldn't change that even if I wanted to. Nothing can change that. You can go with it and experience the pleasure of being mine, or you can fight it and find out what it's like to be on the opposite side of a battlefield from me. It *will* be a battle. I won't stop fighting for you."

I whimper when he sneaks his hand under the hem of my shirt, smoothing a path up my abdomen so he can cup the weight of my breast in his palm. His thumb locates my nipple, brushing over it before he pinches it through the thin material of my leotard. My head falls back, my lips part, and a breathless moan escapes me. Heat travels from my breasts to my pussy, and my core clenches.

"Don't move," he tells me, slowly releasing my hands. "Let me explore what's mine."

I'm too swept up in sensation to push him away, enjoying his touch even though I know I shouldn't be. I can't help it; Mason is skilled. He's already decided where and how to touch me, and each of his caresses lures me deeper into his spell. He grips the hem of my shirt, pulling it up and over my head; I lift my arms to help him. After tossing my shirt aside, he tugs down the straps of my leotard and pushes the material down to my waist, freeing my breasts. A long breath escapes him as he stares at them, then leans down, rubbing the faint stubble of his jaw over the upper swell of my left breast, making me gasp at the rough, erotic sensation. He teases my nipple with his teeth, adding an edge of panic to the pleasure, before engulfing it in the wet heat of his mouth. My fingers creep into the locks of his hair and a whimper escapes me as my breathing speeds.

Mason releases my nipple with a wet pop and pulls back to stare at my body with stark desire swirling in his golden-green eyes. He trails his fingers along the undersides of my breasts, then slides his hands over the flat of my stomach and grips the leotard, dragging it down until it pools around my feet, leaving me clad in only a thin pair of panties. He closes his hands around my waist, lips twitching.

"My fingers almost touch," he observes. "You're so tiny, Chloe, like a little doll made of glass. So delicate and small, which belies the conviction and fiery strength that burns bright in your soul." Mason leans his forehead against mine, his eyes fluttering shut. "You have no idea just how much you belong to me, do you?"

Chapter Twenty-Two

I can't seem to string together any intelligible words when Mason speaks to me in that silky rumble, so all that escapes me is a faint whine. The will to resist him is slowly seeping out of me, inch by inch, leaving behind only breathless desire and burning need for him.

"That's okay, you don't need to say it just yet," Mason goes on, leaning down to brush his lips over mine. "One day very soon, I'm going to need to hear you admit it. For now, all I need is for you to understand it deep down." His hand dips into the waistband of my panties, fingers smoothing over my mound before sneaking lower to run along my slit, making me gasp. "Tell me," Mason says, circling two fingers over my clit, "did you let that incompetent manchild touch you last night?"

When I don't respond fast enough, he pinches my clit. I quickly shake my head and moan, "No."

"You sure?" Mason prods, drawing a moan from me as he slides two fingers inside me, making me wince at the stretch. "You're gorgeous, Chloe. Ethereally beautiful. A man would have to be blind not to wonder what these lips taste like, what this soft, luscious body feels like beneath his hands. Did you let George find out?" He gives me a hard thrust of his fingers.

"No," I whimper. "I didn't, I promise. I wasn't interested in him. I hated the entire date."

"Is that so?" Mason questions, sounding mildly curious.

Feeling the need to placate him, I start to ramble. "It is so. He showed up drunk, ordered both of us food that I hated, and got more drunk throughout the dinner. He spent the entire time talking about his family company and all the girls he seduced with diamonds. He tried to get me to go home with him, even though I wasn't interested. I hated the whole experience."

"Mm," Mason hums, sounding slightly appeased. "I'm glad to hear that. You'll only be enjoying dates that you go on with me, won't you?" When I don't respond, he adds a third finger inside me. A panicked squeak bursts from my lips as any remaining bravado dissipates under the pain and pleasure he's delivering, the foreign sensations he's inspiring. "Won't you?"

"Yes," I blurt, the word coming out high pitched and breathless.

"Good," Mason agrees. He pulls his fingers out of me, and dejection overwhelms me as I sag against the wall. "Kick off your leotard," he commands.

I do as he asks, too dazed to put up a fight. Mason sweeps me up into his arms, wrapping my legs firmly around his waist, and carries me over to the bed. I think I know what's coming next, and I'm not sure how to feel about it.

When Mason lowers me onto the soft mattress and yanks off my panties, I close my legs and cover my breasts with my arms, sitting up. "Mason, wait—"

"Shh," he cuts me off, gently unwinding my arms. "Don't fight me, Chloe. It's high time I make you mine completely, isn't it?"

"I don't know if I'm ready—"

"You should've thought of that before going on a date with another man," Mason says, kneeling on the bed beside me. "Relax, I'll make it good for you." When my breathing shallows and true fear sparks within me, he pauses, then works his jaw. "If you really need more time, I'll give it to you. But I don't think you do. Don't let your fear win, give into me. Let me give both of us what we need."

A loaded silence ensues as I try to decide whether or not to give myself to him. I notice the lines of strain along Mason's neck and arms as he holds himself still, waiting for my decision. I know he's wanted me since the first day he met me, and I also know there have been many occasions when he could've taken me but refrained. Right now, he wants me with a desperation that's both frightening and humbling.

"Tell me you want me," Mason breathes out, shuffling forward and cupping my cheek. "Or tell me that you're not ready, and I'll back off. I'll go jerk off in the shower, just like I have been twice a day since I met you." The idea of him touching himself while thinking of me makes a soft noise escape me, something between a whimper and a moan. "Tell me, Chloe, one way or the other."

"I..." I trail off, blinking. "God help me, I *do* want you. I shouldn't, you're everything I dislike in a man, but I do."

I only catch a glimpse of Mason's victorious grin before he pushes my upper body down onto the soft mattress and straddles my waist. "I'm going to take my time with you today, Chloe. Fortunately, we have nowhere to be until tonight, so I can have all the time I desire with your gorgeous body," Mason murmurs. "I can play with these beautiful breasts and these pretty little nipples for as long as I want." He cups one of my breasts in his hand, molding the soft flesh, then leans down to lick a path around my nipple before taking it into his mouth. My eyes fall shut and a soft moan escapes me as he starts to suck, circling my other nipple with his fingers until it beads, then idly pinching it. "I love the way you taste," he murmurs. "Like crushed flowers drizzled with honey." He moves to my neglected nipple—unable to help myself, I bury my fingers in his hair, arching into his mouth. I yelp when he bites my nipple again, and my eyes open as my brows furrow with confusion. "That," he says, pulling back to look down at me, "was for ignoring my knocks, texts, and calls last night."

"My phone was on do not disturb, and I was listening to classical music," I tell him quietly, briefly wondering if the sensual pleasure he's been delivering has all been a ploy to lure me into a sense of safety or comfort so he can hurt me. I don't *really* know what Mason's like when it comes to sex—in my limited sexual experience with him, all I've learned is that he prefers to drive the show.

"Don't ignore me again," Mason commands, spreading my thighs and kneeling between them. "When I call you, Chloe, I want you to pick up. When I text you, I want a prompt response. If I knock on your door, I want you to open it. I like the chase more than most, but I've caught you now. You're mine."

"We—we should make a new deal," I say. "A new arrangement that suits us better. I need solid parameters."

This seems to amuse Mason rather than irritate him. "Of course you want something new to cling to. Okay, Pixie, I'll humor you. The new deal is, you belong to me. End of story."

I shake my head, sitting up and placing a hand on his chest, stopping him before he can go any further. I try to close my legs, but he places his palms on my thighs, preventing it. I feel ridiculously vulnerable being naked while he's fully clothed, so I say, "We're going to negotiate. First, though, you're going to take off your shirt."

A slow, wicked smile overtakes Mason's lips. "Any time you want to ogle me, Pixie, all you have to do is say so." He yanks his shirt over his head, tossing it aside. Then, he lifts me up by my waist, drawing a squeal of surprise from me, before switching our positions and sitting me on his lap. My legs bracket his waist, and his hands rest on my hips while mine land on his shoulders. My eyes wander over the corded muscles of his shoulders, biceps, and triceps before settling back on his face.

"Alright, my little negotiator. Tell me, what do you want?" he asks.

"First of all, I need a timeline. We can do a trial run next semester, which will keep our new arrangement running until the end of the school year. Same timeline as our last deal." I know he won't settle for less, and besides, I want to explore this thing between us despite my better judgment.

Mason inclines his head. "Fine. For the duration of that time, you're my girlfriend. You will pick up the phone when I call and answer when I text. You'll stop running from me, stop fighting against me at every turn, and consequently find out what life with me could look like. I think it'll be to your liking."

I nod. "I can do that. At the end of our arrangement, you will not force me into more or try to steamroll me. We'll decide whether or not we want to move forward *together*."

"But I retain the right to use my powers of persuasion to extend the arrangement," Mason volleys back.

I don't know that his powers of persuasion will be enough. I think Mason and I could get along, and now that I've cooled down from his tantrum and gotten his word that it won't be repeated, I'm not entirely opposed to giving a relationship with him a chance, but I see it as a trial run.

"But you won't force me, coerce me, or blackmail me," I state. "You also won't throw tantrums when I go out to dinner with others to appease my mom and Bradley—" Mason wraps a hand around my mouth, cutting me off, and his eyes darken into a forest-green, the flecks of gold shrinking.

"Don't," he says curtly. "Don't fucking go there, Chloe. We've been over this. I'm a jealous man and I won't tolerate you going out with others."

I twist my head to the side, freeing my mouth. "It's not because I want to, Mase. It's because I need to. Bradley's willing to pay my tuition if I play the role of a society stepdaughter and let him push me toward an advantageous relationship. The college fund my dad left me won't be enough to cover undergrad and medical school; I need the help."

The anger surrounding Mason dims as he realizes that I didn't go out to shirk him or because I was being a people-pleaser; I went out because I need the help that's being offered.

"I'll pay your tuition," he says.

"No," I disagree. "I'm not asking for handouts; I don't want to feel like a kept woman."

Mason releases a low growl. "Fine, then I'll appeal to Bradley. He wants to arrange an advantageous relationship for you? I'll make sure I look like the best candidate available. I'll speak to my father and see what I can cook up. If it doesn't work, though, I'll pay your tuition. Don't disagree, Chloe, because I am not letting you go out with someone else. If you do, I can't guarantee that the man will be alive the next day, and I get the sense that you wouldn't want to be responsible for someone's death."

I try to think of a way I could be okay with this, a way where I won't feel like Mason's literally paying me for the pleasure of my company. "Make it work with Bradley, or I will have to go on dates. And if I find out you hurt someone because of it, I will be terminating our arrangement immediately—I reserve the right to do that."

"You are so damn difficult," Mason rumbles, even as he leans forward and plants a hard kiss on my lips. "Fine. I'll figure out how to make Bradley like me enough to pay your tuition." He pauses. "Since you're talking about medical school as if it's a given, I assume you're planning to pursue higher education instead of dance?"

I nod. "Most likely. I won't accept offers to be a corps dancer unless I'm on a direct soloist or principal track. I'm passionate about dance, but I'm too sensible to give it my livelihood if it won't be worth my while."

Mason's lips tilt up. "Of course you are, Pixie. You're as clever as you look."

"Thank you, I think."

My lips part on a gasp when Mason slides his fingers between my thighs, his touch gentler this time, but no less insistent. He holds me to him and stares deeply into my eyes as he begins to play my body like a fine instrument, stroking my sensitive flesh until arousal spills out of me. Until I'm suppressing my moans and my head falls back. A tug to my hair forces me to look at him again; I can't contain my moan when his thumb rubs a circle over my clit while he watches me like I'm the most fascinating thing he's ever seen.

"Eyes on me, Chloe," he says. "I want to see your pretty cheeks and neck flush when you come. You're almost there, aren't you?"

I nod, feeling the tension within me rise as he pushes me closer and closer toward the cusp of an orgasm. My muscles tense and my toes curl as I dig my fingers into his biceps.

Everything about Mason is hard, perfectly honed, and pristine. The slope of his muscles, the wicked glint in his eyes, the sharpness of his jaw and the softness of his lips. The immaculate head of auburn hair that looks aristocratic when styled yet even sexier when it's messy, just like it is now. He's a study in flawlessness, and the fact that this man is bending over backwards just to be able to call me his for a few months is almost too absurd to believe, yet incredibly empowering. I might not always like Mason's methods, but I can't fault his determination. After last night, I was ready to never touch him again, yet here we are.

"Oh, fuck," I whimper, shaking my head from side to side. "*Shit.* Mason, I—"

"Come," he cuts me off, leaning forward to run his lips along the column of my neck. "Let me feel you."

I let out a long, low moan as my back arches and my body jerks in his hold. The knot of tension in my core explodes into pure, unadulterated pleasure that rolls over me in languorous pulses, each contraction stronger than the last. My orgasm is intense, made only more potent by the intense feeling of vulnerability as Mason holds me like I'm his most treasured possession, all the while finger-fucking me and whispering dirty words in my ear.

"Lie down," Mason murmurs. "I'm going to feel that around my cock next."

I stiffen as I recall his size from our first encounter—he barely managed to fit even part of himself in my mouth, I don't know how the hell he plans to fit his entire cock in my body. Despite my reservations, I climb off of him and lie down on the bed, figuring that I must be remembering wrong; his dick can't be that—

My thought cuts off as Mason stands, shucking his pants and boxers, and my lips part as I take in his size. He kneels on the bed, fisting his length in his hand, and renewed alarm sparks within me. The haze from my orgasm clears away entirely as I attempt to deduce how the *hell* he plans on getting that monster inside of me when three of his *fingers* were painful.

"Mason," I start slowly, feeling my eyes widen as I stare at his swollen length. It's hard, veiny, and appears terrifyingly engorged, the tip glistening with a bead of moisture. "I don't think you understand basic anatomy. There's no way that... *thing* is fitting inside me."

A deep chuckle rumbles out of Mason as he climbs over me, eyes glittering with amusement. "Oh, Chloe," he says, his tone filled with fondness. "Baby, we'll make it fit. It's going to hurt a little bit at first—"

"A *little bit*?" I repeat, incredulous. "I don't want to end up being rushed to the ER because you puncture my fucking lung!"

Mason *cracks up* at that, his chuckle transforming into a full-body laugh, his features lighting up with mirth. "Pixie, I'm not gonna puncture your lung. I very much like you in one piece, I'm not going to break you. We'll take it slow. If it gets to be too much, tell me and I'll wait. I don't want to hurt you anymore than I have to, I want to make you feel good. Okay?"

I hesitate for a long moment, irritated with his laughter in response to my perfectly reasonable concerns, but soften when he strokes my cheek with his hand. "Okay. Just... be gentle."

Mason grips my legs and curls them around his hips, reaching his hand between us to align the heavy head of his cock with my entrance. I bite my lip, trying to stifle a wince as he slowly pushes the tip inside me. The result is *pain*, much more pain than three of his fingers—more pain than I've ever felt down there. A cry escapes me as I squeeze my eyes shut, fisting the bedsheets and twisting my head away. Mason instantly stills, then strokes his fingers over my face, pushing my hair back. "Look at me, Chloe."

I crack my eyes open, trying to blink back the tears welling in them. Mason rubs his thumb over my bottom lip, gazing down at me with a heartbreakingly soft expression. "You're okay, sweetheart. You're good." He leans down to kiss me, soothing me with his lips, gently sucking on my tongue while sliding a hand down to caress my breast and play with my nipple.

"Take a deep breath for me," he murmurs, pulling back. "Hold onto my shoulders. It'll only hurt for a bit." As soon as I dig my fingers into his shoulders, he slides forward, breaking through the barrier in my body; my vision blurs with the shock of pain. I choke on my cry as tears spill onto my cheeks, shaking my head and biting down on my bottom lip so hard I taste the tang of copper in my mouth, but I don't tell him to stop. I want to get the worst of it over with.

Mason stills inside me once more, giving me another thorough kiss before sliding the hand playing with my nipple lower until it comes to a stop on my clit. He begins rubbing smooth, tight circles over the sensitive bundle of nerves, and the pain of my lost innocence begins to ease.

"Okay?" he murmurs.

I nod. "You can keep going."

Despite him toying with my clit, it hurts as he sinks in deeper and deeper until I'm stuffed so full I can barely inhale a breath. After what feels like an eternity, he bottoms out, his cock fully seated inside me. There's still pain, but it lessens by the second, and what replaces it is a strange sense of connection. I can't tell where Mason ends and I begin; it feels like our bodies are fundamentally entwined.

I gasp as he draws his hips back, sliding part of the way out, then sinks back in. His clever fingers on my clit help me forget about the pain and focus on the small spark of pleasure that ignites as he begins to thrust. I'm hypersensitive, which allows me to feel every ridge and vein along his length, feel the way he pulses inside me. It feels unexpectedly... *good*.

I thread my fingers through his hair and pull him down for another, deeper kiss. I suck on his tongue, marveling at how full I feel as the pain continues to abate. It's not long before I start craving something more, craving the speed, intensity, and vigor I know he's withholding.

I pull away from his lips to murmur, "Go faster, Mase." He pauses, thrusts stuttering, then arches an eyebrow at me.

"Yeah? You want more, Pixie?"

I nod, and he obliges, leaning down to kiss me once again as he speeds up his motions. His renewed pace is faster, sharper, more jarring, and each forward surge feels like a claim that I revel in. A knot of pleasure begins to pulse low in my belly, winding tighter with each kiss, each twirl of his fingers, each rub of his tongue over mine.

"I can feel you starting to flutter around me, Chloe," Mason says, jaw clenching as he pulls back to lock eyes with me. "Come for me, beautiful girl—*fuck*," he cuts off with a curse as my orgasm sweeps me under. Sound and light become muted, all dimmed beneath the weight of my pleasure. I never knew sex could be *this* satisfying, this pleasing, deliver this strong of an orgasm, but now I'm starting to understand why other girls seem to lose their mind over it. My legs tighten around Mason's waist, pulling him deeper inside me, my back arches, and a series of depraved, broken moans escape me as I ride out wave after wave of my orgasm.

I feel Mason stiffening inside me before his length starts to twitch, and I belatedly realize that he didn't put on a condom. I'm too far gone to care about it right now, though—I cling to him as we both succumb to pleasure.

Mason kisses a path along my jaw, then murmurs in my ear, "You were damn well worth the wait."

Chapter Twenty-Three

Chloe

The rest of my time in New York flies by. Every day, Mason takes me out to explore different parts of the city, keeping me thoroughly entertained. The new dynamic between us puzzles me, mainly because it feels so *natural* to be his girlfriend. His inner asshole significantly recedes, leaving behind a doting boyfriend. He touches me freely—tucking my hair behind my ear, wrapping an arm around my shoulders or waist, intertwining our fingers—and seems completely at ease around me.

We sleep beside each other every night, with me nestled safely into his side. We don't have sex again, probably because I spend several days after our first time wincing and swallowing back Tylenol to help alleviate my soreness. We *do* kiss a lot, and Mason kisses me in several choice places.

On New Year's Eve, we attend another one of his family parties. Raegan and Amara are there, and they once again pull me away from the adults and onto a sofa in a quiet corner. Mason stays with us for the entire party, holding Raegan on his lap and humoring her impressive ability to talk endlessly. The seven-year-old only ever pauses in chattering long enough to suck in a breath, then gets right back to it. I cradle Amara in my arms, quietly wondering if I can steal her away from her monstrous family and take her back to Greywood with me.

Mason and I leave New York on the second of January, heading back to school. Though Mason tries to persuade me to do an impromptu trip to Europe, I'm adamant in my refusal. Several dance company members are staying on campus and meeting up at headquarters for daily practice, and I'm eager to return to them. There are rumors that Pandora's Box might go on tour again this summer, so I can't let my dancing lag.

On the flight back to Vermont, I sit beside Mason, my head resting on his shoulder. One of his hands is planted on my thigh, while the other holds his phone as he reads on the device.

Halfway through the flight, Mason's phone rings, and he stiffens. I lift my head when he takes the call, blinking away my drowsiness.

"Hello?" he greets. "Yes, this is still my number." He pauses for a long moment, and menace begins to roll off him in potent waves. "Are you sure? *Fuck*, okay. Send me pictures and see if anything was left behind. I'll send my guys to check it out, then take a look myself once I'm back."

He hangs up and turns to look at me, brows furrowed with displeasure, eyes darkened with a brewing storm.

"What's wrong?" I ask him, sitting up. "What happened?"

Mason exhales a long breath. "Ian got a notification—he still has access to the security system alarms in your new dorm room. There was a break in. He sent someone to look at it for him, and it looks like whoever broke into your first dorm has now targeted this one. They used a *sledgehammer* to break in the door, and... well, apparently the mess they made isn't pretty. I should be getting pictures any second—" he cuts off as his phone buzzes in his hands, lifts the device, and swears under his breath.

Cold chills me to the bone. I was so swept up in the New York trip that I'd momentarily forgotten about my problems on campus. A fine shiver sweeps over me, quickly transforming into a continuous tremor. The cabin's temperature is perfectly controlled, kept at a comfortable 75 degrees, and yet I suddenly feel like I'm in the North Pole. Someone broke into my room; my *new* room, which was reinforced with security by the previous owner's boyfriend. If whoever's after me is able to do that, what *aren't* they capable of?

"Show me the photos," I tell Mason as he glares at his phone.

"You don't want to see this, Chloe," Mason replies, shaking his head.

With a trembling hand, I reach out and snatch his phone from his grip, glimpsing the photo pulled up on the screen.

"What the hell?" I breathe, taking in the picture of the wall above my bed. There's a message written on it with what appears to be *blood: Get out or get dead, bitch.*

"Fuck, Pixie," Mason says, snatching his phone back before I can look at the other photos. "I said you don't want to see the pictures."

I'm too far gone in my terror to pay his ire any heed. Somebody not only broke into my room *twice,* they also decided to create a scene straight out of a thriller movie the second time around. The first break in could be written off as a scare tactic; this is a *dangerous* escalation.

"There's blood..." I trail off, shaking my head. "Why is there blood? Whose blood is that?"

"Pixie, you're going to pass out if you don't calm down and get your breathing under control," Mason says, setting his phone aside. Lips thinning, he unfastens my seatbelt and pulls me onto his lap, wrapping his arms around me. His warmth is a welcome contrast to the cold plaguing me, but it isn't enough. I press my head to his chest, listening to the sound of his steady heartbeat, focusing on it until my breathing starts to calm.

"You might not completely trust me, Chloe, which is something I'll work to change. What you should trust is that I'm the scariest person in your life, and I'm committed to protecting you."

There's a certain comfort to be found in his words, because Mason *is* the biggest terror in my life, the worst monster I've met to date. The only thing that can take down one monster is another, bigger one, and I think my boyfriend might be the person for the job.

***

Mason

It takes an hour for Chloe to settle. I give her a few sips of the scotch I order for myself, and she eventually drifts into a restless sleep. I gently set her back on her seat, then start making preparations. It's clear that she can't stay in Greywood's dorms, it isn't safe for her, so I have several tasks to get through before we land.

I contact the team of people I have stationed in the city by Greywood and dispatch them to Chloe's dorm. I don't often have use for the trio of men who work as my fixers and researchers, but times like this are exactly what I pay them for. They'll execute my tasks discreetly and without asking questions, and they'll make sure that campus security and the local police department give them a night to investigate before moving in.

Chloe wakes up not long before we land, and much to my pleasure, she climbs back onto my lap. I put my phone away and hold her close, enjoying her cuddliness while it lasts. She's going to be in for quite the shock soon enough, and I don't think she'll be in a touchy-feely mood after that.

Once we land, Chloe's withdrawn. She doesn't protest when I pull her to my car, doesn't protest when I drive her to my apartment building, says nothing until she gets inside and sees what's waiting for her.

In my living room sit two cardboard boxes that contain all the belongings that my people could salvage from her dorm room. Sitting beside them are the numerous shopping bags with the clothes I bought for her on the trip, and perched on my couch is the lone duffel bag she took with her to New York.

She walks up to the cardboard boxes and wrenches them open, her face paling as she sees her things inside. "Mason," she says slowly, "what the fuck? Why are all my belongings here?"

"You can't stay in dorms," I respond. "It's not safe. Considering the new nature of our arrangement, I figured that now would be the ideal time to officially move you in with me." While I'm not happy that Chloe's room was desecrated, I am happy that I have an excellent excuse to keep her here indefinitely.

"No," she says, shaking her head. "*No.*"

"Baby," I say, "it's done. You're safe here in a way you wouldn't be anywhere else. The security in this building is excellent, the security in my apartment is even better."

Some women would shout at their partner for making a move like this; others might try to run. Chloe's response is to sink into my forest green sofa, fold her arms, and ignore me. She's probably already deduced that if she attempts to run, I'll catch her, and if she yells at me, I'll calmly enumerate all the reasons why my apartment *is* the best place for her to be.

I keep an eye on her as I take a seat at the mahogany dining table in the corner of the room and make a few calls, but she doesn't move from her spot. Doesn't speak to me, doesn't unpack, just alternates between staring at her hands and staring at the flatscreen TV mounted on the wall in front of her. I think she might be in shock.

Once I'm done with my business, I stand and take a few steps toward her. I sense that she needs her distance, so I stop a few feet away from the couch. Her eyebrows are furrowed, her expression is pensive, and I can practically feel her anxiety. I want to take her into my arms and comfort her, but I also don't want to scare her. She's already had a frightening day; I don't wish to add to her fear.

My eyes flick over to the entrance hall, and a tendril of shame swirls through my chest. My girl has only been here once before, on the night when I first met her and accidentally triggered her so intensely she had a panic attack. This environment alone could be enough to amplify her terror.

"Chloe," I say, looking back at her. She slides her eyes sideways, lips thinning as our gazes lock.

"Do you want to look around?" I ask. "Get to know the place where you'll be living?"

She shakes her head. "This isn't my home, Mason, it's yours. I don't feel any better here than I would back in the program dorms."

I glance around the living room, taking in the minimalistic décor. Aside from the dining table, TV, and sofa, a small coffee table sits in front of the couch and a study desk occupies the corner of the room, stationed beneath a window. There are two doorways along the far wall, one leading to my bedroom and one to the unused spare. The apartment doesn't have any pictures or paintings or knickknacks, it's a bare space empty of character. I loathe soulless places, so it's startling to realize that I live in one.

"So make it your home, as well," I say. "We'll go shopping to pick out some items together, and you can browse online. Art, knick-knacks, whatever. I want you to be comfortable here."

Chloe wrinkles her nose, shaking her head. "I *don't* feel comfortable here, Mase. I don't want to be here. I don't even like shopping."

"You liked shopping just fine in New York," I point out.

She releases a sigh of frustration. "I was uncomfortable with it."

I do recall her being a bit flushed during our shopping trip. "I'm going to buy you things and spoil you, so you should get used to it." When she says nothing, I sigh. "Come on, Pixie. I want you to be happy here."

I think that her decorations, *our* decorations together, would make me warm to this apartment and see it as more than just a gift from my parents. I've only ever used it as a place to sleep, study, and occasionally, fuck. Now, it could be something more; it could become an actual home.

So much is changing with Chloe's presence...

When Chloe drops her gaze to her lap again, I try a different tactic. "What do you want to be happy here?"

I understand her discomfort—my pursuit of her hasn't been terri-bly conventional. In truth, my underhanded methods are a side effect of her being like a goddamn siren to me; impossible to resist. Chloe's shaping up to be far more than just an object of desire, she's becoming an obsession. I know deep down that my obsession with her isn't going to be short-lived; I don't see my need for her dissipating, possibly not *ever.*

"I don't want to be here," she grumbles, not deigning to look in my direction.

"I understand that, but it truly is for your safety," I tell her.

It's become clear that Chloe's situation with whoever's after her is more dangerous than I initially anticipated. In addition to breaking into *both* her dorm rooms, the person has been stalking her for some time, as evidenced by the candid photos of Chloe that were left on her dormitory bed. The item placed next to the pictures was even worse, something so macabre I don't even want to think about it.

I don't burden Chloe with this information; she already has plenty of worries, and I'm determined to shield her from unnecessary fear. What she doesn't know can't hurt her.

"If you were worried about my safety, you could've put me in a hotel or something," Chloe says.

I sigh and take a seat on the arm of the couch. Since I won't give her unnecessarily gory details, I switch subjects. "I don't want you miserable, Pixie, so what do you need to be happy? Other than good sex."

"I'm *not* having sex with you," she says, even as her eyes drop to my body and linger just a beat too long.

"We'll talk about that later. For now, what will make things easier for you? What can I give you or do for you?" I'd usually have somewhere in the vicinity of zero fucks to give about a woman's comfort, but Chloe isn't *a* woman, she's *my* woman. Ergo, her comfort and happiness matter a great deal more than I'm used to.

Chloe stares at me for a long moment, brows furrowed. Then, she says petulantly, "A cat. I want a kitten."

A chuckle of surprise bursts out of me, but that's an easy request to fulfill. "We'll go to the shelter tomorrow to pick one out."

"And I want my own bed," she demands.

That's a stone too far. "Yes to the pet, no to the bed. You'll be sleeping with me." I won't give up the pleasure of feeling her weight in my arms as we slumber.

"I don't want to," she says firmly. "I'm mad at you."

"I'm not asking," I respond, just as firmly. "You can be mad at me while we share a bed."

When I see desperation flicker through her eyes, and her gaze darts to the door, I shake my head. "Don't, Chloe. Don't run. You won't get very far. What else do you want?"

Chloe slumps into the material of the couch, head thumping against the cushion behind her. "I don't know. I kind of hate you right now, I know you're leveraging the situation to have me closer to you."

"True," I admit freely. "I want you with me at all hours of the day and night. You've quickly become my favorite person. That said, I want this to work for both of us, and I think that it can. Help me make it work, please."

My phone buzzes in my pocket with an incoming text; I feel Chloe's eyes on me as I read over the message, clenching my jaw at the contents. My team *still* can't find whoever broke into Chloe's room, which means I'll need to enlist outside help. For now, I need to get both of our minds off of this shitstorm.

"I'm going to give you my credit card tomorrow—no, don't protest. I want you to buy decorations, make this place your own, add accents of yourself to it," I tell Chloe. "For now, though, we're taking a trip."

She frowns, dubious. "Where?"

"I know I said we'd go to the shelter tomorrow, but I've changed my mind," I say. "Let's go get you a kitten."

CHAPTER TWENTY-FOUR

Chloe

The shelter Mason takes us to is just a twenty-minute drive from his apartment. After being greeted by a receptionist, we're instructed to wait a few minutes until a staff member can show us to the kitten nursery. Mason and I sit on an uncomfortable wooden bench propped against a wall; he scrolls on his phone while I glance around the sterile room, which feels cold and deeply impersonal. Linoleum flooring, white-painted walls with spiderweb cracks, no pictures, knickknacks, or decorations.

"Chloe?"

My head snaps up at the familiar voice; a bright smile splits my lips when I see Mira standing at the end of a hallway beside the receptionist's desk.

"Mira," I say warmly, rising to approach her. We meet in the center of the room and share a quick hug. "How's your winter break going?"

"The usual; lots of work. I've been picking up shifts here left and right to help out." She glances to my side as Mason joins me and wraps a possessive arm around my waist. "Who's this?"

"Mason Sieger," Mason responds. "Chloe's boyfriend."

Mira's eyebrows practically hit her hairline. "*Boyfriend?*" She meets my eyes, her gaze startled. "I didn't know you were even dating someone, let alone in an official relationship!" She gives Mason a longer, more searching look, taking a step toward him. "You…" she trails off with a shake of her head. "Are dangerous. *Very* dangerous, and capable of causing great harm." Her head tilts to the side as her eyes narrow, but then a slight smile tips up her lips. "But you won't hurt Chloe. Got it." She turns to me. "I don't like being near him, I'm pretty sure he could disembowel a man with a straight face, but he's no threat to you."

Mason's arm tightens around me, and he gives me a startled glance. "What the *fuck*?"

"Mira's weirdly intuitive," I explain. "She can *feel* people." It startled the shit out of me when, within fifteen minutes of meeting her, Mira told me she was sorry for the passing of my father and remarked on how profoundly he'd impacted my life. "I think she's an empath."

Mira shudders. "God, no. That word has too many supernatural connotations. No, I'm just terribly sensitive. It's more irritating than useful." She sighs. "But my roomie, Cara, does find it helpful. She has me vet guys for her before embarking on her infamous one-nighters. Anyway, I take it you guys are here looking to adopt?"

"A kitten," the blonde receptionist pipes up helpfully.

Mira smiles. "Wonderful. Are you two living together? I ask to ensure that the kitten will have a stable home environment."

Mason clears his throat, seeming deeply unnerved. "Yes."

"Makes sense," Mira says with a nod. "Your possessiveness of her is a physical force." She winks at me. "Good thing it's tempered with equal parts protectiveness, or you'd be *screwed*, and not in the good way." She claps her hands together. "Alright, lets go see the kittens!"

Mason's stiff beside me as we follow Mira down a hall and into a room brimming with kittens. Each kit is housed in a glass crate integrated into a cubby-like system on the walls; they all have water, food, blankets, and even little toys. Some of their dwellings are covered with blankets, but most are visible.

"What sort of personality are you looking for?" Mira asks me. "Wait, I know. Intelligent, clever, and a kitten that will like you more than Mason. Right?"

A grin spreads on my lips. "Right."

She squeals. "I have *just* the one for you! A Russian Blue, part of a litter rescued two weeks ago. The kitties were just a few days old when we found them, the mom wasn't around. The one I have in mind is an adorable little dude who's feisty, full of love, and ready to be adopted."

As Mira approaches a wall of the dwellings, all of the cats begin meowing for her attention. She smiles and coos at them but focuses on one glass case in particular. She unlatches the glass door and slides it open before reaching in. When she withdraws her arms, she has the most adorable bundle of grey fur, perky ears, and inquisitive yellow-green eyes clutched in her hands.

"Animals usually love me, but this guy's a bit dubious," Mira says. "I get the sense that he'll vibe with you, Chloe. Your energies should mix well." She walks over to me, shoes tapping along the floor, and stops just a foot away from me.

The kitten leans his head forward, adorable black nose twitching as he scents the air. In a blur of motion, he leaps from Mira's arms and flies at my chest; I yelp and catch him just in time, cradling him close.

"Knew it," Mira says, her smile softening when she hears the loud purrs this little grey bundle is emitting. She looks between me and Mason. "Should I draw up the paperwork?"

Mason holds his hand out for the kitten to scent; after a moment, the kit hisses and swipes out a at Mason, then burrows his head into my chest, ignoring Mason entirely.

"No," Mason says. "We'll find another one."

"We'll take him," I decide, ignoring Mason's objection. "He's perfect. Thanks, Mira, you're a doll."

"What?" Mason questions. "*No*, Chloe. We're not getting a cat that hisses and claws at me. We can find one of the nicer ones." He looks at Mira. "There *are* nicer ones, right?"

Mira tilts her head to the side. "You should stop pretending that Chloe doesn't have stupid amounts of power over you. She does. There's nothing you can do to change that fact." To me, she says, "I'll get started on the paperwork. You should give the little guy a name. He's already forming a bond with you." She smiles brightly. "I really am the *best* matchmaker for adoptions." With a happy sigh, she flits out of the room.

"Who the fuck *is* that girl?" Mason breathes.

"Fantastic," I respond, then turn my attention to the little fluffball clinging to my shirt. "What should we name you, hmm?" After a moment of thought, the perfect name comes to me. "Loki," I decide. "Mischievous and clever. You look like a Loki to me." The kitten meows and blinks slowly, which I take to be his agreement. Smiling, I lean down to nuzzle his furry head.

"We're *not* keeping him," Mason says tersely.

I pin him with a steady gaze. "You've just *kidnapped* me, Mason. We are going to get the cat *I* want. Then, we're going to the nicest pet store in the city to get supplies for him."

I hold my breath while Mason glares at me, wondering if Mira's right—if I really *do* have a great deal of power over him. I've never known Mira to be wrong, but Mason seems so powerful, so in control, that it's hard to imagine *I* hold any significant sway over him.

After a long, tense stare-off, Mason looks to the ceiling and sighs. "*Fuck*. Fine, you can have the goddamn cat."

"And I'm going to clean out the pet store," I say, emboldened by his reluctant agreement.

Mason shakes his head, eyes fluttering shut. He inhales a deep breath, and a faint smile steals across his lips. When he meets my gaze, his eyes are more gold than green. "I'd expect nothing less, Pixie."

It takes an hour to complete the necessary paperwork and finalize Loki's adoption; another hour is spent at the nearest pet store. I get a plethora of things for my new furry friend—toys, food, treats, an elaborate cat tree that Mason will have to assemble, several beds, and even a few outfits. To my faint surprise, Mason doesn't once complain or tell me that it's too much. When we check out with an overflowing cart, he swipes his card without protest.

"Why aren't you irritated?" I ask him as we're driving back to his apartment. "I just spent over a thousand dollars on cat supplies. Most of the things I insisted on getting are frivolous and unnecessary."

Mason lifts a shoulder, glancing over at Loki, who dozes on my lap. "I like taking care of you. I already told you I'm going to spoil you; if that comes in the form of spoiling the cat that I didn't want, so be it."

Huh. "I still haven't forgiven you for moving me into your apartment without asking," I inform him.

"I'll be sure to make it up to you in every way I can think of." Mason pauses. "I do expect you to start decorating the apartment soon, Chloe. I want the place to feel like it belongs to both of us, because it does now."

"I don't recall seeing my name on the deed," I say, though my words are empty of any real rancor.

"I'll put your name on it as co-owner, then. The documents should be drawn up in the next few days."

I'm puzzled by Mason's easy acceptance of my demands and his desire to draw me into his life. I haven't had someone want me and work for me in many years—I've become used to existing on the periphery of the lives of the people around me. Despite my frustration with Mason's presumptuousness, I can't deny that being the center of his attention is heady. I'm afraid I could get addicted to the feeling if I don't tread carefully.

Back at Mason's apartment, we work together to unpack all the items I bought for Loki and set them up in the living room. Mason spends over an hour working to assemble the cat tree, while I set up Loki's litterbox, bed, and crate. Then, I feed the kitten and snuggle him, stifling my laughter each time Mason curses up a storm, claiming that the cat tree must be missing a part.

Loki eventually falls asleep on my lap, leaving me with nothing better to do than watch Mason grapple with the multi-tiered cat tree.

"If this isn't a symbol of my commitment to you, Chloe, I don't know what is," Mason says once he's finished, shooting me a look brimming with exasperation. He checks the time on his phone, then shakes his head. "It's late; I'm going to order dinner. Since the cat's finally fallen asleep, you have a chance to put away your things."

"My things that you had transported here without my knowledge or consent?" I ask.

Mason shrugs. "The things that belong here, since we're living together."

"Until the end of our arrangement," I clarify.

"At which point we'll renegotiate," Mason says with a nod. I open my mouth to disagree; he holds up a hand and gives me a censuring look. "I just spent the better part of two hours setting up comfortable living and playing quarters for your cat, Chloe, all the while listening to your giggles. Don't think I won't be getting you back for that later. For now, put the damn cat away, unpack your shit, and let's enjoy a nice meal together. I'm ordering from a family-owned Italian place Carson recommended."

Deciding that now isn't the time to argue, I carry Loki over to his crate. The exhausted little guy doesn't even wake up when I gently set him on a small cat bed and close the bars of the crate. "I'll be back soon," I whisper.

I pick up one of the cardboard boxes containing the things from my dorm room, pile it with as many shopping bags as I can carry, and walk toward the wall with two bedroom doors. One leads into a bare bedroom with only a single mattress, while the other leads into Mason's bedroom. I glance longingly at the spare but know better than to try to settle there.

"Do you need help unpacking?" Mason asks.

"Nope, I'll be a good little captive and fold everything neatly." I can't help the bit of snark that peeks through my tone.

Mason releases a soft snort. "Okay. Let me know if you change your mind."

Mason's bedroom is large, with a four-poster bed leaned against the far wall, accompanied by a polished bedside table. A dark red couch, flanked by two matching armchairs, faces a sleek flatscreen TV. Sunlight filters through a bank of windows on the left wall, casting a warm glow across the room. The right wall features two doorways—one leading to a spacious walk-in closet, the other into a bathroom. After making a second trip to the living room to retrieve the rest of my belongings, I carry the box that holds my toiletries to the bathroom and begin unpacking.

As I place my facewash and makeup in a drawer built into the two-sink counter, I can't help but ponder the astronomical differences between Mason and me. Even this bathroom, with its gleaming floors, polished faucets, and shower equipped with *three* showerheads, attests to Mason's wealth. He grew up with the sort of opulence that's astounding to me, and I have to wonder if our lifestyles can mix together.

I give my head a shake as I walk into the closet, reminding myself that my concerns are exactly why I put an expiration date on our relationship. I'll admit that I'm attracted to Mason; his physique is stunning and his personality is surprisingly appealing. He's domineering and used to being in charge, but he's also thoughtful, considerate, and vulnerable. To the world, he presents himself as a wealthy playboy, but I've glimpsed what lies beneath that armor, and the real Mason captivates me. The one who indulges Raegan's ability to talk for hours on end, the one who glares at Amara's father for ignoring her, the one who holds me like I'm his favorite person and isn't put off by my intense bouts of anxiety.

It takes an hour for me to finish unpacking; just as I'm putting away my last pair of underwear in the closet, Mason walks in, startling me. "Dinner's ready," he announces. I blink as he lifts up a bag he holds in his hand; one stamped with the name of a very expensive *lingerie brand.*

"I assume they didn't deliver the food in that," I say drily.

CHAPTER TWENTY-FIVE

Mason smiles, shaking his head. "No, Pixie, the food's on the table. This is a little gift I got you, one I hope you'll enjoy. From my understanding, most of the clothes in your room were destroyed during the break in." His jaw clenches, and he inhales a subtle deep breath before continuing on. "I had a courier pick these up. Consider them replacement items."

I'd already assumed that I wouldn't be getting my clothes back from my room, but the confirmation still makes my heart sink. I've worked hard to preserve every t-shirt and pair of pants in my wardrobe for the last years, since I don't want to waste money on clothes unless I need to.

Swallowing, I try to lighten the mood. "It's very like you to be focused on lingerie instead of serviceable things such as shirts and pants."

Mason's lips twitch. "You have plenty of outfits from New York, but we neglected to stop by any lingerie stores. I figured picking up some bras and panties worthy of your body was prudent."

"All the outfits we bought are high end and polished," I point out. "They're appropriate for your family, but far too nice for school and dance."

Mason appears to contemplate this for a moment before nodding. "Fair enough. I'll have my courier pick up more practical items for daily use." He walks up to me, handing me the lingerie bag. "I'm sure these will have plenty of uses, though. Why don't you put them away while I set up dinner? Meet me in the living room once you're done."

My cheeks flame as I rummage through the bag, finding an array of multicolored bras, thongs, garter sets, and sheer nightgowns. I can imagine that Mason would *love* to see me model these items, and I think I might enjoy wearing them for him. Imagining the way his eyes would darken with desire sends a low pulse through my core.

After splashing cold water on my face to cool my blush, I head to the living room. Mason stands by the dining table, pulling containers from a plastic delivery bag. My mouth waters at the delicious aromas that float through the air—a tantalizing blend of pasta sauce, garlic, and baked cheese.

A few soft meows draw my gaze to Loki, who's woken up from his nap and is pawing at the bars of his crate, demanding my attention. Smiling, I walk over to him and lift him from his crate, holding him to my chest and scratching under his chin, loving the rumbly little purr he releases as he snuggles into my touch.

"Am I going to have to start competing for your attention?" Mason questions, arching an eyebrow at me.

My smile widens. "Yup, you've got me. I adopted Loki so I'd have less time for you. Not because I spent my childhood begging for a cat, only to be denied."

With a chuckle, Mason disappears into the kitchen and returns two minutes later, holding a silver bowl filled with a serving of wet food for Loki. I notice it's sprinkled through with kibble, as per Mira's recommendation. My heart flutters as Mason sets down the bowl by Loki's crate—he's taking care of the kitten *I* made him get. It's a small gesture, but a meaningful one.

I set Loki down by the bowl; instead of going straight for his food, the kitten spends several moments staring at Mason. After a long pause, Loki gives a slow blink and buts his head against Mason's ankle in a gesture of affection. Then, the kit turns his attention to the food, making adorable little noises as he feasts.

"Alright, I guess he *is* pretty cute," Mason says. "When he isn't hissing or clawing at me, that is."

Mason takes my hand and leads me over to the table. He pulls my chair out for me, then attentively fills my plate with several of the offered dishes, listing their names as he goes. He fills his own plate as an afterthought, then sets about opening a bottle of red wine. The dinner feels intimate, domestic, yet oddly natural, as if we've been doing this together for years.

"I'm not old enough to drink," I mutter half-heartedly as he fills our glasses. Despite my words, I reach for my wineglass and inhale deeply, savoring the notes of dark berries and rich oak.

"The legal drinking age in most civilized countries is eighteen," Mason says mildly. "Besides, you're a responsible young woman. You're one of the most mature people I've ever met, actually." He takes a sip from his glass. "You don't *have* to drink, but don't let a ridiculous law stop you."

"You seem to have an interesting perspective on the letter of the law," I murmur, even as I take a sip of my wine and hum with pleasure.

"That's because the laws in this country are a house of cards that can easily tumble," Mason says. "The whole legal system is arbitrary and largely meaningless, created to suppress the poor and empower the rich. It's corrupt in too many ways to count, and there's no accountability for people who can pay their way out of facing justice. I am *not* a fan of this country's justice system."

"I can see that," I say, faintly amused. "We'll have to revisit this conversation when I'm not tired from a stressful day and hungry as hell. I'd like to pick your brain more, talk about our world views."

"I'd like that, too," Mason says.

We eat in comfortable silence for a while; I keep an eye on Loki, who quickly finishes his food, then climbs into his crate, curls up on his little bed, and falls asleep. I step away from the dining table long enough to close his crate, then join Mason once again. We talk a little more as we eat, and once we're done, I help him clear the table and load the dishes into the dishwasher.

"How many kids do you want?" Mason asks as I'm shutting the dishwasher door. Startled at the question, I spin around to face him, finding him leaning against the kitchen island across from me.

"Right now? None," I tell him with a pointed look.

Mason smiles faintly. "Not right now, Pixie, I mean in the future. Once you're ready to be a mom. How many kids do you want?"

I pause. "Two or three. I'll definitely want to wait until I'm settled in life, with a good job and a trustworthy, stable husband to build a family with."

"Hmm," Mason hums. "That sounds reasonable. Funny enough, I'd like two or three kids as well—maybe more, if my future wife would be amenable."

"Your future wife will certainly have a lot to deal with," I say, keeping my tone light. "Maybe she'll be too overwhelmed by you to consider bringing more mini versions of you into the world."

Mason closes the distance between us in two swift steps and slowly braces a hand on either side of my hips, clutching the counter and caging me in. My breath hitches at the heat in his gaze and the nearness of his warm, hard body. "When I marry that very special woman, I'd dedicate myself to taking stress out of her life, not adding to it. I'd see it as my responsibility to keep her happy, content, and thoroughly pleasured. I wouldn't repeat the mistakes of my parents by holding her at a distance."

"Maybe your wife would want distance from you," I say quietly.

A faintly amused smirk steals across his lips. "But you see, Pixie, I wouldn't allow that. I'd keep her very close to me. If she tried to put distance between us, I'd do whatever it might take to close that gap. If she tried to run, I'd chase and catch her. If she tried to fight, I'd subdue her. I'd even lock her up in a tower if that's what it took to keep her with me." He pauses, letting those words sink in, and I try to ignore the low pulse of fear that grips my chest at the meaningful glint in his eyes. I think we both know that our hypothetical discussion isn't truly hypothetical; Mason is delivering a warning to me, telling me not to run or push him away. More, he's warning me that he might want me on a *permanent* basis. "That being said, I'd prefer to go a different route," he murmurs, picking up a lock of my hair and twirling it around his finger. "I'd work my hardest to make her dreams come true and give her the fairytale that she deserves. I'd want to make her happy—I would do everything to avoid giving her a reason to run."

"It sounds like you're imagining quite the perfect woman—one I'm not sure exists," I observe, a fine tremor in my tone.

"She *is* perfect," he says, emphasizing the present tense and confirming that he's talking about... *me*. "All I could ever want in a woman and more. I'll do what I can to make her happy with me, but I won't let her go."

"Mason," I whisper. "You're starting to scare me."

"There's no need to be scared, Pixie," he replies. "Don't run and I won't have to chase. Enjoy what I can give you; what I want to give you. Give us a chance. At the end of the year, renegotiate terms that are to your liking." He leans down until his lips are hovering right above mine, until we're breathing each other's air. "Give me a chance like you promised you would, and everything will work out." He plants a kiss on my lips, a gesture that's almost chaste. "Now, onto a more titillating topic: I want you, Chloe. I want to make both of us feel good. Would you like that?"

Despite the somewhat terrifying threats he just delivered, I still want Mason. I crave him even though I know I shouldn't.

I nod slowly, and Mason gifts me a smile of satisfaction. "I want to try something tonight," he says. "You're going to ride me, but the position will be somewhat... *enhanced*. You'll be on top, but I'll have all the control."

"Okay," I murmur.

"Okay," Mason repeats. "You'll like it."

He takes me by my hand and leads me into the bedroom. Feeling like I'm in a trance, I go willingly. I let him strip off my clothes and brush his fingers over every inch of my body as he goes. I let him play with my nipples, kiss my neck, and stare at me with a reverence that makes me feel beautiful and powerful. I sit on the bed when he tells me to, and quietly wait as he goes into the closet.

When he returns, it's with two pairs of leather cuffs held in his hand. Each pair has two cuffs attached by a short strip of leather. I stiffen at the sight of them; Mason places them on the bedside stand, then thoroughly distracts me from their presence as he begins to shed his clothes, revealing a body that exudes raw power.

He climbs onto the bed and leans against the headboard, then reaches for the cuffs and drops them beside him. I spend an inordinately long amount of time staring at his cock, which is so hard it almost looks painful.

"Straddle me," Mason commands softly.

Swallowing thickly, I follow his instructions, climbing up the bed and straddling his waist. Mason adjusts me so that his cock rests against my navel. The tip, glistening with a pearl of liquid, reaches my belly button. It's no wonder it hurt to take him last time, our anatomy quite simply doesn't add up. He's too big and too hard, and yet, I know I'll take him again. I want to take him again—crave it, even.

"Give me your hands," Mason says. When I don't move to obey, he gives my ass a sharp slap, drawing a yelp from me. "Hands, Chloe." I lean away from him, frightened; his eyes soften and he gently squeezes my hip. "I'm not going to hurt you. I think I've proved I like making you feel good, haven't I?"

I can't deny that he has. The cuffs are intimidating, but he's never given me a reason to doubt my physical safety with him, and there's something about the idea of having my movements restrained that's unexpectedly arousing.

"Will you stop if I ask you to?" I question, gazing at him.

Mason nods. "Yes. If you say the word *red*, everything stops immediately, and we talk."

I inhale a deep breath, steeling myself, then hold out my hands. My heart races as Mason picks up one of the leather cuffs and attaches it to my right wrist, tightening it until it's snugly wrapped around my skin. He takes the cuff on the other end of the leather strip and leans forward, then lifts my right ankle and wraps the cool material around it. He pauses to lick a path along my breast, tongue lashing at my nipple, making my eyes flutter.

"Too tight?" he asks, his voice gravelly.

I shake my head.

"Good. Rest your palm on my leg. Get comfortable, Pixie."

I follow his instructions, then watch with widened eyes as he secures my left wrist to my left ankle. Once he's done, he leans back to survey his handiwork, eyes darkening with desire. My body is arched backward, hands resting on Mason's legs, and my mobility is extremely limited. Just as he promised, he's in control now, and judging by his expression, he has me exactly where he wants me. What takes me off guard is my own arousal at the position, at the bondage. Liquid heat steadily gathers between my thighs, and my nipples harden into beads under Mason's stare.

"Now that," he breathes, "is a gorgeous fucking sight. You should see yourself right now, Pixie. Chest heaving, tits bouncing, bent to my will and ready to get fucked." He gives a pause. "And you are about to get fucked, Chloe. Last time, we had sex; this time, I'm going to *own* you. Because you're mine, aren't you?"

"For now," I murmur.

Mason's eyes darken. "For now," he repeats. "We'll see about that."

He clasps my hips in his big hands and lifts my lower half up. I clutch his legs tighter, tensing in preparation for him to impale me on his length, but he doesn't. Instead, he starts rubbing my pussy against his cock, back and forth, slow slides that spread my wetness over my clit and tease it. My breaths speed up as pleasure builds within me. The taboo nature of this position combined with Mason's manhandling and the way he slides the tip of himself over my clit again and again is enough to drive me half out of my mind. I release a quiet whimper as a coil of tension gathers in my core, and I start shivering with pleasure and anticipation.

"There's my good girl," Mason murmurs, making warmth spark in my chest. "So fucking pretty in your submission, Chloe. Letting me move you the way I want, pleasure you the way I want. I very much look forward to spending the rest of my life figuring out how to continuously bring that blush to your cheeks, make you squirm and moan and scream for me."

"Oh god," I murmur, biting my bottom lip.

"Not god," Mason corrects. "*Me*. Say my name, Chloe. I want to hear you moan it."

I make a low noise of dissent, shaking my head. I don't want to give into Mason any more than I already have.

"No?" Mason says, his tone mocking. "Fine. I'll be sure to make you scream it, then."

He adjusts his erection, pressing his tip at my entrance, and slowly begins lowering me onto his length. I gasp as my inner muscles stretch to accommodate his intrusion, making me tense. An ache starts up within me, a sensation that I quickly realize is my need for him, a burning desire to feel him deeper inside me.

When he's about halfway in, Mason mutters, "*Fuck this,*" and then abruptly slams me all the way down on him, making me cry out with pain. My eyes squeeze shut as a sharp, stabbing burn ripples through my pussy and travels to the rest of my body. I instinctively try to lift myself off him, but my bindings and his firm hold on my hips keep me in place. My body feels stretched to its very limits, causing tears to sting my eyes. Slowly sinking onto him was a bit prickly but felt good; getting forced down so suddenly does *not* feel good, it *hurts*.

"Shh," Mason soothes. "You're good. You took all of me like a good girl, Chloe." His tender tone is at odds with the way he holds me in a bruising grip, keeping himself buried inside me. I can feel his heartbeat through his cock—or maybe it's my own, I can't tell. I can't differentiate where he ends and I begin.

Mason drags his tongue over my nipple in a long, wet lave, before latching onto it with his lips and suckling. He strokes his thumbs up and down my sides, switching from one nipple to the other, gently sucking and nipping until the pain within me starts to ebb, morphing into a liquid heat that causes wetness to gush out of me and coat his cock.

"Open your eyes, Chloe," he whispers, kissing a path up my neck and to my lips. "Show me those gorgeous teal orbs. I want you to look at me while I fuck you."

My breath shuddering in and out, I force my eyes open, blinking several times. "That hurt," I whimper.

"I know," he responds, lips brushing against mine with his words. "I couldn't help myself, Pixie. Sometimes I'm gonna want it rough. I think you will, as well. Won't you?"

"I don't know," I say softly, shaking my head. "I don't know anything right now." My thoughts are scattered and confused; all my focus is centered on our bodies, our connection, the feel of him inside me.

"That's okay," he murmurs. "All you need to know is that you belong to me, and I will take care of you. How is the pain? Better?"

I nod slowly. "You didn't put on a condom. You need to start wearing them. I need to get on birth control."

Mason's eyes glimmer with something feral and possessive. "Set up an appointment at the school clinic, then, because there's no fucking way I'm letting a piece of rubber get between us." He kisses me as he starts to slide me up and down his length, tangling his tongue with mine while his cock touches places inside me that I hadn't known about before Mason. He sets a slow pace, allowing me to adjust to him with each slide in and out. After a few minutes of that, the last traces of pain fade, replaced by a brimming feeling of fullness. The coil in my core starts to build once more, and I release a soft moan.

"Go faster," I urge Mason between kisses. He pulls back, offering me a sensual smile that makes me clench around him.

"My pleasure, Chloe," he says, sliding me up and down his length faster and starting to thrust his hips in time with my downward motions. Whimpers, mewls, and moans of pleasure escape me at how frighteningly good his cock feels as it rubs against my inner muscles, hitting a particular spot inside me that makes stars burst in my vision. I start to pull at my wrists as my pleasure builds and builds, moving toward a peak that I know will be more intense than any other orgasm I've experienced.

"Are you almost ready to come?" Mason asks me through gritted teeth. I nod quickly, then cry out when Mason presses his thumb to my clit. "Ride me," he commands. In the throes of abandon, I follow his instructions, lifting my hips up and down, my moans climbing in pitch as he starts to rub my clit with firm, knowing strokes.

"Come," he barks, and my body helplessly obeys his command. My channel clenches and convulses as I cry his name, then scream it when he speeds up his action on my clit. "There's a good fucking girl," he growls, and I feel him twitch inside me as he also finds release.

My body slumps after my orgasm ebbs, awkwardly folding backwards. Mason's quick to release the leather cuffs, then pulls me against his chest. I whimper as his cock slides out of me, and he kisses my forehead.

"You good?" he asks.

"Mm," I reply, not having the strength to speak.

I feel languid and cuddly, so I bathe in the way Mason cradles me close, soaking up his warmth and attention. For several long moments we lie together, both drugged from pleasure. Mason plants butterfly kisses over my nose and cheeks, murmuring soft words of praise that practically make me glow.

After several minutes, I become aware of noises coming from the living room—little meows and grumbles being made by Loki, who's apparently awoken from his nap. I can imagine Loki is confused and maybe a bit scared to wake up alone in a strange place.

"Don't go," Mason grumbles. "Let the cat entertain himself."

I press a kiss to Mason's chest. "I adopted that kitten, so I'm going to take care of that kitten. Let me up, Mase, I have mom duties to attend to."

Mason lets out a sigh. "If I must."

Chapter Twenty-Six

I roll out of Mason's bed, grab my phone, and head to the closet, retrieving a satiny pair of silk pajama bottoms and a matching button-up top with a collar. Even the *sleepwear* Mason bought me in New York is elegant and top-tier. I clean myself up in the bathroom, running a warm washcloth between my thighs, and get dressed before making my way to the living room. Loki's clawing at the front of his crate, yowling at the top of his lungs for attention. My heart clenches as I scoop him up and take a seat on the couch, settling him on my lap.

My kitten calms after a few minutes of being held and begins kneading at my legs with his adorable little paws. I turn on the TV, clicking over to a national news station, content to wait until Loki tires himself out and falls asleep. Mason emerges from the bedroom after a little while, joining me on the couch and casting a glower at Loki.

I smack his arm. "Stop glaring at Loki. He's still a baby, just two months old, and he needs attention."

"Your attention should belong solely to me," Mason sighs. "But I suppose I can share it. Temporarily. For short periods of time."

I roll my eyes at him, shaking my head. "You just fucked me to within an inch of my life and you're still not satisfied?"

"I'll never be satisfied with you, Chloe. I'll never get enough of you; I'll always want more. You're mine."

"For now," I remind him. "Don't push it, Mason."

"Don't push me, Pixie," he returns. He opens his mouth to say something else, but falls silent when Loki hisses at him, sensing the tension between us and responding in kind. I bite my lip to hide a smile; Mason rolls his eyes.

"Looks like I finally have someone else on Team Chloe," I muse, scratching beneath Loki's chin and reveling in the little purr he releases.

"I'm Team Chloe *and* Mason, as you should be. That cat needs to get on board, or we'll have problems."

"You *do* have problems if you feel threatened by a tiny little kitten," I say with a faint smile, even as goosebumps rise on my skin. Mason's capability to make indirect threats is impressive; he just dresses them up as casual conversation.

Before Mason can respond, the shrill ringing of a phone sounds from the bedroom. Recognizing it as his ring tone, I raise my eyebrows at him, silently asking if he's going to take it. Considering the late hour, I imagine anyone calling right now must have a good reason.

With a low, "This isn't over," Mason leaves to take the call.

I hold Loki against my chest, rubbing my cheek against his furry one. "You're the cutest thing ever, you know that? I've always wanted a kitten, but I wasn't allowed to have one. My mom's allergic, and she wouldn't even entertain the idea of getting a hypoallergenic cat. Now, because of Mason, I can have you." *Because of Mason, I can have many things I couldn't before.*

Mason returns after a few minutes, his expression sober and eyebrows knitted.

"Who called?" I ask, scratching behind Loki's ears. "Is everything okay?"

Mason purses his lips, schooling his expression into a mask of neutrality. "Nothing to worry about."

I frown. "Don't do that. If you want to give this relationship a chance, you're going to need to be open with me. Otherwise, I won't feel comfortable being open with you."

Vulnerability is meant to go both ways; honesty and openness need to be extended on both ends of a relationship. If Mason's serious about keeping me, then he needs to give me a compelling reason to keep him.

Mason releases an irritated sigh. "I heard from the guys I have going through your dorm room for evidence. They're leaving for the night; they were just checking in with me to pass on their report. They collected samples of some fingerprints and... *fluids* found at the scene, which they'll send over to a lab for testing. Hopefully, the results will help us find whoever's been after you. My team will clean up the mess first thing in the morning."

"First thing in the morning?" I question, shaking my head. "No, I want to see the state of my room before they fix it." Mason barely let me glimpse a single picture of the scene, and while I have no real *desire* to see the carnage of my dorm room, I need to. I have to understand what I'm up against.

"No," Mason says immovably. "Absolutely not. The scene is fucked up, Chloe, you don't need to see it. I don't want you to see it. All the ugliness will be cleaned and scrubbed. I'll see if any of your belongings can be salvaged and have them brought here."

My hackles rise as I stare at him. It feels like he's trying to keep me out of this business because he doesn't think I can handle it. As if I'm a delicate trophy wife who's meant to be kept on the periphery of his dealings. The problem is, these aren't *his* dealings, they're *mine.* The threat is to *me,* not him. It's *my* room—*rooms*—that were broken into twice.

"Mase," I start slowly, "don't try to keep me out of this. It's *my* life, I deserve to be in the loop about it."

Mason shakes his head. "No, Chloe. I will handle the situation. I don't want you anywhere near the crime scene. You're mine now, which means I will take care of your problems."

"Please don't push me on this," I say firmly. "It won't endear me to you. It won't make me trust you. The only thing it will do is make me feel like I'm a little girl you're protecting for her own sake, as if my delicate sensibilities can't handle the truth. That isn't fair." I inhale a deep breath, trying to rein in my temper and indignance. "I want to see my room before it's cleaned."

"*No,*" Mason snaps, giving me a hard look.

My lips thin. "Then at least let me see the pictures of it."

"No!" Mason repeats. "*Enough.* I won't talk about this anymore. I was giving you the courtesy of the openness you asked for, but I will *not* put you in the line of fire. I'm not keeping you away because I want to belittle you, I'm doing it because it is my *job* to protect you, and I won't let anyone get in the way of that—not even you."

I swallow past the knot in my throat, my brows furrowing at his complete shutdown of the topic. It takes me a moment to recognize the emotion that's causing my throat to swell: pain. Mason might think he's protecting me, but instead he's making me feel inept and unworthy of handling the problems in my own life, which hurts. His demeanor tells me that saying as much won't have any effect—his jaw is clenched, his eyes glint with warning, and his entire body is tense.

"Okay," I say after a pause. If he won't take me to my dorm, then I'll just have to find another way to see what I need to see. "I'm going to stay out here for a little while to try to get Loki to bed. Go to sleep, we can talk in the morning."

"I'm not going to bed unless you're coming with me," Mason says.

That's a step too far. "No," I snap harshly. "No, you don't get to cut me out of the dealings in my life and then expect me to play house with you. I'm mad at you right now, I need space, and if you want there to be *any* hope of our relationship extending past its expiration date, you need to give me some breathing room."

Mason opens his mouth to argue, then seems to think better of it. He stares at me for several long moments, his gaze burning a hole in my head. I think he's considering plucking me off the couch and carrying me to his bed. If he does that, I'm going to swallow my pride and ask April or Elia to help me get away from him for a while. I hate the idea of imposing on my friends, but the man in front of me is not being reasonable right now.

"Fine," Mason says. "If you're not in my arms come morning, Chloe, we're going to have a big fucking problem."

"If you don't learn to back the hell off, Mason, I won't be around to solve those problems. You've already pushed me to my limits today. *Go.*"

He stands from the couch and goes to the bedroom, shutting the door behind him. Once he's out of sight, I let out a long, irritated growl.

Mason has been equal parts wonderful and infuriating today. He moved me into his apartment without asking, then spoiled me by getting me a kitten. We had a lovely evening with good food and excellent sex, only for him to turn around and try to push me out of my own life. There are parts of him that I like, that I could even see myself falling for, but they're tempered by the domineering asshole in him.

"Can you believe what a jerk he is?" I ask Loki. "What am I going to do with him?" The kitten blinks at me drowsily, releases a quiet meow, then falls right to sleep. Even that adorable gesture isn't enough to soothe my anger.

I inhale a steadying breath, then force myself to stop seething and start thinking. Mason said that his people will scrub my dorm room in the morning; that gives me between six and eight hours to glimpse the state of it. I could try to get into Mason's phone and look at the photos he has of my room, but I don't know his password, and seeing the scene in person would be more useful. I want to try to understand whoever's after me—get a sense for their mindset or emotions.

I set Loki back in his crate, then order myself an Uber, determined to regain at least a modicum of control. If I bend to Mason's will now, I can easily see him finding a way to overtake my life entirely, which would be catastrophic.

I take care to keep quiet as I sneak out of the apartment, grabbing the keys on the entryway table as I go, so I can let myself back in once I return. If all goes according to plan, Mason will never know I left.

My Uber driver is an elderly gentleman who makes polite conversation throughout the ride—I give him one-word answers, a mixture of anxiety and fear churning my stomach. If Mason finds out that I left, he won't take it well. He might even see it as a betrayal of his trust. Then again, by trying to bar me from my own life, he's betrayed *my* trust, so turnabout's fair play.

The closer I get to Greywood, the heavier my chest feels. When the driver drops me off right in front of the program dorms, I'm almost hesitant to get out of the car. I force myself to, not willing to concede when I'm so close to finding out firsthand what my room looks like.

If anything goes wrong, I'll scream at the top of my lungs and wake everyone in the building.

Since I don't have my student keycard on me, I enter the six-digit code into the pin pad below the electronic scanner on the front door of the building, unlocking it. I do the same in the elevator. When I make it to my floor, I take a deep breath to steady my nerves, clutching my phone tightly in my hand, then head to my room.

The wooden door to my room is cracked ajar, splintered in several places. The locks on it have been smashed to bits, rendered useless. The frame is covered with red cautionary tape that warns everyone to stay out, a warning I don't heed. Steeling myself, I give the door a push inwards, duck under the tape, and step inside.

The sight that greets me is gruesome enough to make nausea rise in my esophagus. Blood is *everywhere*—staining the floors, the walls, the torn-open drawers of my dresser, and there's an excessive amount of it on my bed. The mattress and sheets are soaked through with the dark red liquid, and there are several dried puddles of it on the floor beneath the bedframe. I can smell and almost *taste* the metallic tang of it in the air, threaded through with a disgusting rotting scent.

I blink several times, pushing away my horror and forcing myself to view the room through an analytical lens. My clothes are scattered on the floor, and most of them have been deliberately splashed with blood. My study desk is splintered in half, probably by the same sledgehammer that broke the door, and the mirror above it is shattered. The scattered shards show a distorted reflection of my horrified expression.

I inch forward when I notice sheets of paper on my bed, startled to realize that they're pictures of *me* going about my daily business around Greywood. A closer look reveals that they span several months and track me in multiple locations—outside dance HQ, through the window of the campus café, studying at the park. Whoever did this to my room has been stalking me since the *beginning of the year*.

A yelp escapes me when I look to the side of the photos and see a *dead raccoon* laid on my bed. *Jesus Christ.* Its furry belly is split open, intestines strewn around it, and its glassy eyes stare up at me, filled with accusation. I take a startled step back, heave, and clap a hand over my mouth to contain my vomit.

Whoever did this wanted me to find my room in this state, wanted to inflict maximum terror, and they are succeeding.

My eyes fixate on the bloodied writing staining the wall behind my bed, the message that I already glimpsed in one of Mason's pictures: *Get out or get dead, bitch*. My gaze drifts lower as I notice more words scrawled on my headboard, and my stomach flips as I read them: *Leave or end up like him*. Beneath the message, there are arrows pointing to the mattress, directing my attention back to the poor raccoon.

Having seen more than enough to last me a lifetime, I turn and run out of the room, a sob of horror escaping me as I take the stairwell down to the first floor. I burst out of the building and onto the stone platform in front of it, panting, unable to get enough air in my lungs. Flashes of the blood, the writing, and the poor raccoon play on a torturous reel in my mind.

I can see why Mason didn't want me to come here. The scene is beyond jarring; it's downright traumatizing. If he'd talked to me instead of shutting me down, I *wouldn't* have come here. Right now, all I really want is to go back to him and spend the rest of the night in the comfort of his arms, trying to forget what I've seen.

I'm in a daze as I pull out my phone and order another Uber, my hand shaking so badly I can barely click around my phone screen. I force myself to breathe deeply and try to calm down; being hysterical right now won't help me. Unfortunately, no amount of deep breathing seems to make a difference as the minutes tick by in silence, trapping me with my terrible thoughts and those awful images.

I walk down the steps leading to the building, deciding to wait right by the road so I can get into my Uber as soon as it arrives. I need to get the hell away from here.

"You're not supposed to be here, Chloe," a gritty male voice says from behind me, making my blood run cold. "Though I'm happy that you are." I try to turn around to see who's there, but an arm curls around my neck, preventing me not only from moving but from *breathing*. My phone clatters to the ground, bouncing a few feet away as I claw at the arm for dear life.

Chapter Twenty-Seven

Panic grips my throat as tightly as the arm does. Adrenaline surges through me, giving me wings, kicking my fight-or-flight instinct into gear. It's late, the nearest lamppost barely illuminates my surroundings, and I know if I don't get away right now, I might not make it out of here alive. After I was assaulted at that party in high school, I took a year of self-defense classes at a local martial arts studio. We covered how to break free from a rear chokehold on the first day.

I shift both my hands to the crease of my attacker's elbow, digging my fingers into the joint, then swing my body sideways with all of my strength, breaking his hold. Before he can grab at me again, I slam my elbow into his side, sending the breath gusting out of him, and drive my knee into his crotch. He falls to his knees with a shrill cry; I try to glimpse his face, but he's wearing a ski mask. All I can see through the black material obstructing his features are his angry, devious brown eyes.

I don't want to waste time unveiling his identity and risk giving him a chance to recover. Spotting headlights flashing up the road, probably belonging to my Uber, I snatch my phone from the ground, shove it into the pocket of my pajama pants, and break into a sprint. Unfortunately, I barely manage to get half a step before his hand cuffs my ankle, sending me crashing face-forward onto the pavement. I use my palms to cushion my fall, hissing at the stinging pain that tears through them.

"*Fucking bitch*," the man rasps, dragging me backward. I release a piercing scream, praying that someone hears and comes to help me, which startles my attacker. *Did he expect me to stay silent?*

I kick my foot hard, managing to break his hold, scramble to my feet, and run toward the headlights in the distance. Almost immediately, I hear his footsteps pounding on the pavement behind me. He releases a string of blistering swearwords that push me to run harder and faster. I'm certain that my attacker is the same man who left the horrific scene in my dorm room, and I'm desperate to escape the same fate that befell the raccoon. The car's getting closer, driving in my direction, and I pump my arms, ignoring the ache in my lungs as I sprint as fast as I'm capable of.

"Get back here!" My attacker's roar is momentarily drowned out as the car puts on a burst of speed, then veers off to the side of the road not fifty feet away from me and comes to a screeching halt. The footsteps behind me falter, then grow quieter. I chance a brief glance over my shoulder, glimpsing my attacker running in the opposite direction, away from the car.

The driver's side door opens and *Mason* steps out of the car. He probably discovered my absence and guessed my intentions to come to Greywood to see the result of the break in myself. I put on a final burst of speed and crash right into his arms; he catches me with a faint *oomph*.

"Are you fucking *insane?*" he demands. "Sneaking off in the middle of the night, wearing only your goddamn *pajamas?*" He takes a moment to look at me, then stiffens. "Chloe, what's wrong? Why are you running?"

"Someone attacked me," I say, gasping for breath, "in front of dorms. After I saw my room. I don't know who, he was wearing a ski mask. He was right behind me, chasing me, but ran when he saw a car coming." I spin around, peering into the distance, trying to locate where the burly man who was just chasing me went, but he's disappeared without a trace. Mason lets out a low growl.

"I'll deal with you when we get home," he says, grabbing my arm. The aggressive gesture is too much; I jerk out of his grip, my breaths turning even more shallow as images flash through my mind. *My bloodied dorm, the raccoon, the masked man, the party...* all of it coalesces into a ball of trauma that overwhelms me.

Mason takes my arm again, marches me to the passenger side of the car, and deposits me in the seat before slamming the door. I sink into the cool leather, feeling chilled down to my bones. The images crowding my mind replay in an endless loop, drawing me deeper into a state of panic.

I can still smell the scents of blood and death from my room, along with the rancid breath of my attacker. I can still *feel* the sheer menace radiating from him. Moreover, I can still hear the slurring of the boy from the party all those years ago, feel his sloppy, harsh touch moving over my body. Bile rises in my throat, and I swallow several times to prevent myself from throwing up.

I try to focus on something from the present. The smooth dashboard, the steering wheel, the gear stick, Mason pacing outside the car as he yells at someone on his phone, but none of it seems to be enough. I'm shivering so intensely my teeth are chattering—I feel like I'm in the middle of an arctic tundra, yet my clothes are drenched with sweat, as if I'm in a sauna. I'm a mess, and I don't know how to calm myself down.

I switch over to thinking about my favorite memories. Skiing with my father, letting my mother dress me up when I was younger, the time when I found a baby bunny in our garden, but it's not enough.

When the driver's-side door opens, I'm so wound up I scream. Mason gets in, casting me a startled glance that quickly morphs into a look of concern.

"*Fuck*," he mutters under his breath. He reaches across the center console, smoothing my damp hair back from my forehead. "Pixie..." he trails off. "I need you to breathe for me."

"I—I *am*," I say between shallow pants.

"Not like that," he disagrees. "Breathe deeply, in and out. C'mon, breathe with me." He inhales several exaggerated deep breaths, and after a moment, I force myself to follow his lead.

Several minutes pass as we breathe together, and my breaths gradually even out. My full-body shiver subsides into a smaller tremor, and though I'm fuzzy and not altogether present, I'm no longer in the grips of a panic attack.

"I'm c—cold," I manage to say between chattering teeth.

Mason quickly turns on the car and blasts the heat. "We're going home," he says slowly, enunciating each syllable. "You need to get some sleep—"

"*No sleep*," I cut him off, shaking my head. I know from experience that if I try to sleep right now, terrible nightmares will greet me.

Mason nods. "Okay. You can warm up in a bath while I figure out what the *fuck* just happened." He pauses. "Why would you sneak out like that, Chloe?"

"Because it's *my life*," I emphasize. "You can't... take it over."

He works his jaw for a moment, then releases a sigh. "We'll talk about that later. For now, let's go home."

***

Back at Mason's apartment, I spend an hour in a piping-hot bath, warming up while Loki prowls around the rim of the bathtub, meowing and batting at the water. Eventually, he falls in, and I quickly fish him out. He sneezes, then runs out of the bathroom, abandoning me. My trembling's calmed down, as has my heart rate—the crash after the adrenaline high is hitting me hard, leaving my body exhausted even as my mind remains restless.

I step out of the bathtub, dry off, and wrap myself in a robe. It takes me a moment to gather the courage to face Mason. I know he's furious with me for sneaking out, and part of me wishes I'd listened to him and stayed home. The other part of me refuses to let him take control of my life.

When I walk out of the bathroom, I find Mason seated on the edge of the bed. In one hand, he holds his phone to his ear; in his other hand, he holds *Loki* by the scruff. Loki spits, hisses, and tries to claw at Mason, who merely squints at the kitten with a perplexed expression. Despite the severity of the evening, a small smile pulls on my lips.

"I see," Mason says into the phone. "I don't care what it takes, figure out what happened. ID the attacker at any cost." He glances at me, then inclines his head at Loki, who's now taken to yowling.

I walk over to them and scoop Loki into my hands. The kitten promptly crawls up to my chest, clinging to my bathrobe with his tiny claws, and buries his head in my armpit. His tiny body shivers, so I return to the bathroom to grab a washcloth to dry him off.

"Call me first thing in the morning with an update," Mason says in the bedroom. "Yup, take care."

He hangs up the phone just as I walk back in, with Loki wrapped in a hand towel.

"I am *furious* with you," Mason says, meeting my eyes. His words are empty of any real rancor, he appears more relieved than angry.

I nod. "I'm pretty pissed off with you, as well." I also kind of want him to hold me, but I don't say that out loud.

"You say you don't want me to exert control over your life, but what option am I left with when you do things that put you in danger?" Mason questions.

"Tonight was a one-off," I reply, frowning. "It's not like I make a habit of getting into dangerous situations, Mason. I'm usually a very cautious person. If you'd been willing, I would have asked you to take me to my dorm room. Since you wouldn't even let me see pictures, I went alone."

"I didn't take you because I wanted to protect you!" he snaps. "I wanted to avoid traumatizing you!"

"I wouldn't have been in danger if you'd gone with me. Whoever attacked me might've thought twice with you by my side—"

"The entire *world* is a danger to you, don't you get that?" Mason demands. "Everything. Everywhere. It's all fucking dangerous, Chloe. The world you'll get pulled into once your mother marries Bradley Rodgers will be even *more* dangerous. Members of high society might drape themselves with the finest clothes and appear to be the epitome of civilization, but we're nothing more than well-dressed predators. How am I supposed to protect you there if I can't even protect you on a college campus?"

I'm momentarily taken aback by the vigor of his words. This isn't just a point of pride for Mason—I can see in his eyes that he is genuinely invested in my well-being.

"Mason, it's not your job to protect me from the world," I tell him. "I appreciate the help with whoever's after me, but you can't keep me safe from everything, and I don't expect you to. I don't want to be bubble-wrapped and locked up in a tower for my own good. If you try to do that, it'll only show me that you don't respect me. I get why you're mad, but I need you to understand *why* I snuck out. I've been independent for a long time, since my dad passed away." I pause, looking down at Loki, rubbing the towel behind his ear. "I didn't have a lot of support after his death. I can't just become dependent on someone overnight. I don't *want* to."

Life taught me a painful lesson about the perils of relying on another person a long time ago. After my father's death, my mom wanted to forget about him, and by extension, me. The few times I relied on her for anything more than my basic physical needs, I was crushed.

"I get that," Mason says. "I don't like it, but I get it. The thing is, you don't need to be scared to rely on me, Chloe. I'm serious about you, about *us*. You agreed to actually give us a chance; that won't work if you're still functioning as a one-woman show. I'll try to dial back my protectiveness, even though it'll grate on me, and in return I need you to trust me enough to rely on me, if only a little. I *do* respect you, Pixie. I respect you a lot. I think you're an incredible woman. Hardworking, intelligent, and so beautiful it's painful to look at you." He stands from the bed, slowly closing the distance between us. "Give me a little trust, Chloe. Lean on me, trust that I'll catch you when you fall. I promise you won't regret it."

His words chip away at my armor, burrowing beneath it like seeds sinking into fertile soil and taking root. I swallow past the knot in my throat and force myself to meet Mason's gaze, which is earnest and open.

I sigh. "You ease up on your protective bullshit, I'll try to extend more of my trust."

Mason inclines his head. "That works for me." He reaches out to slide an arm around my waist, his eyebrows furrowing. "I hate fighting with you. Let's not do it again."

A soft puff of laughter escapes me. "I hate to break it to you, but that wasn't a fight. It was an argument—a pretty *mild* argument."

Mason's nose scrunches in an adorably boyish gesture. "What the fuck would qualify as a fight?"

I smile, reaching up to stroke my fingers over his jaw. "When you hear me start yelling and when things start getting thrown, you'll know it's a fight."

Loki releases a low purr, eyes flicking between me and Mason. The little guy even leans forward to rub his cheek against Mason's shirt.

Mason chuckles, gives Loki a little pet, and kisses my forehead. "So, when you and I are in good standing, this cat likes me. When we're fighting or arguing, he's ready to claw my guts out."

I smile down at my new pet. "I know what you're thinking, Mase. I chose damn well."

CHAPTER TWENTY-EIGHT

On the last Friday of winter break, just three days before the start of spring semester, I engage in my usual evening routine of cuddling up to Mason on his couch. A movie plays on the TV in front of us, Loki plays on his cat tree behind us, but my attention is wholly absorbed by Mason, and his focus is lasered on me. Nestled into his side with his arm wrapped around me, I bask in his warmth and undivided attention as we converse.

"Favorite color?" Mason asks me.

"Blue-green," I respond.

"Like your eyes?" Mason questions, brushing a lock of hair from my forehead.

I shake my head. "Not quite. Have you ever visited any of the Caribbean islands?" At his nod, I continue. "I went there for winter break when I was ten. My dad chartered a boat and took me for a ride around the coast. There's this little stretch of water where the dark color of the ocean's depths meets the shallow waters that lap against the shore. The intimidating deep blue transforms into a stunning light blue, tinged with a greenish sparkle. I was fascinated by the color, and

I wanted to stay in those waters forever. It's been my favorite hue ever since."

Mason smiles. "I'll have to take you there again. I can picture the way your eyes would light up at the sight of the luminous waters."

I snuggle closer to him. "I'd like that. What about you? What's your favorite color?"

"It used to be black," Mason murmurs, running a finger over my cheek. "Now it's teal, like your eyes."

My heart warms at his words, and I press a kiss to his chest. "Flatterer."

"Just being honest," Mason replies. He lowers his hand to tug at the hem of my shirt. "Why are you wearing so many clothes?"

"Because every time I'm *not* fully dressed, you take it as an invitation to fuck me." In the mornings, I almost always wake up to the sensation of Mason's tongue lapping at my pussy. Sometimes, he takes me when I'm getting dressed in our closet. I've barred him from joining my morning showers because he takes me then, as well. In the evenings, same deal. His stamina is off the charts, his appetite for me is endless, and he's completely insatiable.

"I can't help myself," Mason murmurs, leaning down to brush a kiss over my lips. "You're irresistible. *Delectable.* I think I'm obsessed with you, Chloe."

My chest flutters at that. If he had said those words to me a few weeks ago, I would have been deeply unnerved. Now, I like the sound of them very much, because I'm growing increasingly fond of him, as well.

"I think you're pretty irresistible, too," I tell Mason, leaning toward him for a deeper kiss. Mason starts to pull me onto his lap but pauses when his phone buzzes on the coffee table.

"One moment," he says with an irritated sigh. "Only a few people are allowed to call me today, and those are calls I need to take."

He presses a kiss to my head, then swipes his phone from the table and answers. Feeling a bit mischievous, I flutter kisses along his neck and chest, making him grip my hip tightly and shoot me a warning look.

"Hello?" he says, his tone faintly choked as I pull his shirt collar to the side and scrape my teeth over his collar bone. Whoever's calling says something that makes him stiffen, and his hold on me turns lax.

Mason casts me an apologetic glance before standing up and heading into the spare room, leaving me battling a sense of emptiness. Thankfully, Loki leaps down from his cat tree and pads his way over to me, bracing his front paws on the side of the couch and meowing for my attention. I pick him up and cuddle him close to my chest, idly stroking his soft fur.

Mason steps out a few minutes later, his face set in a blank mask. I've learned that he only wears that expression when something's wrong, but he doesn't want me to notice.

"Who was it?" I ask, sitting up. "Is everything okay?"

"Stuart Croms," Mason says, leaning against the bedroom doorway and folding his arms across his chest. "Does that name ring a bell?"

My brows knit as I think for a moment, then shake my head. "No. Should it?"

"He's a student at Greywood. Junior. Economics major." Mason clears his throat. "He's also been stalking you for months. He's broken into your room twice. He left a dead raccoon on your bed. Attacked you in the middle of fucking campus."

My chest tightens. "You found my stalker?"

Mason inclines his head. "I found your stalker." He clicks his tongue. "I'm going to make a few calls, then I'm heading out for the night. I'll be back by morning."

I set Loki aside and stand from the couch, taking a step toward Mason. "Please don't do anything crazy."

"Stuart's the crazy one for going after you," Mason says softly. "What I'm about to do is perfectly sane."

I regard my boyfriend nervously. I have absolutely no idea who Stuart is or why he targeted me, but the fact that he's made my life a living hell is enough to make me despise him. While my hatred and indignation make me want to see him imprisoned, Mason's ire could mean something far more permanent.

"Are you going to..." I swallow. "Get rid of him?"

Mason's prolonged silence makes anxiety wash over me as flashes of him getting caught for murder flit through my mind. Strangely, the actual thought of Mason killing Stuart doesn't bother me as much as the possibility of him going to prison for it.

"*I'm* not going to do anything to Stuart," Mason says. His deliberate emphasis on *I'm* makes me suspect that he might stand by while others do.

"Will you give the order?" I ask.

"Do you really want the answer to that?" he questions. His words themselves are answer enough. Despite the apprehension washing over me, I cross the room and plant my hands on his shoulders, leaning against him. He softens, wrapping his arms around my waist and holding me close.

"I don't want you to get caught," I murmur.

His lips tip up at the sides. "You're adorable," he replies. "I'm not going to get caught for anything."

"I'm pretty sure that conspiracy to commit murder carries a maximum sentence of life in prison," I retort, frowning.

"Chloe," Mason says calmly. "This is not my first rodeo. I assure you, I won't get caught. Stuart is going to vanish, and that'll be the end of it."

I take a deep breath, stepping back. I know that Mason has questionable morals and is willing to do many things that most people wouldn't. I also know he's extremely well-connected and could probably get away with committing murder in broad daylight with multiple witnesses. Those parts of him scare me. They don't terrify me like they used to, but they still make me nervous.

Mason's arms tighten around me, keeping me in place. "Don't," he says quietly. "Don't back away from me. Don't let fucking *Stuart* come between us. You know who I am. You know the darkness that shadows my world. Don't let it push you away. You're stronger than that. *We're* stronger than that."

I let my eyes flutter shut as I lean against him once more, resting my cheek against his chest. "I want to be a doctor, Mase. I want to *help* people."

"I help people, too," Mason says. "I earn my work credits in the business program by working remotely at my father's investment firm. I make people a *lot* of money."

I laugh softly. "Your client list probably includes mobsters. I don't think making them wealthier counts as helping people."

"True, but I also have a Supreme Court Justice among my clients. I think that balances the morality scale." His phone buzzes again, and my heart sinks as he pulls back to check it. "I have to go," he says. "Eliana and April are going to come over and keep you company tonight. Feel free to order dinner, watch a movie, whatever you like."

"Mason," I say, taking a fistful of his shirt. "Just please be careful. And..." Memories flash through my mind: my rooms being broken into, getting attacked, the fear that's been haunting me for weeks. "If you're going to get rid of him, make it hurt." Stuart's made my life a living hell; I want Mason to return the favor.

Mason smiles. "That's a guarantee, Pixie."

After changing into a dark sweater and black slacks, Mason gives me a final kiss and leaves. I sink back into the couch, holding Loki close, worry suffusing me at the thought of what Mason might be doing right now. Of who Stuart is and why he wants to scare me into leaving Greywood. A quick search of his name on social media confirms that I've never met him. He's unremarkable—average height, a little on the heavier side, with flat brown eyes that send a chill down my spine. I remember glimpsing those eyes when he attacked me, though I don't understand *why* he did that. Why he did any of it. As far as I know, we're complete strangers.

I only have a few minutes to ruminate before thunderous knocks sound on my door.

"Open up, bitch!" April's voice calls. "I've brought you Elia, Elia's cat, and a bag full of margarita supplies." A smile pulls on my lips as I put Loki back on his tree and let April in; she gives me an exaggerated kiss on my cheek with a loud *"mwah"*, then marches right into the apartment as if she owns the place, a plastic bag clutched in her hand. As she starts unloading bottles of liquor on the dining table, I turn to Eliana.

"Hey," I greet, giving her a smile before turning my attention to the fluffball in her arms.

"Who is this?" I question, holding my hand out for Elia's cat to scent. He's adorable, with dark grey fur and striking green eyes. He sniffs my hand, then nudges his head against my fingers.

"Mewlius Caesar," Elia says proudly.

A startled laugh bursts out of me. "Mewlius Caesar?"

Elia smiles. "He's Carson's cat, and Carson named him when he was a boy." Elia scratches Mewlius's chin, and he releases a loud purr. "Carson calls him Caesar, but I call him Mewlius; I think it's a cute name."

"Get in here, bitches!" April calls out. "Let's get tipsy!"

I usher Elia in and close the door. "Mason and I just got a kitten, but I can put him away if Mewlius isn't social—"

"No need," Elia says with a laugh. "Mewlius is friendly with other cats. He can probably help socialize your little guy."

We introduce Mewlius to Loki; the two take to each other immediately and cuddle up together on the cat tree.

"Where are your glasses?" April asks me. "I'm gonna pour all of us a drink, then you're going to explain how you're suddenly living with Mason *fucking* Sieger. Last I heard, he refused to make a deal with you, and you parted ways. That fiasco happened..." She pauses to think as she shakes up a margarita in a cocktail shaker. "A month ago? Less?"

I groan. "It's complicated."

Elia rubs her hand up and down my arm. "That's kind of how it goes with these sorts of boys. Spill."

Two margaritas later, we're all seated on Mason's couch, and I've explained my situationship-turned-relationship with Mason. Both of my friends are surprisingly supportive, though that might be because they're halfway through their *third* margarita while I'm still nursing my second.

"So, Mason just moved you in here without asking?" April questions. "Dude must be obsessed. Like, *obsessed,* obsessed, you know?"

I clear my throat. "He said he moved me in to protect me from the campus threat, but I think that was just an excuse to have me here." I bite my bottom lip. "I like him a lot, when he isn't being a jerk. There are moments when his darker side peeks through, and it terrifies me so much I want to run away, but the rest of the time, he's amazing."

Elia gives my hand a squeeze, shifting in her spot beside me. "I get having to deal with a man who can be a dick. Carson is wonderfully empathetic, but Seth can be difficult. The most important thing I've learned about him is that communication is key. He has... *darker* instincts, and to subvert them, he needs to understand what's going on in my head. When he tried to break up my friendship with April to have more time with me, I told him it was hurting me. He stopped pretty quickly."

"Seth's a psychopath," April points out from the other side of Elia. "His brain does not function normally *at all*."

Elia shrugs, sipping her drink. "You're the one who's engaged to a sociopath."

April smiles. "True, so I get how it goes." She trains an intelligent gaze on me. "Ian and Seth can't really grasp most emotions, so it's different with them. I don't think Mason's on the anti-social spectrum, but from what I've seen and heard, he's extremely calculated and motivated. He wants you. He's obsessed with you, quite possibly falling in love with you. If he isn't already there." She laughs. "I can see why. You're hot as fuck, smart as fuck, and genuinely kind. I bet that's like a beacon to him."

I blink slowly. "Thank you? I think. I don't see how this factors into how I should deal with Mason being a jerk. He's not like Seth or Ian; their darkness is permanent, it's who they are. Mason's darkness ebbs and flows."

"Mason's smart enough to know that if he wants to keep you, he needs you to like him and *want* him as much as he wants you," April says. "If he does things that push you away, let him know. He might not be a sociopath or psychopath, but emotions can get lost in ambition, and Mason is clearly *a very* ambitious person. He's certainly ambitious in his quest to keep you."

My cheeks heat, and I glance to the side. "He does tend to ease up when I communicate."

April points at me. "Exactly. See? I always know best." She releases a happy sigh.

I laugh lightly. "I'm surprised your boyfriends let you come hang out with me tonight," I remark. "They seem pretty attached to you, and we're in the last days of winter break. I imagine they'd want to spend as much time with you as possible."

"Oh, Carson's working late, and Ian and Seth are out with Mason," April says. "Apparently, Mason invited them to help take care of a problem."

I blink several times as understanding washes over me. Mason told me explicitly that he wouldn't do anything to Stuart, but implied that other people would. I hadn't realized that he was referring to Ian and Seth.

"You know something?" April asks, arching an eyebrow at me.

I release a short, empty laugh. "Yeah. I know something."

April makes an impatient waving gesture with her margarita. "Well, don't keep me in suspense! I asked Ian where the fuck he was going, but he only said to 'take care of a scumbag.'" She tilts her head to the side. "Oh, wait, I think I already know. Mason found whoever broke into your dorm room—*both* your dorm rooms—and attacked you. Since Mason's designer clothes are too nice to get blood on, he invited Seth and Ian out to beat whoever hurt you to a pulp, maybe even kill him. Am I right?"

I bite my lip. "I don't know if we should be talking about this. It's not exactly legal."

"Neither are half of Ian's dealings," April volleys back. "Or Seth's, for that matter."

"Everything that's said here will stay here," Elia assures me.

Fair enough. "Yeah, Mason found the guy who's been targeting me. He's a student at Greywood, actually—Stuart Croms, an economics major. I've never met him before, and I didn't recognize him when I looked up his picture on social media, but Mason seems certain it's him." I frown. "I don't know *why* Stuart would come after me."

"Ah," April nods. "That's probably why Mason brought Seth and Ian. They both have violent and highly effective methods of persuasion; they'll extract whatever information Mason wants *and* get to play for a bit." She shakes her head. "I swear, the only time Ian's happy is when he's fucking me or hurting someone else."

"Same with Seth," Elia agrees sagely. "He also seems pretty content when I'm posing for his art."

"Welcome to the dark side," April says, leaning over Elia to clink her glass against mine. "Mason might not be a psycho, but he's certainly fucking dark."

***

Elia and April leave at around midnight, after making me promise to hang out with them more often this semester. Since I'm unable to fall asleep, I spend the next few hours reviewing my spring semester schedule and setting up a study regimen. Once that's done, I move on to organizing my personal email on my laptop. As I'm creating folders to categorize my emails, a new message pops into my inbox, coming from my *mother's* email address. Brows furrowing, I click on it, and my heart sinks into my stomach.

Chloe-

Bradley and I are getting married! I'm not sure where to send your wedding invitation, so I decided to email it.

Mom.

I open the attachment and read over the official invitation. They've chosen to have a destination wedding at a small resort in Italy in mid-March. I *want* to be happy for my mom, but I can't muster any joy for the occasion. I've only met Bradley a few times, and each time I was struck by his controlling nature. He even tried to control *me* by setting me up on dates with trust fund assholes. To Bradley's credit, he agreed to stop after I sent my mom a detailed text about George's lewd and inappropriate behavior, *and* he agreed to still pay my tuition this year. So far, those are the only nice things he's done for me.

Sighing, I shut the laptop and recline on the couch, feeling sick to my stomach. I want Mason to be back already; I need to ensure he's okay, to hold him and be held by him. It's concerning just how quickly I've formed an attachment to him, but I'd be a lot more worried if I wasn't certain that he's also forming a strong attachment to me.

April's words about Mason being in love with me float across my mind, bringing a blush to my cheeks. I don't know if she's right; I don't know if he's falling for me or has already fallen for me, but I do think I'm starting to fall for him. If things don't work out between us, the breakup will undoubtedly be painful. *I hope they work out.*

I sit up as the sound of the door unlocking echoes through the apartment. Setting aside my laptop, I get to my feet. A moment later, Mason walks in.

"Hey, Pixie," he greets when he sees me, a small smile pulling on his lips. "You should be asleep—*oof.*"

His words are cut off when I crash into him, wrapping my arms around his shoulders and hugging him close. "You were safe?" I ask. "Careful?"

He clasps my waist, giving it a squeeze. "Always. Did you stay up because you were worried about me?"

"Of course, you moron," I mumble against his shoulder.

Chuckling, Mason hoists me up into his arms. I wrap my legs around his waist with a squeal, then bury my face in his neck. He carries me over to the couch, taking a seat and situating me on his lap. I pull back to study his expression—he's smiling, but lines of strain crease his eyes and forehead.

"Is the problem... taken care of?" I ask.

"The immediate one is," Mason says, rubbing his thumbs over my hips. He looks down, then gives his head a shake. "Stuart won't ever bother you, or anyone, again. Unfortunately, there are other problems that have to be considered."

I stiffen. "What do you mean?"

He releases a long sigh, leaning forward to run his lips along my neck. "Stuart wasn't acting alone. Someone was paying him very good money to fuck with you."

I jerk back. "*What?*"

"I don't know many details, but I'm already working on finding them," Mason murmurs against my neck, pressing a kiss to my pulse. "Stuart had a lot of student debt. Someone offered to help him pay it off if he agreed to scare you into leaving Greywood. Violently, if need be."

My thoughts start to race at his words, and my heart follows suit. Why would someone pay a student at Greywood to torture me? To try to scare me into leaving school? I don't have any enemies—none that I know of, anyway.

"Who would pay him to do that?" I breathe. "And *why?*"

"I don't know," Mason sighs. "Stuart was a troubled kid; he was arrested for animal cruelty in his youth." Recalling the dead raccoon on my bed, I grimace. "Someone anonymously contacted him several months ago, telling him to follow you around campus and take pictures of you. Stuart didn't know who, but he needed the money and he didn't seem to have any problems stalking a girl to get it. Then, a few weeks before winter break, whoever had him following you also told him to break into your room and threaten you, with the goal of scaring you off campus." Mason pauses. "They made the same request on the day we returned from New York."

I clutch his hair, pulling him away from my neck as I think. "The day we returned from New York?" He nods; I frown. "That seems... rather specific. Almost planned." My blood runs cold as I scramble to figure out who could've done this. It could be someone from Mason or Bradley's social circles, but I don't get why they'd want me away from Greywood. To cause a scandal, maybe? No, that doesn't make sense—*none* of this makes any sense.

Mason strokes a hand up and down my back, attempting to soothe me. "I'm going to find out who put Stuart up to this shit, Chloe. No matter what, I'll keep you safe."

I give him a featherlight kiss on his lips. "I trust you." I just wish my safety wasn't in question to start with.

Chapter Twenty-Nine

The first half of the spring semester flies by in a blur of school, homework, sex, getting lost in Mason's attention, and so many orgasms I have to look up if I'm at risk of getting brain damage. The physical intimacy is great, but what's even better is *him*. His thoughtfulness, his attentiveness, the way he picks me up from school every day to take me to his apartment and indulges my random food cravings. How he buys me a heat pad for when I'm on my period and stocks his cupboard with my favorite snacks. How he always brings Loki his meals and shamelessly bribes my cat, even though Loki still hisses and claws at Mason whenever he feels like it.

Before I know it, spring break is upon us, and we're flying to Italy for my mom's wedding. Mason receives an invite, as do several members of his family, so he and I take one of his family's private jets to Italy, then drive from the airport to a small, *stunning* resort. I spend the hour-long ride alternating between staring at the mountains in the far distance and admiring the bright blue waters of the nearby beach.

We pass through a charming city close to the resort, and I find myself stunned by several monuments, a gorgeous church, and hole-in-the-wall museums that I'm *desperate* to explore. Unfortunately, we don't have time to wander the city as I'd prefer—all wedding guests are expected to adhere to a strict schedule, attending the various events that Bradley and Mom have set up for us.

After settling into a lovely villa overlooking the glittering ocean, Mason and I walk across the cobblestone pathways of the resort, heading to the welcome breakfast that all guests are expected to attend. It's held in a beautiful one-story restaurant that vaguely resembles a modernized Greek temple, made of faded white bricks and surrounded by pillars. Since the building isn't large enough to seat all the guests, tables have been placed in the courtyard outside. I'm seated at a round table with Mason's family—his parents, his aunt and uncle, and best of all, Amara and Raegan. While I don't miss the fact that I'm not invited to sit with my own mother, I suppose my placement at the Sieger table means that Bradley is finally accepting Mason as a part of my life.

I glimpse the bride and groom through the bank of windows making up the front wall of the restaurant—Mom doesn't notice me, while Bradley catches my eye and gives me a brief nod of acknowledgement. He makes no move to stand and greet me, even though we're about to become family. *No surprise there.*

Despite the lack of attention from my mother and her husband-to-be, I get *endless* attention from Raegan and Amara throughout the breakfast. Raegan remembers me and instantly demands I tell her a story; I promise to do so later. It takes Amara a bit longer to recognize me, but once she does, she abandons her seat beside her mother and climbs right onto my lap, while Raegan takes up residence on Mason's lap.

"Is this what it's always going to be like when there are kids around?" Mason asks curiously, even while he bounces Raegan on his knees, delighting the little girl. "They're going to cling to you, and by extension, me?"

"Probably," I confirm. "Kids tend to like me. I like them. The calculus behind that one is pretty simple." I gently tug on a lock of Amara's light-blonde hair. "Isn't that right, sweetie?"

She glances at me over her shoulder, cheeks pinkening, and offers a shy nod.

After a few minutes, Amara taps my thigh, then points at my plate. A waiter has just delivered my breakfast order: a large, fluffy-looking waffle with a side of fresh cream and fruit. Amara's own plate, filled with scrambled eggs, lies abandoned and untouched across the table. The poor girl was probably too uncomfortable to eat seated by her mother, a woman who ignores her so completely it's painful to watch. I lean forward, mindful not to bump Amara against the table, and cut a small piece of waffle, smearing it with whipped cream and topping it with a raspberry before holding the fork to Amara's lips. She accepts the bite, chewing happily and making an adorable little humming noise that makes me melt.

"Okay, coming here might be worth it just for your cousins," I tell Mason, who watches with bemusement as Raegan helps herself to the bacon on his plate. Mason's eyes flick over to me as I offer another bite to Amara, and his gaze warms.

"They are pretty adorable," he agrees. "Ours would be cuter, though."

"We can return to this conversation in five to seven years, if we're still together," I inform him, popping a bite of waffle into my mouth, then continuing to feed Amara.

Mason reaches out his hand and strokes Amara's arm, smiling at her. "Try not to eat all of auntie Chloe's food, yeah? She's gotta have breakfast, too."

I wave a hand. "We have a fully stocked kitchen in our villa; I'll live. I even found an array of *baking* supplies in the cupboard."

Raegan perks right up at that, turning to gaze at me with wide, eager eyes. "Baking? Cookies?"

I smile at her. "I don't see why we couldn't bake cookies. I think we have all the ingredients we need." I look at Mason. "It's pretty hot out, and it'll only get hotter throughout the day—we could probably plead heat stroke to skip the afternoon cookout on the beach and make cookies with the kids instead. If your aunt and uncle are okay with it, of course. I don't think my mom or Bradley will notice our absence."

Mason shrugs. "Sounds good to me. I'll clear it with Amara and Rae's nanny, have her bring them over in the afternoon."

Amara taps my thigh, motioning to my plate again, requesting another bite. I give it to her, topping the waffle with a strawberry and blueberry this time, then ask Mason, "You'd have to clear it with the nanny? Not your aunt and uncle, their *parents?*"

Mason's lips thin as his eyes wander across the table, settling on his aunt and uncle. "Their mom and dad are... otherwise occupied," he says. "Their nanny does most of the raising, though she's warned not to get too attached to the girls."

My lips thin, and I hold Amara a little tighter. "That's archaic."

"It is," Mason agrees. "I was also raised by nannies and sent to boarding schools as soon as I was old enough. My dad was hands-on compared to other men in the family, but that isn't saying much." He nudges my foot with his own. "That's another reason why you should stick around. Give the babies of my family some much needed socialization and love."

When I arch an eyebrow at his blatant attempt to emotionally blackmail me into staying with him, Mason turns to Amara. "Do you want Auntie Chloe to be around more? Hang out with you when the family is together?"

Amara nods vehemently. Raegan chips in, "Yes!"

Mason's father glances over at Raegan's raised voice. He looks at the girls, offers me a thin smile, gives Mason a nod, then returns to his conversation with his wife.

"It's settled, then," Mason says. "You can't deny the kids."

"You need to cut it with the emotional blackmail," I tell him. "Using your adorable cousins against me won't get you very far."

Mason appears doubtful. "You already look half in love with them. I think trying to use them is worth a shot."

Totally true. "Maybe, maybe not," I say airily.

Breakfast ends soon after, and guests begin to trickle back to their temporary homes. I'm briefly introduced to Raegan and Amara's nanny when she arrives to take the girls back to their villa—Mason tells her to drop them off at our villa before lunch. Just as Mason and I are leaving, we're waylaid by Bradley and my mother as they walk out of the restaurant.

"Chloe!" Mom greets enthusiastically, leaning in to kiss both of my cheeks. "I'm *so* glad you could make it! What do you think of my dress?"

I look over her plum-colored dress, which appears to be straight out of a 50s housewife catalog. Sweetheart neckline, tight bodice, flaring skirt. "It's beautiful," I compliment, then shake Bradley's offered hand. "Good to see you," I tell him.

"And you," he replies with a genuine smile. *Huh.* "I thought I made the right call booking a villa for you and your... boyfriend. I'm glad to see the two of you are still going strong." I'm not sure if his words are genuine, but I accept them nonetheless. After exchanging a few pleasantries, we head off in separate directions.

Mason and I take a winding path back to our villa, soaking in the beauty of the resort. We pass a gorgeous belltower that looks to be hundreds of years old, a few courtyards surrounded by vibrant gardens, and several villas made of rough stone and topped with red, sloped roofs.

"Your stepdad's kind of a prick," Mason says. "A really clever one, but a prick nonetheless."

"He's not my stepdad yet. And besides," I shrug, "he might be a prick, but at least he gave us our own villa. I heard your aunt complaining that she has to share her three-story villa with the rest of your family."

Mason snorts. "Our villa only has one story and one bedroom, theirs has *six*, but I see your point."

I turn to examine him, noting the lines of strain on his face and the rigidness of his shoulders. He's been tense all week, and it's been gnawing at me, though I didn't want to bring it up. Mason talks when he's ready to talk; trying to rush things isn't helpful. "Mase, are you okay?"

He glances at me. "I'm with you. Why wouldn't I be okay?"

I give him a small smile. "You've been tense as a bow for a while. Is it because of the wedding? I know you don't want to be here, and honestly, neither do I, but at least we get a free trip to Italy."

Mason releases a deep breath, wrapping an arm around my waist to pull me close. "I've been tense about the wedding, but not for the reasons you might think. You've been jittery because it's tough to see your mom remarry; I've been on edge because this might be enemy territory." He squeezes my hip. "There haven't been any more incidents on campus, and no one has tried to target you again, but that doesn't mean the danger has disappeared."

The topic instantly darkens my mood as my thoughts go to Stuart and the unknown person who paid him to fuck with my life. Nobody's tried to hurt or frighten me at Greywood since Mason took care of Stuart, but that could be because Mason's made it abundantly clear that I'm under his protection. Few people are foolish enough to cross Mason Sieger.

I swallow. "How does... *that* situation have to do with the wedding? What do you mean, this is potentially enemy territory? Do you think that—" I cut off as my heart starts to race. "That someone here put Stuart up to what he did?"

"I don't know for sure," Mason says. "But Stuart was paid a significant sum of money to mess with you. Most people don't have hundreds of thousands of dollars to throw around. So, we're looking for someone with wealth and a motive to harm you, possibly even kill you. We're currently attending a wedding full of people who might dislike you simply because you weren't born into their world. Some might even despise you enough to try to knock you out of it."

I shake my head. What he's saying doesn't make sense—the timelines don't add up. "Stuart started stalking me at the beginning of the year. Nobody here knew about me back then; I made my unintentional society debut at the Christmas party with you."

Mason pulls me even closer, tucking me into his side. "Actually, Chlo, two people knew about you. Your mom and Bradley."

CHAPTER THIRTY

I blink slowly as Mason's words burrow under my skin, sending a chill through my bones. "You think... you think that my mom or Bradley could possibly..." I trail off, unable to verbalize the thought. It's too much; the idea alone is terrifying.

My steps falter as we approach our small villa that overlooks the beach. Mason unlocks the door, ushers me inside, and leads me straight to the plush white couch in the sitting room. He takes a seat and pulls me down next to him, holding me close to his side.

"Yes," Mason replies. "Well, I doubt Grace is involved, but Bradley? I think he might see you as an impediment to their relationship, to their lifestyle. You could be viewed as the hidden daughter capable of making problems. A liability."

"But... but Stuart broke into my room the second time *after* Bradley offered to pay my tuition," I argue. "And he *still* paid for my tuition, even though I only went on one date." If Bradley was intent on getting me to leave Greywood, why would he pay for my time there?

"He offered you a deal that you didn't follow through on," Mason says. "Tuition in return for treating you like a high society stepdaughter—a bargaining chip in his business dealings. You went on one date before I swept you up. Then, the day we came back to Greywood, there was a dead raccoon on your bed."

"He booked this villa for *both of us!*" I exclaim. "Why would he do that if he's the one trying to scare me? What would be the *point* of frightening me? Besides, the first break in happened before we saw him in New York, before I broke our deal after a single date. His involvement wouldn't make any sense."

"Your situation is certainly an elaborate puzzle with several pieces that are difficult to put together," Mason agrees. "I'd be a lot more certain that Bradley's the culprit if it wasn't for the first break in before we went to New York." He strokes a hand up and down my arm. "At first, Stuart was just stalking you and taking photos of you; photos he uploaded to a server that was accessed by one other person, though I don't know who. It could've been Bradley trying to keep an eye on you. But you're right, the first break in doesn't make sense—scaring you away from Greywood back then doesn't make sense. The second break in, however, could be explained by Bradley trying to frighten you away from Greywood and away from *me*. That way you'd have to turn to him for help, and he could have you play the part he wants you to play in return for his protection." Mason smiles bitterly. "He's never much liked my family. He does business with my father and is on polite terms with him—hence the wedding invite—but Bradley has never *liked* Grant Sieger."

"The first break in, though," I whisper, pulling my legs up and holding my knees to my chest. "I don't get why Bradley would want to scare me then."

Mason shrugs. "He could've just wanted to fuck with you. You're the daughter from your mother's first marriage. He might be a sadistic piece of shit who wants to torment you for being a living reminder that your mom had a life before him."

I inhale a sharp breath. "My mom... Grace wouldn't let him come after me. She might not like me, but she's still my mother; she loves me." *I think. In her own way.*

"Your mom wouldn't necessarily know about all of Bradley's dealings," Mason replies. "Honestly, there was a moment when I suspected her, but then I realized she doesn't have the right connections to pull this off, and she has no motive to harm you. She might not know how to relate to you, but you're still her daughter."

I sink back into the couch cushions, crossing my arms over my chest, trying to take deep breaths while my mind spirals out of control, taunting me with every worst-case scenario imaginable. I hate to admit it, but Mason might be right. He's viewing my situation through an impartial, practical lens that's untainted by emotion; mine is chock-full of emotion. While there are some unexplained variables, I can't deny the possibility that Bradley might be the person who hired Stuart.

"Oh my god," I whisper. "My god, Mason. Jesus *fucking* Christ—"

"Shh," Mason hushes, clasping my waist and pulling me onto his lap. I go willingly, craving physical comfort. I straddle him, wrapping my arms around his neck and hiding my face in his shoulder, trying to breathe deeply and stave off a panic attack. At this stage in the proceedings, Mason has to know that I have an anxiety disorder, and he's not fazed when I have particularly anxious episodes or even panic attacks. He never calls me hysterical, never says a cruel word; instead, he holds me until I calm.

"Chloe," he murmurs in my ear. "You have my protection. You're safe with me, no matter what. I'll *always* protect you."

"How am I supposed to face Bradley tomorrow?" I ask him. "God, what am I supposed to *do?*"

"Trust in me," Mason replies. "That's all you have to do. Bradley isn't the only suspect. There are other people who could know about you through him and have any number of reasons to want to hurt or scare you. You're new, you're unpredictable, there could be old grievances at play. Whatever it is, whoever's after you, I will find out, and I'll put an end to them." His hand soothingly strokes my spine, and he presses kisses against my cheek, forehead, and neck while I cling to him, trying to draw on his strength.

"I'm sorry I'm so needy," I murmur.

"Don't apologize," he says with another kiss. "I'm not sorry. I like your neediness; I like that I can show up for you and make a positive difference, both emotionally and otherwise."

"But I'm bringing problems into your life," I say. "Not just with my constant anxiety, but with the threats surrounding me. The ones you have to work to take care of for me." I release a groan. "I'm a mess."

"You're not a mess," Mason disagrees. "And even if you were, then you'd be my *favorite* mess, Chloe. *I'm* sorry that I still haven't been able to figure out who's after you and why. The situation is more complex than I ever could've anticipated."

"Thank you for being here and helping me," I murmur, pressing a kiss to his neck. "I don't think I could do this alone."

"You won't have to," Mason assures me. "You'll never have to, because you'll always have me. I'll always have your back, Chloe, come hell or highwater." He pauses to kiss my cheek again. "I know that I can be intense when it comes to you. There are times when I overdo my possessiveness. I just *really* want to keep you. I like you more than I've ever liked anyone."

The longer we're together, the more I want to keep Mason too, but I'm scared of what a future with him would entail. His world, the world my mom's about to marry into, frightens me. Mason can also intimidate me with his forwardness, but a part of me likes the certainty of knowing that I'm wanted so much. There haven't been many people in my life who have truly wanted me. There are many who want *things* from me, but not just me. Mason's the first in a long time.

"I get it," I tell him. "I'm growing pretty fond of you, too. I like you when you're not being a jerk. I like how protective you are of me. I love how much you want me—not just for sex, but for who I am."

Mason lets out a low groan. "Don't start talking about sex while you're straddling me with your lips brushing against my neck, Chloe. I'm strong, but I'm still a man, and I'm trying to support you right now."

I smile. "Okay. Thank you. Just... hold me like this for a bit longer."

"However long you need," Mason assures me. "We can chill. There are American movies on demand on the TV; we can watch something if you want."

I sigh, shaking my head. "I have a bunch of schoolwork I need to do."

"We're on spring break, Chloe. What schoolwork could you possibly have?"

"I have a busy schedule next term, Mase. If I get started on some of my projects now, I'll be less swamped when school starts back up."

Mason grunts. "You're overachieving tendencies are taking up too much of your time."

I laugh softly. "I know, but that's what makes me who I am. I like schoolwork."

"No, you like praise. You like knowing that you're doing the right thing, you like having certainty about your future. You relish the exhilaration that accompanies getting straight A's, because it gives you a better shot of getting into a good med school and having a successful career."

I'm not entirely comfortable with how spot-on Mason is; I *do* like the warm feeling that accompanies an A+ in a class. I like having an impressive resume, I like knowing that performing well academically will give me a better shot at a fruitful future.

"You might be right," I agree.

After my anxiety has dulled, I disentangle myself from Mason and walk through the small villa, admiring the white and blue décor, the oil paintings hanging on the walls, and the stone floor covered with fluffy carpets. After retrieving my laptop, textbooks, and notebooks from the small bedroom I'm sharing with Mason, I set them up on the coffee table in front of the couch. Then, I curl up against him and work for a few hours. Mason also pulls out his laptop and clocks in a few hours of remote work for his dad's firm. We stay in comfortable silence for a few hours, until our doorbell rings.

"That'll be the girls," Mason tells me. "I'll get the door, why don't you start gathering the baking products in the kitchen? Raegan loses her mind over cookies, and her favorite kinds are chocolate chip and vanilla. Amara likes anything sweet, but she goes crazy for vanilla frosting."

I nod, shutting my laptop and closing my textbooks. "I'll get to it."

The modernized kitchen boasts of a six-burner stove and two ovens, along with cupboards and drawers filled with kitchenware and cooking supplies. I start assembling mixing bowls, measuring cups, and ingredients on the large Italian-marble island. Only two minutes pass before Raegan bursts into the room, bringing a flurry of excitement with her.

"Hey, Raegan," I greet, smiling down at the young girl. She's dressed in an adorable blue dress; her honey-blonde hair is pulled back into a ponytail, and she wears blue sandals to complete her outfit. "I'm thinking about making a batch of chocolate chip cookies and another batch of vanilla. Maybe some brownies, too. How does that sound?"

"*Awesome!*" she exclaims. "I wanna help!"

"That's good, because I'll need your help," I tell her. "I'm not all that good at mixing, so you'll definitely come in handy then. Sound good?"

"Yeah!"

Mason comes in a moment later, holding the hand of little Amara, who looks around the kitchen with wide blue eyes and an unsure expression. When she sees me, her lips stretch into a smile; I smile back, waving her over. "I hear you like vanilla frosting," I tell her as she toddles from Mason to me and grabs a hold of my leg. Her arms reach upward, and I melt, picking her up and settling her on my hip. She shyly hides her face in my neck, clinging to me.

"Holy *shit* is that cute," Mason says quietly, shaking his head.

"Bad word!" Raegan exclaims. "Put a dollar in the swear jar, Mason!"

Mason leaves the room, returns with his wallet, and pulls out a 20-dollar bill, handing it to Raegan. "Will you take an advance payment?"

The seven-year-old pockets the cash. "Yup. Okay, cookies!"

"Right," I say, nodding. "Mase, you gonna help out?"

"Will *you* feed me later?" he questions.

The insinuation in his words makes me blush, and I nod.

"Then yes, I'm at your service, milady. What do you need?"

Chapter Thirty-One

For the next two hours, I boss Mason around the kitchen. He helps me measure ingredients, crack eggs, and stir the cookie dough. He enlists Raegan's help to add as many dark chocolate chips as she wants and lick the spoon once the dough is ready. I focus on making Amara feel involved; I sit her on the counter and have her hand me some eggs to crack and hold the bowl while I stir, chatting with her. She giggles and smiles but doesn't say a single word as we work, which worries me. She *has* a voice—her laugh is the most adorable thing ever—but she just doesn't seem to want to use it.

After we have everything in the oven, Raegan settles on the couch to watch a Disney movie that Mason puts on for her, while Amara gets a bit fussy. Deciding it's time for her nap, I bounce her on my hip, hum to her, and stroke my fingers through her hair while taking her to the bedroom and drawing the curtains. She falls asleep in my arms, and I try not to move her too much as I set up a fort of pillows on one side of the bed and seat myself on the other. When I attempt to peel her off me to set her between my body and the pillows, she wakes and starts crying again, clinging to me.

I should probably let her cry herself to sleep, but she's in a strange, foreign place, and my heart can't bear the sight of her tears, so I let her hold onto me. I prop some pillows against the headboard and recline against them, circling my arms around her.

I've been around enough children to understand the basics; they're unable to regulate their emotions, and they get upset with any internal or external disturbances. If they're too cold or too hot, they'll cry. The same goes if they need to use the restroom, feel sick, or are simply tired. All of them get clingy when they're emotional, and they usually seek comfort from family members. Since I've yet to see Amara's parents give her a drop of attention, I assume she relies on nannies for affection.

When Mason comes into the room to check on us a while later, I whisper to him, "Does she have anyone to give her emotional support?"

Mason sighs. "Her sister."

I shake my head. "Raegan's seven, I'm asking about adults. I know their parents aren't hands on, but what about the nanny?"

A grimace steals across his face. "Their nannies are switched out every three months. Their mom doesn't want them to become too attached to anyone."

My chest tightens, and I brush a few strands of golden hair away from Amara's cheek, holding her closer, feeling deeply protective of her. "That's barbaric. Children *need* stability."

I know from pictures and stories that both of my parents were very hands-on when I was a child. I always had someone to hold me, console me, and read me bedtime stories. The distance between my mother and me didn't appear until I was a bit older, and it became a chasm when Dad passed away.

"I know," Mason says. "It's not my place to intervene, but believe me, sometimes I want to. Rae and Amara are treated like dolls to be carted around, not like actual small humans who need affection and support."

I sigh, nuzzling Amara's forehead. "We should steal her away. She's so... so *precious*. She can't be ignored like she's nothing."

"The sad thing is that her parents wouldn't even notice her absence until the next family event," Mason says.

"Can we... I don't know, find a way for the girls to keep one nanny?" I ask. "That could give them at least one stable, dependable figure in their lives."

Mason shrugs. "I can talk to my dad about it. Ask him to tell his brother—Jason—to clean up his household. I think it's the girls' mother, Laura, who's the real problem, but she'll listen to her husband; she married him for money, and he controls her bank account."

My head jerks back at the casual way Mason says that. Catching my expression, he chuckles. "That happens a lot in my world, Chloe. Marriages are business arrangements more often than not. Sometimes they're mutually beneficial, other times not so much. Laura got pregnant with Raegan when she was dating Jason. Jason ended up marrying Laura because *my* dad wanted his brother to have a stable home life." He shrugs. "That hasn't worked out all too well, as you can see. Jason and Laura still do whatever they want, now they just share custody of an apartment and happen to have two kids together."

"Huh," I say quietly, trying to wrap my mind around such a cold, impersonal arrangement. After a moment, I ask, "Where's Raegan?"

"She fell asleep on the couch," Mason replies. "The nanny told me that the girls would probably want to nap for an hour or so around this time. How much longer will the cookies and brownies need to bake?"

I check the timers I have set on my phone. "Cookies are done in two minutes, brownies will take another forty. Vanilla frosting's chilling in the fridge, ready to use whenever. You want to take over so I can check the oven?"

Mason smiles softly. "Sure." He slowly takes a seat on the bed, leans against the headboard, and opens his arms, inclining his head. Amara stirs a bit as I hand her over to him, hands reaching for someone to hold onto. As soon as her little fists clutch Mason's shirt, she falls right back to sleep.

"How does she sleep the rest of the time?" I ask him. "She seems to like being held."

"She has a stuffed hippo she clings to at her apartment. One of her former nannies left it for her."

I'm dubious. "She accepts a stuffed animal as a substitute for a human?"

"It's fancy and can be warmed up like a heated blanket. She makes do with it." He tips his chin at my phone. "Your alarm will go off soon; go get the cookies and check on Rae, I'm good here."

I leave Mason and Amara in the bedroom and pass through the living room. Rae's curled up on the couch, snoring softly, head resting on a pillow, so I continue on to the kitchen. The cookies are perfect—fluffy and giving off heavenly aromas. I set them on the stove to cool, check the brownies, then take a seat on the couch beside Raegan, pulling my laptop onto my lap and plugging away at some schoolwork while I have the time.

Another half hour passes in comfortable silence. After finishing up on my laptop, I take the brownies out of the oven and quietly order some lunch from room service, knowing that the girls need to eat some actual food before indulging in sugary treats for dessert.

The meal arrives just twenty minutes after I place the order. A server silently sets half a dozen dishes on a circular dining table next to a window that overlooks a gorgeous white-sand beach. Just as I'm closing the door behind him, Raegan sleepily blinks her eyes open.

I smile at her in greeting, walking over and taking a seat on the arm of the couch. "Hey," I say. "I ordered us some lunch; we can eat while the goodies are cooling. Are you hungry?"

She shoots up into a sitting position, frantically looking around. "Where's Amara?"

Startled, I put a hand on her arm. "She's in the bedroom napping with Mason, sweetheart. She was a bit tired, just like you."

Raegan visibly calms, releasing a deep, shuddering breath. "Oh. Okay."

The sisters are obviously extremely close and even a bit codependent. While I'm glad that Amara has a wonderful older sister to look out for her, I wish Raegan didn't feel responsible for her sister at such a young, tender age.

The bedroom door creaks open, and Mason steps out, holding Amara's hand.

He smiles at me and Raegan. "Hey, guys. We've just woken up, and I think Amara's a bit hungry. Are we ready to eat?"

"Cookies!" Raegan exclaims.

I tap her nose. "Some real food first, please." Raegan pouts, bringing a small smile to my lips. "Don't you want to grow to be big and strong like Mason? Brownies and cookies are delicious, but if you only eat them, you'll stay small forever."

Raegan appears contemplative at that, glancing over at Amara, who releases Mason's hand and toddles over to us, holding her arms out. I lift her onto the couch, where she promptly cuddles up to her sister.

Raegan nods, putting her arm around Amara. "You're right. I need to be big and strong to protect Amara. Let's eat."

Protect Amara. That strikes me as an interesting phrase because it indicates that Raegan doesn't think Amara's being protected. I lock eyes with Mason, whose brows furrow at his cousin's words.

He gives me a meaningful look, silently telling me that we'll talk about it later, then dons a casual smile. "Right, girls. Let's get some food in our bellies, then we can have as many sweets as we can stomach."

I frown at him. "Not *as many* as we can stomach, but certainly a few."

I uncover the dishes at the table and set up plates for the four of us while Mason ushers the girls over. Raegan takes a seat on the chair closest to the window, eyes widening as she looks over the selection of pastas, lasagnas, and of course, a burger for Mason—something I've learned is his favorite food. She reaches out to snag a fry from the burger plate and dunks it in ketchup. Meanwhile, Amara approaches me and taps my thigh again, blinking up at me. I set her on my lap, drag a second plate over to us, and start loading both up with food.

As soon as Mason takes his seat, Raegan starts chattering away about the pretty weather, the clear sky, and how she wants to do some stargazing while she's here. Amara's a little more self-sufficient this meal, picking up food from her plate and munching away. Mason seems unusually relaxed, especially considering the difficult conversation we had just a few hours ago. It dawns on me that he might be more of a family man than I assumed, especially when it comes to family members he likes.

Once we've all eaten our fill, we move our party of four to the kitchen. Together, we frost the dozen sugar cookies, and Raegan insists on frosting a few of the chocolate chip cookies as well. She gobbles down three cookies—an impressive feat—while Amara nibbles on a sugar cookie. The nanny comes knocking all too soon and takes the girls away.

"Something's up with them," I say after we've kissed the girls good-bye. "Something's not right in their household."

Mason nods his head, lips pursing. "Yeah. Things have always been a bit off with their branch of the family. I thought it was the usual issue among the rich—parents ignoring their kids—but I think there's something more. The way Raegan looked at Amara and talked about protection..."

"She also panicked when she woke up and couldn't see Amara," I add on, frowning.

Mason gives my hand a squeeze. "I'll look into it, make sure the girls are okay."

I let out a sigh. "I don't like your family. Amara and Raegan are fantastic, so are your other cousins, the twins. I'm happy to see the kids whenever, but the adults suck. Can we avoid the grownups in the future? Only see them on major holidays? Maybe just for Christmas?"

Mason gives me a strange, lingering look. I tilt my head to the side. "What? Do *you* want to spend more time with them than what's absolutely necessary?"

He shakes his head, a half-smile pulling on his lips. "No, Chloe," he says. "That's just the first time you've talked about our future extending past our arrangement."

My breath hitches as I realize he's right. I've always assumed we'd part ways at the end of the school year, even if part of me hopes we'd somehow stay together. Now, though... now my mindset has shifted. Maybe it's the theoretical future talk we engage in, when we paint pictures of a house full of *our* kids, the vacations we'd take, the ways we'd support each other. Whatever the case is, I *am* thinking about a future with Mason.

Mason wraps a hand around my waist, pulling me close. "Fucking finally, Chlo."

Chapter Thirty-Two

The following evening, Mason and I attend the rehearsal dinner. The very idea of the dinner makes me jittery; so far, I've managed to avoid all the scheduled festivities aside from the welcome breakfast. I don't want to be near Bradley when there's a chance that he's the one who hired Stuart. Unfortunately, I can't skip out on such an important event without drawing attention and questions.

Mindful of the black-tie dress code, I put on a dark red satin gown with a beaded bodice and flowing skirt. Thin straps hold up a plunging neckline that I would've never had the confidence to wear before Mason. A sash wraps around my waist, tying into a bow at my back. My makeup is minimal—a hint of blush and a touch of highlighter, paired with a lipstick shade that matches my dress.

Mason wears an obscenely expensive and devastatingly sexy tailored suit the color of charcoal, complemented by a red tie knotted at the collar of his crisp white button-down. As we make our way to the resort's restaurant for the rehearsal dinner, I can't help but admire what a power couple we are. He dispels my fears and replaces my anxieties with the certainty that I'll never have to face the world alone.

I feel strong when I'm with him, capable of achieving anything I set my mind to.

The courtyard in front of the restaurant is littered with large round tables draped in pristine white tablecloths. Once again, I find myself seated with Mason at his family's table. Amara sits to my left, Mason to my right, and Raegan's seated on his other side, babbling away as usual. I exchange pleasant greetings with Grant and Jade Sieger, graciously accepting Jade's compliments on my dress, before turning my attention toward the bridal table.

Tonight, Mom and Bradley sit next to each other at a rectangular dining table right in front of the Cupid's fountain, facing their guests. They converse with the men and women sharing their table, but every so often, they break their conversations to smile at each other and share a kiss, which makes my stomach twist with discomfort. I should be happy that they're happy, but with my suspicions of Bradley, I *can't* be.

Amara tugs at the skirt of my dress, blinking up at me with her beautiful blue eyes. She nods at my lap, and as always, I melt at her silent request. I help her off her seat and lift her onto my lap, holding her with an arm around her waist. When she reaches for the woven breadbasket in front of us, I grab a slice of fluffy ciabatta bread, dip it in a small dish of salted olive oil, and split it with her.

"You really need to become a mom," Mason tells me lowly. "How attached are you to your five-to-seven-year timeline?"

"It's a realistic timeframe," I tell him. "I'd love to be a mom, I actually can't wait for it, but I need absolute security in my career and finances. I want to be a mom, but I don't want that to be my *only* identity."

"Hmm," Mason hums. "I guess we'll revisit this topic later."

Servers emerge from the restaurant with perfect uniformity, each pushing rolling carts laden with food. They begin distributing an appetizer course among the guests: a small regional salad and a slice of toasted bread topped with delicious bruschetta. Amara eats from my plate, probably growing accustomed to how easily I share. Once she's done, I wipe her mouth with a napkin and finish off what's left.

The meal consists of five courses, each of them small. After the salad comes a classic bolognese pasta, followed by a perfect fillet mignon, another pasta, and finally, a decadent tiramisu dessert. By the end of dinner, Amara has fallen asleep on my lap, and Raegan's curled up in her chair, also half asleep. That's when champagne glasses are brought out, and Bradley rises to his feet, clinking his glass with a knife to get everyone's attention.

I straighten in my seat, mindful not to disturb Amara as I turn my gaze toward my future stepfather. Fear stirs in my chest as his eyes briefly lock with mine, and he inclines his head. Swallowing, I offer him a nod in return.

"Ladies and gentlemen," he begins, speaking in a loud, clear voice. "Thank you all for coming tonight and for joining us in Italy to celebrate my union to a phenomenal woman. I know we're all stuffed full after dinner, and most of us are a bit tipsy, so I'll keep this brief." He offers the crowd a charismatic smile before turning his attention to my mother. "I'd like to thank my lovely bride, Grace, for being such a wonderful partner to me these last years. I know I'm not always an easy man to be around; I like most things just so, and your accommodation means the world to me. *You*, Grace, mean the world to me, and I cannot wait to embark on the journey of life together." He pauses, lifting Mom's hand and brushing a kiss over her knuckles. After giving her a soft, intimate smile, he turns back to the crowd. "Family is the very essence of life; reproduction is as vital to human nature as greed, and we have been given the gift of not only the ability to procreate, but also to develop a bond of love to bind families together." Back to my mom, he says, "Grace, I love you very much and can't wait to build a family with you." Mom blushes like crazy, staring at Bradley with hearts in her eyes. Bradley turns to look at me. "And to my soon-to-be stepdaughter, Chloe, I hope you know that you will always have a place with us and support from us." He clears his throat. "Thank you all again and have a wonderful evening."

I sink back in my seat, sipping from my flute of champagne and absently stroking Amara's hair, confusion clouding my thoughts. I did *not* expect to be mentioned, and while there's a chance Bradley only gave me a shout-out for the sake of the crowd, I think I sensed sincerity in his voice.

I look over to Mason, who also appears contemplative, arms crossed over his chest and eyebrows furrowed as he stares in Bradley's direction. My boyfriend must feel my gaze on him, because he looks over to me and shrugs his shoulders, as if to say *I don't know, either.*

I'm still in a thoughtful mood when we get back to our villa. As soon as Mason shuts the door, I flick on the lights and say, "That was really freaking weird."

"It was," Mason agrees. "Bradley's little ode to you in his speech doesn't clear him as a suspect, he could just be keeping up appearances, but it seemed genuine." He removes his tie. "I'll take a closer look at people around Bradley who might've known about you before the Christmas party. Give more consideration to other potential suspects." He releases a deep breath. "For now, though, I want to forget about Bradley and everyone else." He walks up to me, wrapping his arms around me. "I've been dying to be inside you all night, Chloe. I've been trying to decide whether I wanted the dress on or off when I took you."

Heat curls low in my belly, and I feel my nipples harden into tight peaks at the suggestiveness in his tone. "Did you make a decision?" I ask, my voice unaccountably husky.

Mason nods slowly. "I did. First, I'm going to hike this skirt up around your waist, tear off whatever panties you're wearing, and eat your pussy until you're sobbing. *Then*, I'll do away with the dress so I can touch and tease every single part of you while I fuck you until you're incoherent."

I swallow thickly. "I can get on board with that."

Mason's lips hike up at the corners. "Glad to hear it." He sweeps me into his arms so quickly I yelp, then carries me to the bedroom, tossing me onto the bed.

I bounce once before he's on me, pushing up the skirt of my dress and tearing off my panties with a harsh tug. He spreads my thighs and settles himself between them, then sets about driving me out of my mind with his *extremely* talented mouth. I moan and writhe and bury my fingers in his hair as he licks, nibbles, sucks—*plays*, really, making these little masculine groans of pleasure that get me off as much as his tongue does. It doesn't take me long to come with a low cry and convulsions that shake my entire body.

Mason rolls me onto my back, unzips my dress, and shoves the fabric off me as if it's somehow offended him. My bra is swiftly unclipped and tossed over my shoulder. He pulls me up to my knees, braces a hand on the back of my neck to hold my upper body down on the mattress, and slowly sinks inside me, inch by thick inch. There's always a prickle and burn with him when we first start; it's a bite of pain that I've come to crave, as it carries with it the whispered promise of impending pleasure.

"*Fuck*," Mason growls. "Fuck, Chloe, you feel like heaven." He sets a steady, brisk pace, pumping in and out of me with measured strokes that draw small noises of pleasure from me. All the while, he continues to speak, punctuating his words with thrusts. "You feel like home. You know what you really feel like, beautiful girl? *Mine*." He circles a hand around my neck and uses it to lift me up, plastering my back against his front, hot breaths fanning over my cheek and neck. "I can't get enough of you, Chloe. I never will." He gives my neck a squeeze, momentarily restricting my breathing; my eyes roll into the back of my head.

"You know what I think every time I see how good you are with children?" he whispers, sliding his other hand down my body, finding my clit with his fingers. "I think about just how fucking badly I want to put a baby inside of you. See your belly swell with life *we* created, make my own family with you."

Even while my mind reels at his admission and I want, *need* to tell him that it's too soon, we're too young, I can't manage to say the words. Instead, a low, desperate moan escapes me, and he chuckles in response. "Yes, you want that too, don't you? But you're too perfect to be a young mom, aren't you? You can't trust anyone aside from yourself. Well, Chlo, you are going to learn to trust me, and there *will* come a day when I'll put my baby inside you. Just as soon as you're ready."

"Oh god," I whimper. His words are turning me on as much as his actions; I'm on the cusp of an intense orgasm even though I just came. Mason's thrusts speed and intensify, telling me that he's getting ready to come, as well. He releases my neck to pinch and twist my nipple *hard*, creating a stab of pain, all while rubbing the side of my clit up and down in the way he's learned I like. With a loud cry, I come again, clawing at his hands, unable to control my trembling.

"One more," Mason says as soon as the worst of my convulsions have died down. "I want you to come one more time for me, baby."

"I can't," I whine.

My body feels wrung out, I'm positively drugged on pleasure and almost afraid that I can't handle any more of it, but Mason isn't stopping or slowing. When my eyes flutter closed with a low groan and I shake my head, he collars my throat with one hand and spanks my clit with the other, forcing a yelp from me.

"Mason, please—"

"You know how this goes, Chloe," he says. "You take what I give you and you do what I tell you. I'm telling you to come again."

He releases my throat, pulls out of me, and rolls me onto my back. He hikes my legs up, hooking them under his arms, and slides back into me; the angle of his position allows him to go even deeper.

"Fuck," I whimper.

My inner walls feel sensitive and each of his thrusts brings with it a burning sensation; my entire body feels like it's on fire. Sweat slicks both of our skin and I'm past the point of exhaustion and approaching the territory of total annihilation. Mason takes my lips in a deep, passionate kiss, sipping from my mouth while his thrusts speed up. My heart drums in my ribcage like the wings of a hummingbird, so fast I think it might explode. Even as I'm sure I'm not capable of coming anymore, I feel my pleasure start to build again, approaching another crest that's terrifying in its promised intensity.

"There we go," Mason murmurs. "Don't fight it, Chloe."

He releases one of my legs, slides his fingers between our bodies and finds the nub of my clit with his fingertips, circling them over my most sensitive spot. That's all it takes; I orgasm again with a scream that Mason swallows with a kiss, and a few thrusts later, he also comes. We stay with our bodies joined together for several minutes, catching our breath, before Mason rolls off me and pulls me close.

"You have a knack for showing me that I'm capable of crazy things," I mumble, curling up against him. His arms wrap around me, and I rest my head on his shoulder. My hand lands on his chest, and my legs twine with his.

He chuckles. "You mean I have a knack for making you come until you're incoherent? I'll take the compliment."

"Hmm. You *are* very skilled in the bedroom. Enough so to make me forget about—" I cut off, sucking my bottom lip into my mouth and internally berating myself. My guard is always down after sex with Mason, and times like this, I don't filter my words as well as I should.

Mason strokes his hand up and down my shoulder. "About what, Chlo?" he asks gently.

I shake my head, then scoot closer to him and bury my face in his neck, hiding from his questions.

"Chloe," he says again, patiently. "Are you ready to talk about it?"

"About what?" I try to speak the words casually, but there's a tremor beneath them that betrays me. The warmth coursing through my body slowly seeps out of my system, leaving behind a chill and a feeling of fundamental uncleanness.

"About *him*," Mason says. "The other one. Whoever hurt you."

I swallow. "You already got Stuart."

"You know I'm not talking about him," Mason tells me. "I'm talking about the guy who traumatized you before then. The guy who's the reason you got a panic attack from giving me a blowjob the first time we met."

Mortification swirls through my chest, heating my cheeks. I try to pull away from Mason, but he doesn't allow it; his arms contract around me, keeping me close. "You don't have to tell me anything," he assures me quietly. "I'd like you to, but you don't have to. When you're ready to talk, Chlo, I'll be here."

Something in me softens at his words. My reflex is to clam up when I even think about that wretched party, but with Mason, it's different.

He might have a domineering personality, but he isn't *forcing* me to talk; he's *asking* me to. And, despite my anxiety around the very idea of digging up that grave, I want to tell him. I'm tired of keeping it to myself.

"It happened at a party," I say slowly, speaking into his neck. I don't have the emotional strength to look him in the eyes as I tell this story—*my* story. "A house party to celebrate my school's dance team making it to nationals." I inhale a shaky breath. "I was on the dance team, and while I wasn't usually one for parties, the girls on the team insisted I should go, so I did. I put on a dress that was about a size too small for me—not because I wanted such a tight fit, but because I didn't have many dresses." I release a small, sardonic, empty laugh. "I wasn't used to getting much attention at school—I always had my nose buried in a textbook. I got a *lot* of attention at this party, though. All the boys were looking at me, winking at me, and their gazes made me uncomfortable. So, I started drinking. I was not an experienced drinker, but the girls around me were downing shots in between cocktails, so I figured a few beers wouldn't affect me. They did." I dig my fingers into Mason's chest, trying to ground myself. "The captain of the lacrosse team, Roan, started talking to me when I was on my second beer. He was nice enough, casual, but I was still uncomfortable with the male attention, so I just... kept sipping beers, which he kept refilling. They made me feel fuzzier and less awkward. The next thing I knew, I was *very* drunk, and Roan was pulling me upstairs and into a bedroom. Things got bad."

I grimace at the memory of his grubby hands coasting over my flesh while he murmured something about the shortness of my dress, about how I was *asking* for it. "I could barely talk, but I said multiple times that I did *not* want to do anything, and he ignored me. I realized that if I didn't give him an alternative, he'd rape me. So, I offered him a blowjob." I squeeze my eyes shut, then force them open when flashes of Roan's face appear in my mind. "It was disgusting. I was barely conscious, so he pretty much just used my mouth to get off. I threw up as soon as he was done, which grossed him out. He ran out of the room like it was on fire. I managed to get to the bathroom and purged the contents of my stomach, then stayed wrapped around the toilet bowl for the better part of an hour, until the dance team captain found me. Clara.

"Clara wasn't a *nice* girl, she was strict and kind of bitchy in school, but she was good to me that night. She ensured that Roan had left the party, then she gave me water, Gatorade, and drove me straight to the police station to file a report. The policeman I spoke to took one look at me and determined that I must've been asking for it. They took my statement, but they didn't take me seriously. A few hours later, I went home. My mom was at the house, and I tried to tell her what happened, but she didn't want to hear it. She didn't want me to start any scandalous rumors that might haunt me. She just told me that it was best to forget incidents of men being *inappropriate,* and then went to bed." Belatedly, I realize that tears are wetting my cheeks, and Mason's grip on me has turned to steel. I can feel the tension radiating from his body, feel his anger as if it's my own. Instead of frightening me, there's something soothing about it, because he cares. He's listening, and he cares.

"*Fuck,*" Mason mutters. He squeezes me even tighter, as if he's afraid I'll disappear. "Christ, Chloe. That should *not* have happened to you. It shouldn't happen to anyone." He gently slides a hand into my hair, cupping the base of my skull and tilting my head up to look at him. He swipes at my tears with his thumbs. "You know that it was not your fault *whatsoever,* right? It doesn't fucking matter what you were wearing or how much you drank. None of it matters. That piece of shit took advantage of you." He lifts me on top of him, leaving us chest to chest and heart to heart as he wraps his arms around me in a tight hug. I cling to him, accepting the comfort that I desperately wished for the night I was assaulted.

"It could've been worse," I mumble. "It could've gone all the way—"

"Stop," Mason says gruffly. "Stop internalizing what this fucked up world has taught you. You went through something terrible, and you had to deal with it yourself. It doesn't matter that it could've gone differently, it was still awful. You were touched when you didn't want to be." He kisses my head once, twice. "You'll never have to go through something like that again. You'll never have to face the world alone again." He gives me a squeeze of assurance, as if he's cementing his promise.

For a long moment, silence stretches between us. As my tears slow and stop, a strange feeling washes over me. The sensation is calm, restful, and cathartic. It feels like a weight's been lifted off my chest; the silence that I kept for years is no longer a necessity. This burden isn't only my own to bear—I can share it now.

"Mason?"

"Hmm?"

"Thank you," I say quietly. "For listening, and for validating me. I didn't know how much I needed that."

"Always," he says firmly. "I'll always be here to listen. I'll always be here to share the weight. You'll never be rid of me, Chloe."

I like the sound of that.

CHAPTER THIRTY-THREE

Mason

Long after Chloe falls asleep, curled up against me, I lay awake, thinking of the revenge I'm going to exact on the scumbag who hurt her. Roan. The lacrosse captain. I'll have some of my people look into him and find him—then, it's anyone's guess what I'll do to him. I might orchestrate a scheme to put him in prison, though that feels too nice for him. A much more pleasant thought is contacting the mob fixer that my father occasionally makes use of—a man who turns torture and death into a genuine art form. A small smile tilts my lips, and I make a mental note to get in contact with the fixer.

My phone buzzes and lights up on the nightstand, distracting me from my thoughts. I reluctantly shift away from Chloe and pick it up, eyes narrowing when I see a text from an unknown number.

We need to talk. Meet me in the courtyard outside the restaurant. 10 minutes. -Bradley Rodgers

I click my tongue as I read the message, trying to figure out what the hell Bradley wants to discuss with me at such a late hour. I never gave him my phone number, but there are many ways he could've obtained it. The real question is, why would he take the trouble? What does he want to talk about? Or is his true intention to lure me into a trap? If Bradley's the one who sent Stuart after Chloe, he might have found out that I'm taking a closer look at him. He could want to get rid of me before I can cause problems for him.

Bradley's not known as a violent man in our circles, but he is known to have some connections with darker people in the business world. There's no guarantee that I'll be meeting with *him;* he might send one of his underlings or bodyguards to kill me. This resort is old and doesn't have cameras set up, so there'd be no evidence of my murder.

Even though my cautious nature recoils from this midnight meeting, a larger part of me wants to hear what Bradley has to say. After all, his speech tonight—including the bit about Chloe—seemed surprisingly sincere.

I decide to go to the meeting, but put some precautions in place first. I shoot off a text to Seth, giving him a recap of my current situation and attaching a screenshot of Bradley's message. I tell Seth to forward our conversations to the authorities if I don't send a follow up text by morning, and to look after Chloe in my absence. Then, I forward our conversation to Carson. Carson will show Eliana, and Eliana will make Seth follow through. Seth Balor won't do me any favors for free, but he's helpless when it comes to his girl.

In the off chance that I end up swimming with the fishes tonight, Bradley will get put under a microscope, and Chloe will be taken care of. That's enough for me. I brush a kiss over Chloe's forehead, get dressed in dark clothes, grab a small switchblade from my suitcase and tuck it into the pockets of my slacks, then quietly exit my villa.

Outside, the sky is bright with millions of glittering stars—a view that's rarely seen in America, thanks to the endless pollution. As much as I'd like to take Chloe out here right now for some stargazing, I keep my eyes on the path before me as I make my way to the restaurant.

The courtyard in front of the restaurant has been stripped of all the circular tables that were set up for dinner. Only the rectangular table beside the fountain remains. Bradley sits at the center of it, a laptop open in front of him, a phone lit up beside it, and a tumbler of dark liquor cradled in his hand. He doesn't look up at my approach, merely waves at the chair beside him with his free hand.

"Mason Sieger," he greets. "Thank you for coming."

As I sink into the available seat, Bradley shuts his laptop and turns his full attention to me.

"To what do I owe this pleasure?" I question mildly.

Bradley smiles thinly. "It's come to my attention that the girl who's going to become my stepdaughter in less than twenty-four hours has been experiencing difficulties on Greywood's campus. Difficulties that are *extremely* troubling." He takes a sip from his tumbler, then sets it on the table. "I've also found out that you are aware of these difficulties."

Unsure of where this is going or what Bradley's angle is, I incline my head. "That is correct."

"My question to you is simple, then," Bradley goes on conversationally. "Why the *fuck* have you not made me aware of her problems?"

I blink slowly, taking a beat to try to read him. He could be lying his ass off in a ploy to make himself look innocent, but I don't think he is. I decide to roll with the conversation and see where it takes me. "Why would you *want* to be made aware? You didn't know anything about Chloe until she was thrust under your nose over the winter holidays."

Unless you're the one who hired someone to make her miserable—then I'm sure you'd have done your research first. "You've made no effort to create or maintain a relationship with her. You don't appear to have any regard or affection for her."

"I don't have much regard or affection for anyone, save for Chloe's mother. I love Grace very much, and because I love Grace, I also care for the well-being of her daughter. Even if I didn't *like* Chloe, I'd still have a sense of duty to the family I'm creating. If Chloe's in trouble, it's my responsibility to help resolve it."

This is... unexpected. Bradley speaks with passion and sincerity—there's no hint of deception on his features, merely irritation. The speech he gave earlier tonight was in front of an audience; I couldn't be sure that his words were genuine. What he's saying here and now rings true. I think he actually feels a sense of duty toward Chloe.

"Then why did you never speak to Chloe before Christmas?" I ask him. "Why did you only offer to pay her tuition if she agreed to let you send her out on dates? If you claim to care about her, why did you know *nothing* about her life or achievements until that painful lunch we all suffered through?"

"Tread carefully, boy," Bradley warns quietly. "You come from a respectable family, but you only have so much leeway for your insolence. You want to know the answer to your questions? Grace is the answer. She loves her daughter, but she also struggles with how little she has in common with Chloe."

Chloe's echoed similar sentiments to me. I've occasionally noticed Grace staring at Chloe with longing in her eyes, as if she *wants* to connect with her daughter but doesn't know how to and isn't willing to put in the effort to find out what it'd take.

"Have you ever considered that Chloe is a painful reminder to her mother? Grace loves me, but she also loved her first husband *dearly.*

One day he was home for dinner every night, the next, he was in a closed-coffin burial because his body was too fucking disfigured for an open casket. Chloe is a living, breathing reminder of her loss; combine that with Grace's free-spirited nature, and it is a recipe for disaster." He inhales a deep breath, cracking his neck. "I've been seeing Grace for years, as you know. For some time, I wasn't sure if marrying her was the right path because of her problems with her daughter. Eventually, my love for her left no other option. I've offered to get to know Chloe many times. Christ, Sieger, who do you think signed the bills on Chloe's school and extracurricular activities? Who do you think paid for her *dance classes?* I didn't pay for her university education because Grace insisted that the college fund her late husband left behind was more than sufficient. When I found out that wasn't the case, I offered to help."

I try not to show my surprise; I had no idea Bradley paid for Chloe's high school and dance classes. *Chloe* didn't know about his involvement, either. He could be lying, but surely he knows that I can verify his words within hours—all signs point to him telling the truth.

"I don't know Chloe well for the simple fact that Grace never thought to properly introduce us. I've only met her a few times in passing. Now that circumstances are shifting, it's my responsibility to remedy that." Bradley shakes his head. "Jesus, Mason, why the fuck would I book a villa for the two of you if I didn't care for Chloe? I don't particularly like you, which is why I initially pushed Chloe to allow me to set her up on a few outings with suitable young men, but I do respect her choice now that she's made it."

Much of my suspicion toward Bradley recedes with his explanation and genuine indignation. He appears downright *offended* that I dared question his sense of duty toward Chloe.

Bradley clears his throat and shakes his head. "Enough of that. You're here to tell me everything you know about what's been going on around Greywood campus, and then I am going to take over whatever half-assed investigation you've been running."

"No," I disagree. "If you want to be read in, I'll read you in, but you will not take over. I'm open to combining resources to find the root of the problem, but I won't tell you shit if you try to push me out."

Bradley's jaw flexes as he stares at me. "What exactly do you want from Chloe, Mason? From what I've heard, the two of you are living together, and you seem to be... attached to her. What's the plan in the long run? You're graduating in a few short months, what then? Are you serious about her?"

I let out a puff of laughter. *Serious* is a mild way of describing my intentions toward Chloe; I've contemplated impregnating her just to ensure that she'd never be able to leave me. The thought still bounces around my mind each time I see her take one of the birth control pills she was prescribed at Greywood's student clinic. Since she seems amenable to extending our relationship, I work to hold myself in check. We'll get around to having kids eventually; there's no need to rush so long as we're together.

"I want nothing *from* Chloe, but I do want everything *with* her," I say with complete honesty. "I'm in love with her. I want to protect her, provide for her, support her, and build a life with her."

I can tell Bradley's taken aback by my assertion, but he doesn't dispute it. He just stares at me for a while, perhaps gauging my sincerity. I let him look, willing him to see that I mean every word. I've never cared about anyone like I care for Chloe; I've never felt more *right* about supporting another person. I never thought I'd *enjoy* supporting someone, both emotionally and physically. I'm proud to know how to calm Chloe down when anxiety gets the best of her. I like everything about her; her clinginess when she's anxious, her cuddliness the rest of the time, how goddamn *adorable* she is. We're the perfect example of opposites attracting—my pieces fit hers seamlessly.

"Well, then," Bradley says. "I'd offer you my condolences for succumbing to that horrible disease called love, but I'm terminally ill with it as well. Tell me what you know, and we'll put our heads together to figure out next steps."

I spend a long time staring at him in silence, thinking on whether or not I should trust him. He's given me facts that can easily be checked, such as paying for Chloe's high school and dance classes; if I find any discrepancies, he'll be back to being prime suspect, but... for some reason, my instincts push me to trust him. After a long moment, I give a nod, then spend the next half hour explaining the details of Chloe's situation. I tell Bradley about what Stuart did to Chloe, and the fact that he was hired to torment her. I also provide him with a vague outline of my general pool of suspects, and freely admit that Bradley himself was a suspect up until a few minutes ago. That makes him chuckle.

Once I'm done, I ask, "How did you find out about Chloe's issues on campus?"

"I have resources everywhere, and I've been taking a closer look at Chloe recently."

I have no doubt that Bradley is a *very* resourceful man, so I nod. "Tell me, who would be at the top of *your* suspect list?"

Bradley tilts his head from side to side. "Stuart could've been hired by a fellow student at Greywood University who has a bone to pick with Chloe, though I doubt it. My understanding is she mostly keeps to herself."

"I vetted the students on campus," I tell him. "Nothing came up."

He gives a curt nod. "There are people who know about Chloe through Grace or me, who knew about her before she debuted at the Christmas party. I'm not sure why they'd want to scare her away from Greywood, but I'll do research on my end, and I expect you'll continue doing research on yours. We'll keep in contact to discuss. Clearly, we both have an interest in Chloe's well-being."

"More than can be said for her own mother," I comment.

Bradley gives me a warning look. "Grace is complicated. She loves her daughter, but she doesn't *like* her daughter for reasons that could be difficult for some to understand. That's no longer going to be a problem; I'll work on creating some closeness within our family, before it starts to expand."

I purse my lips. "While you do that, maybe consider the fact that you've also hurt Chloe," I advise.

Bradley frowns. "How do you mean? I've been nothing but cordial to her."

"In the one recent interaction you had with her, you were *controlling* of her," I retort. "You tried to dictate her dating life and held her tuition over her head so she'd fall in line. That might seem fine to you, but it wasn't to her, *or* to me. Your offer made it seem like her only value to you was as a bargaining chip. I appreciate your willingness to help me figure out what's going on around her, but if you want Chloe to be part of your family, *start acting like it*," I emphasize. I won't tolerate anyone hurting Chloe.

Bradley considers me in silence for several moments, mulling over my words. Finally, he gives a small incline of his head. "I'll see you tomorrow, Mason," he says.

I tap the table twice. "See you then."

Chapter Thirty-Four

Mason

I return to my villa enveloped in a fog of thoughtfulness and mild confusion. It's difficult to reconcile my preexisting notions of Bradley with the man I just had a conversation with. Beforehand, I saw him as an unnecessarily wealthy asshole who might harbor enough resentment for Chloe to harm her. Now, I can see that *despite* his wealth, Bradley Rodgers has admirable core values—ones that are often absent in most people who share his tax bracket.

Bradley cares about Chloe simply because she's the offspring of his fiancée. He doesn't demean Grace or see her as lesser because of her quirks and issues—instead, he seems to love her enough to be not only what she needs, but also what her daughter needs.

The varying dynamics required in different relationships puzzle me. Grace seems to need a guiding hand to keep her on the right path, perhaps because she never learned to be independent—she married her first husband when she was very young. Chloe does not need to be guided; instead, she needs support to achieve her dreams, and a calm, dependable anchor for her anxieties. *My* mother requires space and a blind eye to her affairs, much like my father. As for Raegan and Amara's parents... well, they're a shitshow of such epic proportions that it's probably best they spend as little time together as possible.

Once I've locked the villa door behind me, I make my way into the kitchen, intending to grab myself a stiff drink and then return to cuddling Chloe. I'm surprised to find Chloe standing at the kitchen counter, meticulously frosting a neat brownie slice. In front of her stand three glass bowls, each containing frostings of different colors—black, white, and blue. Her brows are furrowed as she focuses on her task, eyes narrowed in concentration.

She glances up at me, then returns her attention to the intricate, flower-shaped design she's creating with the white and blue frosting, meticulously swiping a butter knife across the surface of the brownie.

I study her for several moments. Her eyes are a bit puffy from crying earlier, but aside from that, she seems fine. *Good*, even, despite the heavy conversation we had. It's profoundly relieving to see that telling her story didn't cause her pain—instead, it seems to have lifted a weight off her shoulders. I'm struck anew by her bravery and courage, her unwavering ability to continue forward despite the trials that her life has thrown at her.

"Hey," she murmurs. "You were out late." The unspoken question of where I was hangs in the air.

"I got a midnight summons from Bradley," I say, opening the pre-stocked liquor cabinet and withdrawing a decent bottle of bourbon.

Chloe's knife clatters to the counter. "*What?*"

After pouring myself a drink, I give her an outline of my late-night discussion with Bradley. Once I'm done, Chloe blinks several times before slowly picking up the frosting knife, her frown deepening as she gazes at her brownie.

"Oh," she says. "Well, that's pretty weird."

"Understatement," I grunt.

"Did he seem sincere?" she asks, adding a few strategic swipes of blue frosting to her brownie.

"From what I could see, yes," I reply. "Surprisingly so. I think I'm going to put my head together with his to look for whoever hired Stuart."

"If you think you can trust him," she murmurs. She adds a perfect black dot to the center of the flower, then sets aside her knife and places the brownie on a plate.

"Do you?" I ask.

She shrugs. "I don't really know him. I didn't like how he behaved when we had lunch together, but his controlling nature could be a byproduct of his job and the world he lives in. To be fair, I didn't like you all that much at the beginning of our relationship; you were certainly an acquired taste."

"And they say true love is dead," I quip. "I'm glad you did acquire a taste for me. It would've been quite the challenge to keep you with me if you'd never started liking me back."

"They have a word for that, Mason, it's called *kidnapping*."

"Don't tempt me," I reply, setting my empty tumbler down on the counter and stepping up behind Chloe. I brace my hands on the countertop, bracketing her waist and effectively caging her in. She doesn't stiffen or become flighty like she once would've, which pleases me. "Nice frosting skills," I say, admiring her brownie. A canvas of black frosting gives way to the textured, slightly raised white petals of a flower, embellished with blue lines that blend seamlessly with the petals. "That actually looks professional."

"You already got laid tonight, you don't need to keep flattering me."

I chuckle, dipping my head to press a kiss to her neck. "It's a genuine compliment, babe. The brownie looks beautiful and delectable. Almost as edible as you."

Chloe softens, casting me a gentle smile over her shoulder. I lean down to steal a kiss before she turns back to the baked good.

"I enjoyed painting when I was younger, even though I wasn't very good at it. My dad would paint whenever he could find the time, and he taught me. He loved the versatility of oil paints, and he always incorporated texture to add dimension to his art. I still have a painting he made for me in my childhood bedroom, a canvas filled with flowers, their petals raised just like this," she explains. "It's fun to replicate some of his techniques when I bake. Frosting isn't the same as oil paint, but it's both pretty *and* edible. I wish I had more time to bake."

"I'd have loved to meet your dad," I tell her sincerely. "He sounds like an incredible man, and he did an outstanding job raising you."

Chloe snorts. "Flatterer."

"Why are you up so late?" I ask her, rubbing a hand up and down her arm. "Or early, as it were."

She shrugs. "Bad dream."

"Was it about..." I trail off, guilt twisting my chest. If she had a nightmare because I encouraged her to talk about a painful part of her past, I'll never forgive myself.

"No," she says. "Not about that. I was being chased by a demon, actually. Woke up startled. You weren't there, I assumed you were out on a walk or plotting revenge, so I decided to distract myself."

Thank god.

I rest my chin on her shoulder as she cuts the brownie into two pieces, then spins around to offer me one half. Pushing the brownie plate aside, I hoist her up and seat her on the counter before once again caging her with a hand on either side of her hips. She raises her eyebrows at the swift change in position but doesn't protest as she holds the brownie up to my lips. "Open. You ate so many cookies earlier that you didn't even bother to try the brownies."

I plant a hand on her thigh and part my lips, allowing her to feed me a bite. Rich dark chocolate goodness melts on my tongue, perfectly fluffy and fudgy, complemented by a bite of vanilla from the frosting.

"Holy *fuck*, that's good," I say with a full mouth.

Chloe smiles, eyes glittering with pleasure. "Thank you. I used to bake a lot more in my free time. I didn't have many friends in high school—I never had enough time to build and sustain friendships. My mom wasn't home much, so I often found myself alone with a few hours of free time. When I wasn't babysitting or studying, I'd bake and bring whatever I made to my next babysitting gig or to a nearby animal shelter."

"For the dogs?" I ask, nodding at the brownie for another bite. I could pick it up myself, but I like having Chloe feed me.

"God no, they can't have chocolate. For the staff and volunteers who kept that place running. Wherever I thought the baked goods would be appreciated."

My eyes nearly roll into the back of my head with the next bite. Once I've swallowed, I say, "You're *absolutely* wife material, just so you know. This is only making me want to keep you more. You're amazing with kids, your brownies are to die for, and you make this world seem a whole lot less shitty."

Chloe's cheeks turn a delicate pink at the compliment, and she looks down shyly. I like her shyness as much as I like everything else about her; it's utterly endearing. She's adorable. I'm determined to do everything I can to keep her. She brightens the world around her with her wit, personality, beauty, and even baked goods.

"Just so you know, I'm a disaster in the kitchen," she admits, looking back up and offering me another bite. "I can't cook for shit, I never learned how to. Baking is a science, though, and I like science. Once you understand the functions of the ingredients, it's easy to bring them together into something like a pastry or cake. Cooking requires more creativity, and creativity is not my strong suit."

"Hmm. Well, I guess that when we get married, I'll cook the dinner, and you can make the dessert. How does that sound?"

"Not bad, *if* we ever get married," Chloe says, offering me the last piece of brownie before picking up the other half for herself. I pluck it from her hand, wanting to feed her just like she fed me.

When I hold it up to her lips, she frowns. "I'm not a child, I can feed myself."

I arch an eyebrow. "Does that mean I *am* a child since you fed me?"

A mischievous smile pulls at her lips. "You're definitely a manchild sometimes."

"Could a true manchild do the things to you that I can?" I query.

Chloe presses her lips together, looking down, that adorable blush making an appearance again. "Come on, Chlo, let me feed you. If you really don't want to, I won't force you, but I'd like to. I enjoy taking care of you."

I place two fingers beneath her chin and use them to tilt her head up. She parts her lips, allowing me to feed her a bite, then hums with pleasure. "Oh, that *did* turn out well. We should bring some slices over to Raegan and Amara's villa, I think they'll enjoy the brownies. Of course, nothing can match Raegan's love for cookies, but hopefully the brownies will be a close second."

"I think the girls would like seeing us regardless of what we bring," I counter. "I'm pretty sure Amara's almost as in love with you as I am."

Chloe stiffens, eyes widening. Everything inside me tenses as I internally berate myself for letting that slip. I hadn't intended to tell her that I love her until we were closer, until I was reasonably certain that she's also in love with me. I know she *cares* for me right now, but that doesn't mean she loves me. Our relationship is only a few months old, and before we formed our new arrangement, she was determined to fight me at every turn.

I don't bother retracting my words now that they're out. I *am* in love with this girl. I didn't fall for her immediately; our story isn't one of love at first sight, though it was certainly *lust* at first sight on my end. The love, however, was a slow build. It started out as intrigue, an emotion that I don't usually feel toward people. Then it progressed into a deep interest with a looming possessiveness and a feeling of absolute disgust at the thought of her with anyone other than me. The more I got to know Chloe, the more I understood the way her mind works and glimpsed the *kindness* and *goodness* that live in her very soul, the more invested I became in there being an *us*. At this point I'm a complete goner for her, to the extent that there's no line I wouldn't cross to keep her.

"Oh," Chloe breathes out. "Um..."

"You don't have to say anything," I assure her. "*I* didn't even mean to say anything, it just slipped out. I'm not going to take it back, though, because that would be a lie. I do love you, Chlo, and I don't expect you to feel the same way yet, but I hope that you will someday."

Chloe swallows, nodding. "I can't say that I love you, but I can say that I care about you a lot, and I'm definitely starting to see a future for us. I also think there's a good chance that I *will* end up in love with you, which irritates the shit out of me, because I was never supposed to even like you."

That's more than I hoped for from her, so I'll take it. For now. "I'm gonna make you fall in love with me," I inform her. "It's inevitable. You might as well just accept your fate now."

Her lips quirk. "You know, I don't doubt you."

CHAPTER THIRTY-FIVE

Chloe

The wedding takes place on my third afternoon in Italy. The ceremony is held on a wooden patio perched atop a pristine beach with stunning white sands. The sun shines brightly, its rays reflected off the cerulean waves that lap lazily at the shore. Sitting beside Mason in the fourth row of wooden chairs on the bride's side of the aisle, I find my attention drawn by the ocean more so than Mom and Bradley's nuptials.

There was a time in my life when seeing the four bridesmaids standing beside my mother would've hurt. Both tradition and general decency dictate that my mom offer me a spot as a bridesmaid, and a few years ago, being cut out of her wedding would've brought tears to my eyes. Now, I'm mostly desensitized to my mother's utter lack of regard for me. There's still a faint pang of pain in my chest, but it's a hollow ache, barely noticeable.

Mason looks unreasonably dashing in his tuxedo. His hand rests on my leg, just over the stretch of thigh exposed by the slit in my green chiffon dress. He appears bored with the ceremony—every so often, he leans over to whisper gossip about one of the guests in my ear.

Amara sits on the other side of me, with Raegan on her right. Little Amara tried to climb onto my lap when we first arrived for the ceremony. In a rare bout of attentiveness, Laura hissed at her daughter to sit in her own seat. Amara teared up at that, but her tears were silent, and she seemed to perk up when I offered her my hand. Now, she's fallen asleep, her body leaning against my side. I ignored Laura's glare when I wrapped my arm around Amara to keep her from falling over.

After what feels like an eternity, the time comes for vows. Bradley delivers a thoughtful, heartfelt speech about spending the rest of his days building a worthy life and a beautiful family with my mother. Mom, crying, gives a much shorter speech about her love for Bradley and dedication to bringing light and happiness into his work-intensive life.

They share a passionate kiss, and then the newlyweds make their way down the petal-strewn aisle and head to the beach, where they'll have their wedding pictures taken. I don't get invited to the photos, which doesn't surprise me—though Mason seems to genuinely believe that Bradley intends to try to make me a part of their new family, I see no point in getting my hopes up. I follow the rest of the guests as they start to flit back to the resort's restaurant, where the reception will be taking place.

Buffet-style tables line the walls of the restaurant, and additional ones are set up on the edges of the outdoor courtyard. The selection of food is vast; there's a diverse array of delectable traditional Italian dishes, with a few American and even French ones thrown into the mix. Pastas, pizzas, craft hamburgers, savory souffles, cream soups—the sheer variety is enough to make my head spin.

Raegan and Amara's nanny is present for the reception, so I'm not overly concerned about the girls. I do, however, get a touch nervous when Mason's father approaches us.

"Mason," he greets.

"Dad," Mason responds.

Grant trains his gaze on me. "Chloe, I'm sorry we haven't had a chance to talk the last few days. I understand you've been keeping my nieces good company."

"Better than their parents," I agree, then nearly slap a hand over my mouth at my rudeness. Perhaps the deliberate neglect I've observed during this trip is getting to me, or it could be that the monotony of the wedding has simply bored me into impropriety. Whatever the case, my usual filter seems to be absent.

"My apologies," I quickly add on. "The time difference hasn't been kind to my sleep schedule, and I'm spending my limited free time working ahead in my classes for next term."

"Ah," Mason's dad replies, eyeing me carefully, as if he doesn't quite know what to make of me. I don't think he *dis*likes me, but I'm not sure he likes me, either. I do know that he likes the idea of a marriage between me and Mason, as it will provide him with a permanent connection to Bradley Rodgers.

I don't like Grant very much; from what I've heard, he's been more present in Mason's life than most parents in the Sieger family are with their children, but Mason was still raised by nannies and in boarding schools.

"Well, it's good to hear you're still working hard. I hope that Mason's following your example," Grant says.

Mason stiffens beside me; I take his hand in mine, twining our fingers. His father tracks the gesture with narrowed eyes, tilting his head to the side as he watches us. "Mason's an extraordinarily hard worker," I say firmly. "He doesn't have as many classes as I do, but he's at the top of the business program. He does excellent work in your firm, clocking in long hours at the end of every school day. Correct me if I'm wrong, but by all appearances he's a remarkable progeny to carry on your legacy."

A tense silence ensues, and I begin to second-guess the vigor behind my words. It probably isn't the best idea to be so forward with a man like Grant Sieger—he has the means to crush me without lifting a finger. I don't even think that being the stepdaughter of Bradley Rodgers could protect me if Grant decides to destroy me. I swallow nervously, but force myself to maintain eye contact, resisting the powerful urge to shrivel under Grant's withering stare.

"You're not wrong," Grant finally says. Mason releases a nearly imperceptible breath of relief; *my* breath of relief is much less covert. Grant's eyes warm by the faintest margin, and I think I might've just earned a bit of his respect. "Do keep an eye on him, Chloe, laziness can strike at any time. You appear to be an excellent candidate to keep him on track. Mason," Grant turns to face his son, "hold onto this one. She might actually make your life bearable." With those words, he takes his leave.

I turn to Mason. "I'm not sure if I just made a mortal enemy of your father or if I can sleep safely tonight."

Mason chuckles, lips quirking. "You can definitely sleep safely. My dad likes you as much as he's capable of liking anyone; you're safe from him." He pulls me closer by my hand, smiling down at me, pleasure glimmering in his eyes. "I like it a lot when you defend me. I'm going to reward you later."

"No, you're not—we have a flight to catch tonight," I remind him.

Mason shrugs. "It's a private plane. There's a bedroom. You told me that you've finished all the work you possibly can for next term, so we have time. I wanted you to join the mile-high club on our way here, but you were being stubborn."

"I was doing a chemistry assignment, and then I fell asleep," I remind Mason. "That's not stubbornness; it's exhaustion."

"All the same, I *highly* recommend you become a member of that club sooner rather than later," Mason says, snaking an arm around my waist.

I frown. "Are you speaking from personal experience? Are *you* already a member?" For some reason, the idea of him sleeping with someone else bothers me.

"I like the jealousy in your tone. It's sexy as fuck."

"It's not jealousy—"

"I promise to forget all my previous forays in that particular club. I'll be like a virgin all over again, ready for you to ravish," Mason goes on.

I sigh, shaking my head. "You're insufferable, you know that?"

"I think the regular orgasms I give you make up for my behavior. If you want, you can chastise me like a naughty schoolboy." When I pull a face, Mason chuckles. "Or perhaps *you'd* like to be chastised like a naughty schoolgirl. Then rewarded and praised for taking your punishment so beautifully."

My nipples pebble in response to his words, and my core begins to pulse. You need to stop," I whisper. "We're in public."

Mason abruptly releases me and steps back, smoothing a hand over the lapel of his jacket. "My apologies, I wouldn't want you to get *too* flustered. I'll save that for later."

I pat his chest. "You still need to talk to your dad about whatever's going on with Jason and Laura, have him check on the welfare of Raegan and Amara. And *I* need to eat something. Someone distracted me with sex this morning, preventing me from eating breakfast."

Mason shrugs. "What can I say? *I* was pretty hungry, and a man's gotta eat." He lets out a faint *oomph* when a small body crashes into his; Raegan smiles up at him, arms wrapped around his waist.

"Do you still have some of those cookies?" she asks, looking between us.

"No, Sanity-Eater, we sent them home with you, remember?" Mason pauses. "Rae, don't tell me you've already eaten *all of them?* There were at least twenty."

Raegan shrugs. "I shared some with Amara."

As if summoned by her name, Amara toddles through the crowd of people, and promptly wraps her arms around my leg, blinking up at me.

"Where's your nanny?" Mason asks the two of them.

"Ditched her a few minutes ago. She was trying to read me a really boring book," Raegan explains.

Mason thinks for a moment. "You mean the Bible? The one she's always carrying around?"

"I think so," Raegan agrees. "All the characters have boring names and say weird things. It puts me right to sleep. So... can we make more cookies?" The question is directed at me, paired with wide, hazel doe-eyes that are impossible to resist.

"We don't have time to bake anything new, but there are some leftover brownies," I tell her. "If you eat a good meal, maybe I'll drop some off with you before we leave tonight."

Amara tugs on the skirt of my dress, signaling that she wants to be held; I lift her in my arms, settling her on my hip. She promptly hides her face in my shoulder, clinging to me. Remembering that the little girl is not comfortable in large crowds, I tighten my hold on her and press a kiss to her head.

Watching us, Mason remarks, "I *really* want to knock you up."

"Don't you dare," I warn.

"What does knocking someone up mean?" Raegan asks cheerfully.

I wince, then give Mason a pointed stare. "Yeah, Mason, what does that mean?"

"It means playing sports," Mason replies smoothly. "You know, knocking around a ball."

"Oh," Raegan says, frowning. "Then why is it knocking *up* instead of knocking *around*? That sounds weird."

Mason shrugs. "Turn of phrase."

"Well, it should be knocking around," Raegan says decisively.

"Okay, Sanity-Eater, let's get you back to your nanny—"

"*No!*" Raegan says emphatically. "I'm sick of her reading, I wanna hang out with you guys."

Mason gives me a questioning look; I smile and nod. "I don't think the little one is letting go of me any time soon, and I'm totally okay with that. We can eat with them."

"Alright," Mason agrees. "You fix a plate for the two of you, since Amara seems to only want to eat from your plate. I'll take care of me and Raegan."

Nuzzling Amara's hair, I ask, "Can we keep her?"

Mason chuckles. "Unfortunately not, but we can make some of our own."

"How?" Raegan demands. "How can you make another person? Nobody will tell me."

That's a question I've had to answer many times during babysitting gigs—children are surprisingly curious to find out where they come from and how adults create them. "Well, we'd start out by writing a letter to a stork," I explain. Amara lifts her head from my shoulder as I pick up a large plate from the nearest buffet table, surveying the food options.

"What's a stork?" Raegan asks, following behind Mason as he grabs two plates and starts loading them with food.

"It's a bird," I answer. "There's a whole organization of them, kind of like a business. I write to one of the storks in that business, and they decide if I'm ready to have a small human of my own. Then, they do one of two things; put that small baby in my belly so it can nest until it's time for birth or, more commonly, a stork will put a baby in a basket and fly it to me."

"Oh," Raegan says. Her focus quickly shifts to Mason, and she starts demanding that he get her more of this or less of that. I load my plate with a little bit of pasta, chicken, and a few side dishes, hoping that Amara will enjoy the selection.

"Chloe! There you are, darling." My mom's voice rings out just as I turn away from the buffet table. I look up to find her and Bradley making their way toward me. Mom looks splendid in her diaphanous white wedding gown, beaming brightly and clutching Bradley's arm. I suppress a sigh as I paste a smile on my face, hoping that this interaction will be a little less awkward than our other most recent ones.

CHAPTER THIRTY-SIX

M om and Bradley stop right in front of Mason and me, and for a moment, I'm struck silent as I stare at my mother. She looks stunning in her billowy white gown, and her smile is so incredibly happy, it brings warmth to my chest. Despite our strained relationship, I still love her and wish for her to find joy—I can't begrudge her now that I can see she's truly found it. Bradley also looks to be very happy, and perhaps more importantly, he seems *content* as he stands with my mom.

"Who is your little... friend?" Mom asks, peeking at Amara, who once again hides in my shoulder.

"Mason's cousin, Amara," I explain. I nod to Raegan, who's hiding behind Mason's legs. "That's her sister, Raegan. We've all become close."

"How lovely," Mom says, a genuine, warm smile tipping up her lips.

"Rae, why don't you go find us a table?" Mason asks, turning and handing her one of the plates he holds.

Raegan doesn't need to be told twice. Apparently, the outspoken girl is shy when it comes to certain strangers. She dashes into the crowd, and I spot her making her way to the exit, presumably to grab us a table in the courtyard.

Amara slowly lifts her head and gazes at my mom, curiosity and interest lighting up her sparkling blue eyes.

"Hi, sweetheart," Mom greets with a wide smile. "My goodness, you are just the cutest thing in the world, aren't you? You remind me so much of my Chloe when she was your age. Glimmering, inquisitive eyes."

The warmth and nostalgia in Mom's tone hits me square in my chest, and I almost take a startled step back at the impact. I haven't heard her mention my childhood in many years, and I never expected her to speak about me with such sentimentality.

Amara smiles shyly, and Mom beams at her, reaching out to give her hair a stroke before turning her attention to me. There's something wistful in her eyes as our gazes meet, almost as if I'm a young girl again, one who adored both her parents and was adored by them in return. Before Dad died and Mom tried to forget about him, and me.

Mom delicately clears her throat. "How did you like the ceremony?"

"It was beautiful," I say amiably. "Very well thought out and executed. This reception is also great." A strange awkwardness overtakes me, and the air between me and Mom almost seems to come alive with memories of the connection we once shared.

"We just wanted to drop in and say hello before we're swept up in formalities for the rest of the afternoon and evening," Bradley says, offering me a nod. "I also want to express how happy I am to have you in my family, Chloe. You're an exceptional and bright young woman, and I'm proud to have you as a stepdaughter."

I blink a few times, taken aback. "That's very kind of you, thank you."

Bradley nods, gazing at me for a few beats. "We're off to our honeymoon tonight, but I'll be in touch. Pick up when I call, I'd like to get to know you better." He turns to leave, taking Mom with him.

I glance at Mason, then lean closer to whisper in his ear. "That was weird."

Mason offers me a half-smile. "Not weird, Chlo, that was an olive branch. Keep an open mind and see where things go." His expression hardens. "But if either of them hurt you, I'll personally cut them off."

I press a kiss to his jaw. "I love your protectiveness."

Amara tugs my hair, drawing my attention back to her, and points at the plate I'm holding. "Alright," I say with a chuckle. "Let's go find your sister and eat."

Dinner is pleasant enough; I end up sharing a table with Laura and Jason, neither of whom notice their daughters. Amara eats a few bites from our shared plate, then cuddles up to me. After a while, Laura and Jason's impressive ability to ignore their own flesh and blood begins to irritate me. Their daughters are adorable, beautiful, and so much fun to be around. Amara is a cuddle bug with the sweetest smile and giggle, and Raegan's boundless energy and ability to talk nonstop is endlessly amusing. They're both wonderful and worthy of love—how are their parents so blind to that?

Jason flits off to speak with guests half an hour into the reception, while Laura stays behind, loudly complaining about a myriad of things.

When she gets up to refill her wine glass, grumbling about having to serve her own alcohol, I call out to her. "Laura, would you like to spend some time with Amara and Raegan? They're delightful, and I think they could use a mother's touch."

Laura pauses by my seat, casting me a condescending look down the ridge of her fake nose. Mason tenses beside me, planting a possessive hand on my thigh, silently warning Laura to tread carefully. Amara's grip on me tightens, and she buries her head in the crook of my neck, hiding from her own mother.

"They have a nanny for that," Laura says sharply. Something resembling hatred flashes through her perfect blue eyes as she regards me. It almost feels as though she's personally offended at my presence here, despite this being *my* mother's wedding. "If you're trying to get close to the girls for money, it won't work. I suppose I could pay you for the hours you've spent with them, but it's not like you need the cash with your new stepfather."

My head jerks back in affront; Mason says lowly, "Laura, that's enough."

Laura scoffs. "Adorable how you protect your little girlfriend. If you two want to play the babysitters, go ahead, but don't you *dare* criticize my parenting style."

I'm tempted to say, "*what parenting style?*" Instead, I try to backpedal, not wanting to fight with Laura in front of her daughters. "I'm not criticizing you—"

"*Right,*" she says sarcastically. "You're just holding *my* daughter in *your* peasant hands."

Jason, standing a few feet away from the table and scrolling through his phone, looks up at his wife's rudeness. He's a pudgy man with a suit jacket that strains at the seams, and despite being on his fourth cocktail, his decorum far surpasses Laura's.

"That's enough, Laura," he says tiredly. "Leave my nephew and his girlfriend be, there's no point in throwing a tantrum."

Upper lip curling, Laura rolls her eyes and walks away. Jason meets my eyes, offering me a vaguely apologetic smile. "Don't mind her," he says. "She's just used to being the center of attention."

I hold back a mean quip that threatens to escape, instead sealing my lips and nodding. I don't bother asking Jason if he wants to spend time with his daughters—I don't want his inevitable refusal to hurt the girls.

I glance over at Raegan, whose arms are crossed over her chest, her expression pensive and downturned. Amara continues holding me tightly, her breaths shaky. I didn't mean for them to hear their mother's blatant rejection; I certainly won't subject them to the same thing from their father.

After a while, I manage to coax Amara into eating a few more bites of dinner. She dutifully opens her mouth and allows me to feed her, nodding when I ask her if she likes the food.

Once we've all finished eating and dusk has splashed across the night's sky, Mason and I take Raegan and Amara back to our villa. We're already packed and ready for our trip back to Greywood, our luggage standing neatly in front of the door. I wander to the kitchen with Amara propped on my hip and Raegan following behind me, then pick up one of the plastic containers where Mason placed the leftover brownies and hold it up. Mason, leaned against the kitchen doorway, watches with a faint smile.

"Share with your sister, okay?" I tell Raegan.

"Yes!" She jumps up and down with excitement, beaming. The skirt of her dress rises with the movement, and I notice a splotchy, black and blue bruise on her thigh.

"Oh my gosh," I say, startled. The bruise is yellow around the edges and appears painfully swollen. "Are you okay, Raegan?"

Raegan instantly stills, smoothing down the skirt of her dress, her energy shifting from excited to nervous. My brows draw together as I regard the sudden change in her personality, and an unpleasant feeling niggles at my chest. A strange intuition that I can't quite place yet.

"Yeah," she says. "I fell while I was playing with Amara yesterday."

Her words are convincing, but I don't think I'm getting the full story. I look to Mason, who's frowning at his cousin. Since Raegan's facing away from him, he couldn't have seen the bruise, but he still looks concerned. "You want me to take a look at it, Rae?" he asks.

"No!" she snaps. "It's just a little bruise. It's fine."

Mason and I exchange an uneasy glance at Raegan's sudden defensiveness, but neither of us say anything. Instead, I give Raegan's hair a quick stroke before handing her the container with brownies. I open my mouth to try to ask about the bruise again; a knock sounds on the door before I can.

"That'll be the nanny," Mason murmurs. "She'll want to take the girls back. They're leaving in the morning."

Sure enough, their nanny waits for the girls at our door. She's an older woman with greying hair and kind eyes. I almost smile when I see the small Bible sticking out of the pocket of her dress. I pass Amara off to her; she accepts the little girl and also takes a hold of Raegan's hand. Amara stirs, frowning, and reaches for me; the nanny thanks me and Mason before hurrying off. The last thing I see as they disappear down the path is Amara's look of sheer betrayal and despair, her eyes welling with tears as she reaches for me.

"Mason," I say. "Something's fucked up with that family. Their mom is bitter, their dad doesn't give a shit, and their nannies are switched out too often for them to form healthy attachments." I turn to look at him. "The bruise on Raegan's thigh doesn't look accidental, like she tripped and fell. If it were a bruise on her knee or shins that was paired with a scrape, I could believe it, but it was on her thigh, where her dresses always cover her."

Mason's lips thin. "She could've bumped into something."

I shake my head. "You don't believe that."

"No, I don't," he agrees, taking my hand in his and closing the door. "I couldn't get my dad alone during the reception, but I'm planning on calling him once we're back at Greywood to see if he'll force Jason and Laura to get their shit together. I'll also have him look into whatever might've caused Raegan's bruise." He sighs. "I wish I could handle this myself, but I don't hold anywhere near as much sway in the family as Dad does."

I lean against him, resting my hand on his chest and head on his shoulder, silently offering my support.

He wraps his arm around me. "There's so much shit going on, and I feel like I'm failing everyone. You're not safe until we figure out who hired Stuart, and there's something wrong in my extended family."

I wind my arms around his neck. "Don't take on responsibility that isn't yours. You can't control everything, Mase. You're doing what you can for me, but you're not omniscient or all-powerful. Certain things take time. As for your cousins... since your dad has the role of the family patriarch, it's *his* job to make sure things are running smoothly with his brother. Give him a push in the right direction." I rise on my toes and kiss his neck. "Be nice to yourself. You're a wonderful boyfriend and cousin."

Mason kisses the top of my head. "Everything seems brighter when you're around. You make me feel... *whole*. Complete, and capable of anything. Even world domination."

Smiling, I suggest, "Let's hold off on world domination for now."

Chapter Thirty-Seven

After returning to Greywood, Mason and I spend the remainder of spring break having sex, binge-watching TV shows, playing with Loki, and video chatting with his cousins every day.

The night we get back to our apartment, Mason speaks to his father about his concerns regarding Amara and Raegan. Grant subsequently has a serious conversation with Jason, telling him to sort out his family matters and start stepping up as a father. Grant also starts visiting his nieces twice a week to keep a closer eye on them, which earns him a good deal of my respect.

To my surprise, I receive a call from Bradley just a few days after the wedding, while he's on his honeymoon with Mom. Our first conversation is a bit awkward, but he continues calling me every few days, and often, my mom also says hello. As time goes on, my talks with them become easier, almost natural. I begin to trust Bradley's intentions more and more; he seems sincere in his desire to bond as a family.

School resumes all too soon, and I once again find myself swamped with a hyper-busy schedule. Mason and I fall into the same routine we developed the first half of spring semester—we eat breakfast together in the mornings and dinner in the evenings, and we spend every weekend either heading to the mountains or exploring the city.

I meet up with Elia and April twice a week, and they both seem genuinely pleased when I tell them about the developments in my relationship with Mason. Elia cautions me to be careful, as she believes that Mason is a wolf in sheep's clothing. I respond to that by telling her that Mason is a wolf in wolf's clothing—there's nothing sheepish about him—and yet I'm falling for him anyway.

On the last Friday of April, I receive a call from Bradley while I'm sitting beside Mason on our couch, with Loki slumbering away on my lap. I pick up immediately, a small smile curling my lips.

"Hey, Bradley," I greet. "How are you?"

"I'm fine," he replies, his tone unusually terse. "Your mother, on the other hand—"

"What's wrong?" I ask, sitting up straight. "What happened? Is she okay?"

"She's unharmed, but there was a shooting attempt this morning," Bradley replies. "A sniper tried to take her out from afar. Is Mason there?"

"Jesus Christ," I whisper, a shiver of fear creeping down my spine. "Can I talk to her?"

Mason shoots me a questioning look; I wave a hand, unable to focus on him right now.

"She's sleeping at the moment, I'll have her call you when she's up," Bradley responds impatiently. "Chloe, is Mason there? I need to talk to the both of you."

"Yeah, he's next to me. I'll put you on speaker." Nerves churning in my stomach and hands shaking so much I almost drop my phone, I manage to hit the speaker button. "We can both hear you."

"Good. Mason, there was a failed attempt on Grace's life this morning. The would-be shooter was apprehended and interrogated by my security." Bradley pauses. "I was interested to find out that the second-rate assassin works for a mercenary company. He doesn't know who his employer is, but something familiar came up."

Mason slings an arm around me, rubbing my shoulder, trying to soothe my anxiety. "I'm glad Grace is okay. What came up? What happened?"

"Under interrogation, the shooter gave up an account number where payment for the assassination was wired. I had my tech people look at the account and found that the shooter was paid by a shell corporation." Bradley pauses. "The same shell corporation that paid Stuart Croms to terrorize Chloe."

The phone falls from my grip as shock overcomes me; Mason snatches it up, holding it steady while drawing me closer to him. My thoughts whirl at a blinding pace as I try and fail to connect the dots between what Stuart did to me and an *assassin* trying to kill my mother. *What the fuck?*

"You're suggesting that the same person came after both Chloe and Grace by proxy?" Mason asks.

"I'm not suggesting, I'm *stating* that the same person came after both of them," Bradley confirms. "The remaining question is, who has a motive to want Chloe harmed and Grace dead?"

"The only connection I can see between the two of them is you," Mason says quietly. "You're Grace's husband and Chloe's stepfather." His throat clicks as he swallows, glancing at me. "I assume they're both officially your heirs now that you and Grace are married. If all three of you were dead, one of your enemies could launch a hostile takeover of your companies and assets." He blinks slowly. "Or there could be someone else who would have a claim to your assets if you and your heirs were gone—a relative, perhaps."

After a short pause, Bradley says, "Grace and Chloe are my heirs, but Stuart didn't try to kill Chloe, only scare her and run her off campus. And, so far, nobody has tried to kill me."

Mason gives me a squeeze. "Stuart's attacks were escalating. He might've been instructed to kill Chloe later on. As for you, you might have been the final target."

"What did Stuart say when you… questioned him?" Bradley asks.

I snuggle closer to Mason, drawing on his warmth and strength. He presses a kiss to my head before responding to Bradley. "He said that his employer instructed him to shake Chloe up *badly* for the second break in, scare her enough that she'd be desperate to get away from Greywood. He took… liberties when he physically attacked her. By all accounts, Stuart wasn't a very stable person; maybe whoever hired him had hoped that he'd escalate to killing her without prompting. Or maybe they intended to have her killed once she was away from Greywood. I don't know for certain, but what's clear is that you're the connecting link between what's been happening to your wife and stepdaughter. You're one of the richest men in the world, which makes you a natural target. Doesn't it seem likely that there might be people who are desperate to get their hands on your money? Chloe may not have been out in high society when Stuart was first hired to fuck with her, but when we spoke on the night before your wedding, you said that there were people who knew about Chloe before her debut."

Bradley clears his throat. "I'll take a closer look at potential suspects. We'll talk again tomorrow."

"You said you'd do your research the last time we spoke about Chloe's troubles," Mason says sharply. "Look harder, and send me your suspect list. I'd like to do my own digging."

After a long pause, Bradley concedes. "Fine. You'll have the list in a few hours."

"Bradley, I need to see my mom," I say, my voice shaky. "I need to talk to her and make sure she's alright. Can I come visit you?"

Another pause. "Yes, that'd be good for Grace. Come stay with us in New York for the weekend. Mason, you'll come as well—we can talk more in person. I'll send my jet for you in the morning." He hangs up with a resounding click.

Mason sets my phone down beside him, then turns his full attention on me. Without preamble, he pulls me onto his lap. I collapse into him, clutching his shoulders and resting my head on his chest. His theory about someone being after Bradley's money seems plausible, and the fact that my mom, Bradley, and I are all in mortal danger because of it fills me with dread.

"You okay?" Mason asks, resting his chin on my head.

"Not really," I answer honestly. "I'm scared, Mase."

"You know that I'll protect you against anything and everything, right?" he asks. "You don't have to be afraid. You have me, you'll always have me, and I'll always protect you. Yeah?"

I swallow. "Yeah. Thank you. I'm sorry I'm... like this. Annoyingly clingy and perpetually anxious. I don't know why you put up with me."

Mason gives me a light thwack on my ass. I barely feel it through the material of my baggy sweatpants, but his message is clear: stop talking shit about myself.

"Stop," he tells me. "I'd be pretty shaken in your shoes, too. Besides, I love your clinginess. I don't love that you struggle so much with anxiety, but I do love how cuddly you get. I love being able to help you through your worries. I love everything about you, Chloe, so don't you dare talk badly about yourself. That'll get you turned over my knees, pretty girl. You're mine, and I take *excellent* care of my things."

My eyes start to burn. I've never experienced such unreserved acceptance from anyone; not from anyone who *truly* knows me, anyway. It's ironic how our relationship started with me being terrified of Mason, and now I turn to him in times of terror. He's intimidating and forward, but he's also caring, protective, and so loving. At this point, I don't think I can imagine a life for myself without him in it, and I've gone beyond the scope of *just* caring for him.

I tilt my head up to look in his eyes, nerves fluttering in my belly. "I love you too," I tell him. "A lot. I didn't want to, but you gave me no choice. You accept me, you support me, and you make me feel strong and safe."

Mason inhales a quick breath, his lips parting and eyes widening. His hand winds into my hair, cupping my skull with a heartbreaking gentleness.

"You better mean it," he tells me, gaze flicking between my eyes and my lips. "If you love me, the arrangement's over. You're mine, permanently. You don't get to take it back. You don't get to change your mind."

I smile softly, feeling my heart swell. "I know. You're not exactly subtle, Mase, and I might've hated that at first, but now I love it. I love everything about you, even your irritatingly domineering personality, because I know you soften and melt when it comes to me." I bite my lip. "I want to have babies with you. Not now, not any time soon, but in the future. I've seen you with Raegan and Amara, and I can't imagine a better dad." Mason's eyes narrow and travel down to my belly. I say loudly, "No, you cannot switch out my birth control. There's a reason I keep it hidden." I know Mason all too well; if he had the chance, he would've knocked me up already. With him in my life, I might be open to kids sooner rather than later, but *not* now. Not yet.

"Damn," he murmurs. "Well, I guess we'll just have to practice for when we do make babies together, won't we? Open your mouth and let me have a taste."

***

The flight to New York is a quiet affair. I spend the majority of the time engrossed in my finals project for one of my classes, a twenty-page essay that is, admittedly, *not* particularly fun to write. While I like numbers, I'm not quite as good with words.

When we land, a limousine picks us up right from the tarmac and takes us straight to Bradley's apartment. My mom's been living with him for a year now, but I've never seen the place—I never got an invitation.

Under different circumstances, I might be impressed with the sky-scraper building that looks at once modern and tasteful, the stunning crystal chandelier in the lobby, or the fact that, when the elevator opens, it lets us directly into the penthouse apartment. I barely glance at the famous painting hanging in the entry hall, or the gleaming marble floors.

A woman greets us at the elevator, fine wrinkles forming on her face as she offers Mason and me a slightly sad welcoming smile. "Ms. Richardson, Mr. Sieger," she says. "I'm Riley, Mr. Rodgers's house-keeper. He's in the living room, awaiting your arrival. Please, follow me."

I follow Riley through a small hall that leads directly to a large living room that's decorated in forest green and silver tones, practically reeking of wealth. A velvet sofa, embroidered with silver detailing, faces a fireplace. Positioned in front of it is a finely carved, dark wood coffee table. One of the walls is lined by bookshelves, while another showcases several original paintings by renowned artists. The back wall is made up entirely of windows, offering a stunning view of the city, with a glass door that lets out onto a large balcony.

Bradley stands behind the couch, attention on his phone. He looks up when Riley announces Mason and me, pocketing his phone.

"Chloe, Mason," he greets. "Thank you for coming."

He crosses the room and kisses me on my cheek, then shakes Mason's hand. The familiarity of his greeting is unexpected, but it warms me. Maybe once we've figured out who the hell tried to kill Mom, we might have a shot at becoming a family.

"I know you're eager to see your mother, Chloe," Bradley says. "Please try to be casual. Don't let her see your anxiety; she's been worked up since the shooting, and I'd prefer to avoid upsetting her any further."

"Of course," I agree. I know what it's like to be stuck in a spiral of anxiety; it's important that others around me are calm, otherwise my anxiety can become debilitating. "She's okay, though?"

"Perfectly fine physically," Bradley confirms. "Riley will show you to our bedroom, where your mother is. Mason, you will stay here with me. We have a few matters to discuss."

Riley smiles, gesturing for me to follow her. She leads me through a labyrinth of hallways and *up a staircase*, to the *second floor* of the apartment. There, she knocks on a closed, cream-colored door.

"Come in," Mom says softly from within, her voice sounding a bit hoarse.

Riley nods. "Go ahead."

I inhale a deep breath, push down my own anxieties, and open the door with a casual smile, as if visiting Mom in her home is routine.

CHAPTER THIRTY-EIGHT

The bedroom is large; the walls are painted a soft, calming aqua color. A grand, king-sized bed stands at the head of the room, and an antique silver vanity is propped against the wall across from it. A bathroom lies through one door on the side wall, a closet through another. Mom sits on a chaise lounge at the foot of the bed, wrapped in a dark red silk robe. Bags shadow her eyes, and her face is devoid of its usual makeup. She looks exhausted and worried, her features sunken and eyebrows furrowed. When she sees me, a small smile spreads on her lips.

"Chloe," she greets, a strange note of something that sounds suspiciously sentimental in her tone. She pats the cushion beside her. "Thank you for coming, sweetheart. Sit with me."

I blink slowly, thrown by her use of the endearment, but pad across the Persian rug covering the floor, wringing my hands. I take a seat on the far end of the lounge, leaving a cushion of space between us. Mom *scoots closer* and wraps her arms around me in a hug, kissing my cheek. For a moment, I'm stiff, unsure how to respond to this unexpected familiarity, but after a few beats I hug her back, eyes fluttering shut as

I give her a squeeze. *I've missed this.* I haven't received a genuine hug from her since the day Dad died.

"Hey, Mom," I say quietly. "It's good to see you. I'm glad you're okay."

"Thank you," she says, pulling back. She reaches out to tuck a stray strand of hair behind my ear; I flinch at the unfamiliar gesture. Her eyes briefly widen and her hand falters, but she completes the motherly motion before folding her hands on her lap. An awkward silence ensues as we gaze at each other, both of us unsure of what we're supposed to do. This is the first time we've acted like a real mother and daughter in too many years to count.

"How's school?" she asks me.

"*You care?*" I almost respond. "Good. Busy, but good. How are you? How was the honeymoon?"

She smiles softly. "It was wonderful. We toured France, England, and Scotland for two weeks. You'd have loved it, they're such beautiful countries."

"I saw some pictures on your social media, it did look beautiful," I agree. "I'm glad you enjoyed it."

More awkward silence; more of me not knowing how to act around this version of her.

"Tell me more about school," Mom says. "What's it like to be a double major? Bradley told me that the dance program you got into is a major in itself, and that you're doing biochemistry alongside dance. It all sounds very daunting and hectic."

I swallow, blinking a few times. The last time we discussed school, before I left for college, she told me that I was wasting my time and college trust fund. Now, she's asked me about Greywood twice in the span of a single conversation.

"It's pretty busy," I tell her. "My dance classes go from 6 a.m. to 12 p.m. every weekday. After that, I rush to get to my biochem and general education courses, I have those until 5 or 7 p.m. The other girls in the dance company can do their gen-ed courses online, but since I'm enrolled in biochemistry, I have to attend some of them in person with the rest of the plebians." I pause in case Mom doesn't want to hear more; she nods encouragingly. "I'm part of a dance production that's an original by one of my ballet masters, who's also a director and choreographer, Mr. Sanders. It's a retelling of Pandora's box, I have a soloist role. This semester, the ballet runs every Friday and Sunday, with the occasional weeknight performance."

"That sounds wonderful," Mom says, smiling. "You were always a talented dancer, and a bit of a... what do they call it? Mathlete?"

I smile back, a bit sadly. "Yeah, that's thanks to Dad." I wince as soon as I've spoken. "Sorry, I didn't mean to bring him up. I know you don't like talking about him." I clear my throat. "What was your favorite part of the trip?"

"Chloe," Mom says slowly. "While I was traveling with Bradley, we had a few serious conversations that brought me to some realizations. We love each other very much, but Brad isn't one to beat around the bush, and he brought several of my mistakes in recent years to my attention."

I'm stunned to silence by the sincerity and contrition in Mom's tone. On the rare occasions we speak, she only wants to talk about vain topics with me.

I think back to my conversation with Mason the night before Mom's wedding. I was skeptical when Mase told me that Bradley seemed to care for me and wanted to help strengthen my relationship with Mom, but perhaps my boyfriend was right.

"Um... we don't have to talk about anything serious," I hurry to say.

Mom holds up a hand. "Please, sweetheart, let me get this out." I fall silent, and Mom sucks in a deep breath. "Bradley forced me to see some truths that I've been avoiding. At first, it was frustrating, but when a bullet whizzed by my head a few days ago…" she swallows hard, eyes starting to glisten. "One thing was on my mind through that chaos. When Brad's security guards were hauling me away, my thoughts were with you. I've had a lot of time to think, and my biggest regret if I'd been hurt, if I'd… *died*," she shudders, "would've been that I'm not close with my daughter. I hate that I don't know enough about you, and that's because I haven't asked in years."

She reaches out to take my hand; shocked, I let her. "Your father was the first love of my life. He was my sun and my center. You might look more like me than you do him, but your personality takes entirely after his. Motivated, focused, and bound for great success in life. For a long time, you served as a painful, living reminder of what I lost, of the man I loved with everything in me, a man who was abruptly taken from me. I couldn't bear it." She shakes her head. "I tried to turn you into someone I could be around more easily; someone like me. You know I was pulled into modeling right after high school and met your father soon after. I left the modeling world behind for him. *He* became my world, and without him, I was lost. I thought that if you and I could have more in common, if you were less like your father, it'd become easier to spend time with you. But you've always been an independent soul, Chloe, which is the complete opposite of me. I need someone to stabilize me and be my home; you only need yourself and your own motivations and convictions to make your way. I couldn't understand that, and we both know that I didn't try to. Instead, I pushed you away. That's one of my greatest mistakes in life."

My eyes begin to prickle with oncoming tears. I almost question if I'm dreaming right now, somehow imagining her saying all of these kind things to me, but my dreams are never this positive.

"Another mistake was not being there for you regardless of our differences," she goes on. "You're so smart, Chloe. So bright, with such an intellectual mind. You don't care about things like appearance or physical pedigree because you have a brain that'll get you through life. While I'm certainly not stupid, my mind doesn't work even half as quickly as yours. I have an eye for visuals: colors, design, and cut. You have an eye for numbers and equations. I like it when things look pretty; you like the mechanics of *why* something looks the way it does." She smiles faintly, lips wobbling. "Bradley put it in the best terms, I think. I see a flower and admire the vibrant colors of the petals and the sweet scent; you see a flower and admire the biological structure of it, how the colors evolved over thousands of years to make it more attractive to bees for the sake of pollination. You understand the chemical compounds that create the sweet scent. We might both see the same things, but the way we perceive them is different, and that's a beautiful thing." She sighs. "I'm sorry for not being there to support you when I should've, sweetheart. I was so stuck in my pain that I didn't think to acknowledge yours; I just wanted to forget about everything painful and move forward. I shouldn't have done that."

Jesus Christ. The tears I've been holding back spill over my eyes and trickle down my cheeks. Mom makes a soft noise and reaches out with her free hand to wipe them away, before swiping at her own.

"I'm sorry I'm so similar to Dad," I say quietly. "I know it's painful for you, I wish I could be more like you—"

"*Don't,*" she cuts me off firmly, "apologize for being who you are. *Ever.* You're amazing, Chloe, and I never meant to make you feel otherwise. My discussions with Bradley happened when we were talking about having children, and they opened my eyes to my faults with you. I didn't want to see my mistakes, but my near-death experience made them glaringly obvious. *I'm* sorry for pushing you away and not providing you with the support and attention you deserved. I'd like to try to be there for you now, as would Bradley. I don't want to *pretend* to be a family, I want to actually *be* a family. I know I've made mistakes and that I'll make many more, but I couldn't live with myself if I didn't try."

"I'd like that," I tell her. "I'd like that a lot."

Her words don't make years of pain disappear, but they do soften the hurt ever so slightly and open the possibility of a new, bright future that I wholeheartedly wish for.

She cups my cheek, brushing away the last of my tears. "Thank you. I won't promise you that I'll be perfect because that'd be a lie, but I can promise you that I'll be there through all the imperfections."

"That's all I ever wanted," I choke out. "I miss Dad so much, too. He loved me fiercely; the two of you loved me fiercely, and then I lost both of you."

Mom's brows pinch. "I know. I'm so sorry for that." A small, sad smile touches her lips. "Remember how he'd bring you into his office weekly? Have you sit in on his meetings with patients? You'd fill notebooks with your observations." She stands and moves to her bedside table, opening a drawer and withdrawing three pocket-sized Moleskin notebooks, bringing them over to me. "I found these when I was moving a year ago, but I never gave them a second glance. I read them cover to cover yesterday. You'll make an excellent doctor, if that's what you want to be." She hands them to me; I open the one on top, and glance over the notes I made when I was all of nine years old.

June 11th, 2014. Observation of Patient #1 of the day. Male in his forties, reporting with arrhythmia (heart palpitations, irregular heart-

beat, sweat). Duration of issue: approx. 9 months. Height: 6'1. Weight: 235.

Tests done pre-visit:

- *Blood work. Results indicate dyslipidemia (high cholesterol, elevated LDL & VLDL, low HDL, high ESR, indicators of pre-diabetes, type 2) Conclusion: predisposition for cardiac issues.*

- *Echocardiogram & stress-test. Results indicate abnormal cardiac markers.*

Patient is at high risk of cardiac events.

Medication prescribed: Fluvastatin (cholesterol treatment, blocks enzymes in liver that produce cholesterol).

Plan of Care: Follow up in three months, repeat blood work and tests to reassess.

A soft sob escapes me as I read through the notes. I remember Dad peeking at my notebooks at the end of each day. He'd always ask, *"What'd you see today, Brains?"*

"Thank you," I whisper, closing the notebook and clutching it to my chest. "Thank you. I forgot about these; I'll treasure them."

Mom nods. "I still love your dad, sweetheart. He'll always have a piece of my heart, but some people are fortunate enough to have two great loves in their life, while most don't even get one. I hope you'll come to care for Bradley. He's a good man, and he respects you and wants to help you."

I could never accept another father in my life—Dad was everything to me, the best father anyone could ask for, and I can't replace him. But I think I could accept Bradley as a father *figure* of sorts, one who makes my mother happy *and* gives her reality checks when nobody else can get through to her. That's worth a lot.

"I'd like to get to know him more," I say. "I'd like to get to know both of you more."

Mom smiles. "Good." She stands, nodding. "We'll be having an early dinner in about an hour—will you and Mason be around? I know you're staying with us, but you probably have your own plans in the city. I'd just like for all of us to get to know each other better. Brad was a bit skeptical of you dating a Sieger at first, but Mason obviously cares for you very much. And, my gosh," she presses a hand to her heart. "His cousins, those two girls. Most adorable little humans I've seen in far too long—especially the youngest."

I smile in turn. "We'll be around for dinner. Mason's cousins are named Amara and Raegan—Amara's the baby. Her parents are... not very hands-on, to say the least, and she's formed a bit of an attachment to me. She's the sweetest girl in the world. I think Mason and I will stop by their place while we're visiting; Raegan likes to bake, and Amara just likes to be held." My eyes lower. "I don't think she gets held very much."

"The cold distance is exactly why Brad was wary of Mason at first," Mom says. "According to him, the Siegers are cold as ice. Mason is a cool one, too, but not with you—at least it doesn't seem that way." She walks over to her vanity, taking a seat. Looking at me through the mirror, she asks, "He treats you well?"

"Like a princess," I assure her. *Unless we're in bed. Then, he treats me like his toy.*

She nods. "Good. As long as he keeps treating you that way and caring for you, hold onto him. Why don't you put a movie on while I get ready? It's been so long since we watched something together."

"The Devil Wears Prada?" I query, thinking of the film we watched the last time we cuddled up together. I think I was eleven back then.

"That sounds lovely."

This reminds me so much of when I was a little girl, sitting on my parents' bed, watching with wide eyes as my mother prepared herself. Although I'll never be a big makeup person, she turns it into an art; not overdoing it, putting on just enough to enhance her prettiness without making herself look like she stuck her face in a bucket of paint.

"Mom?" I ask once I've navigated to our chosen movie and started it.

"Hmm?"

"Will you do my makeup?" My voice wobbles, because I never thought we'd be here. Talking openly about our lives, spending time together like we used to. I always thought that Mom's love for dressing me up and doing my makeup was a reflection of her vanity. Now I'm starting to understand that she truly loves design, color, and fashion, so she was trying to connect with me, not control me or mold me into her image.

Mom beams. "I'd love to. Come over here, we'll get you glowing for Mason."

An hour later, Mom and I emerge from her bedroom. She went full throttle on me, doing my eye makeup, putting lipstick on me, and even curling my hair. With my Moleskin notebooks in my hand, I follow Mom through her maze of an apartment and to the dining room.

A long wooden table, large enough to seat twelve people, takes up the center of the room. A modern chandelier made of glass prisms hangs from the ceiling, and a bank of windows on one of the walls offers a beautiful view of the city. Four placemats have been set up around the head of the table; Bradley and Mason are seated at two of the placemats, conversing quietly. They fall silent when Mom and I walk in, and Bradley rises and kisses Mom's cheek. Mason also rises, smiling at me.

"What have you got there?" he asks me, nodding at the notebooks.

I hand one to him, placing the others beside my plate as I take a seat. "Notes I took when I was younger, shadowing my father's appointments with patients."

Eyebrows raised, Mason flips open the notebook, releasing a puff of laughter as he scans a page. "Jesus, you were what? Nine?" He shakes his head. "Too smart for your own good, even back then."

"You look lovely, Chloe," Bradley tells me. "Did you ladies have a good time?"

"We had a wonderful time," Mom replies, leaning in to kiss his lips. "Absolutely wonderful."

Chapter Thirty-Nine

Our first evening in Bradley and Mom's apartment is surprisingly enjoyable. Dinner is an intimate affair, and Mason and I spend hours after the meal simply talking with Mom and Brad. Mom takes liberties to share embarrassing childhood stories about me, and Mason and I tell my mother and stepfather about our school lives.

Mason surprises me by revealing that he sent in an application for Greywood's graduate MBA program. Although he's a third-round applicant, he has a stellar record at our university and is about to graduate Greywood's undergrad business program with four years of work experience under his belt. I hope to hell he gets into the MBA program, so we won't have to do a long-distance relationship.

I spend the following morning with Mom, going through old scrapbooks filled with photos of me as a child. After sharing a quiet brunch with everyone, Bradley hands me a platinum American Express credit card, telling me not to exceed the monthly limit, which is *forty thousand* dollars. When I tell him that I have no use for even a tenth of that limit, he advises me to put all school-related expenses on it, along with any recreational activities and shopping trips. He refuses to take the card back, so I'm left with no option but to add it to my wallet.

At around noon, Mason and I leave to visit Amara and Raegan, who live in an apartment building that's just a thirty-minute walk from Mom and Brad's place. Bradley, who seems hypervigilant after the failed assassination attempt on Mom, sends three security guards with us. I'm grateful for the additional protection, though it does feel a bit odd to walk down crowded New York City streets with burly men trailing behind me.

Unfortunately, I haven't been able to video chat with Mason's cousins on a daily basis since the start of school—now I only really have time to talk to them on weekends. By the time I return from school and finish my homework on weekdays, the girls are usually already heading to bed. I'm excited to see them again, to cuddle with Amara and entertain Raegan with stories.

While we walk, Mason tells me that Laura's away on a vacation for the next week and a half, and Jason's golfing in the Hamptons for the weekend. Apparently, Laura often takes off on spontaneous vacations, and Jason also enjoys flitting about the state and country. His efforts to be more present for his daughters are tenuous at best.

I insist on stopping by a baking store and a grocery store to pick up baking supplies for Amara and Raegan. Naturally, I get carried away; by the time Mason and I emerge from both stores, one of our personal security guards has to help us carry the numerous bags. I apologize to the guard, who introduces himself as Gordon, for the inconvenience. He assures me it's no bother and mentions that he also has a daughter who coincidentally loves to bake.

When we arrive to Jason and Laura's apartment, I'm at once underwhelmed and overwhelmed by it. While Bradley and Mom's apartment is opulent yet tastefully decorated, *this* apartment is like a poorly curated museum. It's all marble and cold stone, high ceilings, and walls adorned with mismatched paintings by famous artists. A nanny greets Mason and me at the door and leads us through the vast apartment, giving us *and* our guards a short tour of the place. The guards take the opportunity to ensure the apartment's empty of threats, much to the nanny's consternation. Gordon sets our baking supplies in the kitchen before tipping me a smile and telling me that he and the others will station themselves outside the front door to give us our privacy.

The nanny then takes us to the playroom, which is cozier than the rest of the apartment. The floor is covered in a fuzzy blue rug, and there's a large L-shaped couch facing a TV. Three dressers, bursting with toys, line one of the walls. When I stop in the doorway, I see Raegan and Amara sitting together at a wooden desk in the corner of the room. Raegan's bent over a coloring book, scribbling away at it with crayons, while Amara's seated beside her, silently watching her sister work.

Raegan looks up when Mason clears his throat; her expression turns from one of intense focus to sheer delight. She leaps off her chair and runs up to Mason, wrapping her arms around his waist in a hug.

Mason chuckles, mussing her hair. "Hey, Sanity-Eater—whoa, what happened to your arm?"

I glance at Raegan's left arm, brows furrowing when I see that it's covered in a pink cast that spans from her hand to her elbow.

"I fell while playing in the park," Raegan says. "A doctor told me I broke a bone."

"Are you alright?" I ask, stepping closer. "Does it hurt?"

"I'm okay, it doesn't hurt too bad," Raegan says, glancing at her arm.

"When did it happen?" Mason questions, eyebrows furrowed with concern. "You didn't have that cast on when we had our video chat last Sunday."

"Monday," Raegan replies. "It hurt the first few days, but it's good now. I'll just have to wear this cast for the next six weeks."

A niggle of worry tugs at my chest. I'm not sure that Raegan's telling us the full story, but I don't think pressing her will get us anywhere. Swallowing, I offer her a smile and drop a kiss on her forehead, then make my way over to Amara, kneeling beside her chair.

"Hey, sweetheart." I reach forward to tuck a piece of her hair behind her ear. Amara blinks at me, then holds out her arms expectantly. Smiling, I stand and settle her on my hip, tapping her nose. She clings to me, resting her head on my shoulder, though her attention seems to be on Mason and Raegan. More specifically, I think she's staring at Raegan's wrist.

She's probably worried about her sister. Heart clenching, I kiss Amara's head, gently sifting my fingers through her hair. Something definitely strikes me as off in this household, but I can't say that in front of the girls.

Instead, I opt for a brighter topic. "Okay, ladies, I brought supplies for baking. I'm thinking we'll make some cookies, then maybe also pudding or banana bread—"

"*Yes!*" Raegan exclaims. "Cookies!"

Smiling, I follow Raegan as she rushes out of the room, running right past her amused nanny and bolting into the kitchen. She helps me find bowls and all the necessary tools for baking. I have her and Mason work on making cookie dough while I seat Amara on the counter and enlist her help with the banana bread. The nanny briefly stops by to tell Mason and me that she needs to go out and run a few errands while we're here—I assure her that we're planning to stay for a few hours, so she can take her time.

Once we've got all the goodies baking in the oven, I notice that Raegan and Amara are tired from the excitement, so Mason and I settle them down for a nap. We let them rest in their bedroom while we return to the kitchen, taking seats at the small kitchen table. Comfortable silence stretches while we wait for the treats to finish baking.

Mason's phone starts to buzz; frowning, he pulls it out of his pocket and checks the screen.

"It's my dad," he says, sounding irritated.

"You should take it," I tell him.

He shakes his head. "No, I'm spending time with you right now. I don't want to waste it on him." He declines the call. A moment later, the phone starts buzzing again.

"Mase," I say. "Just pick it up and tell him you're busy."

With a sigh, Mason complies, answering the phone and putting it to his ear.

"Hello? Yeah, I'm in the city. No, I can't, I'm busy." His expression grows serious at whatever his dad says. "*What?* Are you sure? Fuck... no, I can't just—" he cuts off with a sigh, casting me an apologetic glance. "Half an hour. That's what I have for you. *No*, I can't spare more time, *I'm with my girlfriend*. Half an hour or nothing. Okay. See you soon." He hangs up, working his jaw.

"Let me guess," I say softly. "You have to go."

Mason nods. "Yeah. My father said he might be close to figuring out who the shell corporation that paid Stuart and your mom's would-be assassin belongs to. He doesn't want to disturb Rae and Amara, so we'll be meeting briefly at a café."

"Your dad knows about the shell corporation and the attempts to hurt me and kill my mom?" I ask, surprised.

Mason nods. "I asked him to have his tech guy look into the shell corporation, though I didn't specify why." He shrugs. "The more people looking, the better our chances of finding something." He picks up my hand, pressing a kiss to my palm. "You'll be good here?"

I nod. "I'll be good. Go ahead, tell me what he says. I'll take care of things for now."

His lips thin. "I hate leaving you while there's danger hanging over your head, Chlo. I wish I could stay with you." His expression hardens. "You know what? I'm staying. Fuck my dad."

I lean forward to kiss him. "I'm safe, Mase. I have guards here with me. You should go, find out what your dad has to say. It could be helpful. Speaking of guards, you should take two of them with you. Leave me Gordon—I like him the best."

Mason looks torn between wanting to stay with me and wanting to hear what information his dad has to offer. "Are you sure?"

"Positive," I confirm. "Go. Take two guards and go."

He shakes his head. "I'm not the one in need of protection, Chlo, you are. I'll be fine."

"Someone could get to me through you," I point out. "If anything happened to you, I'd run after you to try to help—I wouldn't be able to stop myself. I love you too much. *Take the guards and go.*"

His eyes soften at my words, as does his expression. Finally, he nods. "Okay, fine. I'll leave Gordon and take the others if it'll make you feel better."

"It will," I confirm.

He leans in to kiss my lips. "I'll be back soon. Don't let the cookies burn."

"When have I ever burned something while baking?" I question, arching an eyebrow.

Mason chuckles. "Well, there was that one time a few weeks ago. I distinctly recall the smoke alarm going off."

I gape at him. "That's because you sat me on the counter and *went down on me*! I was too distracted to pay attention to the time! I tried to tell you it was unsanitary to do that on our *kitchen counter*, while there were cookies in the oven!"

He shrugs, completely unashamed. "What can I say? I wanted an appetizer. But, seriously, don't set off the smoke alarm here. The security in this building is crazy; if the alarm goes off, the police *and* fire department get called at the same time. They'll show up within seven minutes."

He plants another kiss on my lips, then strolls out.

I sigh, shaking my head. I check the time on my phone; the cookies have another ten minutes, and the banana bread has over an hour. I have enough time to peek in on Raegan and Amara, make sure they're sleeping comfortably.

I head through the winding, tasteless, *soulless* apartment and make my way to the bedroom the girls share. Mason told me that Raegan refuses to sleep in a separate room from Amara and vice versa, so they bunk together. I slowly creak open the door to their room, glancing around. Curtains are drawn over the windows on the back wall, but small nightlights are plugged in by the two princess beds taking up either side of the room, casting enough light for me to see the girls.

Amara's curled on her side, clutching her stuffed hippo—a cute stuffed animal that's bigger than she is. Raegan's on her back, her injured wrist laid out beside her, while her other hand rests over her chest. I smile when I see she has a stuffed rabbit tucked *into* her shirt, its little head resting on her neck. These girls are too adorable to be real.

I quietly close the door again, making my way down the hall, wanting to get back to the kitchen before the cookies start to burn. I pause when I hear the echoes of the front door opening and closing. It must be Mason, already back from his meeting with his father. My assumption proves to be wrong when the sounds of high heels clacking along the floors reach my ears.

Frowning, I pause, waiting to see who's home. A moment later, *Laura* comes into view. She stops at the end of the hallway, staring at me, not looking altogether surprised to see me. *Isn't she supposed to be out of town?*

"Hi, Laura," I greet. "Sorry if I'm in your way, I'm just here for the afternoon to bake with your daughters."

"Where's the nanny?" Laura asks, clutching the designer bag she holds close to her chest, gaze darting around.

"Out running errands for the afternoon. Mason's grabbing coffee, he should be back soon." When I take a closer look at her, I notice that her eyes are slightly bloodshot, her pupils are dilated, and there's a residue of some white powder beneath her nose. *Jesus Christ, is she high?* I think she might be. Sheer disgust washes over me; Laura's not just unfit to be a mother, she's an unfit person altogether. Coming home—to the place where her two *daughters* are—while high out of her mind makes her a horrendous individual.

I want to chew her out, but instead I force myself to say, "I'll get out of your way."

"No, you won't," Laura says, reaching a hand into her bag. I see a flash of glinting steel a second before she takes a *pistol* out of her Chanel purse and points it at me with a shaky, unsteady hand.

What—the—fuck?

Chapter Forty

"What are you *doing*?" I gasp, taking a few steps back, darting my gaze around. I have no understanding of what's happening right now; all I know is that Laura's high, armed, and looks ready to shoot me.

"*Don't move!*" she hisses, halting me in my tracks. "Don't. Fucking. Move. You've been in my way for a while now, *Chloe*, and so has your *whore* of a mother."

I blink several times at her words. *My mother and I being in her way...* recently, the same person has tried to frighten me and kill my mother. Sheer horror freezes the blood in my veins as I look at Laura through a new lens—as the person behind the shell corporation. I'm 90% sure it's her. I don't understand *why*, though. I'd assumed that there was financial motivation behind the attacks on my mother and me, but maybe I was mistaken. Laura has plenty of money, what more could she want? Could she be angry with Mom for some reason?

"I don't know what you're talking about," I say carefully, needing her to lower her weapon so I can escape. "You're not making any sense. Why don't you put the gun down and we can talk all of this over?"

"No!" she snaps. "No more talking. I've tried fucking *talking* for *years!* I've tried talking to him over and over again, but he never *listens!"*

"Who?" I ask, taking a step back.

"You're brand-new fucking *stepfather*, that's who," Laura seethes.

I blink, struggling to comprehend how Bradley factors into Laura's rage. My gaze drops to her gun, which is shaking in her grip. The safety's off, but the weapon isn't cocked; even if she pulls the trigger, I don't think a bullet will fire. At least, I'm praying it won't.

"What about Brad?" I ask carefully.

Laura cocks the gun, and my heart rate shoots into the stratosphere. *"Don't* call him that!" she warns. "He isn't *your* Brad. He isn't your *anything!* Your mother *stole* him from me, and I won't let her have him. Her or you—neither of you can have him. He was mine first, it was supposed to be me and him!"

A slow breath rushes out of me as realization dawns. At some point in the past, maybe before Laura got with Jason *or* after, she had a relationship with Bradley. Now, Brad has married my mother and is legally related to me, and Laura thinks we're at fault for his decision to be with my mother. Laura struck me as bitter at the wedding, but I never would've guessed her instability or her past.

"You and Bradley," I breathe.

"It was always supposed to be us," she repeats. "He was mine first. He was always mine, not yours. Brad and I were endgame. It was always supposed to be us." She's babbling, repeating sentences, coked up out of her mind and pointing a deadly weapon at me. I don't think I've ever been in such a dangerous situation before, not even when I was attacked outside of dorms—when *she* sent someone to attack me. *This is fucked.*

"My guard, Gordon, is outside the front door right now," I warn her. "He's due to come in and check on me any minute."

She releases a crazed laugh. "The door's *locked*, stupid girl, and your guard doesn't have a key. It's reinforced with steel and completely bulletproof, thanks to my husband's wealth and paranoia. Even better, this whole apartment is soundproofed. Nobody's coming in here until I'm done with you. Not your *boyfriend*, not your guard, and not even my fucking nanny, the bitch that I can't fire anymore."

Done with you sounds like Laura's way of saying once I'm dead. All I can think to do right now is keep her talking—anything to prevent her from deciding to pull the trigger. Conversation might risk escalating her mood, but it could also distract her. I can only hope it'll distract her.

"Why are you doing this? You and Bradley are in the past. You're married now, you have two daughters and more wealth than you could possibly spend—"

"Shut up!" she interrupts. "You don't know *anything*. The wealth I *had* was gambled away by my imbecile husband. I only stayed away from Bradley so I could have Jason's money, but then the fucking asshole drained it all! As for my *daughters*, those little bitches are worthless. Sniveling children who don't do anything but cry and complain. Raegan isn't even Jason's!"

My head jerks back. "*What?*"

"Oh, yes, stupid girl," Laura sneers. "I had an affair with Bradley when I was dating Jason eight years ago. I got pregnant with Raegan a few weeks later. Bradley and Jason both demanded paternity tests like the absolute fucks they are. I knew Bradley would never marry me, so when I realized he was the father, I doctored the test to make it look like Raegan belonged to Jason. Jason married me a month later, and Bradley never spoke to me again." She shakes her head, upper lip curling. "I tried to get with Bradley again over the years, but he started dating others. Eventually, he settled with your gold-digging whore of a mother—I *told* Bradley to stay away from her, but he didn't listen. He chose *her* over *me*. Do you know how ridiculous that is? Nobody chooses me as second—I was on the cover of Vogue nine years ago!"

I bite my tongue to withhold a scathing quip. The truth of the matter seems to be that nobody chooses Laura first, and rightfully so. She's horrendous, delusional, and convinced that she deserves everything she wants—she's willing to resort to *murder* to achieve her goals.

"But Bradley fucking Rodgers chose your mommy and you instead," Laura goes on. "I was mad when they got engaged, so I started to look for ways to fuck with Grace, but I couldn't get anyone close enough. You, though, were left totally unprotected, so I thought I'd have some fun with you." Laura really *is* behind my torment—she hired Stuart because she was angry at my mother for getting chosen by Bradley. Her logic is so backward and twisted, I don't know how to start untangling it. "But then Bradley actually *married* your mother, and I realized I had to do something about her now, before things spiraled further. I tried to get rid of Grace a few days ago, but Brad's fucking guards protected her and now he's tripled her security. I'll find a way, though. Maybe at your funeral." She releases a disturbing cackle. "Yeah, maybe I'll finally get rid of her when she's burying you. Then I can tell Brad the truth about Raegan. He'll take us back."

I shake my head, baffled. "No, Laura, he won't. He loves my mom, and he cares for me; he wouldn't take you back even if you weren't the one to kill us. Besides, everyone will know you killed me, you'll be going to jail—"

"*No!*" she screeches. The gun goes off with a deafening bang. I tense in preparation for searing pain or total darkness, but after a moment I realize that she didn't shoot me, she shot the floor right in front of me. A glinting bullet peeks out of the marble, surrounded by several cracks. I release a shuddering breath, looking back to Laura. I'm not sure if she shot the ground intentionally or if she missed while aiming at me—I'm not sure if she knows, either. Something tells me that the next bullet she fires will find its way into my body.

"If Brad doesn't take me, I'll just have to kill him too," Laura rants. "Then his assets will revert to his last living blood relative: Raegan. I'm her guardian, so that means his money will be mine until she's of age." Laura continues talking, rambling, her words cyclical and recursive yet sporadic at the same time. I tune her out and try to focus on finding a way out of this. Nobody's coming to my rescue, it's up to me to get out of here alive.

The cookies, I realize. A glance at an ornate clock at the end of the hall tells me that I should've taken them out of the oven two minutes ago. A few more minutes, and they'll start to burn and smoke. The fire alarm will blare to life, and Mason told me what'll happen then. I can use the noise as a distraction to get away from Laura. Go to the girls' bedroom and barricade us in there while waiting for the police.

Just then, the worst possible thing happens; I hear a door creak open and close behind me, followed by quiet, familiar footsteps pitter-pattering down the hall. A startled gasp draws Laura's eyes over my shoulder; I cast a glance behind me, seeing none other than baby Amara, frozen in fear and shock, staring at her mother.

"*You,*" Laura sneers at her daughter. "You... I can't have you. Brad won't take me back then—he'll take me back with Raegan, but not with you." Her gun slowly shifts away from me and toward Amara.

My eyes widen as I realize that Laura's contemplating shooting her *own daughter*, the sweetest, most adorable three-year-old girl who deserves to be *protected*, who *has* to be protected.

Several things happen at once; the fire alarms screech to life around us, so loud I think my eardrums might burst. I throw myself in front of Amara, turning away from Laura and covering the little girl with my body, dropping to my knees. Laura's gun goes off again, and a searing heat explodes on the outside of my left arm, drawing a cry from me.

Amara screams; Laura gives a crazed laugh; I don't think as I scoop Amara into my arms and sprint down the hall toward her room. More bullets whiz past me as I run, clutching Amara so tightly I'm afraid I might hurt her. Blood spills down from my arm, staining my clothes and even getting on the poor child. Adrenaline overtakes the pain I *should* be experiencing, and while I'm dimly aware that I'll need to get medical attention soon, my focus is taken up by protecting the girls from their deranged mother.

The door to the bedroom opens, revealing Raegan standing in the doorway, her eyes wide. As gently as I can, I push her back into the room, set Amara down, and close and lock the door.

"Raegan, Amara, go to the bathroom," I tell the girls loudly. In case they don't hear me over the blaring of the fire alarm, I point at the bathroom and make an urgent waving motion with my hand.

As they scurry to follow my directions, I look around for something to push in front of the door to keep Laura out. She could shoot the lock open, but she'll have a harder time getting in if the door's blocked by a heavy object. My eyes zero in on a heavy chest of drawers that should serve as a decent enough barrier. I grab onto the edges of the wardrobe and use all of my strength to tug it in front of the door, hissing at the pain searing its way through my arm.

I yelp when another bullet pierces through the wood of the door and the drawers, narrowly avoiding my waist, embedding into the wall behind me. Fuck. The wardrobe is only halfway in front of the door, but I don't have time to finish the job. I hurry to the bathroom, where

Amara and Raegan stand in the doorway, and hustle them inside, shutting and locking the door. I don't know how long the locks will keep out an armed and psychotic woman, but hopefully, it'll be long enough for the police to get here. *It has to be, or all of us are dead.*

CHAPTER FORTY-ONE

The bathroom is primarily made of white tiles and marble countertops, with a glass shower in the corner. Across from it is a large, antique metal bathtub that looks somewhat out of place. Its presence must be a gift from a higher power, as the metal looks thick enough to protect from bullets.

"Get in the tub, Raegan!" I yell at the seven-year-old.

She's either frozen in shock or doesn't hear me—she throws herself at my waist the same way I've seen her do with Mason, eyes welling with tears as she stares at my arm. A crash outside the bathroom indicates that Laura's gotten into the bedroom, and these girls need protection from bullets. I lift Amara up again, groaning as the pain in my arm *really* starts to make itself known, then grab Raegan's uninjured hand and pull her to the bathtub.

I climb in, holding Amara to my chest, then help Raegan step in as well. I settle Raegan between my legs and pull her upper body down, resting the back of her head against my stomach. I sink as low as I can, trying to make sure that all of our bodies are beneath the rim of the tub, so we're protected by its thick metal. Clutching Amara close, I pray that the tub is strong enough to stop any bullets that might hit it.

A bullet shoots through the door and whizzes across the bathroom, burying in a tile wall. Another shatters the mirror over the two-sink counter, and one more destroys the glass shower.

Raegan's screaming and Amara's wailing; the sounds of their cries break my heart. I pull Amara closer, placing her hands over her ears so the noise from the alarm doesn't hurt her, then do the same with Raegan's good hand and use one of mine to protect her other ear. My blood starts to pool around us—I glance at my arm, wincing when I see a gaping hole in my skin. It looks like the bullet tore through the outside of my arm, just beneath my shoulder, but at least it didn't get lodged in my muscle or bone, though it did a fair bit of damage. I'd take a hundred of these wounds if it meant protecting a child as sweet and innocent as Amara from her psychopath of a mother.

Chaotic noises sound from beyond the door, though no more bullets pierce it. I count the seconds, praying that the police or fire department have arrived. Something heavy slams against the door once, twice, and on the third time, the wood splinters. I pull my bottom lip into my mouth, holding the girls close, desperately hoping it's not their mother.

I glimpse a flash of blue uniforms above me as several figures storm into the bathroom. A whole lot of shouting ensues, and I risk a peek over the rim of the bathtub. A sob of relief escapes me when I see the startled faces of four NYPD officers.

I can see their mouths moving as they yell something at me, but I can't hear what they're saying over the screeching of the alarm, Raegan's terrified screams, and Amara's sobs. The noises are overwhelmingly loud, everything is too much, and my panic finally settles in despite my relief.

The fire alarms abruptly shut off, and now the only things filling the air are the shouts of the police officers, Raegan's frantic wails, and Amara's low sniffles as she clings to me and hides in my shoulder.

"Shh," I whisper to Raegan, rubbing her arm while rocking Amara in an attempt to soothe her. "You're okay, sweetheart. It's over. You're okay." I turn to the police, trying to unfuck my thoughts long enough to speak a coherent sentence. "I'm fairly certain I'm about to go into shock, and these girls are *definitely* in shock, so *please* stop yelling. None of us can take that right now."

The four officers fall silent, exchanging glances of concern with each other.

One of them, a younger man with warm brown eyes, steps forward. He opens his mouth to speak; I cut him off with the most pressing question. "Did you get Laura?" I ask. "She had a gun, she shot me and shot at her daughters. Is she gone?"

The officer nods. "Yes, we've detained the woman with the gun. The three of you are safe. Ma'am, I need you to get out of the tub."

Another officer asks, "Who's blood is that?"

"Mine," I respond, forcing myself up on shaky legs. My head swims and my vision wavers, but I swallow and gather my strength. "The girls are fine, for the most part. Terrified and shocked, but fine." My words are reinforced by the way Amara holds onto me with all the strength in her little body, head hidden in my shoulder, and the way Raegan clings to my leg like a little monkey.

As my legs buckle, I clutch the edge of the tub for stability. Now is *not* the time to fall.

"Raegan, I need you to let go of me so I can—"

"*No!*"

Okay, then. I inhale a deep breath. "Sweetheart, I'm woozy. I might fall over, and then you'd get hurt. Can you please step out of the bathtub? You can hold my hand."

"You won't let go of me?" Raegan asks, tears streaming down her cheeks.

I swallow thickly, brushing away her tears with my thumb. "Not for a second. I've got you, Rae. You're safe. These nice men are here to help us. Okay?"

Her wide eyes do a slow scan of the room, glancing at each officer before she turns back to me and nods. "Okay," she whispers. "I trust you."

Jesus. After the life she's led, I can't imagine what I've done to deserve her trust, but I sure as hell won't betray it. Even if that means forcing myself to be strong while I'm on the very verge of passing out.

The officers continue looking at each other, unsure of what to do, while Raegan reluctantly releases my leg and grabs my hand, holding it tightly as she steps out of the tub. I force my feet out of it next, then half-sit, half-fall onto the edge of it, clutching Amara tightly. Raegan immediately takes a seat to the right of me and hides her face in my chest.

The brown-eyed officer catches a glimpse of my wounded arm, and his eyes widen. He activates the radio clipped to his shoulder, requests a medic from whoever's on the other end, then yells for someone from the fire department to get in here. I already informed the officers of my injury, but I don't think they'd realized just how bad it is.

Brown Eyes grabs a washcloth from the counter, kneels in front of me, and claps the washcloth over my wound, sending a fresh burst of pain coursing through me. I grit my teeth against the cry threatening to escape, determined not to show how much pain I'm in. I don't want to further traumatize the two girls clinging to me like I'm a lifeline.

"I need Mason," I try to say, though the words are slurred. "The girls trust Mason, their cousin. My b—boyfriend." *I think I'm about to pass out; I can't pass out yet.*

"Mason Sieger?" Brown Eyes questions. "He's in the lobby, raising all hell to try to get up here."

"Please let him up," I say. "For the girls. They need someone they trust right now."

"*You* need medical attention for that tear in your arm," the officer says. "We gotta get you to a hospital, miss...?"

"Chloe Richardson," I manage, my breaths shortening into shallow pants. "Bradley Rodgers's stepdaughter." I don't like name-dropping Bradley, but it seems like the right thing to do.

"You're Mr. Rodgers's kid? *Shit.*" He shakes his head. "This is gonna be a fuckin' nightmare."

I can't muster the energy to reprimand his language in front of the children; I'm too busy trying not to keel over. Brown Eyes turns to look over his shoulder, addressing the other officers. "Bradshaw, go down to the lobby and bring Sieger up, and for god's sake, find a damn medic. Price, Eckers, secure the scene and get started on evidence. Call in backup and get a hold of Mr. Rodgers. Brief him on the situation. He's gonna raise hell over his stepdaughter getting caught up in this, keep it calm."

It dimly registers in my mind that the NYPD knows of Bradley—not entirely surprising, since he is a man of great influence. Hopefully, that'll work in my favor.

"Gordon," I say. "Where's Gordon? My guard?"

"Bring him in, too, Bradshaw," Brown Eyes says. When the other officers stay in place, Brown Eyes snaps, "*Move your asses, now!*"

He turns back to me. "Can you tell me what happened, Chloe?"

"Laura, the girls' mom, was psychotic." I give my head a shake as my vision swims. "Can we t—talk later? I need..." I blink several times, trying to remember my training. "Transfusion, maybe, and IV. Now, please. And Mason."

Gordon bursts into the room before Brown Eyes can answer. His eyes sweep over the scene; two children holding onto me, an officer kneeling beside me with a blood-soaked washcloth pressed to my arm, and me swaying back and forth on the tub. A shattered mirror and shower, a bullet buried in the tile wall.

"*Fuck*," he mutters.

"Yeah," I agree. "Call Bradley, please. Tell him Laura... lost her mind. I—" I cut off as my vision briefly goes black. When it returns, I find that the police officer is now holding me upright with a hand braced on the shoulder of my uninjured arm, right by Amara's head. Gordon has his phone out and is speaking rapidly into it, probably talking to Bradley. "I think I need to sit somewhere more stable," I finally say. "The floor."

A woman wearing an EMT uniform appears in the doorway, a medical satchel slung over her shoulder. She strides right through the room and shoos Brown Eyes aside, taking his place kneeling in front of me and holding the washcloth to my arm.

"Hello, Chloe," she greets. *I wonder how she knows my name.* "My name is Alina, I'm going to help you out today." A young male also in an EMT uniform enters shortly after her, standing by the door.

Alina drops her satchel, checks under the washcloth, then calls out some medical shorthand to the male, something I'd be able to follow easily if I wasn't half-passed out already. Brown Eyes tries to get the girls to let go of me again; Raegan screams her refusal while Amara doesn't bother responding.

The male EMT, who I assume is Alina's assistant or fellow, rushes over to me and opens Alina's satchel, rummaging through it and retrieving what I recognize as a tourniquet. Together, they place the tourniquet on my left arm, a few inches above my wound; I wince at the ensuing pain but try to keep my wits about me.

Thankfully, the next person to arrive is Mason. He makes a beeline to me, looking pale as death as he sinks to his knees. "Jesus Christ," he says, the words little more than a horrified whisper. "What—"

"Mason, take Rae," I slur. "Please."

"We need to get Chloe to the hospital," Alina tells him, her tone irate. "For that, the two children need to release her. *Now.*"

Mason sucks in a deep breath and nods. "Hey, Sanity-Eater," he greets Rae gently. "Chloe needs to get looked at, is it okay if I take you? I promise to get you cookies."

I release a manic laugh. "They burned." That's precisely what saved me.

Raegan lifts her head and peeks over her shoulder, giving Mason a cautious look. As soon as she sees him, she releases me and wraps herself around him.

"The little one too," Alina says. "Chloe's lost a lot of blood, we need to go."

Amara's arms tighten around me in response. I muster what strength remains in me and whisper into her hair, "Hey, sweetheart, I'm kinda hurt right now. Mason will take *really* good care of you. Can he hold you for a little while? I promise I'll be back soon."

Amara pulls her head back, and the tears streaming from her eyes break my heart. She gives me a short nod, lower lip wobbling. Mason lifts her off me; she keeps staring at me even as she latches onto him.

Alina glances at Mason. "You—Mason? Get the girls out of here." She turns to her assistant. "Adam, go get the stretcher." Adam's quick to follow her instructions, running out of the bathroom.

Mason says, "I need to stay with Chloe."

Alina gives him a hard look. "You need to give the professionals room to work. Focus on the two traumatized girls holding you. Get in contact with their guardians and be ready to speak with police. I'll take good care of Chloe." She turns to Gordon. "Guard Dog, go help Adam with the stretcher." *I think I'm starting to like her.* Finally, Alina addresses Brown Eyes. "Officer, I'll take it from here. You can meet us at the NYU ER."

Chapter Forty-Two

The next hours are a mess of absolute insanity. I'm taken to a hospital in an ambulance, where Alina puts me on an IV. In the ER, I'm wheeled directly to a private room, where my wound is swiftly cleaned, stitched, and the tourniquet on my arm is removed before I receive a blood transfusion. Gordon stays with me the entire time, from the ambulance to the private room, and I think his presence intimidates the doctors and nurses into doing their very best work.

With the help of the transfusion and IV, I start feeling better. Although I'm exhausted, lingering worry and adrenaline keep me wide awake and alert. I'm asking Gordon where Mason is when Bradley enters my hospital room with no fewer than four guards. My stepfather gives Gordon a dark look that raises goosebumps on my arms. "We'll have a discussion regarding your failures later," Bradley tells him, then turns his attention to me.

"Christ, Chloe," he mutters, shaking his head as he crosses the room and takes a seat on my hospital bed. He glances at the IV I'm connected to, the clip on my finger monitoring my vitals, and then meets my eyes. "Are you okay?"

"I'm better after the transfusion," I tell him. "My arm hurts like hell, though. How are Amara and Raegan? Where are they?"

"They're fine," Bradley says. "They're with your mother and Mason at our apartment, safe and sound. The older one still won't let go of Mason, though the little one has accepted your mother as a substitute. Grace is delighted."

I smile softly. Mom was always great with me when I was a kid, Amara's in good hands with her.

"Bradley... Laura talked before she got down to shooting. She said that Raegan's your daughter."

Bradley goes entirely still, eyes narrowing as he stares at me. "Excuse me?"

"She told me about the affair you guys had eight years ago. She said Raegan's yours."

Bradley exhales deeply, shaking his head. "That's not possible. I was with Laura for a short time, yes, and when she got pregnant, I requested a paternity test. Raegan is Jason's daughter, though that doesn't have much meaning anymore." He pauses, gazing at me. "When the police contacted Jason about his daughters, he didn't answer. They had the local PD where he's staying check on him; he's dead. Died of poisoning a few days ago. Laura's work. She's confessed to everything under interrogation."

I wince a little at the thought of Jason being killed by his psychotic wife. I didn't know him well, but he seemed like a decent enough person, just not a very good father. With Raegan and Amara's future up in the air, it's imperative that Bradley believes what I have to tell him. "Bradley, I think Laura was telling the truth about Raegan. She told me she didn't think you'd marry her, so she doctored the test to make it look like Rae was Jason's biological daughter. That's why Laura wanted me and my mom dead; without us, Raegan would be your only heir. Laura ranted about wanting you back but planned on killing you if you refused to be with her. With you gone, she intended to use Raegan to seize your assets." I give him a recount of the horrific debacle in Laura's apartment, relaying everything she said to me. Bradley grows increasingly tense as I talk, his eyes alternating between widening and narrowing.

When I'm done, he says, "*Shit.*"

Staring at Bradley now, I start to see the resemblance between him and Raegan. They both have the same hazel eyes, and similar shades of honey-blonde hair.

"Check if you need to. Rush a paternity test, but I'm fairly certain Raegan's yours."

Bradley stands from the bed and starts pacing the room. "*Fuck.*"

I'm not sure if he's worked up over not knowing he's had a daughter all these years, or because he doesn't want to take responsibility for her. If it's the latter, it would break my heart.

"Raegan's lovely," I tell him. "Bright, talkative, upbeat, an actual ray of sunshine. Anyone would be lucky to call her theirs."

Bradley pauses in his tracks, turning to stare at me. "You think I'm cursing because I don't *want* her?" he asks, stunned.

I give a hapless shrug. "I don't know what to think. I'm still a bit woozy from almost bleeding out."

"Dammit, Chloe, I'm not pissed because I don't want another daughter, I'm furious that I might've had a daughter for *seven years* who was raised without me in her life. Raised by the *Sieger* clan." He shakes his head. "Why do you think I was so wary of you and Mason? That family is cold as ice. Most families in our circles are, but the Sieger's put a whole new spin on it, and Laura is *famous* for being a shitty mother with a bad temper." He shakes his head. "If you're right—"

"I think I am," I interrupt.

"Then I have failed a daughter of mine for *seven years*. God dammit—" he shakes his head again, then turns to one of the five guards flanking the door. "Get a hair sample from Raegan, the seven-year-old, immediately. Do a test, check if she's mine. I want results in an hour."

The guard nods. "Right away." He turns and jogs out of the room.

Half an hour passes in tense silence. Bradley glares at a wall while I pretend to watch the muted TV. He gets a call, answers it, and demands, "Results?"

Whatever he hears causes him to pale before he hangs up the phone. "*Fuck*." He turns to me with a grim smile. "Congratulations, Chloe. You have a sister."

When he stands to leave, I say, "Wait. If you take responsibility for Raegan, you need to take Amara, too. They're very close, and Amara's also wonderful. They have to stay together."

Bradley doesn't think twice before giving me a nod. "You're right. I have a whole new set of matters to attend to, not the least of which is rushing two adoptions and discussing this with your mother." He pauses to swallow, exhaling a shuddering breath. For a moment, his expression cracks, revealing a flash of fear—fear of failure, I think. It only lasts for a heartbeat before his features harden into his usual mask. "I spoke with your doctor on my way in. As soon as your IV is finished, you're free to come home." He nods at two of his guards. "You're with me." He turns to the other two, Gordon and one of the ones he came in with. "You two stay with Chloe. Protect her. Gordon, if there is a single fucking scratch on her, I will ruin you. We'll talk tonight."

Bradley nods at me. "I'll see you at the apartment. Call if you need anything."

***

After promising Gordon that I'll ensure he isn't fired—it's not his fault he got locked out of a soundproofed apartment, and he had no reason to suspect Laura of anything—I return to Bradley and Mom's apartment, which is a hub of activity.

Raegan and Amara are in one of the living rooms with Mason, Mom, and Mason's parents. Jade and Grant are seated on one sofa, looking supremely uncomfortable. Mason and Mom are seated by each other on another sofa across from them. Raegan is on Mason's lap, curled up and asleep, while Amara is awake on Mom's lap, staring wide-eyed at my mother, who smiles at her. As soon as I walk into the room, Amara's attention turns toward me; with a little gasp, she climbs off the couch and crosses the room, tugging on my pants. I lift her with my good arm and carry her over to the couch, taking a seat next to Mason.

"So," I say into the strained silence. "It's been one heck of a day."

"There's one way of putting it," Mason agrees, worried eyes scanning me. He looks like he wants to touch me but is afraid to, so he settles for kissing my cheek. "Are you okay? I wanted to come to the hospital, but the girls—"

"Needed you," I finish for him with an understanding smile, stroking my hand through Amara's hair. "It wouldn't have been a good place for them. I'm glad you stayed with them."

Grant stands up, clearing his throat. "Chloe, I'd like to apologize for what you went through with Laura. I can't imagine how scary it was. None of us could've guessed that she'd ever try to..." he trails off, unable to finish his sentence. Clearing his throat, he presses on. "Let us know if there's anything we can do for you." Jade nods along with her husband, offering me a strained smile.

When I look a little closer at Grant, I notice that his eyes are red rimmed, as though he's been crying recently. That's when the belated realization sinks in that he just lost a brother.

"I'm sorry for your loss," I tell him sincerely. "I didn't know Jason well, but he seemed like a decent man."

Grant smiles thinly, a wealth of pain swimming in his eyes. "He was an eternally free spirit. Jason and I were close when we were younger." He swallows, nodding at the girls. "We should take them. They need to be with family now—"

"They are with family," Bradley interrupts, striding into the room. He raises a stack of papers he holds, presumably the paternity test. "Raegan's mine. We've discussed this at length in the last hour, Grant."

Grant's lips thin. "Just because you suddenly found out you have a daughter and feel some honor-bound bullshit to take responsibility does not mean that you're fit to be a parent—"

"Neither are you, Dad," Mason says quietly, shocking me. All eyes turn to him; Raegan stirs at the commotion, blearily blinking her eyes open, then shrinks back from the many adult gazes bouncing between her and Mason.

"Mom?" I prompt, nodding at Raegan.

Mom does what she always did when I was a little girl; slips straight into nurturing mode. She stands and smiles at Raegan. "Why don't we go paint our nails? I think you need some pampering after the long day you've had."

Amara looks from me to Mom, then holds out her arms to Mom, signaling that she wants to join. Mom picks up Amara and takes Raegan's hand, leading them from the room.

Grant remains perfectly still as he stares at Mason, a mixture of shock and betrayal evident in his expression.

Mason gazes steadily at his father, unfazed. "I love you and Mom. I respect you both. But I think you're self-aware enough to admit that you weren't around when I was young." He looks between his mom and dad. "I don't blame you for that, you lead busy lives, but the fact is I got stuck growing up at boarding schools and being raised by nannies. You only acknowledged my existence when I became old enough to take an interest in business." Mason shakes his head, releasing a deep breath. I take his hand in mine, silently offering my support. He gives my hand a squeeze before continuing on. "Raegan... we just discovered she's been getting physically abused by her mom for years." I suck in a sharp breath at that tidbit of information—the bruise I saw in Italy and the cast on Raegan's wrist make sense now. Raegan must've confided in Mason while I was away. "Laura *shot* at Amara, who might've died if not for Chloe. They need parents who will be there for them and help them heal. Who have plenty of time for them."

"And you think he has time?" Grant asks tersely, waving to Bradley. "He's busier than I am."

"I'm also a man of priorities," Bradley says. "It doesn't matter how busy work gets, I am never too busy for family. I spoke with Grace, she'd be happy to stay with the girls and be hands-on, as will I. I'll be here every morning for breakfast, and I'll be home in time for dinners most nights of the week. I'll adjust my schedule so I can do some work remotely and spend more time with them. If you honestly believe you can offer them more care and attention, let's take this to court and allow a judge to make a ruling, but I think you know that my family is better suited to the girls than yours. You saw how distant Jason and Laura were with their children and did very little to remedy the situation." When Grant's expression grows severe and he opens his mouth to rebuff, Bradley holds up a hand. "I'm not faulting you; you didn't see it as your responsibility. I understand. Now, Raegan and

Amara *are* my responsibility. More importantly, they are a *privilege*. The necessary papers for them joining my family are already being drawn up. Get on board or don't, but if you attempt to settle this in court, I will make it my mission and joy to destroy your reputation."

Grant sinks back down to the sofa. Jade places a hand on his shoulder. When he meets her eyes, she inclines her head, glancing at Mason. "Our son speaks harshly, but he's right, Grant. Raegan and Amara will always be our nieces, but they require *parents*." Jade's eyes shift to me. "Make sure they're looked after properly, Chloe."

I'm a little humbled that she turns to me with her instruction, as though she trusts me the most out of anyone in this room. In all fairness, I did save Rae and Amara's lives just a few hours ago and was grazed by a bullet for my efforts. I suppose that merits recognition even in the upper circles of society.

"I will," I promise. "So will my mom, and Bradley."

Grant releases a long sigh, gives his wife a nod, and stands. He approaches Bradley, giving him a hard look. "I want free access to visit them, freedom to spoil them, and assurance that they'll be seeing a child psychologist on a weekly basis to process the trauma they've endured."

"You have it," Bradley replies with an ease that leaves no doubt he's telling the truth.

After several tense moments, Grant extends his hand. Bradley's eyes glimmer with respect as he shakes it. Mason and I stand from the couch when Grant makes his way over to us.

He hugs Mason and whispers something in his ear that I don't hear, then turns to me. "I'd hug you as well, but I don't want to hurt you. Thank you for saving my nieces' lives. If you need anything from my family, reach out to me." He takes my hand in his and kisses it. Jade stands from the couch and kisses her son's forehead, then both of my cheeks, before following her husband out of the apartment.

Bradley exhales a deep breath, then turns to me. "How are you feeling?"

"Tired," I admit. "In pain."

He nods. "The hospital prescribed some pain medications for the next few days; I'll have Riley bring them to you. I need to go finalize some details." He pauses, a hint of nervousness briefly flashing in his eyes. "Could you... work with your mother to turn this apartment more child-friendly? Bedroom's, playrooms, whatever the girls," he swallows, "*my daughters* need. Your mother's told me you've always gotten along with children."

"Of course," I agree. "I'll work with Mom and Riley to get everything handled. But, if I can be blunt?"

Bradley nods. "Please do. You don't need to censor yourself here, this is your home as much as mine."

I like the sound of that. "What they need most is connection. If you're truly aiming to be a father to those two, this is a critical time. Finish your work and come join us—I think we'll be making a mess of your bedroom and bathroom in the meantime."

Bradley's lips stretch up. "Strangely, I look forward to it." He looks at Mason. "Come with me, there are a few things I'd like to speak with you about."

***

When I get to Mom's room, I find my mother painting Raegan's nails in the bathroom. Dozens of nail polish bottles line the counter, and Raegan beams at my mom, chattering away as if nothing's amiss. As if she and my mom are old friends. Amara sits on the edge of the white bathtub, staring at the display, wide-eyed and intrigued. Seeing her on the edge of the tub makes a much different bathtub flash through my mind. I blink away the images of that terrible metal bathtub where I thought I might die, and walk over to Amara, scooping her up with my good arm. She melts into me, resting her head against my chest, and stares at my bandaged arm hanging by my side.

She reaches out a hand to touch it, withdraws, and then reaches out again, as if she wants to trace the bandage but also doesn't want to hurt me. "It's okay," I assure her. "It hurts a little, but I'd have taken a lot more pain if it meant protecting you."

Amara blinks up at me slowly, then turns to my mom. She points at Mom, then raises her eyebrows at me as though asking, *"who's that?"* I smile gently, bouncing the toddler on my hip.

"That's our mom," I whisper, leaning my forehead against Amara's. "A *real* mom who will love you like crazy, just like I do."

I think I first fell in love with these girls during the Christmas party when I met them. Spending time with them in Italy only cemented my love for them. With an actual gun to my head, my biggest concern was these two wonderful sisters—I didn't care about anything other than protecting them.

I kiss Amara's cheek. "You know what that makes me?"

She blinks.

"Your sister," I tell her.

A slow smile blooms on her rosebud lips, melting whatever's left of my heart. I release a soft noise low in my throat, planting a flurry of butterfly kisses over Amara's face, making her giggle.

"Chloe!" Raegan screeches, startling me. "We should paint your nails *blue!*"

I smile at her. "Whatever color you choose, Rae."

CHAPTER FORTY-THREE

I return to Greywood after a week spent at home with my family. Before leaving New York, I make sure Bradley's apartment is child-friendly, help him locate an appropriate child therapist for Raegan and Amara, and emphasize the importance of him spending as much time with his daughters as possible.

Mason and I spend the rest of the school year traveling to New York City every chance we get. Often, we only have time to spend a single day there, but I cherish every hour I get with the girls. The sisters—*my* sisters—settle in well with Mom and Bradley. It only takes them two months to start referring to their new parents as Mom and Dad. The first time Amara speaks, she calls Mom, "*Mama*," which delights her.

After a swift trial, Laura is sentenced to life in prison with no possibility of parole. Bradley ensures that she's placed in a maximum-security prison where she's only allowed to leave her cell for a few hours each day and will never see sunlight again. It's a harsh but entirely appropriate punishment for someone as wretched as Laura.

Not long after her biological mother's arrest, Raegan admits the full extent of Laura's abuse over the years. Laura would take her daughter's arm in bruising grips, slap her, shove her to the ground, and threaten to hurt Amara if Rae didn't stay silent. My heart breaks to hear of everything the seven-year-old has had to endure in her life. The fact that Rae's maintained a bright and sunny disposition despite suffering through Laura's abuse is a miracle.

Summer arrives after a hectic yet fulfilling end to the school year, bringing with it Mason's acceptance letter to Greywood's MBA program and a second tour for Pandora's Box that lasts two months. Mason travels with me around the world as I dance my way across stages in Europe, Russia, Asia, and the States.

The last leg of the tour is spent in none other than New York City, where Greywood's Dance Co. performs in Lincoln Center for a week. Mason and I stay with Mom, Bradley, and the girls for the week. I'm delighted to finally have plenty of time with my sisters, who are equally as delighted to see me. Amara refuses to let go of me unless it's bedtime or I have to leave for a performance, and Raegan keeps Mason constantly engaged with her rambling.

I'm pleased to see that Bradley is up every morning in time to wake the girls and is home almost every night in time for dinner. Mom is also wonderful with them, doting and caring yet strict when she needs to be. I can see her love for her adopted daughters, and their love for her.

On the Sunday afternoon of the last week of my tour, Mason and I join as Mom and Bradley take Raegan and Amara to Coney Island for an afternoon trip.

"This is someone's version of *fun*?" Mason asks tersely, speaking loudly to be heard over the cacophony of roller coasters and carousels whirring, children screaming with delight, and the noise of footsteps thumping along the pavement as people run from one attraction to the next.

I elbow him. "Yes, it is. It's a wonderful day out with a nice breeze. There are plenty of child-friendly rides, classic games with huge stuffed animals awarded for minimal success, and all sorts of amusement park foods offered at vendors. This is *fun* for children, Mason. I can't believe you've lived in New York your whole life but have never been to Coney Island."

Mason nods at Amara who's clinging to me as per usual. "She doesn't seem to be enjoying herself. She has her headphones in."

"She doesn't like loud noises," I remind him, pressing a kiss to Amara's head. "Notice how she's looking around with wide eyes, and pointing at things she wants to get a closer look at? She *is* enjoying this."

"Hmm," Mason hums doubtfully.

I smile when I see Raegan hurrying through the crowd, leading Mom toward us by her hand. Bradley is close behind them, holding a stuffed elephant that's about as large as he is, looking both puzzled and bemused. The toy casts a stark contrast against his three-piece suit and designer sunglasses; he looks wonderfully out of place, and the fact that he's willing to go so far out of his comfort zone for his kids makes me truly appreciate him as a person.

There was a time when I dreaded becoming part of Brad's family, but he's proven to be a good and decent man with a strong sense of honor, responsibility, and a surprising amount of love to offer Amara and Rae.

On cue, Amara reaches a hand out to Mom. "Mama!"

As always when I hear her refer to Mom as Mama or Bradley as Daddy, my heart warms. The sisters have spent their entire lives without stable parental figures, and they're embracing their new family with open arms and hearts. Of course, Raegan still has her fair bit of trauma to work through; she sees a child therapist twice a week.

Amara also has a therapist who's helping her with her speech troubles. According to Amara's therapist, Amara has a strong vocabulary and is *able* to utilize it, she just doesn't seem to *want* to.

"Hi, baby," Mom greets, smiling softly as she takes Amara from me and presses a kiss to her forehead. Mom taps Amara's headphones, silently asking permission to take them out. When Amara nods her agreement, Mom removes them and puts them in her purse.

Amara smiles shyly and hides her face in Mom's neck, turning her head sideways to stare at the stuffed elephant Bradley holds. Bradley motions to someone in the crowd surrounding us; Gordon emerges from the throng of people and takes the elephant from Bradley. It took some convincing to keep my stepfather from firing and blacklisting Gordon, but I managed. After all, Gordon did nothing wrong; nobody could've guessed that Laura was crazy enough to try to kill me *and* one of her own daughters.

"'Fant," Amara says quietly, pointing at the elephant.

"That's right," Mom agrees, beaming. "It's a nice big elephant. I'm thinking it would pair well with your pink hippo. Would you like that?" Amara nods animatedly.

"I want funnel cake!" Raegan exclaims.

"We can get some after we eat lunch," Bradley tells her patiently.

Raegan's head swivels right over to Mason and me. "I want funnel cake *now*. Can I have funnel cake?"

Mason thins his lips to hide a smile, while I wag my finger at Raegan. "Sorry, Cookie Monster. No cake for you until you've eaten something. Listen to your father."

Frowning, Raegan turns back to Bradley. "Daddy, *please,* can we have it now? I promise I'll eat later. I can even have some salad," she tries to bargain.

Bradley taps her nose, shaking his head. "No can do, Rae. Food first, fried dough later. Why don't we head over to the food vendors? They have tons of interesting options."

Raegan crosses her arms, but huffs out an agreement nonetheless. Bradley takes her hand and begins steering her toward the section of the park lined with food stalls. Mom and Amara are right beside them, followed by me and Mason. We end up settling on fantastically unhealthy loaded hot dogs and fried pickles, a treat for the girls, and set up at the only vacant table in the area. For half an hour, we eat, talk, and laugh, until Amara grows tired and becomes fussy, lips wobbling and eyes filling with tears.

Mom scoops her up, puts on her headphones, and rocks her from side to side, looking at Bradley. "I think it's time we get her home," she says softly, brushing some strands of hair from Amara's forehead. "We've been here a while, she's getting tired."

"Funnel cake first!" Raegan practically screams.

Bradley rises from the table. "I'll go get us some to take home." He nods at her half-eaten hot dog. "I expect that to be finished once I'm back, young lady."

Raegan lifts her hot dog and takes a huge bite, smearing condiments all over her cheeks and chin. Mom's quick to pull a wet wipe from her purse and use it to clean Rae up with one hand, while still rocking a fussing Amara with the other.

"Chloe, why don't you come with me?" Bradley offers. "You can help me pick out which funnel cake we should get."

"Nutella, strawberries, whipped cream!" Raegan says loudly.

I give her ponytail a light tug. "You got it, Cookie Monster. Be good and finish your lunch."

I rise from the table and follow Bradley as we head over to the stall selling all sorts of fried desserts, from doughnuts to churros to funnel cakes of every variety. Bradley places our order of two funnel cakes, then we step to the side, waiting for our dessert.

"Tomorrow's your last night in New York, and the last night of your tour," Bradley comments, glancing at me. "Then you're off to travel with Mason for the next two weeks. Excited?"

"Very," I confirm. "A little nervous for tonight's performance, since there'll be a lot of pressure for our grand finale. We have to be perfect."

"You will be," Bradley says confidently. "You're an excellent dancer." He pauses for a long moment. "Your solo variations in the ballet are all beautiful and executed with remarkable professionalism. I've heard chatter that, once you've graduated Greywood, you might get some offers from a few well-known ballet companies to dance with them as a soloist and perhaps even principal. Are you considering taking that path?"

I bite my bottom lip, my gaze drawn back to the girls, Mom, and Mason. I always thought that I'd choose ballet if I were taken into a company as a soloist or principal, and I'd assumed that would never happen. Now, with the possibility looming, I still find myself unsure. I love dancing, it's a passion of mine, but I know I'd love being a doctor even more. Both careers will require long hours, but one is relatively short lived while the other can be lifelong. If I take fifteen years of my life to dance, there's no guarantee that I'll end up becoming a doctor with such a setback in my schooling. I could live knowing I gave up ballet, especially since I've already had the privilege of dancing on most of the major stages in the world, but I don't think I'd be happy putting my schooling and the potential to become a practicing doctor or surgeon on hold.

"I don't think so," I say, shaking my head. "I love ballet. It's the most beautiful art form to me, I'll always love it, but..." I don't know how to say that I'm far more inclined to follow in my father's footsteps without offending Bradley.

Bradley nods with understanding. "But you grew up with a brilliant role model who made you fall in love with medicine."

I clear my throat, relieved that he's not upset by the idea. "Yeah. My biochem classes are going to pick up and become even more challenging next year, I honestly don't know if it's a good idea to stay in the dance program."

Bradley shrugs. "So don't. You've already made your mark worldwide over the last two summers. You have several impressive achievements under your belt. If you left now, it would be on a perfect high note."

He's right, but... "My two closest friends are in the dance company."

Bradley arches an eyebrow. "If leaving the company would dissolve those friendships, then they aren't real friendships, and you're better off without them." He sighs. "Look, Chloe, you're an adult. I'd never tell you what to do or presume to boss you around; that isn't my role. It *is* my role to offer advice, guidance, and support, so here it is. You're one of the smartest and brightest people I've ever met. You're talented in too many ways to count; both in creative and technical pursuits. As a ballerina, I think you could potentially be a soloist for a few years. As a doctor or medical researcher, I think you could change people's lives, maybe even the world. Whatever you do, make sure it's what's most satisfying to *you*, because you're the one that counts at the end of the day." He casts a glance at our table, lips thinning. "Besides, you have a lovesick boy who will follow you anywhere and have your back through everything."

I grin. "Admit it, you're warming up to Mason."

Bradley grunts. "Slowly, and under duress. Since he refuses to detach himself from you, it seems like the two of you come as a package deal." A slow smile curls his lips. "He's still bitter that I tried to encourage you to go out on dates with other men when I first met him. I hope you know, Chloe, I genuinely thought I was working in your interest. He comes from a cold family and has a reputation that makes most playboys look wholesome."

Remembering the first day I met Mason, exactly *how* I met Mason, and how much he scared me at first... yeah, I'm not surprised. I'll never tell my stepdad that when I first showed up at Mason's door, he assumed I was a prostitute.

"Whatever you choose, you'll have my family's support, and Mason's as well," Bradley tells me. "Do what gives you the most fulfilment, Chloe. If that's dancing, excellent. If that's something in medicine, excellent. The most important factor in your decision should be *you*."

I swallow, nodding, "Okay. Thank you."

Mason stands from the table and makes his way over to us, wrapping his arms around my waist from behind and resting his chin on my head. "You two look very serious," he says. "Is everything okay?"

I spin around in the arms of the boy I've come to love *so* much, smiling up at him. I know beyond any shadow of a doubt that, whatever comes next for me, whatever course my life ends up taking, Mason will be right by my side for the whole of it.

"Yeah," I say. "As long as you're here, everything's wonderful."

Bradley coughs into his fist, probably uncomfortable with our blatant PDA, but Mason and I ignore him.

"Well, it's a good thing I don't plan on going anywhere, isn't it?" Mason says lightly, leaning down to kiss my nose.

"It is," I agree, my heart warming. *It really is.*

Afterword

Thank you so much for reading Starlets and Savages! Chloe and Mason were an absolute blast to write.

If you enjoyed this book, please leave a review! Reviews are critical for visibility and growth, and I read every single one of them to get an idea of what readers do and don't enjoy.

Greywood Elites is far from complete! Next up will be Mira's book, Luminaries and Legionnaires, featuring a very intriguing anti-hero, and a new journey into the underworld of organized crime. Pre-order for Luminaries and Legionnaires will be live very soon!

If you're interested in seeing more stories set in the Greywood University world, check out the other books in the Greywood Elites series! Muses and Monsters is a dark menage MFM romance; Primas and Predators is a dark dark romance with a book-long redemption arc.

Muses and Monsters link: https://www.amazon.com/dp/B0D6X14VW1

Primas and Predators link: https://www.amazon.com/dp/B0CW1DWT1P

ABOUT THE AUTHOR

Rose likes to write about complex, oftentimes twisted main characters who grow stronger together on whichever journey they take. Watch out for sexy morally grey heroes and sharp, intelligent heroines within settings ranging from fantasy to academia to the underworld of organized crime.

When Rose isn't writing or listening to the whispers (or shouts) of her characters in her mind, she's drinking coffee, throwing herself at anything nature-related (especially in the winter, when there are no spiders or mosquitos to attack her), and reading.

If you'd like to connect with Rose, join her Facebook group: https://www.facebook.com/share/1AgAcE5efaztPjLq/

To stay updated on her upcoming releases, you can subscribe to her newsletter: https://dashboard.mailerlite.com/forms/892614/130136824777541065/share

If you'd like to browse her books and get access to VIP content such as excerpts from upcoming books or deleted scenes, visit her website: https://rosegravestone.com/

If you're interested in reading her works-in-progress (pre-edits and re-writes for publishing) she has a Patreon where she posts chapters of books she's working on: https://patreon.com/rosesreaders